ADVANCE PRAISE FOR *HOLLOW PLACES*

"*Hollow Places* by Michelle Massaro offers heart-wrenching angst along with beautiful redemption. I wanted to rescue every one of her characters, but she didn't need my help. Will appeal to fans of Nicole Deese."

—Angela Ruth Strong, author of *Husband Auditions*

"*Hollow Places* brings together the beauty of a sweet romance with the heart-tugging emotional experience you'll find in the best social justice stories. Michelle Massaro brings her characters to life, from the hunky pastor with the speckled past to the haunted heroine searching for meaning. And let's not forget the charming and precious Thomas, a little boy desperate for a family to call his own. If you like stories that both warm your heart and keep you turning the pages, you'll love *Hollow Places*. This is one of the best contemporary romances I've read in years."

—Robin Patchen, USA Today bestselling author
of *Glimmer in the Darkness*

Hollow Places

By

Michelle Massaro

Orange Grove
Press

Cover design by Michelle Massaro

Orange Grove Press logo by Michael Massaro

Published in Corona, California, by Orange Grove Press.

Scriptures taken from the Holy Bible, New International Version®, NIV®. Copyright © 1973, 1978, 1984, 2011 by Biblica, Inc.™ Used by permission of Zondervan. All rights reserved worldwide. www.zondervan.com

Scripture taken from the New King James Version®. Copyright © 1982 by Thomas Nelson. Used by permission. All rights reserved.

Publisher's note: This novel is a work of fiction. Names, characters, places, and incidents are either products of the author's imagination or used fictitiously. All characters are fictional, and any similarity to people living or dead is purely coincidental.

ISBN-13: 978-0-9973273-7-3 (Orange Grove Press)

Produced in the United States of America.

For El Roi, the one who sees.

And for the hurting child in each of us.

"But you do see trouble and grief. You consider it to take it into your hand. You help the victim and the fatherless."

(Psalm 10:14, New Heart English Bible)

Chapter One

Alli Johnson sat at one of the tightly packed tables filling the karaoke bar—laughter emanating from those crammed into the room, drinks in hand—and knew exactly who she was supposed to be tonight: fun, happy, carefree, up for anything.

Twisting her grin to one side, she shook her head and wagged a finger at Janelle—the neighbor who had inserted herself into Alli's life a year earlier and now stood holding out a microphone to her. With a playful squint, Alli groaned and accepted the mic—to the whoops and cheers of the crowd. Her would-be friends. "Okay, fine." She looked back at those seated closest to her. "But don't say I didn't warn you."

A collective chuckle rumbled, and a male voice shouted from the back of the room, "Relax, girl. You've got this."

She looked to her date, the decent-looking attorney Janelle had set her up with — Garrett something-rather, his name was. From up on the stage, he wiggled his eyebrows and shot off a dashing smirk as she dragged her feet to join him. Janelle sat perched on her date's lap and glowed like a Bieber fan backstage.

The music started, a catchy, driving beat. Alli closed her eyes and counted to five, and when she opened them, she was no longer Alli Johnson, social worker, she was Sandra Dee—and her date was Danny Zuko. She tapped her thigh to the beat as Garrett started the first verse of "You're the One That I Want."

When he squealed out the word "electrifyin'," Alli brought her mic up, lifting one side of her mouth, and began singing her part—with total commitment. She draped her wrist over her date's shoulder and sang directly to him. Their eyes locked while she channeled her sexy persona. The crowd cheering as Garrett flawlessly played off her performance. He placed a hand at her hip and stared down at her like she was a hot slice of caramel apple pie, and he hoped to earn a taste.

Eyes hooded, Alli poured out the melody as if she were considering giving him one.

She almost believed it, too.

Then right in the middle of the song, it happened. Like she knew it would. That hyper-awareness of how pointless this was. How deep her performance ran. She was a mere spectator of her own life.

Emptiness opened its jaws, tried to swallow her up. Her voice faltered, though no one but her probably noticed. Lashes beating the air, she tamped down the overwhelming sensation that this wasn't really *her* and threw herself back into the lyrics proclaiming the title of the song.

Though she wasn't sure of *anything* down deep inside, she bounced around on the stage, sashaying this way and that as the song drew to a close, then matched Garret's breathless laughter as they finished the final note. He grabbed her hand and took a bow before leading her off the stage and back to their table.

Janelle was beaming. "You two were great out there! What a pair you make. Fantastic!"

Garrett chuckled and pulled out Alli's chair for her. "*She's* the star."

Alli's mouth slid sideways as she took her seat. "Aw, thanks." She tucked her loose hair behind her ears. "It was fun."

It *was* fun. But as usual, she couldn't completely relax and enjoy it. She stretched out her neck, hoping to shake off the tension threatening her muscles.

"I'm guessing you've done this before." Garrett leaned toward her and grabbed a tortilla chip from the basket in front of them.

She gave him a demure smile and shrugged. "Once or twice maybe."

"Once or twice?" Janelle swung her head toward Garrett. "Dude, she's hustling you. First time I took her, back when she'd just moved here and still had red hair, she won best performance of the night."

"Red hair, huh?"

Alli waved off Janelle, ignoring the hair commentary. "Pfft. Fluke."

Garrett shook his head. "Oh, I doubt that. I'm sure you had them mesmerized. Just like you do tonight."

His gaze traveled from her forehead to her mouth and landed back on her eyes. Throat dry, Alli blinked and twisted her lips to the side. She flipped up a palm and raised her shoulder. "Well, what can I say? I'm a woman of hidden talents."

"You're certainly a mystery I'd like to solve." The air hummed with the combined energy of the patrons in the room, spiked by the unmasked look of interest in Garrett's eyes. In the distance, the DJ announced the next song, and a soft ballad began to play.

Janelle shot a conspiratorial look toward Alli, then grabbed Eric's hand. "Babe, I feel like dancing."

Alli squinted at her.

Eric gave her a clueless look and shrugged. "Uh, okay. Sure."

Alli rolled her eyes. Subtle, Janelle. Smooth exit there.

When Janelle led Eric to the dance floor, Garrett scooted his chair closer to Alli's and ran his index finger across the back of her hand. Her eyes traveled there, reflexive instinct fighting her will to not flinch or pull away.

His gaze on her went melty. "I'm having a good time tonight."

"Me, too." She grinned and let him take her hand. He was a decent guy, handsome, made a good living. Could even carry a tune. She should be interested. He squeezed her fingers and tilted his head, his blue eyes shining in the light of the fake candle on their table. He had great eyes. Yes, she should be really interested.

Her phone rang and relief eased from her lungs. She slipped her hand from his to look at the screen. Tim, her supervisor. She lifted her face to Garrett. "Sorry, it's work." She pointed at the screen. "I have to take this."

"Of course." Garrett nodded as she turned away and pushed the 'answer' button on her phone.

"Hello?" She pressed her finger to her other ear to block out the background noise.

"Alli. Sorry to interrupt what sounds like a good time, but you need to head over to the McMillan house. Pronto."

Her spine straightened, and she pressed the phone tighter against her ear. "McMillan's? Tim, do I hear sirens?"

"There's been an incident. Thomas will need to be taken somewhere for the night."

Oh, no. Adrenaline spiked through her veins. "I'm on my way." She palmed her phone and turned back at Garrett. "I gotta run. Thanks though, this was . . .nice."

"Oh." His brows hitched. "Okay. Maybe we can do it again sometime?"

Alli stood and shoved her phone into her jeans pocket. "Yeah. Maybe." She tossed him a quick grin, then hurried past him to the entrance doors. Cold October night air greeted her. She relished it as though she hadn't had a full breath in hours. Probably hadn't.

Alli pulled her long hair out from the back of her leather jacket as she approached her car. The Karaoke bar had to put her a good twenty minutes away.

She'd make it fifteen.

Alli started the engine and flew down the road, bracing for whatever she'd find when she arrived. Experience told her it could be ugly. Sirens were never a good sign.

Just a couple weeks ago, she'd visited the McMillan's place, and the household seemed stable. They were a newer foster family, less than a year of service, but they'd appeared to be handling things well. Thomas was adjusting better than she'd dreamed. He loved living with the McMillans, and they had nothing but good things to say about him as well. She'd hoped this would be it for the kid. That he'd found himself a long-term family. But now . . .she had no idea what to think.

A ribbon of concern spiraled up her back. This kid had bounced around so much. And he affected her like none of her other cases did. Emotional distance eluded her. She strained to focus on the road.

Why him? What was it that made this boy stand out amongst so many? Was it the glimmer of hope that still shone in his eyes, or the growing emptiness threatening to consume it? The way it had to her.

She pressed her lips together and gave herself a shake. Better not to even go there. Just do her job, that's what he needed. A champion. And she had plenty of fight in her.

She pulled up behind a squad car with its lights flashing. A deputy was taking a statement from Mr. McMillan, and several people were bustling about the scene, coming in and out the front door. One carried an evidence bag containing what looked like a kitchen knife.

Alli's gut clenched. Suiting up in her protector role, she marched toward an officer and pulled out her identification. "Excuse me. I'm a social worker. What happened here?"

The officer nodded toward the squad car. "Kid took a knife to the mother. She's been taken to the county hospital."

Alli's eyes rounded. "What? Will she be okay?"

"A flesh wound to the forearm, she'll be fine. Physically."

Doris was lucky. Alli's tongue soured as she formed the next question. "Which kid?"

"Uh, Paul" — he checked his notes — "Paul Cooley."

Paul Cooley. Age fourteen. Yes, she remembered him. Highly abusive background, bad temper, and a bully. The type of kid with little hope left of turning his life around, though the system would keep trying. He wasn't one of her cases, and she'd had reservations about him joining the McMillans—and Thomas—a couple months ago. Looked like she'd been right.

She surveyed the area. "Where's Thomas?"

"Who?"

"The younger child. I'm here for him."

"I'm not sure. Check with my partner." He nodded toward the porch.

Alli crossed the lawn to where the other officer spoke with Greg McMillan. Mr. McMillan had his arms crossed, hands gripping his biceps. Worry lines etched his forehead.

Alli pulled her brows together as she approached him. "Hi, Greg. I'm so sorry this happened." Was she expected to pat his arm or something? Instead, she looked to the officer—Cartwright, his nameplate read. "I'm Alli Johnson, Thomas's social worker. I'm here to take him. Where is he now?"

"Thomas?" Greg lifted a shaky hand to his forehead. "Um. In his room, I think."

"You think?" She looked from the officer to Greg and back again. "Isn't someone with him? Has anyone talked to him?" Not waiting for an answer, she pushed between them into the house, a growl forming in her throat. What had the poor kid seen, heard? And why was he left to process it alone? He'd be terrified. Traumatized.

"Thomas? It's Miss Johnson." Not in the den. She moved down the hall to his bedroom, passing the kitchen along the way. Large drops of blood were smeared on the counter and floor, and a bloody dishrag lay discarded by the sink. But judging by the amount of red Alli saw, Doris was probably in no serious danger.

Alli pushed open Thomas's door. "Thomas?" Flipping on the light revealed a blue-checkered bedspread and matching curtains. But no seven-year-old boy.

She checked his closet and under the bed but didn't find him. Where was he this time? Alli's gaze raked his room, hoping for an idea to spark. An empty space on his dresser sent her pulse speeding.

He'd taken it.

Oh, no. No, no, no. She darted through the rest of the house to finish her indoor search, before jogging back out the front door "He's gone."

Officer Cartwright glanced up from his notepad. "Gone? Are you sure?"

"Yeah. I've checked the house. And he has a history of running." Frustration tightened her neck muscles. "Why wasn't someone *watching* him?"

Greg McMillan's head jutted back. "My wife was stabbed, Miss Johnson. Stabbed! My kitchen is covered in her blood." He paused and began again, calmer. "Thomas must have slipped away unnoticed during the chaos."

Covered was an overstatement, but Alli kept the observation to herself and steadied the anger from her voice. "I'm sorry about Doris, truly. But that's no excuse to lose track of a child. We need to find him." She stared at the cop. "*Now.*"

Officer Cartwright spoke into the communicator on his shoulder. Within minutes, the house was crawling with officers and paramedics searching every cupboard and broom closet in search of little Thomas. Alli moved outdoors and shined a flashlight along the row of shrubs in the backyard, calling his name. At the sound of a sniffle, she cocked her head. Then followed the sound until she came to the small storage shed on the side of the house. She pushed the door open, and there he was. Hunkering down with his knees pulled to his chest, a small, clear plastic box beside him.

"Hey, kid." Alli knelt in front of him, her heart racing in that dark, confined space. Barely enough room for her to fit inside. "You okay?"

He hung his head. "You're here to take me away again, aren't you?"

Alli's chest tightened. "You just need somewhere to stay while Doris is at the hospital. Shouldn't be more than a few days."

He took a big, shuddering breath. "Nobody ever keeps me."

A deep, aching pain rolled over Alli, the echo of her own childhood thoughts resonating through her. Her gaze skittered away, then back to him as she retreated from the memory. At a loss for words, her forehead creased. The ugly truth was, so far, it had been true.

Alli picked up the clear box beside Thomas and peered inside. "Herman seems to be doing well. You've taken good care of him. He'll need a new shell soon probably, huh?"

Thomas took the box from her and held it up to his face. "Yeah. We're supposed to go to the pet store on Saturday." He sighed and a quiet moment passed between them. She had to get him out of there.

"Come on. Let's go hunt down a couple of milkshakes." That would give her the time she needed to find an emergency placement for him tonight. And hopefully put a smile back on the boy's face.

Thomas wiped his hands across his cheeks, then dried them on his jeans before pushing himself to his feet. "Okay."

They emerged from the shed and headed for the house. "We're here!" Alli called with a practiced casual air. Thomas was not in trouble, and she didn't want him to believe otherwise. A collective sigh of relief could be felt rippling through the group, and walkie talkies buzzed the news to any not within earshot. Alli pointed a smile down at Thomas and held tight to his hand.

After a brief conversation with the lead officer, she walked Thomas to her car and buckled him into the booster seat in back, his hermit crab safely on his lap. A trash bag holding his few belongings sat on the floorboard beside him. She reached out awkwardly and gave his shoulder a squeeze. He said nothing as she'd shut his door.

A crisp breeze lifted her hair and swirled it about her throat as she gazed up at the dark night sky. Life wasn't fair. Not to her, and not to kids like Thomas. Born to an addicted mother, he'd suffered neglect his whole life. Nothing in his world was solid, safe. Kids *needed* solid and safe. Was that too much to ask? It shouldn't be. Not if there was anyone up there actually listening.

She plopped into her seat and started the engine.

All the boy wanted was something real to hold on to. She'd thought she'd found it. For him, at least. For her, she wasn't sure she ever would.

She glanced at him in the rearview mirror. His eyes were glued to the animal in the acrylic box. His hermit crab. Something else that made her feel particularly connected to him. Their shared love of the creatures who moved from shell to shell, never finding a permanent fit. Alli blinked dry eyes, tucked her hair behind her ears, and turned on the stereo. "Ready for that milkshake?"

Though his attention stayed fixed on Herman, his lips curved up in an encouraging display. If ice cream could still bring on a grin, things were okay. "What do ya want, buddy? Chocolate?"

He shook his head. "Oreo."

One corner of her mouth lifted. "Oreo? You got it, kid."

His smiling brown eyes connected with hers in the mirror and she caught a glimpse of hope, shrinking though it was. Alli would fight tooth and nail to keep that hope alive.

Hope could be a funny thing. Sometimes found in the most unusual circumstances. Like right now as youth pastor David Porter, while keeping a keen eye on the man before him, thought of how far he'd come over the past few years.

His attacker held an expression of intensity and single-minded focus that told David everything—he was about to lunge.

Not too long ago, David's body would've been pulsing with aggression, heart pounding, limbs twitching. At the first whiff of threat, the adrenaline spike would've propelled him toward violence beyond his own control. And God help anyone who tried to get in his way.

But that was before.

Tonight, his breaths came steady as he side-stepped an attack, threw a roundhouse kick and snapped a hand strike toward his opponent's neck. The man stumbled to the ground and David turned to the onlookers.

"See, the key is not always force, it's balance. If you can throw off your attacker's balance, you then control his momentum and can direct it away from yourself. Then grasp the opportunity to deliver a defensive blow and end the assault." He turned back around and offered to help his opponent off the floor. "Thanks, Adam." His buddy was a good sport for showing up to assist him tonight. Luckily, his wife didn't mind him getting knocked around by the local youth pastor.

Adam acknowledged with a tight nod and bow, then took up a spot at the perimeter to stand at attention, fists anchored in front of him.

"Cool!"

"Yeah man, that's pretty impressive."

A handful of teen boys stood round-eyed as they absorbed what they'd just witnessed.

David smiled. "It's fun, too. But martial arts take a lot of discipline. If you want to learn, I'm happy to teach. But be prepared to be challenged, and to challenge *yourselves.*"

Heads bobbed and the thrill of accomplishment sizzled in David's chest. These boys . . .he'd had been trying for months to get them to connect, to come out of their shells. Finally, through karate, he sensed a breakthrough.

"Great," he said in his firm, instructor's voice. "If you embrace that D word, discipline, you'll get a lot out of it. Kenpo was a lifeline for me. It helped bring my life into focus." Palms facing his temples, he gestured toward an invisible road ahead. The boys nodded. "Cleared the jumbled mess in my mind." After his time in the military, the things he'd seen and done, he'd had difficulty processing it all—until he'd walked into the dojo. "As I disciplined myself with my training, I found an inner strength I didn't know I had—even when I was serving in the army. And with it, clarity, and control of my life. Plus,"— He dipped his ear toward his shoulder— "it looks cool." He grinned, and in return, smiles split the faces of the three teens.

Fourteen-year-old Kevin bounced on his heels. "Can you teach us something now?"

David checked the wall clock and calculated how much time he'd need to get his laundry done at home. He could get it all into a single load this week. "I can give you a short preview lesson, sure. Remove your shoes first, as a sign of respect." He paused to look them each in the eye, raising his pointer. "Respect is essential. You never walk on this mat with shoes on, and you never step onto it without bowing. Even if there's no actual mat, it's the same." He demonstrated the customary bow before entering or leaving the training area.

The kids complied then spread out across the space, enthusiasm lighting their expressions. When had David ever seen them this engaged with their surroundings, this eager to do as instructed and learn? *Never.* Already their respect for him had multiplied and he hoped they'd find it for themselves as well. And for things outside their personal bubble.

He clapped his hands once. "We don't have a lot of time but I'm going to walk you through the Five Star Block Set." He demonstrated the wide stance with his fists chambered at his hips, then went through each of the five blocks that formed the set. The boys remained attentive, focused, and picked up the basics quickly. Next time they came, he'd focus more on form and crispness. Tonight was just to whet their appetites.

The clock drew David's attention as it ticked the top of the hour. "Okay guys, that's all the time I have. Good job. Now you face me and bow." They did, and he bowed back to them. "In Kenpo, bowing to the instructor is like saluting a superior officer. You should stop and bow any time a higher rank arrives on the mat. No matter what. Take this seriously. If you can't show respect, *you* won't receive respect *or* be taken seriously."

Josiah, the tallest of the lot, gave a crisp nod. "Got it."

"Proper response will be *yes, sensei*. Everyone?"

"Yes, sensei!" the group chorused.

"Very good." He grinned and gave them a wink. "Dismissed."

The teens went back to put on their shoes, and David slipped his feet into the sandals he'd left by the door.

"When can you teach us again?"

"I'm not sure. This was one of the rare evenings this meeting room isn't in use."

"Aw man. What about Tuesday? There's nothing happening here Tuesdays."

"Intercessory prayer. But I'm hoping to work something out where I can train more often, see who else might want to join us. Just waiting for the right opportunity."

The boys followed David out to the parking lot. One parent's car was waiting—Kevin's foster mom. The other two had driven themselves. David turned the key to lock up the doors of New Life Worship Center.

Sixteen-year-old Declan zipped up his hoodie and fished his keys out of his pocket. "G'night, Pastor David. Have a good one."

"Yeah, you too. See ya tomorrow night for Heir-Born Youth?"

"For sure." His eyes connected with David's, a spark of life in them that David had never seen there before. And the smile was genuine, not the stiff kind the kid usually offered him. Declan raised his fist and held it suspended mid-air.

David bumped his knuckles and gave a swift upward jerk of his chin in salute. "Drive safe."

Halfway to his car, Declan paused and called back over his shoulder. "Hey, Pastor, Josiah and I were gonna grab a bite to eat . . . you wanna come?"

David's heart warmed. Declan and Josiah were admitting him into their circle, into friendship. He smiled. "I appreciate the offer, Deck. And I wish I could, but I can't tonight. I'd love a raincheck though. Next week maybe?"

Declan's lips curved up and he nodded. "Sure thing. Take care."

Josiah twisted his ballcap then raised a hand. "Goodnight, Pastor."

The teens pulled away from the lot as David stood under the winking stars, the brisk air filling his lungs with anticipation. With hope.

Alli pulled into the parking lot of Jack in the Box. The music silenced as she cut the engine and she threw a grin over her shoulder to Thomas. "Well, I'm ready for my shake, how about you?"

He nodded and unbuckled himself. They crossed the lot to the entrance, and she held the door open for him.

He paused and looked up at her with soulful eyes. "You're my best friend, Miss Alli."

Alli's thoughts tripped, and she pulled in a stuttering breath. "You're not so bad yourself, kid."

They entered the restaurant, nearly empty this time of night, and stood in line behind a couple muscular teens. Their voices resonated through the otherwise quiet room. One in a hoodie and one wearing a sideways cap, they dripped with attitude and exuded trouble.

Alli's jaw tightened in annoyance, and Thomas pasted himself to her side, eyes flickering in anxiety. Did these swaggering peacocks remind him of Paul Cooley?

Alli patted Thomas's back to reassure him. These were just a couple punks who thought they were the center of the universe, like most boys that age did.

The teens took a table against the south wall, so after ordering, Alli picked out a spot on the north side. Problem solved.

When they were seated with their shakes, Thomas seemed to relax a little. He pulled the cherry off the top and bit it off the stem.

Alli pinched hers and dangled it tantalizingly. "You want mine?"

"Sure!"

Smiling, she passed it to him. "Here ya go."

"Mr. McMillan can tie a knot in the stem while it's inside his mouth. With his tongue. Isn't that cool?"

"Very cool."

"Yeah. I wish I could do that."

"You've got two to practice on right there. Maybe you'll get it figured it out."

As Thomas placed a cherry stem on his tongue, Alli pulled out her phone and began scrolling through her contacts. Who could she ask to take him in for a few days? The Duvalls? They were one of the agency's designated emergency homes, often taking children for just one or two nights. They had two older boys with them already but could probably make room. Alli twisted her mouth, thinking. She hated to put Thomas in another environment with troubled teens. Too much risk of exposure to things he needed shielding from, especially in the aftermath of tonight's ordeal. And she didn't get a good vibe from that house. The kids there now would eat Thomas for lunch, she just *knew* it. Bad fit.

Stem abandoned on a napkin, Thomas swung his legs and sucked on his straw, his hermit crab habitat sitting on the table between them. He stuck his finger through the plastic top of the cup into the whipped cream, swirled it around, then brought it to his mouth. "Too bad hermit crabs can't eat whipped cream."

A smile bent her mouth as she took in his little face. "Yeah. It's too bad." She looked back at her phone. No, not the Duvalls. There had to be someone else. She chewed her lip as she continued scrolling, pausing on the Andersons. They had a full house of little ones right now, but Alli was only asking for a few days. They'd be a good choice.

As she hit the 'dial' button and slid out of their booth, she gave Thomas a reassuring wink. "Just give me a second. I'm not going anywhere."

"Okay."

She took a few steps away, keeping her eye on him but gaining some privacy—she hoped. The phone rang and a woman answered. "Maria, hi. It's Alli Johnson." She kept her volume low. "Listen, I have a boy who needs a place tonight—"

"Alli, hi. I hate to tell you this, but I don't think it would be a good idea to send us any kids tonight. We have three with really bad flu. I mean, puking all day long. It's bad. Really bad. I'm so sorry."

"Oh . . ." Alli's shoulders drooped. "Oh, that's okay. I hope you guys feel better. I'll just call someone else." She rubbed the spot between her eyes. "Get well soon."

"Thank you."

She ended the call and looked over at Thomas, chin resting on his hand as he whispered to Herman. It would be easy to take him home with her, let him crash on her futon in the living room. It was already nearing eleven o'clock. And unless she wanted him to catch the mother of all flus on top of witnessing a stabbing . . .

But she couldn't do that. Policy.

She grunted. He'd have to stay the night at the shelter.

Alli slid back into her seat across from him and brought her straw to her lips. Thomas mirrored the action, their gazes connecting, and tenderness swelled in her chest. "Like your shake?"

He nodded. "Uh huh. Thanks."

"Sure thing. We gotta hit the road though."

His dark lashes fell, along with his expression. "Okay."

As they stepped outside, a stiff breeze iced her bones. Why had she thought cold shakes would be a good idea at this time of night? But once she had warm air streaming out of the vents of her car, she pulled onto the road. "All right, let's get you squared away for the night, shall we?" She hoped.

"So. Porter." Adam swung his keys around his finger then captured them in his palm. "Got a second?"

"Sure. What's up?" At the chiming of his cellphone, David held up a finger. He turned off the ringer and looked back at Adam. "Sorry. I'll call them back later. What were you going to say?"

"I've got a question for ya."

"Okay, shoot." David fell into step beside his friend through the church parking lot.

"Well. Ya know with the baby coming, I've had to shift my focus. Take more hours at my desk job." He grimaced. "Bottom line is, I thought you might be interested in taking over my class at the Y."

"Me?"

"Yeah, I already talked to the director; told him all about you. He'd like to meet if you're interested."

"Of course, I'm interested."

Adam grinned. "Figured you would be. Maybe this will solve both our problems."

"It just might. Tell me about the class. Keep it to the highlight reel for now."

"Pretty simple. Class is two evenings per week, hour and a half each . . ." As he went over the basics, David's excitement grew. He'd been itching for regular dojo time for a long while now, and here it was. Adam hit the key fob to unlock his door. "Let's set something up with the director then."

"Sounds good." David's phone vibrated and he checked the screen. "It's a parent. Let me see what's up." He hit the button to answer. "Hi Angie, what can I do for you?"

"Pastor David? Hi. We were just wondering if you've seen Liam this evening. Is he there at the church with your group?"

David furrowed his brow. "No, he's not here and I haven't seen him since church last week. Everything okay?"

"Well, we hope so. He's just not answering his phone, which isn't like him. And it's past his curfew. It's probably nothing, but we thought we'd make a few calls anyway. Let us know if you hear from him?"

"Yeah, of course. I'll make a few calls, too."

"Thank you so much."

He ended the call and turned back to Adam. "Sorry about that. Looks like one of the kids isn't answering his phone. Anyway, thanks for recommending me for this class."

"No problem. I hope it works out, though I gotta say I'm amazed at how much you already do. You're sure you can fit this into your schedule?"

David leaned back against his car and propped one ankle over the other. "It's doable." He nodded thoughtfully. "Definitely doable. Just have to be organized is all. Helps that I'm single." No ball and chain, no drama. He pasted on a smile.

Adam puffed his cheeks out. "Speaking of which . . . Ginger has this friend. Cute. She was asking about you after you dropped by the other day, and Ginger thought—"

David waved his hands in front of him. "Nooo. Sorry dude, not interested. As you know, my busy life doesn't have much time for extras. I'd rather put what little I have into the kids."

"Ginger knew you'd say that. I'm supposed to tell you that 'He who finds a wife finds a good thing, and obtains favor from the Lord.'"

"Yeah, yeah. Psalm 18:22, I know it. You're not the first to quote me that verse. I know another one: 'It is good for a man not to touch a woman.' I think I'll stick with that."

"First Corinthians 7. Touché."

"Tell me something." David folded his arms over his chest. "There are plenty of singles in the church. Why do you guys think *I* need a woman?"

Adam shrugged. "Dunno. Maybe God's speaking to us on your behalf. Or maybe you just have that look."

David shot him a glance from the tops of his eyes. "I won't ask you to clarify."

"Good. I might get myself in trouble." Adam chuckled.

"Look, I appreciate it but—"

"Yeah, yeah. I know. You're a eunuch for the Kingdom."

"Whoa. Hey now. Dude. Let's not go slapping labels around." David socked Adam in the arm and jettisoned a hoarse laugh. "I don't think I could command the same respect in the dojo with that E word attached to my name, okay?" If he wanted a relationship, he'd like to think he could find a willing female—on his own. But romance was messy. Unpredictable. Dangerous.

Adam chuckled along. "Point taken. Look, I promised Ginger I'd mention it. I've done my part. But one of these days the right woman is going to come along and steal your heart."

David shook his head. "My life is in ministry, Adam." His heart had betrayed him once before, throwing itself into the hands of a woman to do with as she pleased. It was the most unsettling state he'd ever endured. The feeling of vulnerability, weakness. Subjected to the whims of his heart like a rag doll in the mouth of a Doberman. He had no wish to go through that again.

Adam reproved him with a click of the tongue. "Ministry and family life aren't mutually exclusive."

They were for *him*. Love was a loss of self-control, plain and simple. And therefore, something David wanted nothing to do with. Not now, maybe not ever. Period.

David's phone buzzed again and as he checked the name, his forehead wrinkled. "It's my neighbor. One sec." He pressed the cell to his ear. "Hello, Mrs. Foulston."

"David. I'm calling you because there's a suspicious-looking fellow hanging around outside your door. Been there a good ten or fifteen minutes, not budging. Looks wily and I don't like it."

David pinched the area between his eyes. He had a good inkling who it was. "Okay, I'll be home in a few minutes and take care of it. Thank you."

"You're welcome. Don't you waste time getting here."

The call ended and David shook his head at Adam. "Looks like I'm on duty tonight. I'll catch ya later."

"Later, man."

David didn't live far from the church, so he arrived back at his place within a few minutes. As he approached his front door, a teen David recognized from Heir-Born Youth shoved off from against the wall of Porter's house, his ball cap hiding his features.

"Hi, Pastor David."

"Hey, Liam. You know, your parents are looking for you. They sounded pretty worried."

"They called you? Figures."

"They said you weren't answering your phone."

"Yeah, I turned it off. They have a thing on there that pings my location."

David furrowed his brow as he pulled his keys out. "And that's a bad thing because . . .?"

"Because I don't want to hear it from them." Tension strained his voice. "I can't go back there."

David scanned the kid's body for any signal of abuse. "Why not? What happened?"

"Something stupid. I screwed up."

David swung open his door and ushered the boy inside. Looked like laundry would have to wait a bit longer. "Have a seat and let's talk."

Liam nodded and strode in with his face pointed at the ground. "I was kinda hoping I could crash at your place for a few days. You've got space, right? I wouldn't be any trouble. I'd stay out of your way. I just don't want to see them right now."

David sat, crossed his arms over his chest and squinted at the boy in front of him. True, he had the space in his apartment, and he wasn't against the idea of taking in a kid if they were in real trouble. Question being, was *this* kid in real trouble? So far, David wasn't sure.

"Tell me what's going on."

Liam sighed and took a moment, then launched into the facts. He'd failed a test, got into it with the teacher, and ended up with a Saturday school and the threat of suspension. As the story poured out, his agitation increased. He swore, expletives bouncing off the walls of the condo with increasing frequency and volume. David calmly listened.

"To make everything worse, I ditched the rest of the day with Brittney. At some point I realized I was being a bonehead but" — he plopped back down onto the couch — "it's too late. They're gonna *kill* me."

His mouth dried. Fingers clenching in reflex, David steadied his gaze. "Liam, I need to ask you. Have they ever hurt you? Has your father or mother ever raised a hand to you or made you fear for your physical safety?" He sat like stone as he awaited the answer.

Liam worked his jaw and shook his head. "No. Nothing like that. But . . ."

The suffocating band around David's chest released. "What exactly is it you think they might do?"

He huffed. "Yell. Cry. Take my license, my phone, my Xbox. Tell me I can't see Brittney. Lock me up."

"Lock you up?"

He rolled his eyes. "I mean ground me, okay? Kill my social life. Lecture me every waking moment and maybe drag me to counseling. I don't know exactly but whatever they come up with will be torture."

David released a slow breath. This kid didn't need a hideout, he needed a reality check. "It's not torture, Liam. It's love. Deep down you know that, right?"

He shrugged and rolled his eyes again.

"I work with a lot of kids who wish they had parents that cared enough to ground them. And ones whose parents *do* threaten their safety. You're luckier than you realize. I know it's hard having to face the music with something like this. But owning our mistakes is a sign of maturity. Would it help if I went to talk to them with you?"

Liam rubbed the back of his neck and stared at his knees before nodding. "I guess."

"Okay. Did you drive over?"

"No, I took an Uber."

"Then I'll give you a lift. Come on."

David spent the next hour in the living room of the Hendrick's home, helping a kid talk honestly with his parents. Felt good to see them through the rocky conversation, to know God was using him in that way, but was there something bigger he was meant to do? He cared deeply about his youth group, about their problems, their struggle to find themselves and decide what path they wanted to be on; he enjoyed walking them through Scripture and watching their faith grow. But was that enough? Lately it hadn't felt like it.

By the time he got back to his place, he was far behind on his laundry schedule. He'd have to settle for one load on the short-wash cycle but so what. He could catch up later.

Later that night, David placed the last folded shirt into his drawer, then stowed the laundry basket in its place in the closet. He shoved away the disquiet in his mind, directing his thoughts instead to the Almighty. His Savior.

He sat on the edge of his bed, knees splayed, and bowed his head. "Thank you for putting me somewhere I can be useful. Me, the biggest jerk of them all. For whatever work You have in store for the kids I work with. So many feeling angry, lost, adrift in this world. Let them come to know You the way I do—as a real, living, powerful God who transforms lives. And however You want me to be a part of that . . . just show me." He stood and rolled out his stiff shoulders.

A decade ago, David never would have imagined he could offer anything of value to anyone. That he'd ever be able to make up for the years of letting his anger and bitterness spew onto everyone he met. But God had had a plan.

David loved those words: *But God . . .*

As he stood in front of the bathroom mirror and reached for the tap, his gaze snagged, as it often did, to the image tattooed to the inside of his right forearm. An empty cross, splintered and stained, and stamped across it the words *I have overcome the world.* It was a message he'd wanted to remind himself of daily, since the night Christ had come into his life and changed everything. It did its job. David would not forget.

He finished up, moved back to his bedroom, and turned on the lamp at his bedside. His fingers brushed the chain of his dog tags, hanging down the lampshade. He ran his thumb over them a moment, the faint echo of explosions ricocheting in his memory, and faces of the fallen parading through his mind. Good men. Honorable. Like family.

With a slow release of air, he said goodbye to them again, turned off the light, and punched his pillow before settling on his side to sleep. Tomorrow he would spend time with some of his favorite people— the foster kids at Grace House.

They arrived at the shelter and Thomas squeezed Alli's hand tightly as they entered. One of the resident workers smiled at them and stepped forward. "Hi, I'm Lilly." She shook Alli's hand then bent toward Thomas and smiled. "And who is this?"

Thomas hid behind Alli's arm.

Alli wiggled his hand. "This is Thomas." She handed Thomas's bag to Lilly, then knelt to see him better. "I'm going to be back in the morning, okay? Lilly is going to give you a nice cozy bed to sleep in. You must be very tired."

"No, I'm not. I don't want you to go. I don't want to stay here." His lip quivered and Alli's stomach clenched.

"I know. But it'll be fine. I promise."

Lilly placed her hand on Thomas's back and ushered him a couple unwilling steps away from Alli. "Don't you worry, things will be just fine." Lilly smiled down at him. "Oh, what's this?" Her forehead wrinkled as she looked at Herman's box in his hands. "Oh, my. Honey, I'm sorry but we can't have living things here. You'll have to leave this with Miss Johnson. I'm sure she can watch it for you."

"No!" Thomas's eyes grew wide with desperation. "I won't stay here without Herman. I won't! You can't make me!" His face reddened and contorted with tears. "Miss Alli, please! Please don't take Herman away. Don't leave me here, please!" He broke away from Lilly and flung his arms around Alli's neck, still gripping the handle of the hermit crab's box. "I don't want to stay here! Don't make me."

Alli blinked, frozen. Tantrums and outbursts she could handle, but hugs? "Shh." Alli gave his back a stiff pat.

"Why doesn't anyone ever care what *I* want? I don't want to be here."

Catching Lilly's apologetic gaze, Alli silently mouthed *please*, then said, "Can't you make an exception about the crab? It's not like you have to worry about it making a mess to clean up."

Lilly's expression deflated further. "We can't. We do it for one, we have to do it for another, and it causes too many problems. Risks, liabilities."

Alli took a gulp of air and nodded.

For once, it would be nice to see the *child* put above the *policies*. Alli scooped Thomas up and straightened, the heft of a child unfamiliar in her arms. She settled him on her hip, his face buried in her neck, and took his bag back from Lilly. "Your hands are tied. I get it. Guess we'll just have to find somewhere else to go."

Lilly's mouth fell open. "Y- you're sure?"

Not at all. "Yes. Thank you anyway."

She carried Thomas back out to her car and he finally relaxed his grip on her, allowing her to get him buckled in, Herman's small habitat hugged to his chest. Face inches from his, she jetted a breath and hitched up one side of her mouth. "Looks like it's just the three of us tonight, kid."

His eyes sparked and he showed the hint of a smile. Alli rustled his hair then climbed into the driver's seat.

"Really?"

She stared at her dashboard for a moment, mouth set in a determined line. "Yeah."

"*Your* house?"

"Uh huh."

It was just a few hours. She'd have some paperwork to fill out, some questions to answer, but this kid needed that hermit crab more than she needed to stay in her boss's good graces. She shot him a smile in the mirror then focused on the yellow divider lines in the road ahead.

Fifteen minutes later, she turned onto her quiet street and into her driveway, then cut the engine. *Funny*, she thought. If it wasn't for Paul stabbing Doris, Alli might have been bringing Garrett what's-his-name back to her place tonight instead of this little boy and his hermit crab.

Yeah, right.

No matter how she tried, she stunk at intimacy.

She looked back at Thomas and raised her eyebrows. "Well. Here we are. Let's grab your stuff."

Thomas clutched the habitat, his sleepy eyes now rounding as Alli pushed open her front door for him. He shuffled inside, stopping in the middle of her living room. Waiting for a cue, no doubt.

"Did you just move here?"

Her forehead crinkled as she shook her head. "No, why?"

He shrugged as she tossed her keys onto an unfinished entryway table. She pointed into the living room. "That couch unfolds to a bed, you'll sleep there."

His eyes traveled toward the futon, taking in the details of the room. Alli set his trash bag down and pushed her thumbs into her back pockets. "Okay, so. I guess go ahead and put on your pajamas and brush your teeth. Bathroom's down the hall to the right. I'll take care of the bed."

"Do I have to take a bath too?"

Start the tub, young lady . . .

Blood rushed to her brain, whooshing in her ears like gurgling water. Alli commanded her lungs to open as she shook her head. "No. You can skip it tonight." She reached for Herman's box and Thomas stiffened. "I'm just going to put him on the counter over here, okay? Close to the heater, and right where you can keep an eye on him all night."

After a moment's hesitation, Thomas nodded and relinquished his friend, then dug through his bag like a bum looking for recyclables. He pulled out a mis-matched pair of PJs and an Avengers toothbrush zipped in a sandwich baggie, then scuttled to the bathroom.

Alli scowled at the bag. Seeing them clutched in her clients' hands always did a number on her. Wasn't there something better to use to hold their belongings when they already felt like garbage being dragged to the curb? Trash bags broke. Trash bags had no value.

She swallowed the bitterness on her tongue and unfolded the futon. Then she went to her linen closet and returned with a pile of blankets and tossed them on the bed. *Pillow.* She didn't keep extras except the second one on her own bed. She retrieved that and returned just as Thomas emerged from the bathroom, his daytime clothes wadded in his arms. He shoved them into his bag, glanced back at her shyly, then pulled out a ratty teddy bear.

Her cheek ticked upward. "Looks just like the one I had at your age."

He smiled back at her, one front tooth still shorter than the other, and climbed onto the futon. "Miss Alli, do you have a family?"

"Nope, it's just me." She fluffed his pillow before he leaned back onto it.

"I didn't think so. If you did there would be pictures and toys and stuff."

She licked her lips and grabbed a breath. "Yeah, probably right." She looked around, seeing the room through a visitor's eyes. Few pictures on the walls, no plants, no china in a cabinet. Or whatever women her age normally filled their homes with. No signs of . . .personality. Identity. Roots. Even after eighteen months, she hadn't yet assimilated the idea of permanence and had no clue how she wanted her home to look. It had never mattered before.

She cleared her throat to loosen its constricting muscles. "But I help take care of lots of kids, like you. Lots of families. That's what's important to me." She shook out a blanket over the width of the futon.

"Don't you want one?"

Someone needed to teach this kid about boundaries.

Then again, he needed someone to teach him about all *kinds* of things, but he didn't have a *someone* like that. Pulse pounding, she shifted her weight. Shrugged. "Don't you worry about me." No need to wonder when she would have a family of her own. She knew the answer: On the twelfth of Never.

Thomas rolled onto his side and Alli gave his back a faltering pat. "My room's at the end of the hall." She walked to the light switch. "Good night, kid."

"No! Leave it on. Please."

Afraid of the dark. She got that, too. "How about I turn the bathroom light on so it's not quite so bright?"

He paused to consider, then hugged his bear. "Okay." He yawned wide. "G'night, Miss Alli."

"Night." Her gaze drifted over the curve of his soft freckled cheek before she turned and trudged down the hall, her body sagging from weariness.

But when she climbed under her own covers, sleep wouldn't come. Memories flashed through her mind and body—impressions, echoes of nightmares that deprived her of air. She stared at the ceiling, tracing patterns in the textured paint and chewing her lip. What on earth was she thinking, bringing a kid here?

Chapter Two

"Miss Johnson?" The small voice pulled Alli awake. "Are you sleeping?"

Streaks of light reached across the room as Alli rubbed her eyes then propped herself up on her elbows in bed. Thomas stood in her doorway, teddy bear under one arm. She rubbed her eyes again with her forefinger and thumb. "I'm awake. What's up?"

"Do you have any food?"

"Um. Food? Yeah. What time is it?" A yawn warbled her words as she grabbed her phone off the nightstand. "Seven? Slept longer than I thought. Guess it's time to get up, huh?" Reluctant but resigned, she dragged back her covers and pushed herself to her feet, running her fingers through her long tangle of hair. "All right. I'm up." She stretched her arms and rolled her neck. "Let's find you something to eat."

Alli tugged at her flannel pajama top and blinked the sleep from her eyes as she made her way to her door.

Thomas's lips bowed up as she drew near. He walked alongside her, transferred his bear to the other arm, and grabbed her hand. Alli blinked down at their joined hands. His was small and soft and sent warmth spreading through her chest. She grinned at him and secured her grip.

The futon was a mass of blankets as they passed. Alli wiggled his hand. "Did you sleep okay? Were you warm enough?"

"Yeah."

"Good." She nodded once. "Okay. Let's fill that belly of yours."

Thomas climbed onto a barstool and propped his bear on the counter beside him. He crossed his arms on the bar and rested his chin on his hands.

Alli opened the fridge and bit the inside of her cheek. A half-full container of almond milk, some plain Greek yogurt, and not much else occupied the shelves. "Uh, looks like I'm out of eggs. And milk. You like almond milk?"

Thomas made a yucky face and shook his head.

Okay, no almond milk. Alli closed the fridge and checked the pantry. The Pringles stared back at her. Beside them, a jar of peanut butter. A can of tomato soup. "Well, I've got Pop Tarts."

His eyes widened.

"But that's not a very good breakfast, is it?"

"Sure it is! I love Pop Tarts."

"Yeah, I bet you do, kid." She laughed. "Here you go. There's one left." She handed it to him on a paper towel then reached for the cannister of coffee.

"Thanks." Thomas bit into the pastry like it was a piece of birthday cake, chewing with the enthusiasm only a seven-year-old boy could have. Crumbs clung to his lips, collected in the corners of his mouth, some falling down his front and onto the floor.

Alli cocked her head as she watched, the image of him cowering in the dark still fresh in her mind. "Thomas… How are you doing? After what happened last night with Paul."

At his somber shrug, Alli was filled with remorse for having ruined his little piece of pop tart heaven. He fixed his eyes on his paper towel. "Fine, I guess. I just went in my room when they started yelling. But Herman got scared." His breathing rate ticked up as he seemed to replay the evening.

"So, you took him to the shed to keep him safe?" The boy still had such a pure heart. Her lip twitched upward even as her blood pulsed warm in her neck.

Thomas nodded as he took another bite of Pop Tart. "I never really liked Paul."

The coffee maker dinged so Alli turned to pour a cup and to steady her voice as she casually asked, "Did he get mad a lot?"

"Sort of. He was just grumpy all the time. And mean. He played too rough."

Alli's brow pinched. "In what way?"

"He liked to wrestle. He was on a team at his old school. So, he always wanted to practice his moves on me but it's not fair because I don't know any moves, and he's bigger than me. When I said I didn't want to, he called me a baby. I tried to be nice though because my mom—I mean, Doris—wanted us to be friends. But we weren't."

Wrestling. Stupid macho displays of domination. Men thinking they were men if they could overpower an opponent. She indulged in an eye roll while her back was still to Thomas. Then, returning to lean on the counter across from him, Alli twisted her lips in a shrug of sorts, and nodded understanding. "I think you did the best you could. You're a great kid, Thomas."

A shy smile appeared, and he looked up at her. Their eyes met and held, and a mystical silence hung suspended between them, like an invisible tether. Some strange, foreign sensation rose in Alli's gut, and her heart hammered for no discernible reason whatsoever.

Befuddled, she blinked, straightened, and gulped at her coffee to break the spell.

Thomas licked the corner of his mouth, then pressed a finger onto the paper towel, collecting the scattered crumbs.

"That's not going to fill you up, is it? Tell you what. After we get dressed, we'll run through the McDonald's on the way to my office. I'll get you an Egg McMuffin and hash browns and some O.J."

"McDonald's? Awesome."

A grin tugged at her lips. "Okay, I'm going to hop in the shower real quick." She glanced around and saw the remote on the coffee table. "I think I have Cartoon Network. Let me check."

She snatched up the clicker and powered on the TV. A minute later she had cartoons playing. Score. "Okay kid, here you go. If you get thirsty, I have bottled water in the fridge. Help yourself."

'Kay."

Thomas climbed back onto the futon with the last bit of his Pop Tart. Alli would have crumbs to clear out, but for the moment, Thomas looked like any ordinary kid doing ordinary kid things. Not like the wounded child nobody kept. Not like a little boy who'd just witnessed such violence the night before. She shook off the thought, then headed down the hallway.

By seven-thirty they were out the door. She carried his bag of things while he held onto his portable hermit crab habitat.

They pulled into the fast-food lane, Alli placed an order, and rolled up to the window to pay and collect their meal. After pulling out her own food, she passed the bag back to Thomas. "Here ya go, kid."

"Thanks!"

He looked so happy, and Alli bit back a smile. Could she just glue him to this moment? Keep that expression on his face forever? She wanted that more than anything else, for all the kids she worked with. But the world didn't work that way. Not for them, not for her.

She ate as she drove, and they got to her office at eight o'clock. At the sight of the office building, Thomas's smile faded, and his eyes dimmed. His armor shot back up into place and there was nothing subtle about it. If he was anything like her, he'd get better at it over time.

"Hey, don't worry. I know it looks boring, but we have a play area with books and stuff. Hopefully, we won't be here too long."

He only nodded in response.

After setting him up with some crayons and paper, Alli straightened her silk blouse and slinked into Tim's office for the reprimand she knew she had coming.

He delivered it at high volume. "You took him *home* with you? Alli, what were you thinking?"

Her shoulders rose toward her ears as her gaze skimmed the ceiling. "I know. I know. But it was the only option."

"What about the shelter? They were all set for him. Or the Duvalls? They could've taken one more."

She leveled her eyes with his. "Okay, look. The Duvalls have a difficult teen with them right now and I wasn't going to put him there. And the shelter wouldn't let him bring his crab in, and if you understood what that means to him, you'd know—"

"Did you say *crab*?" He raised a disbelieving eyebrow. "This was because of a crab? *Alli* . . ." His voice held a patronizing tone that grated her nerves.

"Tim, it's not just a crab, it's his pet, his *family*. It represents consistency, commitment, and I wasn't going to take that away from him."

Her boss planted his hands on his hips and pressed his lips together, stretching out a lengthy pause. "Don't do it again. It leads to problems I really don't have time to deal with."

Alli beamed at him. "Understood."

With a shake of his head, Tim took a seat and waved her away. "Okay, hop to it. Unless you want him to spend his whole day cooped up in an office building with you."

"Yes, sir." She exited his office and blew out a breath on the way to her own. Tim really was a softie under that hard exterior. She'd gotten off easy, but now it was time to buckle down and get cranking.

She rolled her chair up to the desk and logged on to her laptop. Looked like Doris would need at least a few days to recuperate before Thomas could return. An email update from Mr. McMillan explained that the knife had nicked a tendon and Doris would need surgery this morning to repair it. But doctors expected a full recovery with physical therapy. She would be on some heavy pain pills for a couple of days post op. He thanked Alli for taking Thomas for a few days and said to tell him hi.

Alli's lips bunched to the side. The news wasn't as bad as it could've been, but where was she going to put Thomas? She scoured her files for a family with room for him, but each one led to a dead end. Desperate, she made half a dozen fruitless placement calls while filling out the paperwork needed for having brought Thomas home with her. There was no room for him anywhere. The thought of the shelter, of separating him from Herman, made her stomach roil. What was she going to do?

She was about ready to slam her laptop in frustration when Linda poked her head in. "Everything okay in here?"

"No." Alli planted her elbows on her desk and dug her fingers into her hair.

"This have anything to do with the cute little boy out there?" She entered and set a brown bag in front of Alli.

"Yes. I can't find an acceptable temporary placement for him." Her jaw clenched. She'd rather take him back home with her than leave him at the emergency shelter.

"I've been there. Sometimes there's a kid you just want to take home yourself." When Alli spiked her brows, Linda went on, "I overheard you in Tim's office."

"It was a one-night solution. Now I need a better one." Shoulders sagging, Alli peeked into the brown bag and pulled out a muffin. Banana Bran. She could've guessed. For some reason, Linda thought she loved them and Alli hadn't the heart to correct her.

Linda sank into the chair across from Alli's desk. "I know of a good group home that has room."

Alli's spine locked. "No way. I'll find somewhere else; I've just got to think. It's only for a few days. Until Doris comes home." She pulled a bit of muffin off the top and placed it in her mouth.

"There *is* nowhere else," Linda said gently. "Why don't you like group homes?"

Flashes of the past slammed into Alli, and she shook her head to dislodge them. She pinned her gaze on Linda's. "Because I never knew one that wasn't awful. Even if the social workers didn't see it." Blood pounded in her temples, beating like little fists. Like the fists that had bruised her arms and legs countless times when no one was looking. "Group homes are often a last resort, the last stop before juvie, where all the bullies end up once they've been kicked out of every family placement." Her voice had gone to steel, and she crossed her arms over her chest. "And for someone quiet and small, it's the *worst* place you could possibly be."

Linda's eyes went soft. "Are we still talking about Thomas… or you?" Her voice was gentle as a lamb's, and Alli dragged in a deep breath as she looked away.

Her jaw flexed. "I don't like placing kids—especially younger ones—in group facilities if I can help it."

"But sometimes you *can't* help it. And Alli, this one is good. It's privately run, I've used them several times over the past few years. And it's just a few days, right? He can't camp out here and you can't take him home with you. Just think on it."

Frustrated, Alli pinched the bridge of her nose and nodded in defeat. She hated admitting that Linda was right. "What's it called?"

Linda smiled. "Grace House. I'll get you the number."

"*Grace* House? So, it's a *religious* organization?"

Linda bounced a shoulder. "Yeah. Many, if not most, private programs *are* church-sponsored. You have a problem with church, too?"

"I have no problem with people going to church if they want, or having faith." Alli rapped her pen on the desk. "But I refuse to let the kids in my care be taken advantage of. They shouldn't be proselytized while they're not in an emotionally stable place. Right? It can do damage later to have one more . . .entity . . .to let them down. They're vulnerable and the last thing they need is to be sold a false bill of goods." Alli should know.

Linda leaned back in her seat, elbows resting casually on the armrests. "Well, the staff don't think it's false. They have good motives; they want to help. Most of the people there credit their faith for getting them through tough times. They only want to offer that same hope to the kids. But they don't force kids to convert or anything. I've met them, Alli. They're decent people. Really."

Alli's internal diatribe skidded to a halt. She didn't want to offend Linda, implying she questioned her judgment. She swallowed the guilt on her tongue then put on a smile. "I'm sure they are. I'm sorry if I came across judgmental." She rolled her lips together, tension building in her neck muscles.

"It's fine. You're just looking out for the kids."

The kids. Alli bit the inside of her cheek. If she didn't want Thomas to end up in a crisis shelter, sleeping on a cot while waiting for Doris to recover . . .

"Okay." She exhaled in defeat. "Get me their number." She offered a smile as Linda stood. "And hey . . . thanks for the muffin."

Linda employed a satisfied grin and slipped out the door.

Alone again, Alli let her head hang over the back in her chair and puffed out her cheeks. She needed to pull herself together, square things away with Thomas, and move on to the next client. She had to do what she had to do, even if it wasn't ideal.

Alli followed her GPS directions and found the place with no problems. She had to admit it was a lovely property—a full acre at her best guess—plenty of trees and nestled into the foothills. Yet only minutes from shopping, dining, and public schools. Although according to her research, most of the kids here were on home study programs.

The sprawling, single story facility appeared to be a ranch-style home—with considerable square footage added on. Thomas clung to her hand as they made their way up the stone path to the front door. Alli gave him a reassuring grin and rang the bell. "Hey, doesn't this place look beautiful? So many trees, I bet they see plenty of squirrels."

"Really?" Interest sparked in his eyes and Alli was able to take a breath.

"Oh, I'm sure. Probably bunnies too."

The door opened and a woman with red hair and red lips smiled and waved them in. "Come in, come in. It's so nice to meet you."

Alli put on her business smile and extended her hand. "Hi. I'm Alli Johnson and this is Thomas Cooper."

"I'm Regina. The house mom." She closed the door behind them.

Alli gave a curt nod. "Nice to meet you, Regina."

"And you, Alli." She bent at the waist to address Thomas. "And I'm especially pleased to meet you, Thomas."

As she stood in the entry, Alli's cautious eyes traveled the room with its cheery decor and Bible verses on the walls. A fist clenched her gut as a ghostly voice rang in her ears. *We don't spare the rod in this house, missy.*

A full-body shudder surged through her. Thomas noticed and angled concerned eyes up at her. With a mental shake, she redoubled her focus on the task at hand—establishing rapport with the people she'd be leaving her client with. And keeping a lookout for any red flags. She leaned into her job description and turned to Regina. "It's nice and bright in here. I like the open floor plan."

"Thank you. Let me show you around." She veered to the right and came to a den. "This is our family room. Also known as the game room. It's not usually this quiet but it just happens that the kids are all off doing school or various other activities right now. But after lunch, this is the popular hangout. We've got board games over there, art materials in that cabinet, a couple video game consoles, too, but we try to limit screen time."

So far so good. Alli tipped her face down at Thomas and lifted her eyebrows. "Looks fun, huh?"

Thomas gave a reluctant nod.

"Let me show you the back yard." Regina led them around to a sliding glass door that opened to a large grassy area. Sturdy fencing hedged the yard on all sides, separating it from the wooded area beyond. Sports paraphernalia was piled in the shade of an oak tree on one side. At the end of a footpath extending from the patio, a firepit sat on a circular base of pavers.

"Are there any squirrels?"

This was the first interest Thomas had shown.

Regina nodded. "Oh yeah, we see lots of squirrels, chipmunks, and bunny rabbits. They like to hide in all those trees beyond our fence."

Thomas's lips curved up.

Alli took a few steps out onto the grass. "This is a great yard."

"We make good use out of this space. We're blessed to have so much room for the kids to run around in. So, they play sports out here, we have cookouts. When the weather's nice we sometimes even bring out a projector and have outside movie night."

"Sounds awesome. I hope you don't mind my asking, but with a fire pit where do you keep—"

"All the fire-making stuff is locked up in a secure shed, and we have multiple extinguishers on hand at all times."

Alli nodded. "Okay. Good. And . . . what about off-site? Do you take the kids out much?"

"Well, there's a mall about five miles away, and a bowling alley. There's a YMCA close by. In the summer we sometimes take the kids to play and swim at the lake not too far from here."

Lake...

The shudder returned to snake down Alli's spine. "I'm . . .sure they like that." Just don't ask her to tag along.

Regina closed the sliding glass door as the trio stepped back inside. Back into the foyer with its blinding spirituality and the haunting images that came with it. Entering from this side, Alli noted the sign above the front door for the first time. *Precious In His Sight.* The words lanced through her, conjuring a deeper memory. One she'd fought to forget but now came clawing to the surface.

Someone had shared those very words with her once.

She'd been living with Barb and Pastor Roy, and it felt almost like family. How different might her life have been if she'd been able to stay with them forever? She'd played with the church kids at VBS and felt truly happy for the first time in her life. So, for a few weeks the summer she was eight years old, she'd felt precious.

She'd never felt that way again.

Goosebumps raised the hairs on her arms. Would Thomas feel precious here? Or would he sense the emptiness of the words—the promises—woven into most everything in a place like this? Her back went rigid and she struggled to box up the memories before they showed on her face.

Regina gestured them toward the hall. "Let me show you where your room will be. Right this way."

"Good idea." Longingly, Alli eyed the front door again as she walked by. At eight years old, Alli thought God had rescued her. It was later that He'd turned a deaf ear to her prayers.

Thomas, and all the kids in the foster care system, would face the same bitter truth. There was no divine champion wielding a sword for him, no righter-of-wrongs or haloed man in robes with arms opened wide for him.

Just a vigilant social worker who'd fight to the death to keep him from falling through the cracks.

Sunlight poured through the windows, casting a happy glow on all it touched. She rubbed at her forehead with tensed fingers, resenting her inability to conjure the vitriol she wanted.

However fleeting it had been, however ugly the truth about religion turned out to be, that summer still held her best childhood memories. And that fact galled her. Back then, the idea of Jesus was a comfort. And part of her wondered if maybe Thomas should be afforded the same respite, however temporary. Like Santa Clause bringing magic to Christmas, perhaps Jesus could serve as a harmless token of hope.

But when that hope shattered . . .

She twisted her lips to the side, the conflict warring inside her as they passed the kitchen.

"Shut *up!*" The squeak of tennis shoes on linoleum preceded a dull thud.

Alli whirled around to see two adolescent boys in a scuffle. Thomas took tight hold of her hand and Alli's jaw flexed. She knew it. Not ten minutes since arriving and already her concerns were playing out in front of her.

The bigger kid had the smaller one on the ground, straddling him. Alli's stomach coiled in response to the memorized feel of a punch to the gut. But she wasn't ten years old anymore, and she wouldn't watch from the sidelines.

"Hey. Hey!" Her feet were carrying her toward the pretzeled arms and legs on the floor when a broad-shouldered man materialized out of nowhere, a black karate outfit pulling taut across a muscular physique. She halted mid-stride as he bent and gripped the shoulders of the aggressor, pulling him off the other kid.

She froze to watch. Just how did they handle bullying here at Grace House?

"Jake. *Stop.*" Muscles coiled, David yanked the teen up onto his feet and looked into his storming, rage-filled eyes. Injury and desperation and raw pain reflected back at him, tightening a cord around David's chest. He fought the reflexive instinct to raise his voice and put someone in their place, and instead pointed a calm but steely gaze at the boy still on the floor. Reuben stared up at him with cold, hardened eyes and a sneer. David tugged the reigns on his frustration and delivered his words in an unruffled tone. "Reuben, why don't you go on to your room." *Lord, keep me calm.*

"I didn't do nothin'." Reuben jumped up, tugged his shirt down in a huff, then stalked down the hall and slammed his bedroom door.

Yeah right, *nothin'.* That kid loved riling people up. Poking at them wherever it hurt most.

Puffing his cheeks out, David turned back to Jake, whose chest rose and fell in rapid succession, brought on by more than the loss of his temper. The boy was unarguably shaken to his core. David gripped the back of the kid's neck and locked his gaze on Jake's. "What happened?"

His tongue darted over trembling lips. "You wouldn't get it."

Oh, wouldn't he? David had seen and heard it all. Right now, he recognized vulnerability. "Whatever it is, you can't let it sink its teeth into you this way. What'd he say?"

A bead of moisture escaped the corner of Jake's eye, further clenching David's gut. The teen bitterly wiped the heel of his hand across it and looked away, planting his hands on his hips.

"Jake?"

Nostrils flaring, Jake shook his head as if to rid his mind of some foul memory. "He said . . ." His throat bobbed, his voice turning to a gritty whisper. "He said I probably liked it."

Scorching heat raced up David's neck into his face and he blinked against the burn in his eyes as Jake elaborated on some of the finer points of Reuben's taunting. Lord help him, David would've probably socked that kid, too. His nostrils distended. *Give it to God. Just give it to God.*

He gave Jake a quick shake. "Listen. Reuben has his own issues to work through. I know he's tough to deal with. He was . . .*completely* out of line." He'd have to talk to the house parents about this. "But . . ." David shook his head and shot up a prayer for the right words. "If you don't learn how to let it go, you'll always be controlled by the anger . . .and by what was done to you."

Eyes averted, Jake pressed his lips together, his jaw muscle spasming.

"Your abuser had power over your body." The walls of his throat tightened around a growl. "Don't let him have power over your soul. The only way to beat this, is to not let it define you. God wants to give you that victory. Let Him worry about Reuben's problem. You just focus one day at a time on letting God's love heal you, okay? You can overcome, through Christ. I believe that."

Jake shifted his weight and met David's gaze without a word. But his eyes said he was listening. Hearing. He dipped his chin, shoulders slumping as he released the tension.

Good. He was already gaining the upper hand on his life. "Come by my office later and we'll talk more, okay?"

"Yeah." Jake sniffed and, chin high, set his jaw and met David's gaze. "Thanks, Pastor David."

"Any time." David pulled the teen into a firm embrace, clapped him on the shoulder, then sent him on his way.

Walking alongside young men like Jake, victims of their rage on top of all else, David sensed an inner tug, a call to more action. But what was it that God would have him do?

Whatever it was, God would reveal it in His own time. For now, David would keep mentoring the boys who filed through this place. And pray it made a difference.

Alli watched the exchange in stunned silence. After a bro hug from whoever that karate guy was, this Jake kid simply turned to go. She blinked after him. That was *it?*

She looked to Regina, whose gaze was tracking Jake's retreating form. "A pat on the back and he's on his way? I hope the turn-the-other cheek thing doesn't mean that kind of violence is given a free pass around here."

"Of course not, Miss Johnson. David handled the situation perfectly; he knows what he's doing. He's one of our counselors. A volunteer mentor for the boys. He's got a special way of connecting to the angriest ones."

And that was a badge of honor? "Special. Huh."

"He's incredible with them really. Abundantly patient."

Did his *patience* with Jake's temper mean that others were at risk of being subjected to it? He'd pummeled that kid like a punching bag! Thomas fixed his attention on Herman, blocking out the drama, the chaos of his world.

A sour taste coated the back of Alli's tongue, but she strained to keep a civil and professional tone. "What consequences will there be for Jake? And is anyone going to take the time to check on the boy he hurt?"

"David, or my husband, will talk to each of them, I assure you. Don't worry, Alli. All of our staff and volunteers are well trained, and we have a strong record for being a peaceful home."

Alli released her stifled breath and forced her shoulders to relax. That part was true. Grace House *did* have a good reputation; she'd done her research before heading out here. "Of course. Please understand that it's my job to keep you under a microscope. And I take my job very seriously."

Regina smiled the smile of someone impressed rather than accused. "I wouldn't want it any other way. As for what you just witnessed with those two . . . well, things aren't always what they appear on the surface. The situation is complicated. I'm sure that David is writing up a report right now, and later we'll meet to review it and to pray for wisdom in how to proceed with each of these boys."

These people prayed about everything. But Alli mustered a smile. "Thank you for understanding."

"Sure." Regina returned a grin of her own. "Now, let's see Thomas's room."

They spent a few minutes helping Thomas put his things into the drawers assigned to him, then Alli squeezed his shoulder. "Okay, kid, Regina here will get you settled in, introduce you to the others. She told me there's a soccer game today. And I'll swing by and check on you soon."

Thomas looked away, staring into space. "Or I could just go home with you."

Alli twisted her lips. "Can't do that."

His face pointed down at his tennis shoes. "I know."

"He'll be fine," Regina reassured her.

"Yeah. Course he will." She shifted her weight and rested her thumbs in her back pockets. He *would* be fine here. At least for a few days. She had to quit worrying.

"You won't forget to deliver my card, right?"

"Course not, kid. Doris will love it."

Regina called over another volunteer to show Thomas around the remainder of the house, then led Alli toward the kitchen. "Can I get you a cup of coffee before you go?"

"Oh, you don't have to go to any trouble."

"Already made, so no trouble at all."

"In that case, it sounds great." She could sure use an extra jolt of caffeine after the last twenty-four hours. Plus, it afforded her a few extra minutes to case the place.

Regina poured coffee into a large mug and handed it to Alli. "The cream's in the fridge, take your pick."

"Thanks." Alli peered into the fridge at the choices of creamers and her eyes immediately snagged on the one she wanted. "Ah, pumpkin."

"My favorite, too. Love this time of year."

"Same here." Alli assessed the woman in front of her. Sure, she sprinkled a little too much religion into conversation, but Regina had a kind, open face. Soft, bright, but strong. Had to be strong to run a place like this, to make it her life. Alli's hand stilled on the creamer lid as relief seeped through her—though hesitant to admit it, so far, she liked the woman. One thing Alli was good at, was reading people. And she could tell that Regina was "good people."

As Alli lifted her mug to her lips, she caught the words stamped on its side in scrolling font: *This is the day the Lord hath made.* Good gravy, this place was dripping in Jesus.

Regina's gaze shifted beyond Alli, toward the kitchen entry, and recognition sparked in her countenance. "Oh, good. David, I want you to meet Alli."

Alli stiffened at the name. David. Karate dude. She put on her polite face and pivoted his way.

"She's a social worker, just brought in a new boy. He'll be out there with your Soccer group today."

"Oh, hey. Nice to meet you, Alli." The man extended his hand and Alli offered the appropriate smile as she shook it. His grip was friendly-firm, his hand cool and slightly rougher than she expected.

"You, too." Alli squinted into his copper brown eyes, tried to read his face. The guy with the soft spot for bullies. And who'd be spending quite a bit of time with Thomas.

When she pulled her hand from his and wrapped it back around her hot mug, David clasped his hands at his lower back and gave a crisp nod. Ex-military, she'd guess.

She flicked her assessing gaze down the length of him. "I see you've changed clothes." At his quizzical look, she added, "You were in a karate outfit earlier."

One brow winged upward. "That's right. I was. I'd just come from the Y." He looked at Regina. "I hope we're still on for that conversation later today."

"Yep," she answered. "Kyle and I are looking forward to it." She took a leisurely sip from her mug and David helped himself to a cup.

"So… Alli, I know you sent over Thomas's file, but what can you tell us about him?"

Thomas's toothy grin appeared in her imagination. Alli pointed her gaze out the window above the sink and felt a smile soften her face. "He's an awesome kid. A bit reserved and shy. He retreats from conflict. You'll see in his file he does have a history of running away from homes, always after some sort of trigger. To be candid," she ran her tongue along her teeth, "I wish he didn't have to be here. In a mixed environment. He's the kind of kid who is easily overlooked—not that I think you'll overlook him, but he knows how to fade into a background."

"We won't let that happen then," David's said simply.

She paused to look at him. "Good." David seemed to be the type who liked clear-cut solutions. "Thomas is funny. Compassionate. Likes to read. Has a thing for hermit crabs." A laugh spilled from her. "Thank you again for letting him bring Herman with him. That was a non-negotiable as far he's concerned."

Graciously, Regina tipped her head. "I'm glad we were able to make him feel more at home."

Home.

"Yes, well. He'll be back with the McMillans soon. But until then, I'm thankful he has somewhere to go."

Regina wiped the lipstick from the rim of her mug with her thumb, her expression contemplative. "He sounds like a special boy in need of an extra dose of love. Speaking of which, I'm just going to peek on him and make sure he's doing all right with the others in the living room. Be right back." She slipped out of the kitchen.

Alli leaned a hip against the counter, and faced David, noting the outline of his biceps beneath the fabric of his sleeves. She could tell a lot about a person in five seconds flat. This man worked out. Regularly. Though he was dressed casually in a Henley and jeans, neither had been yanked from a pile of dirty clothes—no wrinkles. Two out of the three buttons of his shirt were done up. The man was disciplined, in control, yet also relaxed and comfortable in his own skin.

He grinned at her and held her gaze.

David was also confident and engaged with the world around him. All good traits. For anyone working with her clients that was.

"You look like a lady with a question to ask."

Perceptive. She canted her head. "I admit I'm curious about how you handled that brawl back there earlier. I saw no consequences doled out, no correction."

"Oh, there will be correction, no doubt about it. Reuben is a tough nut to crack."

"You mean Jake, don't you? I thought Reuben was the one on the ground. And quite honestly, I thought he deserved more concern than he got."

"That's because you don't know what you're talking about."

Alli blinked at the blunt rebuke, but he went on. "Reuben has a sharp tongue. Too sharp for his own good."

"Surely you aren't saying it was Reuben's fault he was beat up."

"Jake needs to learn self-control, no doubt about it. But yes, I'm saying it was Reuben's fault." His Adam's apple bobbed, and the muscle of his jaw twitched.

Alli opened her mouth, closed it. "Okay, look." She put her mug down and crossed her arms over her chest. "I'd like to know whatever this insider info is regarding that fight. I'm leaving a young client here and I don't know you guys very well yet and this is going to bug me. What is it I'm missing?"

He nodded, then stepped closer to her. So close she could smell his aftershave. She swallowed and suspended her breath as he spoke in lowered tones. "Short version is that Jake was sexually abused for years, and Reuben teased him about it. Told him he liked it, couldn't get enough. And he used much more descriptive language than I'm comfortable with repeating. I probably would've reacted the same way Jake did."

Alli lowered her gaze, sobered. He was right. She *hadn't* known what she was talking about. She ran her tongue along dry lips. "I guess it *is* more complicated than it appeared."

"Most things in life are." He took a long drag from his coffee and when he lowered the mug, the cloud had lifted from his countenance. "Anything else you want to ask?"

Alli cleared her throat. "Well. I understand you're the boys' counselor?"

He nodded. "One of them. I wear a few hats around here. Counselor, coach, chaplain."

Her eyebrows spiked as shock whooshed over her like a cold bucket of water. "Chaplain? You're a . . . *minister*?" She had *not* seen that one coming. Her people-reader skills bombed that one. She slapped a frozen smile on her face, fighting to hide the uneasy sputtering of her pulse.

"A pastor, yes. For youth. I work at New Life Worship Center, a few blocks from here."

"Oh." Alli's shoulders tensed at the revelation. She didn't cross paths with many pastors. "That's . . . neat." *Neat?* To hide her warming cheeks, she lifted her now lukewarm coffee to her lips.

She shouldn't have been surprised to find a preacher at a faith-based group home, but this man looked nothing like the pastors she'd met in her childhood. With a head of hair to rival James Dean's, a smile like Robert Redford, and those muscled arms. He looked so . . .

Normal, she thought. Yeah, let's go with that.

But this guy had swallowed enough of the Kool Aid to make God his *career*. She searched his eyes for that strange look that people in religious bubbles always had. Yes, it was there; how had she missed it? He had the unmistakable aura of a person from a world full of sunbeams and flowers and easy answers.

An unspannable gulf suddenly opened between them. Noah's Ark felt-boards on one side, dark closets and belt buckles on the other.

David's mouth tipped and his gold-flecked eyes skimmed the angles of her face. "You're uncomfortable with church."

Alli coughed as the brew started going down the wrong pipe. She fought to swallow rather than spew pumpkin coffee on the pastor's shoes. "What? No. Of course not." She cleared her throat again then coughed.

The man was direct. And a little *too* perceptive. He turned his head and gave her a knowing, sideways smile.

He left her no escape. "I just . . ." She bounced a shoulder. "I'm not what you call a believer, okay?"

"Oh. Well, that's too bad."

She balked. "Why? You think everyone has to believe the same as you do? I just don't. I'm too rational for faith. Sorry."

"And I'm sorry you seem to think I have no brain; or that I've checked it at the door."

"That's not what I meant." Her lungs deflated. Why did she have to go and offend him? "Don't get me wrong, church can be great if that's your thing." She again recalled her eight-year-old self, and a reflexive longing to revisit those days pressed on her sternum, reducing her voice to a hoarse whisper. "Thomas could probably use a little Jesus right now." She straightened and stared at him. Why had she said that?

David smiled. "I agree. But hey, relax. You might not believe the same as me, but I won't bite."

The room around her was shrinking.

"Of course not. I didn't think that." Alli offered a laugh, hating the forced sound of it. The clergy was one group of people she could *not* fit in with. And she hated that, too. Friendly Coworker, check. Legal Advocate, check. Party Girl, check. Worshiper? No check.

She stood there, speechless as his gaze pinned hers for several heart beats. The air between them vibrated with mounting tension until the awkwardness was unbearable.

How could she break it, make him smile? Get out of there?

"Um . . ." She gave herself a shake and tapped her watch. "Ya know, I should get going. Court appearance later and some things to get done before that. Busy, busy. You know how it is. Thank you." She set her mug in the sink and turned to go.

"Oh. Yeah, okay. You do have a tough job. An important job. So . . . have a good day. It was nice meeting you, Alli."

She glanced over her shoulder and nodded. "You, too." She hurried the last few steps to the front door, trying not to appear as though she were running. But once outside, she appreciated the relief of cool air on her hot cheeks.

Her neck muscles were tight as she pulled her car out of the driveway.

A couple days. Mrs. McMillan would be recovered and ready to take Thomas back home in a couple days, tops.

Chapter Three

David eyed Alli's exit from over the rim of his coffee mug. That woman had obviously been wounded. Bore scars she blamed on God if he were to guess. But he'd learned some time ago that God was the *answer*, not the problem.

He ran his thumbs up and down the mug in his hands, replaying their conversation. The way she'd reacted when he said he was a pastor, like he was a Martian rather than a man. Worse than that, a Martian out to get her. *I come in peace*, he should've said. Practically did.

His jaw muscle twitched with his irritation. He couldn't help it. Being judged, labeled as the guy to stay clear of—he hated it. For any kind of reason.

He understood why some people felt intimidated by pastors, but it still chafed. What did they think, that he was born holding a communion wafer? His path to faith was far from smooth and he was no stranger to struggle. Just ask Hoffman, Quincy, or any of the guys in his platoon. He was like everyone else. Well, mostly. Was that so hard to believe?

So, share your story.

He grimaced at the prodding. No, he didn't want to get into that. It wasn't like he'd never talked about the war, the toll his military service had taken on him. The restoration of his mind and spirit. He referred to it often enough—without the gory specifics. He just didn't like to trudge through the details. They belonged in the past. Forgetting what lies behind, and all that.

Parts of his story were exactly that—*his*. He'd chosen to put them away. Move on. No discussion. If that meant people might make false assumptions about it, that wasn't his problem.

He polished off his coffee and was rinsing his cup when Regina returned.

"Did Miss Johnson have to leave? I'm sorry I missed saying goodbye."

Dragged back to the present, David turned to face her. "Yeah, she took off a minute ago. What do you make of her?"

"She seems like a good advocate, dedicated. I can tell she cares about Thomas, not like he's just another case number. I like her."

David nodded. "Yeah. I got that from her too. She's also . . ." What word was he looking for?

"Pretty?" Regina's eyes sparkled with mischief and David resisted a groan.

"I was going to say hurting. Or guarded."

"Most people are."

He twisted his lips and nodded. "I suppose that's true." Everyone fought secret battles.

"She's also pretty."

David shook his head. Why did everyone assume he needed a woman? "She doesn't believe in God, so you can put the kibosh on that scheming of yours."

"Well now, that's not something I like to hear."

"That your scheming is thwarted, or that Alli has no relationship with her Creator?"

"Both, actually. But maybe God crossed our paths for a reason."

"You may be right."

"I usually am." Regina grinned, then pointed her gaze out the window for a moment as if she were lifting a prayer right then and there.

David checked his watch. "Don't want to keep the boys waiting, I better get outside."

"Thanks for taking the younger ones today. They adored you last week." She beamed at him, and he dipped his chin.

"No problem."

There was never a surplus of volunteers at Grace House, and since they'd taken in a few younger boys, David went where he was needed. Even if it was out of his comfort zone.

"Thomas should be ready, I'll bring him right out. Let me know how he does."

"Will do. Can't wait to meet him." With a grin, David pushed off from the counter and crossed the living room to the sliding-glass door.

Sports did wonders for kids with so much bottled-up frustration and anger. Ever since he'd begun introducing the boys to different sports, he'd watched confidence begin to replace defensiveness. Didn't matter if they were any good or not. Though some of these kids displayed a surprising amount of talent.

The lawn had been set up with two small soccer goals, and a couple of his boys were already out practicing some footwork. David nodded approval. "Hey, guys. Lookin' good."

"Thanks, Coach."

He lifted an arm to wave them in. "Let's line up for some warmups while we wait for the others."

The boys fanned out and mirrored David as he twisted from side to side.

In his periphery, David caught sight of Regina stepping out the back door with a small, shy-looking boy with brown hair and red tennis shoes. As she led the youngster to the group, David addressed the kids. "Listen, we've got a new teammate today, so I want you to make him feel welcome."

Heads nodded. *Good.*

Regina grinned. "Hey, David. Here's your new recruit."

David knelt in front of the boy and smiled. "You must be Thomas. My name is David."

The boy didn't answer, just stared back at him with a pair of haunted, wary brown eyes. Eyes broadcasting that there was a lot more going on in his head than expressed with his body.

"How old are you?"

"Seven," he answered flatly.

"Seven? Awesome. Listen, we're gonna play a little soccer today, have you played before?"

Thomas shook his head, his face tight. "No. I like T-ball. It's way better than soccer. Mr. McMillan, he's my foster dad, he takes me to play at the park sometimes. And he's real good."

David's eyes crinkled and he breathed a silent prayer. "I'm sure he is. How about we give you something to show Mr. McMillan when you go back home. He'll be proud, I'm sure."

Thomas stared back at him. He didn't speak, but his eyes had lost a bit of their fire. He shrugged a small shoulder.

David shook his head. Like every kid here, this one had been let down. Royally. So, for as long as Thomas remained in the group home, David would do his best to make the boy feel important, welcome. To show him that there were adults who cared.

He stood and placed a hand on the boy's shoulder. "Well, come on then. Let me introduce you to my friends." He pointed to each of the faces standing around. "This is Caleb, Jeremy, Nolan, and Avery. Guys, this is Thomas."

"Hey."

"Hi."

"What's up?"

"Yo."

Thomas lifted a hand and spoke almost too quietly to hear. "Hi."

David clapped him on the back. "Good. Okay, let's get started."

Having gotten past the introductions on a good note, David was able to keep Thomas fully engaged throughout the sessions of soccer and basketball that he ran the boys through. David savored the small victory. He'd cracked the boy's shell. It was a start.

A breeze picked up, swirling a few brown leaves across the lawn. But despite the mild temperature, the boys were sweating.

David checked his watch then clapped his palms together. "All right, hands in!" David stuck his hand out and the boys hurried to gather around and pile theirs on top. "Okay, on three we'll say 'teamwork'. One, two, three—*Teamwork*!" The group tossed their arms in the air as they shouted. "Great job, guys. Let's get a snack! And then, I've got some prizes to hand out." He winked.

The energetic bunch bounded across the lawn to the sliding door and then into the kitchen. They each grabbed a granola bar and a Gatorade from the counter and took a seat around the table.

David rested his forearms on the table and bit into his granola bar. This was usually the time he left them all with an encouraging word.

"Thomas, that's quite a kick you've got. And Jeremy, wow, that goal you scored? Awesome."

"Thanks, Coach!"

Beside him, Avery grunted.

David angled toward him. "Hey, you can't block them all. You were great out there, too. Remember guys, God is still there for you whether you do well or not. No matter what. Right? Let's review our Bible verse."

The boys, except for Thomas, recited in unison, "People look at the outside, but God looks at the inside."

"That's right. He knows us on the inside and loves us no matter what. The Bible says he's our constant friend. Even when we feel alone, or do the wrong thing, or don't play our best."

David stroked his chin. "Now let's see. I think I promised prizes? Wait right here."

He ran to his office and returned with a plastic bag. "Do you guys know what dog tags are?" He pulled out the chains with the Called to Duty solider on them and handed one to Nolan. "Dog tags are worn by the military for identification. These ones here? Identify us as soldiers for God and others."

"Don't you have real dog tags?"

"I do. I keep them hanging by my bedside, and one of these along with them. So, I never forget Who I really serve."

"Cool."

When he got to Thomas, he paused until their eyes connected. "Welcome to Grace House, Thomas. This bunch of rascals here . . .it's like family. When you look at this, I hope it reminds you that you have people who've got your back." He slipped the chain over his head.

Thomas fingered the tag, studying it. Then he looked up at David and quirked his lips. "Thank you," came his small voice.

"Any time."

"Pastor David, do you want to stay and play Mario Cart with me?" Caleb stuck an orange wedge in his mouth and grinned.

David rustled the boy's hair. "I love me some Mario, but I've got a lesson to prepare. Maybe Thomas would like to take my place?"

Thomas's eyes sparkled. He nodded.

David bobbed his head. "Cool. Why don't you guys show Thomas the game room and I'll see ya tomorrow."

"Okay. Come on, it's over here." Caleb and Jeremy walked on either side of Thomas as they headed out of the kitchen, Daniel close behind.

Thomas would do just fine here. His social worker had nothing to worry about. David lifted silent prayers for each of the kids living under the roof of Grace House. But his gut churned as he tossed granola bar wrappers into the bin. Grace House was a family of sorts, but it was far from ideal, and these kids had a lot of unmet needs.

Kyle popped into the dining room. "David, got a minute for a quick chat?"

"Course." He followed behind Kyle down to the office, where Regina was waiting.

"Hey, David. Come on in. Have a seat." Kyle clapped his shoulder and gestured to a chair.

When they were all seated, Regina crossed her legs and looked at her husband expectantly.

David crossed a foot over his knee. "The new kid did fine. A bit standoffish but he'll come around."

"Oh good, that's great. But we wanted to talk about something else. About a proposal we want to make."

"Okay. What's on your mind, guys?"

"Well, we've heard from a few of the boys how much they enjoy the Karate demonstrations and wish they could learn, and so we thought to ourselves, maybe you'd be interested in making it a new program here. We could clear out that sunroom and you could use that space, set up a schedule based on your availability. Put it into rotation with the outdoor sports. What do you think?"

David paused, lips parted. His gaze darted between the two people in front of him. This was nothing short of an answered prayer.

"What do I think?" He licked his lips. "I've been looking for something like this for a while now. It would be great for so many of the kids here. A couple of them in particular."

His thoughts leapt to the scuffle earlier. That fire in Jake's eyes . . . David knew that anger, the heat of it. And he wanted nothing more than to help Jake escape it. To teach him focus, dignity, control. It was karate that helped him tame the inferno. To master it instead of being consumed by it. And it was God who had helped him replace that anger with a vision to serve.

His thoughts raced. He tapped his temple. "I've got it all sketched out in my mind already."

He went on to lay out his vision of weekly Kenpo lessons interwoven with faith messages, sharing how much Kenpo meant for him personally. He answered their questions about logistics and safety, his excitement building as it became more real.

Regina gave a wide-eyed nod. "I'm flabbergasted, David. I wasn't expecting you to have put so much thought into this already."

He lifted his shoulders. "Well, it's gotta be the Lord, right?"

Kyle grinned. "Then let's go for it."

Ten minutes later, David walked out of Grace House with a sense of purpose. A mission. One he was eager to take on.

He spent the following few hours at the church preparing his next sermon, then arrived back home to his condo. He unlocked his door and set the stack of mail on the counter before neatly depositing his shoes in his bedroom closet.

David flipped through his mail, sorting trash from the important stuff. Tomorrow, he'd put together a rough plan for a four-week introductory class. He tossed aside an ad for maid service and as he turned to the last piece of mail, familiar handwriting snagged his eye and stopped him cold.

No. It couldn't be. That man wouldn't dare.

But the return address confirmed the sender. Unwelcome sights invaded David's brain, memories clawing their way out of the grave he'd buried them in. Glowing red. Pitch black. The click of the lock reverberated in his ears, carried to him from years past. Every scar on his body seemed to burn afresh, and his heart and lungs burst into action.

The vein in his neck pulsing, David closed his eyes, willing himself to stay calm. Deep breath in; deep breath out.

It wasn't working.

Heat crept up the back of his neck, inflamed his jaw. Would he forever contend with those horrific years? Would he never be free of them? Not while the man with the power to plunge him back into the torment refused to leave him be. Permanently.

Chest wall spasming, David watched his fingers curl into a fist around the envelope, crushing the unwanted intrusion into his well-controlled life. How dare he send this?

David's fist struck the countertop, sending a shock of pain up into his flexed forearm. Pulse throbbing hot in his veins, he took the two strides into the kitchen, swung open his pantry, and stuffed the offense into the trash bin. He did not owe a thing to this man, and it would be a cold day in hades when he would read a single word from him.

Alli grabbed a new piece of sandpaper and scoured it across the seat of the old dining chair. Her tense muscles appreciated the release as she worked the grain.

Today she'd made multiple home visits, hunched over stacks of paperwork, and stood before a judge to recommend severing a father's parental rights in one of her more abusive cases. It was never easy. Despite what they thought, Alli did not relish severing a parent's rights. But she had no qualms about doing it when necessary. Part of the broken system was not making the call when it needed to be made. Giving strung-out, neglectful parents too many chances to screw up their kids. It was just as bad as being too quick to remove a child and it was one of the parts of her job that Alli was good at—pulling the trigger. The day had been intensely stressful, but most of the knots in her neck came from leaving Thomas at that group home this morning.

With the day now behind her, she wanted nothing more than to get her mind off work. Off the scads of kids waiting for a home, hoping to feel wanted. Whole.

She blew across the wood, sending a swirl of sawdust to the floor, then brushed her fingers along the smooth surface. She'd scored the chair on her last garage sale hunt—the final piece to her eclectic dining set. A smile touched her lips. It would be beautiful once she stained and sealed it. Another mission accomplished.

Scritch, scritch, scritch. The sandpaper moved across the spindles. This chair was going to be brand new. It's what she did—turned trash into treasure.

A blonde strand fell into her eyes and Alli wiped her arm across her forehead, the silence of the house heavy around her. Oppressive. Too much quiet invited too much thinking. About the kids, about the past.

She pushed herself up and stretched, then started her favorite playlist, cranking the volume. The fast-paced anthem hummed through her bones, compelling her to tap her palm against her chest to the beat. Closing her eyes, she let the lyrics pull her in, transport her to another world. One where she was someone else. Someone strong. Someone unbroken.

She mouthed the words, letting them dissolve her worries, and soon her restless feet twirled and danced her across the room as she sang. The chorus hit, and her spirits rose in tandem with the climbing notes as she belted them out, savoring the freedom to make all the noise she wanted. Her favorite perk to living alone. The fear-conquering climax of the song made her heart soar before coming down to end on a final, strong, sustained note that left her feeling invincible.

Blood pumping and mood considerably lifted, Alli sashayed back to her spot on the floor and took up her sanding again, working to the beat, humming along, a smile tugging at her cheeks.

Her private party was interrupted by the buzz of her cellphone and Alli braced herself for the possibilities. Another child found in an empty house? A call from the hospital about suspected abuse? Glancing at the caller ID, Alli released her trapped breath and allowed herself to smile as she pressed the phone to her ear. "Hey, you," she puffed, out of breath from the dancing and singing.

"Hey, Alli. It's Janelle."

She accepted the woman's invading presence in her life. Like it or not, Alli had a friend. "Hey, Janelle. Thought for a second it was work calling."

"Nope, just your friendly neighborhood goddess of fun. I saw you through the window dancing and felt left out."

"What?" Alli hustled to her living room window and yanked the curtain closed.

"Hey, you cut off my view."

"Creeper. I thought I was alone."

Janelle chuckled. "That's what made it so fun to watch."

"Happy to entertain you, I suppose." She brushed dust from her jeans and sank onto her couch, rolling her stiff wrist.

"So . . . you left pretty quick last night; didn't even say bye. Everything okay?"

"Oh. Yeah, sorry about that. I had to pick up a kid. I hope Garrett wasn't too put out."

"Are you kidding? He couldn't stop talking about you. So come on, tell me, what did you think of him?"

Alli's shoulders lifted. "He's nice. Good looking, successful. Doesn't take himself too seriously."

"Yeah, thanks for the resume. Now tell me what you *thought* of him. It looked like maybe there was a spark between you two. Am I right?" She sounded like an over-eager fourteen-year-old.

Alli rolled her lips and shrugged. "Sure, yeah. Maybe. I don't know."

Janelle groaned. "Alli, what is *wrong* with you? Do you want to be single forever?"

What *was* wrong with her? She'd wondered all her life. "You know me . . . I'm careful."

"Careful? Locking your doors at night is careful. Washing your hands during flu season is careful. Alli, you're like Fort Knox."

She huffed into the phone. "That's not true. And I'm not saying I don't like him. I'd go out with him again if he asked."

"Good! Because I happen to know he's going to call you tomorrow."

Alli's lashes beat a handful of times. "He is?" Her voice squeaked at the end. As the shock fizzled, she pressed a palm to her forehead and nodded. "All right. Good."

"Good, huh?"

Alli twisted her lips to the side.

"So, do I get a thank you? I knew you'd like him. It's those baby blues, right? I mean, don't tell Eric I said this, but wow, he's got uh-may-zing eyes. And hair, too." She gasped. "Oh my gosh, I just realized . . . he's Paul Walker's twin!" She paused as if waiting for a reaction. "You know, the actor? Fast and the Furious? . . . Hello?"

Alli smirked and crossed her arm over her chest. "Do *you* want to date him? Because I dunno, I might be more of a Robert Redford kind of—"

"Shut your pie hole."

Alli snickered and tucked her hair behind her ears. Janelle was so much fun to mess with.

"You're going to go out with him, fall in love, get married, and make babies, and then name one after me, okay?"

Mouth dry with saw dust, Alli looked around for her glass of water. She swallowed then licked her lips. "We'll see. Hey, I gotta be up early tomorrow for work."

An exaggerated sigh carried over the line. "Yeah, me too. Okay, catch ya later."

"Bye, Janelle." She tossed her phone onto the coffee table and stood. She did need to be up early for work, but Alli started her music back up and returned to her sanding, her thoughts buzzing, buzzing, buzzing. Garrett was going to call her. That was a good thing, right?

"Robert Redford?" she muttered. Where had that come from? *Don't answer that*, she told herself.

But it was too late. The man's face digitized itself in her brain and dragged her thoughts, kicking and screaming, back to Grace House. To the verses on the walls, the fighting boys, the uncomfortable way that illegally hot pastor looked at her.

Alli tried to shake it off, clear her head. Why should she waste any more time worrying about Grace House? Next time she saw the place it would be to take Thomas away from it. So, she needn't let that Holy Joe get under her skin. She gave a decisive nod, matter settled.

. . .Though seriously, what was with that guy? What kind of preacher looked like that?

She groaned. *Like what, you doof?* Was he supposed to be wearing a pompadour wig or something?

Her eyebrows spiked as she attended to the seat-back of the chair and argued with herself.

Yes! Yes, that would've been better. Instead, he looked like someone who'd work at Models R Us. And she could be mistaken, but she thought she'd even seen a bit of ink peeking out from under the sleeve on his forearm. But who ever heard of a tatted pastor?

She shook her head. It had to be a mole or birthmark or something. And what did it matter anyway? It was none of her business.

The songs shuffled through Kelly, Katie, and Taylor before she'd finished her sanding. Planting herself in front of her pantry, she popped Pringles into her mouth until she reached the bottom of the container. Who cared about cholesterol and sodium intake? Nobody around to tell *her* that junk food and midnight stress eating were bad ideas. She sighed. Nobody ever *had* been.

But what would it be like to have someone care whether she took care of herself or not?

With a flick of her tongue across her salty lips, she tipped the can and let the crumbs slide into her mouth then tossed the can in the trash and headed to bed.

Minutes later, in her sawdust-free PJs, arms wrapped around a puffy pillow, Alli closed her eyes and muscled her way into a fidgety sleep. Though it was anything but restful as brutal memories hunted her down like defenseless prey, strobing flashes of childhood events snapping at her mind as she lay trapped in unconsciousness.

"Smile, Alli. Joe doesn't like sour faces at the table."

Biting her quivering lip, Alli squeezed her eyes shut and counted to five, pushing out real life—the sting on her cheek, the words in her ears, the truth in her heart. She wasn't worth keeping. When she opened her eyes, she was a perfect daughter, part of a happy family. She smiled brightly at her foster mom, all pain successfully buried. For now.

"That's better, darling."

Alli sprang forward in bed with a gasp, thick darkness pressing in around her like an evil, suffocating presence. She fumbled for her lamp and turned it on, squinting against the aching brightness. Invisible fingers slowly retreated from around her pounding heart. She threw off the bedspread and swung her feet over the side, her chest heaving. That rejected little girl inside was trying to claw her way out, still trying to be rescued, but it was much too late for her.

Alli stalked to the bathroom to splash water on her face, then stared at her reflection until the sad, scared eyes looking back at her hardened into steely determination.

"You have a job to do, Alli. And no time to waste with might've-beens." She grabbed a hand towel and patted her face dry.

Feeling sorry for yourself, being weak . . .what did that ever get you?

Nothing. It got her nothing.

Alli slipped back under the covers and managed a couple more hours of sleep. The morning greeted her with nothing but silence from her cold, empty house. She pulled on a warm pair of slipper-socks, tightened the belt of her fluffy robe, and padded to the kitchen for coffee.

Percolating noises and rich aroma layered the air. While she waited for the coffee to brew, her mind wandered to the memories that had poked at her the previous night. Memories that told her she'd always had to pretend. Nobody wanted to see beyond the smile.

These nightmares. Would she ever be free from them?

Worse, this was the fate in store for the kids she worked with, if she missed something, failed them, made the wrong call. As their social worker, Alli was their last line of defense. Who better to help lead them through the system than one of its victims? But she was only one woman and she'd already let so many of them down.

Not this time.

She sat at her refinished table and stared out the window at the colors of sunrise. Loneliness nibbled at the edges of her spirit like the cold weather nipped her fingers. But she wrapped her chilled hands around a hot mug and smothered the loneliness with thoughts of her to-do list. Of going out again with Garrett.

Alli swallowed a sip of coffee, cherishing the warmth as it traveled down her throat into her belly. She imagined being alone with Garrett at a restaurant, without Janelle and Eric as a buffer. Pictured smiling at him across the table. But the face smiling back at her looked a little different. For some reason, he looked a lot like a Robert Redford.

The morning unfolded, and the sun arced higher into the sky, warming the air to a pleasantly brisk temperature, according to her car's thermometer. Alli's cell buzzed and rattled in her cup holder as she pulled into the parking lot of Mercy General. She swung the car into a space before grabbing the phone and pulling her hair over her shoulder. "Alli Johnson."

"Has he called yet?"

"Good morning to you too, Janelle."

"Yeah, morning. I take it he hasn't called yet?"

"It's not even noon yet. Chill."

"I have no chill. Not when it comes to twoo wuv."

"Okay, I think I just threw up a little. I gotta go."

"Oh fine. Call me later. Have a good day-a-ay," Janelle sing-songed.

A chuckle bounced her ribcage. "Bye." With a roll of her eyes, Alli stuffed the phone in her pocket. Garrett would call when he was ready . . . or he wouldn't. Both prospects were frightening.

She reached for the flowers and card on the passenger seat then went inside to find room 212. When she arrived, she rapped her knuckles on the door, waited for the "come in," and popped her head inside. "Good morning!"

Doris sat in a hospital bed, a white bandage wrapping her arm from wrist to elbow, and Greg sat beside her.

"Miss Johnson. Hi. You didn't have to come." A smile lifted Doris's cheeks but didn't reach her eyes.

"Of course, I came. How are you feeling?" Alli set the flowers down and stepped closer to the bed.

"Better, thanks."

"Good. Thomas has been worried. Here . . . he asked me to deliver this." She pulled the handmade card from her shoulder bag and held it out to Doris.

The woman's throat bobbed, and she slowly took the paper and examined it. "Thank you." Her eyes cut to her husband and Greg cleared his throat.

Okay, it didn't take spidey senses to realize something was wrong. Alli tucked her hair behind her ears. "So, what's the latest?"

"Doc says she can go home soon. Hopefully later today, but surely by tomorrow." Greg patted his wife's hand.

"That's awesome news. Thomas will be so happy to hear that. I also got an update this morning on Paul. His caseworker said he's in Juvenile Detention and will go before the judge this afternoon. Aggravated assault."

"Will they get him the help he needs?"

"Yes. But they'll also make sure he's in no position for this to happen again."

Doris nodded. "Thanks for letting us know."

"I have to get back to the office, but do you think it would be okay to bring Thomas by? He really misses you guys."

Doris's eyes filled with tears, and she turned to her husband, throat working.

"Can I have a word with you in the hall, Miss Johnson?"

Alli's heart stuttered. "Yes, of course."

A sense of dread stole over her as they stepped into the cold, sterile hallway.

Hesitance lined Greg's forehead. His crossed arms became a shield. "Doris and I have talked and . . . we've come to the conclusion that we should take a break from fostering."

The air around her thinned. "What?" *No way. No, no, no.*

Greg cleared his throat. "This has taken a toll on my wife, Miss Johnson. Not just physically. We care for Thomas, he's a good kid, but . . ." He hugged his biceps and looked down at his feet. "We're dropping out of the foster program."

A riptide pulled her under, sent her flailing for a handhold as the waters frothed in her brain. "B-but you can't do that." A ludicrous thing to say. Of course, they could drop out.

Greg knew it, too, if the flaring of his nostrils was any indication. Lifting his gaze from the floor, to her, he uncrossed his shielding arms to place his hands on his hipbones. "Yes. We can. We are."

Mouth parted, she stared at him and could practically see him digging his heels into the linoleum. Well, she could too. Thomas was worth it.

"Do you know how devastated Thomas will be? How can you be so heartless to a child you've taken into your *home* and made part of your family for the past six months?"

Red splotches appeared on Greg's face. "I don't appreciate your tone, Miss Johnson."

The reprimand should have should have yanked her back inside the bounds of professionalism, but visions of a ratty teddy bear clutched in the arms of a hurting little boy drove her on. "*Please*, Mr. McMillan. Please don't do this to Thomas. He needs you."

He backed up a step, head shaking. "My wife needs me more. We've made up our minds."

"But—"

"I'm sorry. I really am." Greg turned and pushed opened the door to rejoin his wife, leaving Alli alone in the hall. Looking into the room after him, Alli's eyes connected with Doris's before the woman looked away, her features colored in shame.

The next mother in a long list to abandon Thomas.

Moving from the condo's carpeted living room, David's bare feet registered the kitchen tile as ice. Invigorating, even if unwelcome. Catching sight of the crack in the pantry's door frame, he swallowed a groan and decided he'd rather skip breakfast than open it and face the crumpled letter he'd find there. He really should have taken out the trash the night before.

It had been a long time since he'd lost his cool to such a degree. Apparently, the 'old nature' wasn't as far from the surface as he'd like, and the realization chafed.

Last night it took great effort to master his emotions and regain an even keel. But finally, he'd recaptured a sense of control. A relenting of his anger. His sleep may have been tormented, but the Lord said His mercies were new every morning, and David had latched onto that promise years ago. Today was a day for facing the future, not revisiting the past, especially one he'd worked so hard to put behind him.

Like most days, he'd been up since dawn—exercising, reading the Bible, and now planning his day at the kitchen table. As he wrote out the day's goals and created a checklist of tasks relating to the Kenpo outreach, that buoying sense of purpose returned. Despite David's rough edges, God had work for him to do. An important role in the lives of these teenagers struggling to figure out who they were, to find their identities.

He tapped a pen against the notebook in front of him. How were Liam and his folks doing? He'd follow up with them today. Hopefully,

Liam was staying out of trouble at school. And planning to be at youth group this week. After jotting the phone call onto his list, he got dressed and headed out for the church. He told Kyle he'd be at Grace House that afternoon, but he needed to fit in time to work on his next sermon before the day got away from him.

The New Life Worship Center building was quiet and still when he arrived. A stark contrast to the crowded Sunday mornings and frequent evening meetings. He unlocked the doors, flicked on the lights, and headed down the empty hallway. If he could get the students to show up at 5 am, he might've been able to hold his karate class here. But trying to convince a teen to get out of bed in time for *school* was hard enough. Besides, Grace House was an even better choice for location as far as he was concerned. Affording the foster kids an opportunity they otherwise wouldn't have.

See? God knows what He's doing.

For my thoughts are not your thoughts, neither are your ways my ways.

That's for sure.

In the youth room, the place they called the Launch Pad, he settled into one of the well-worn armchairs and spent a few minutes scrolling social media, checking in on friends he seldom saw but who'd always be brothers. Their unspeakable experiences bonded them, though how each of them worked through it looked vastly different. Some seemed unable to escape the shadows, and their messy lives were the result.

He commented on a few posts, prayed for them, then shut down the app. He opened his Bible and study notes, and for the next forty-five minutes, David sank deep into the Word, drawing strength and certainty. Certainty that God was working— in everything.

The last wisps of morning fog floated past the window as he put the final touches on his next sermon. From beyond the walls, the sound of staff members' voices filtered to his ears, and the smell of coffee worked to override the remnants of the youth's latest popcorn party.

Pastor Ron leaned into the youth room, his thinning gray hair neatly combed. "Morning, David. Got a sec?"

He marked his place with a thumb and closed his Bible. "Of course. What can I do for you?"

The pastor stepped in and lowered his solid frame in the armchair across from David's. "I'm working on the Events Calendar. Wondered if I could talk to you about the next Men's Prayer Breakfast." Crinkles fanned out from the man's smiling eyes.

David had a good guess what was coming, and his stomach muscles coiled. "I only have a few minutes. I'm heading over to Grace House." He slipped his thumb from the pages and stacked the Bible and notebook on his thigh.

Pastor Ron's weathered cheeks lifted. "Again huh?"

"Get to introduce Kenpo to some of the kids today." His chest expanded as he anticipated the sense of control, purpose, normalcy.

"That's wonderful. Having supported them for so long, we're very glad to have someone physically there now."

"Well, I'm glad I get to be that someone."

"I can tell. They're not going to poach you from us, are they? Should I be keeping an eye out for a new youth pastor in the near future?" Mischief sparkled in his kind eyes.

"Well…" David's lips slid into a sideways smirk. "I mean, they do feed me home-cooked dinners a couple times a week. But…" He ran his palm across the stubble on his cheek and cast a pondering gaze from the podium to the ping pong table. "I have a soft spot for this fellowship and the kids in the youth group so… I'm not itching to leave at the moment." The room maybe, not his position as Youth Pastor.

Pastor Ron's thick brows arched in amusement. "Well, gee, that's nice to know."

"It is, right?" David straightened in his seat and shifted his weight forward to signal he was standing up. Maybe he could get out of there before the subject circled back to—

"So, listen. We're putting together the next Men's Prayer Breakfast and I wondered if you'd give your testimony."

"Oh, uh…" He tugged on his earlobe and resisted the urge to fidget.

"David, I know that those memories are hard, and the war isn't your favorite thing to reflect on." Pastor Ron looked at David from the tops of his eyes. "If you really don't think you're up for it, I'd understand. But the little bit you shared on Patriot Day, about your IED encounter," he slowly shook his head, eyes going misty, "It touched a lot of people, myself included. I *know* others would get something out of it too. Yours is a powerful testimony, David. The kind God can use to change lives."

David rolled his lips as he nodded, looking for words. Though his bowels knotted, he wouldn't argue the truth of that. God had rescued him in every way. Much of which had nothing to do with the explosion that nearly took his life. Or the myriad other brushes he'd had with death on foreign soil.

But it was *his* past. And, still fresh from last night's brush with history, David's interest in sharing his testimony was exactly nil, zip, nada.

He caught himself running his thumb over a scar on the underside of his forearm, stopped, and shifted in his seat. "Well… I mean, depends on when it is," he hedged. "I'd have to check my schedule; make sure it doesn't conflict with anything over at Grace House."

He prayed that it *would*. Revisiting his past wasn't something he wanted to put on the calendar, but he wasn't about to try and explain that.

"We're looking at right after the holidays. I'll email you the date and you can let me know. Sound good?"

A groan threatened to rumble in the back of his throat but, not wanting to disappoint Pastor Ron, he forced a smile. "Sounds good."

Like he'd done for years, David would find a way to speak around the details he didn't want to think about. No matter that they'd been pushing harder on the door of his mind lately, trying to bomb their way in and take him down.

Through its half-shuttered windows, the CPS building seemed to be glaring at the neighborhood, seeing the abuse, pain, and injustice hiding in its shadows. Just like Alli.

Tim greeted her the moment she flung open the glass door. He fell in step beside her. "So, I guess you heard, huh?"

She cut him a cold look and kept marching.

"They're just shaken up, Alli. It's like a post-traumatic stress thing. They need time. They'll reevaluate things in six months or so."

"But I have to tell Thomas he was right; they aren't keeping him." A fist clenched in her gut. "He's lost his home. He'd already bonded to them, Tim. The first time in a long time he's done that." A frown tugged on her lips. "I hate this."

"I know."

Bursting into her office, she stripped off her jacket and tossed it at the coat rack. She wanted to scream. Break something. She slumped down into her chair and banged her forehead on her desk, her voice disappearing into the wood. "It's not fair."

Tim's hand came to rest on her shoulder. "This one's under your skin, isn't he? More than average, I mean."

Her whole body drooped. "I don't know." She tipped her head back and stared at the ceiling. "I can't help it. I look at him and—"

"You see yourself."

Her gaze cut to his. "Something like that." The few who knew her full background rarely referred to it. Self-conscious, she straightened in her seat. "He deserves a real family."

"They all do, Alli."

"Yeah." She ran her thumb over the stack of folders in her inbox, counting them. So many kids. The stream never ended. Air dumped from her lungs. "But Thomas is special." She glanced at Tim. "I know, I know. They're all special, but . . ."

"I know what you mean." Tim sat on the edge of her desk and clasped his hands in his lap. "That's how I know you'll do right by him. Because you care too much to give less than your best. Alli, from the moment I read your file, I thought you'd be a good fit for little Thomas Cooper. And the first time I saw you with him, I *knew*—even, I think, before you did. You two are like peas in a pod. He needs someone like you." He stood and looked down at her, sobered. "But your role requires a level head, a measure of personal detachment. So . . . be careful, Miss Johnson."

She gave him a reassuring smile. "Always." It's what she was best at. Being careful. It's why she didn't let people in. She ran her fingernails up and down on her desk. Personal detachment was her unintended specialty. Even when she wanted something more, something deeper: Connection. Family. All the things she would never have.

Unless she made things work with Garrett.

Wait, what? Where did that thought come from? Man alive, what was *wrong* with her?

Tim rapped his knuckles on the desk. "Why don't you get an update on Patricia, hmm?"

Patricia? Ugh. Wasn't this day bad enough already? But she nodded. "Yeah." The next visit with Thomas's birth mother was coming up soon anyway.

Tim exited her office with a salute, leaving Alli to her work. Puffing her cheeks with an exhale, she grabbed the top file from the stack. She reviewed the case and made a few notes, filled out her report, then put it in her 'done' pile. But as she reached for the next case, her mind drifted back to the McMillans. To the latest in an inexhaustible string of losses.

How was she going to break the news to Thomas? Watch the small ounce of hope eke out of his spirit? She rubbed her temples and slouched back in her chair. Alli couldn't fail this one. She *had* to find him a new family. ASAP. Couldn't just leave him in a group home indefinitely.

Determination squared her shoulders as she opened the parent files and began scouring them for a new match. Maybe new families had been added to the register or were about to finish their required courses. Maybe someone had a spot open up since she'd last reviewed the list . . . a child returned home or one aged out.

Her phone rang, sending her thoughts to Garrett's imminent call, and knotting her stomach. A glance at the screen confirmed it was him. She spun her chair around and pressed the phone to her ear. "Alli speaking."

"Hey there, Sunshine."

Alli smirked and crossed an arm over her chest. "Hey, Garrett."

"So how are things?"

"Things are . . ." *Difficult. Complicated. Uncertain.* " . . .about average. How about you?"

"Good. Great. But you know, even better if you'd let me see you again."

An eyebrow twitched upward. "Oh, is that right?"

"Yep. So whaddya say? Saturday?"

"Ooh, Saturday's no good for me." Unalterable plans were already on her calendar.

"Friday then?"

"Sure, Friday works."

"Even better. Pick you up at six?"

"I'll meet you. At seven. Just tell me where."

"You know, the way dates usually work is the man comes to your door, maybe even brings you flowers, then he opens the car door for you, and you slide into his warm leather seats. You let him impress you a little."

Alli chuckled. "Sounds more like a third date kind of deal."

"Stubborn," he teased. "Okay, seven o'clock at Bordeaux Bistro."

Cautious, she thought. "Headstrong. And I'll see you there." After ending the call, Alli smiled and held the phone in her grip for a moment before turning back to face her desk. Who knew, maybe Janelle was right. Maybe this had a possibility of going somewhere if she just gave it a chance. As scary as it was, that was something she could do. Take a chance.

Dread settled in Alli's stomach as Regina opened the door of Grace House and invited her in.

"Hi, Regina."

"Alli, what's wrong? I've been worried since your text came in. I hope you're okay."

"Oh. Yeah, I'm fine. Thank you. But we do need to talk."

"Of course. Just give me a minute to grab Kyle." She offered a tight smile then shuffled off to find her husband.

As she waited, Alli crossed her arms over her chest, her eyes traveling the walls of the foyer and pulling her toward the den. A wall-hanging above the couch read "Let us come boldly to the throne of Grace." Another, on the opposite wall, read "For I know the plans I have for you, declares the Lord." The band around Alli's chest tightened and she looked away.

She started at a loud shout from somewhere in the back of the house. With a bit of a gasp, Alli spun in the direction of the sound. It came again, this time from a chorus of grunting voices. "Hyah!"

Brow tight, she followed the voices until she found their source. Her jaw dropped open. A sunroom had been converted to a makeshift karate room. Half a dozen teen boys stood in a wide stance, fists flying forward from their hips and back again, punctuated by that thunderous karate war cry.

And the instructor standing in front of them—Alli could hardly believe it—was the *minister*.

David Porter.

She blinked, stared. David was teaching these teens—these *angry* teens, many of them—how to be more effective fighters? Wouldn't a non-combative sport be better for these boys?

"When you punch, you want to focus on the first two knuckles for the strike." David tapped the knuckles of his right fist and slowly aimed at a volunteer's face until his fist was a hair's breadth from the guy's nose. "So, for high strikes, above the shoulder, that means you'll want to turn your palm up. See? That way you're striking with those knuckles rather than this part of the hand, which is where your injuries will come from. Your wrist will likely bend, and your weapon will be out of commission fast."

Weapon? Her eyes rounded. What on earth was he doing?

"For lower body punches—say, the bladder or spleen—you will turn your fist palm-down to strike with those knuckles. So, let's do that now—punch high, then low. Palm-up, then palm-down. And I want to hear your kyai with each blow."

"Yes, sensei!"

Alli felt the blows herself. Repugnance punched under her ribs and kicked her breathing up. Her spine straightening. How could anyone think it was a good idea to basically weaponize these kids with karate lessons, especially the chaplain? One of the boys here was the same one who'd tackled a kid to the ground on her first visit. What damage would he do next time?

She blinked away a thousand violent images and rubbed the spot on her belly that still recalled the sensation of having the wind knocked out of her.

"Alli? There you are."

Alli spun at the sound of Regina calling her name. Kyle was with her. She closed her eyes for a moment then gave a closed-mouth smile. "Sorry. I . . . followed the sound of . . ." she gestured toward the sunroom. " . . .anyway, here I am." Lungs full, she planted her hands in her back pockets. The news she was here to deliver had just gotten twice as bad.

"Okay guys, that's it for this lesson. Remember, *A fool always loses his temper, But a wise man holds it back.* Proverbs 29:11. Repeat that back to me. *A fool . . .*"

Maybe David needed to have *this* verse tattooed on his body somewhere. Like his forehead maybe. But life was about progress, not perfection. He knew Who to hand his temper to, and he knew how to help these teens in the same boat he'd always found himself in.

The boys repeated the verse and David nodded. "Good job, guys. Hope you enjoyed the lesson." The first Kenpo session at Grace House had gone very well. He let his gaze wander over the faces in the room, lifting each one in prayer.

His attention snagged on Alli, who stood outside the room with Regina and Kyle. Without intending to, he took notice of her silvery white scoop-necked sweater and fitted dark-wash jeans tucked into tall black boots. Her blonde waves fell simply and effortlessly down her back and caught the light streaming in from the full windows of the sunroom, launching his pulse into a fit of hiccups.

See, this was why he did not need a woman. Nothing but uninvited distraction.

Their gazes caught for one sharp instant, her eyes shadowed in disgust, before she looked away. He popped his head back. What, did he reek? Was he so scary? Or did she recoil from all pastors? Personal or not, she judged him. And *that* . . .he shook his head . . .that pushed his buttons. He exhaled slowly through pursed lips. *Just give it to God, man.*

The sunroom cleared of kids, and David approached the trio of adults. "Alli. How've you been?" He smiled, urging her to quit looking at him like he had two heads. Two *ugly* heads. Or else force her to confront the elephant in the room.

Expression tight, she flicked a response at him. "Fine. Thanks." She swiveled toward Regina. "So . . . your office?"

Brrr . . .cold.

David's forehead creased. They'd just met. How could he possibly have offended her in the few minutes they'd spoken?

"Miss Alli!" Thomas came running toward them, eyes lit up at the sight of Miss Johnson.

At the sight of the boy, Alli's stiff, clinical expression morphed into a hundred-watt smile. She looked almost human as she scruffed his head. "Hey, kiddo. You being good?" She tucked her hands into her back pockets.

David grabbed the chance to jump in, maybe soften her up. "You kidding? He's doing great. Aren't ya, bud? You should see him kick a soccer ball." See, he was a nice guy. Cared about the kids.

"Good." She smiled, but not at David.

Kyle cleared his throat. "David, will you join us in the office?"

"Uh, sure."

Thomas looked up at the circle of adults. "You're going to talk about me, aren't you?"

Alli shot a hard glance at David, who felt completely out of the loop, then at Thomas. "How about you go in the game room while we talk, then I'll come find you when we're finished, and you can let me say hi to Herman."

"Okay." Thomas's tone was flat as he turned and shuffled away.

Whatever was going on did not look good. Curiosity pulled David forward as he followed Alli into Regina and Kyle's office. The door closed and everyone took a seat.

"So, what's the update, Alli?" Regina's forehead crumpled.

Alli's tough exterior slipped and for three heartbeats, he was drawn in by the vulnerability beneath. She looked at each of them, her tongue darting out across her lips, then shook her head and swallowed. "Thomas's foster parents . . . they won't be taking him back."

Whoa, whoa, whoa. Hold up. "Greg and Doris McMillan?" David searched her face, incredulous. "I thought they were a pretty solid unit. I mean, Thomas talks about them all the time." How Greg took him to the park to play ball and Doris baked the best chocolate chip cookies. How they played boardgames on family game night and camped in the yard last summer. Surely, he hadn't made it all up.

She pressed her lips together and pulled her shoulders up toward her ears, as if reluctant to voice the facts. "After the attack, they've . . . declined . . . to take any children back in."

David dropped back in his chair feeling like he'd just taken a blow to the solar plexus. "Wow."

It wasn't unusual for kids to lose a foster placement, but watching it happen from a front row seat was harder than expected. Poor Thomas. David couldn't even imagine.

Alli nodded. "Yeah." She licked her lips and turned on her business voice again. "I want you all to know I'm doing *everything* I can to find another family as soon as possible. But if he can stay here just a little longer than I first thought . . .I'd really appreciate it."

"That's all right with us, his spot is secure." Kyle exchanged a look with his wife. "But he'll obviously be disappointed at this news."

Disappointed? Nostrils flaring, David leaned forward on his knees and prayed.

Alli straightened, her professionalism only thinly veiling her own frustration. "Yes. He'll feel rejected. Unwanted. Knowing Thomas, he'll likely respond by withdrawing, hiding. He may even try to run away. It's hard to say."

Regina nodded. "We'll keep a close eye on him, Alli. Don't worry."

David's muscles eased. Regina had been a house mom for years, and David had seen her in action plenty over the last six months. She'd know what to do. Which was good since David would have no idea what to say to the boy. He'd take a bitter teenager with a chip on his shoulder any day. But a shy seven-year-old? Thomas didn't need help reigning himself in or regulating his impulses. Almost the opposite. David wouldn't know how to help him.

He rubbed his palm over his cheek. "I don't know how useful I'd be but let me know if I can do anything to help."

Alli stared down at her hands and inhaled deeply. "Thank you." Her brow creased, marring her smooth skin, and she bit her lip—that clinical mask cracking, the sensitive girl inside peeking through again. "How's he been?" Her eyes slowly lifted to David's and for once held no ice. Only vulnerability. Warmth spread through his chest as she looked at him.

Hard exterior. Soft heart. *Bruised* heart?

He studied the worry lines on her forehead, wishing he could erase the tension there.

Wasn't that a pastor's wheelhouse? To offer hope and peace?

He swallowed. "First day was a little rough. But after that he started to relax. When I've been with him, he's been great. Mostly happy. Gets along with the other kids, participates in some of the games. He's doing good." The group activities should help him deal with this loss. He hoped.

Alli blinked then nodded briskly. "Okay. Good. Thank you." She smiled at each of them in turn. "I'll keep you posted." She stood and seemed to brace herself for the weighty burden firmly planted on her determined shoulders. She was a tough one. Or trying to be.

At the door, she swung back around. "Call me if you need me." Emotion swirled behind the steel of her hazel gaze.

"We will," Kyle offered. "We're praying for him."

She hesitated, then nodded and turned the knob.

"Alli, hold up. I'll walk you out." David rose and followed her out, falling in step beside her. "Regina and Kyle are good at this, don't worry."

"I know." Alli evaded his sight line and kept walking.

So, they were back to the brush-off. He stretched his neck, rolling his shoulder. *Just give it to God.*

When they got to the game room, Thomas was sitting on his knees in front of a coffee table, crayons spread out in front of him.

"Hey, kid." Alli hooked her thumbs in her back pocket and jerked her chin. "Come let me say hello to Herman before I go. Tell me what you've been up to."

Thomas got up from the table and walked over to her. "I made this for you." Somber, he handed her a folded paper.

Alli's smirk belied the light in her eyes. "Aw." She patted his back then looked at the picture. "This is going on my fridge." She grinned and led him out of the room without a word of acknowledgment to David.

He sighed.

"I don't think she likes you."

David turned toward Cade and crossed his arms over his chest. "What gave it away?"

Cade grinned and came to stand beside David, both of them looking off toward the direction she'd gone.

"I didn't like you when I first met you either."

"Thanks for that, punk."

Cade chuckled. "Don't take it personal, man. You can be an intimidating dude. Especially to someone trying to avoid thinking about God and church and all that. Ex-military *and* a pastor? Talk about a double-whammy."

David raised a brow. "So, what you're saying is, I can take your life, then judge your soul afterward?"

He shrugged. "Something like that."

Alli shot a discreet glance over her shoulder, confirming that, yep, David was still standing watch. The guy was a conundrum. She didn't like him. He set her teeth on edge. But whenever he spoke to her, he was . . . nice. And it wasn't a phony, trying-to-brainwash-her-into-religion, or get-in-her-pants kind of nice. She could sniff out that pile a mile away. The guy was genuine, which chafed. It made him a mystery, and one she didn't have time or inclination to solve.

She did get one question answered though. That wasn't a mole on his forearm. Couldn't quite make out what it was, but that was definitely a tattoo. Certainly fit with the karate-chopping military guy, but he was also a pastor. This did not compute.

Thomas led her to his room and toward the small table where Herman was caged.

"Here he is. He's sleeping."

She cleared her throat. "He's looking good. Looks happy here."

"Yeah, he likes it okay. Regina lets me give him pieces of apple sometimes instead of just his pellets. He likes that."

A smile touched her lips. "Regina's nice, isn't she?"

"Uh huh."

"And…everyone else?"

He nodded. "Kyle can fold paper into lots of neat shapes. And Pastor David gave me this." Reaching under the front of his shirt, he pulled up a chain he was wearing around his neck. "See?" A pair of dog tags swung back and forth as they dangled from his fingers. "It says something about doody." A snicker got loose from his lips.

She raised an eyebrow. "You sure that's what it says?"

He shrugged. "Something like that."

A closer look revealed the words *Called to Duty*. Her radar went up but before she could ask him more about it, he answered with everything she needed to know.

"It means people have my back. Like a family. It's cool." He tucked it back under his shirt.

"Yeah. Pretty cool, kid." Nothing negative to say to that. Alli puffed out her cheeks and lowered herself onto his bed, rubbing her thighs. "I need to talk to you for a minute. Why don't you come sit down?" She swallowed hard as Thomas sat beside her. "It's about Greg and Doris."

"Is she feeling better?"

Alli nodded. "Yeah, kiddo . . .she'll be fine."

"Did you give her the picture I made?"

"I did."

He grinned. "They probably miss me, huh?"

"Yeah." She squinted at him. "But . . . you won't be going back with them." With a tentative reach, she laid a hand on his knee. "I'm sorry."

The news dropped over the boy like a blackout curtain. He picked at something on his pant leg, lifted one slight shoulder and dropped it with a sigh. "I always knew they weren't gonna keep me. No big deal." But his lower lip trembled and when he looked away, the light from the window shimmered in his watery eyes.

Goosebumps poured down Alli's arms and legs. Thomas's gaze dropped to his lap, his lashes damp. She read the deep hurt, the thoughts of blaming himself, the disappearance of another piece of his identity. Like another shell that didn't fit. What if he stopped trying?

Alli crouched in front of him and took his chin between her thumb and forefinger. "Hey. Listen to me." She lifted his face and stared hard into his clouded eyes. "This is *not* because of you. Okay? You couldn't have done anything better, or different, to stop this from happening. Do you understand? You are a strong, *amazing* little boy. And you. Will. Be. Fine." He'd lowered his gaze, so she gave his chin a little shake.

"Look at me, Thomas." He dragged his eyes back to hers. "I promise. Be strong. Like I *know* you are."

Don't break, Thomas.

He stared at her and took a deep breath before speaking. "I don't want to be strong, I just want a mommy and daddy. But none of them ever want me."

Alli's stomach lurched then plummeted. She closed her eyes, exhaled, then blinked them open. A sour taste filled her throat as the words formed on her lips. "You have a mommy, Thomas. And she's trying to get better so she can take care of you. We're going to visit her in a few days."

"Yeah, but . . .she doesn't *really* want me. Nobody does."

"Aw, kid, that's not true."

"Do *you* want me, Miss Alli?"

Her heart flopped strangely in her chest. "I . . ." She licked her lips. "I'm not allowed. It's against the rules."

His gaze rolled down like rain on a window.

"You remember what I told you though, okay? You're *strong*. And you'll be okay."

"And I'm amazing."

A smile tipped her mouth. "That's right. You *are*."

The sun was nearing its peak when David emerged from the Launching Pad and entered the New Life Worship Center foyer. A stocky fellow sat in one of the armchairs lining the south wall, heel bouncing on the carpeted floor. David did a double take. The curly hair, the profile… "Hoffman? Is that you?" He hadn't seen him since their deployment—how many years ago now? "Oh wow! What are you doing here, bro?"

Hoffman stood, grinning wide. "Hey man, how are ya?"

Bursting with affection, David threw an arm around him and slapped him on the back. "I'm good. How 'bout yourself?"

"Pretty good. You know I got a wife and kid now."

"Yeah, man, I saw that. Congratulations."

"Thanks."

"Can't believe you're here. You just driving through the area or what?"

"Sorta." He smiled as a wistful look came into his eyes. "Listen, I don't know if you're busy right now, but I was hoping we could grab a bite to eat. Catch up."

David tried to decode the emotion written on his army buddy's face. "Yeah, that'd be great."

"Cool." Hoffman gestured toward the street. "Think I saw a burger joint up the street that looked good."

"How about something better? I know a sushi sports bar and grill you'd love. Come on, I'll drive."

When they arrived, they were seated opposite the sports bar side, where a crowd was gathered to watch a ball game.

Hoffman settled into his seat and stared at David. "So, look at you, man. A pastor. Whoddu thunk?"

David shrugged. "Guess you never can tell."

"Yeah, man, for real. But you don't look like you've gone *too* soft. I was afraid you'd walk out wearing a preppy sweater like Mr. Rogers or something." A chuckle shook his shoulders. "But you still look like good 'ole Dave Porter."

"I am. Just a mite better, I hope."

Hoffman nodded slowly. "So, you married or engaged or anything?"

"Nope. Too busy for women."

His eyes rounded. "Too busy for women? That's not the Porter I know. Although I do remember you rarely went out with the same chick twice. Didn't want them getting too attached you said."

More like *he* didn't want to get too attached. Still didn't. "Guess some things have changed since our days serving together."

Hoffman's eyes sobered. "Yeah. Yeah, a lot has changed. Listen, I have some news—"

"Are you ready to order?" The waiter had appeared seemingly out of thin air.

Hoffman glanced at the menu. "Think I'll try the tuna roll."

A plain ole tuna role? David shook his head. "You gotta try the sashimi. It's why I brought you here. It's the bomb."

"Uh . . ." He laughed. "I dunno if I can do sashimi, man."

"Oh, come on. You'll love it." David looked at the waiter. "Bring him the fatty tuna sashimi. And I'll have the unagi." He glanced at Matt from the corner of his eye then added, "And a tuna roll on the side."

As the waiter walked away, Hoffman's brows rose. "I know sashimi is raw fish but what the heck is unagi?"

"Eel." The look of disgust on Hoffman's face tugged a smile out of David. "Can't knock it till you try it."

"Sorry I asked."

As David raised his water glass, a familiar face snagged his attention. Alli greeted a brunette at the entrance, and by the looks of it, he'd say this was a friend rather than a client. He watched them slip onto stools in the bar section, chatting like schoolgirls.

"Yo. Porter. See someone you know, or maybe someone you'd *like* to know?" Hoffman wore a wolfish grin and cast an appreciative gaze toward Alli and her friend. "Maybe you aren't too busy after all, huh?"

Something simmered in David's gut. "I know her, that's all."

"Even better. You can introduce me."

David pinned him with a hard gaze. "You're married with a kid now, Matt. I hope you're doing right by them."

Hoffman's brows plunged low. "Of course, I am. I love my family. But I can still be your wingman. Give you an excuse to strike up a conversation. See what happens. She's pretty."

Yes, she was. But there was more to a woman than her looks, and more to David than sensual desires. He watched Alli take a sip from a glass mug, then lick foam from her upper lip. "I'm not interested."

Cheers erupted from the crowd over a home run on the screen and Alli bounced out of her seat, hooting and hollering along with them, turning more than a few heads. David smiled seeing her like this. Happy, light. Relaxed. And seemingly unaware of the attention she was drawing.

Hoffman passed him a dubious look. "You sure about that? No one says you need to let her get attached."

David leveled his gaze on his old friend. "Yeah, I'm sure. I'm all grown up now."

He raised his hands and conceded with a nod. "Understood, Pastor Porter."

They spent the next several minutes eating and making small talk, with David resisting the desire to keep looking over at Alli.

The table jolted and David's glass tumbled, splashing across both his food and his shirt. His jaw hung open in shock for a second before he snapped it shut and released a sigh.

The man who'd just bumped into their table fixed wide eyes on him. "I'm so sorry."

"It's okay, man. No worries." He stood, lamenting his damp shirt, as the waiter appeared with a towel.

"Can I pay for your meal?"

"No that's okay, it's fine. Accidents happen." David offered the mortified man a reassuring smile, despite the irritation trying to tighten his mouth.

"Thank you . . . Again, I'm so sorry." The man gave another apologetic nod before continuing away, leaving the waiter to clean up.

When the waiter finally left, Hoffman shook his head in amazement. "When I saw your shirt, I thought that guy would end up *wearing* the eel on your plate."

"What? No."

"Remember that time you got into it with that big, gnarly dude?"

David scratched his chin. "Which one?" The fact he had to ask wasn't a good sign but came as no surprise.

"Remember he had a long scar on his forehead. You had just bought a drink for a girl, and this guy . . ." he chuckled, "decided to home in on your territory or something. He sure didn't know who he was picking a fight with, though."

David remembered, in the hazy way he recalled most of those days. He really *had* been that bad.

"Took three of us to pull you off him. He's probably walking around with a crooked nose to this day, to go with that scar."

"I really hope not."

Hoffman laughed again, then as it petered out, he quieted and dipped his chin. "Huh. Maybe there's something to this faith of yours."

"Oh, there is."

Hoffman nodded thoughtfully then tucked into his tuna roll.

David's eyes went again to Alli. He watched as her friend gathered her purse, said goodbye, and left. Alli then slumped back in her chair and crossed her legs, face drawn. David's brows pinched together as he studied her. The game went on without her paying the least attention to the screen. The crowd hollered over a strike, but this time Alli didn't even look up. Where did her team spirit go so suddenly? The change was odd. Concerning. Should he go to her? Make sure she was okay?

He gave himself a shake. No. She wouldn't welcome him, and he was with company. David refocused on Hoffman. "Did you say you had some news?"

"Yeah. I do." He cleared his throat and reached for his glass of sake. "It's Ryan Quincy. He, uh . . . he passed away yesterday."

David's face went slack. "No. What happened?"

"Took his own life, sadly. PTSD got pretty bad."

Heaviness pressed down on him, rounding his spine, and David rubbed the scars on his forearm. A contemplative silence stretched between them, each of them testing the weight of the statement.

It was something none of them talked about. Not if they could avoid it. But suddenly David wondered if it could've made a difference. He pushed out a trapped breath. "I wish I'd known how bad off he was. I can't say I don't relate." His past had been tormenting him more than usual the last few weeks. Without his faith, it wasn't hard to imagine himself being in the same dark place that had led to Quincy's end.

"I think most of us can relate. My wife and my kid are what keep me grounded now."

"For me it's serving God."

Hoffman nodded. "I can appreciate that."

David shook his head, his thoughts migrating back to Quincy. "Wow. Didn't he have a girl? What ever happened with her?"

"He married her. They had a couple kids. But she left him about a year ago."

David swallowed. "Sad." That was probably what pushed him over the edge. But loving a man like Ryan Quincy couldn't have been easy.

"It really is." Hoffman took a swig of his sake. "Anyway, I knew you'd want to know."

"Yeah. Thanks for coming to see me and letting me know." Sobering news. Maybe if David had kept in better touch on social media, given Quincy a call once in a while… Moving forward, he would pay closer attention to people. Note signs of trouble, try to help. He glanced back at Alli, who sat staring at the wall. Was the smile fake the whole time?

David turned back toward his buddy just as he pushed his plate away. "Ready to get outta here?"

"Yeah."

David threw some cash down on the table and stood. "So how was the sashimi?"

Hoffman curled his smirking lips. "Raw."

Flashlight in hand, David edged his shoulder under the pipes and pointed a beam of light into the dark crevice under the bathroom sink. A welcome distraction from the pestering thoughts disquieting him recently.

Alli had been on his mind for days. Something had seemed off when he saw her at the sports bar, but he couldn't pinpoint *what* and it clawed at him. Despite how she rebuffed him, she radiated this desperate need for God that wrenched his spirit.

But what could *he* do? She nearly hated him. They weren't friends. Surely there was someone else, someone better qualified to reach out to her. But all the same, thoughts of her poked at him, like a sharp rock in his shoe. So, he'd been praying for direction. Or respite.

Beside him, Kyle squinted at the drain assembly and grunted as he strained to loosen a stubborn bolt. As they worked, something clouded his normally joyful countenance. And it wasn't the effort he applied to the wrench. A worry was eating at him. It was the same look he got whenever one of the kids was going through an especially rough patch.

David's craning neck protested, and he adjusted his position. "So…I know you didn't ask me to lend a hand because you enjoy looking at my pretty face."

"You got that right." Kyle let the wrench clatter to the floor then wiped the sweat from his puckered brow. In these close quarters, the gray dotting his temples was more obvious. "I'm guessing you probably know why I wanted to talk to you."

"I have an inkling, yeah." David wrestled the trap off the drainpipe and plunged two fingers in, clearing out the debris. "Thomas?"

The boy had changed overnight. Wouldn't engage in their games and sports, didn't greet his new friends, didn't join in conversations. And there'd been no hint of that smile of his—one front tooth not fully grown in—for days.

"We're concerned about him." Kyle wiggled the trap back into place then backed out from under the sink and stood. "Regina and I were hoping you might spend some one-on-one time with him today? We're doing everything we can to reach out, but he seems to respond to you. We thought . . .maybe he'd open up with you."

David's shoulders tensed. His specialty was teens. Not little kids. But he stretched his kinked neck and nodded. "Yeah. Of course."

Was he out of his depth? Absolutely. But it was worth a shot. He tightened the compression nut then Kyle cranked the water valve on.

"Great." Kyle wagged his head as he wiped his hands on a towel, then shot him a glance from the side of his eye. "I tell ya…even after fifteen years, it's hard to watch the things these kids have to go through." He jetted a breath. "Let's pray that Thomas's situation turns around soon."

The tile squeaked as David stood. "Amen to that." He turned the tap and watched the water flow freely down the drain as he washed his hands. "Mission accomplished."

"At least this is one thing we can fix, right? Me with my handyman skills and you with . . . well, something other than a pretty face."

David gave a dry laugh. "Try muscle. I think yours are withered away."

Kyle barked a laugh and socked him in the arm. "Don't make me prove you wrong."

"Ouch." He rubbed his arm in mock pain. "Okay, I have a kid to find. See ya, boss." David saluted Kyle and exited the bathroom in search of Thomas. He found him in the den. With an elbow propped on the arm of the couch, his chin resting in his palm, Thomas stared at the television, expressionless.

David relaxed his steel posture and swallowed. "Hey, bud. Whatcha doin?"

The child shrugged, eyes not leaving the screen.

If one of his teens did that, David knew it would be an expression of defiance. He wasn't so sure that was the case for this seven-year-old. *I could use some help, Lord.* He rubbed the back of his neck and tried to think. "I have an idea. What do you say we take a trip to the pet store, just you and me?"

A spark of life flickered in his eyes and David's mouth tipped. "Is that a yes?"

"I guess."

"All right! Let's hop to it, then, huh?" David grinned and led the boy into the foyer.

Regina was there, coffee in hand, smiling down at Thomas with obvious affection. "Did someone mention the pet store?" She bent forward and held out a few folded bills. "Here. So you can buy that new shell for Herman."

Thomas looked at her soberly as he accepted the money. "Thanks." His voice wasn't much more than an exhale.

Regina stood and met David's eyes, the unspoken exchange speaking volumes. "It's just a few dollars, but it should be enough for a hermit crab shell." She passed a smile between the both of them. "You two have a good time."

"It's the pet store, how could we not?" David headed to the door and was reaching for the knob when Regina stopped him.

"Uh, David?" she called.

"Yeah?"

She pointed at the hall closet. "Don't forget."

"Oh. Right." He needed to grab one of the spare booster seats.

Regina smiled over the rim of her mug as she watched him retrieve the seat and tuck it under his arm. He must have appeared just as out of his depth as he felt. When they got to his car, he opened the back door and put the booster in. His fingers felt along the sides and back looking for whatever kind of attaching mechanism it had. The whole thing was smooth, no clamps or loops or latches.

David pulled the seat back out and flipped it over to look underneath.

"What's wrong?" Thomas asked softly.

"Nothing's wrong, bud. Just figuring this thing out real quick. Any idea how it works?"

Thomas took the booster from David and plopped it onto the back seat. After climbing up and buckling in, he looked at David and said, "I just sit on it."

David put on a self-deprecating smile. "Right. Got it. Thanks for your help." At least Regina hadn't been there to see that—or worse, Alli. He slid into the driver's seat and smiled at Thomas in the rearview mirror. His hopes deflated when he didn't receive one in return. "And we're off."

Thomas watched out the window as they pulled away, while David racked his brain for a conversation starter.

Lord, I am way out of my depth here. Please give me the words to say.

Throughout the drive, he did his best. But one-way dialog proved challenging. Relief eased from his lungs when they reached their destination. At least here there'd be plenty to look at.

Thomas made a beeline for the small critter section. He stood in front of a hamster cage, wordlessly watching it nibble its food, the faintest touch of a smile on his face.

The silence made David itchy. Thomas was so quiet. So young. And despite all he'd been through, so . . .innocent. So, this was what a child's eyes looked like before rage and defiance took hold.

After a moment he moved on to the next cage. Didn't say anything, just watched in apparent fascination. David watched him with the same fascination the boy had for the animals, then set his own gaze traveling to the variety of furry creatures on display. Gerbils and guinea pigs and mice. The mice had piled up in their wheel, all trying to run at the same time, with one unfortunate fellow being spun upside down as he clung on for dear life.

David turned to call Thomas over. Swung his head around when he didn't see him. He'd been staring into a habitat a foot away not more than twenty seconds ago.

A sense of dread settled over him as he confirmed the boy was nowhere in his field of vision. He instinctively scanned the perimeter of the store, gaze darting to the entry and exit points. "Thomas? Where'd you go, bud?"

No response. Just the sound of puppies barking nearby.

He unglued his feet and marched to the next aisle. A visual sweep proved fruitless. They always say to never take your eyes off your child, but could he really disappear this fast? Apparently. Also apparent—David was inept at this. "Thomas?"

A woman stood in the next aisle browsing cat toys. "Excuse me, ma'am, did you see a little boy go by just now?"

The woman wore a sweater covered in whiskered cat faces. She smiled at David and pointed. "Is that him watching the fish?"

A lift of his heels gave David a view to the wall of fish tanks on the other side of the last aisle. His heart decided to beat again. "Yes. Thank you."

"Sometimes parenthood is like wrangling cats, isn't it?" A light chuckle shook her.

"Oh. Uh… yeah it sure is." No need to correct the woman. With a dip of his chin, he left her and picked his way to Thomas.

The aftermath of his racing pulse left his underarms damp and his mouth tight. He sidled up beside the kid. "Hey buddy." He knelt and gave him a serious look. "You can't just wander away like that."

Thomas blinked at him. "I just wanted to see the fish. I didn't think you'd care."

"But I do care. Very much. And when I didn't see you, I got scared." For a second, he was even thrown back to the time he'd lost sight of Hoffman and Quincy on a mission and thought they'd been taken out. Not a topic to share with Thomas. Instead, David placed a hand on his shoulder. "You need to stay with me from now on, okay? If you want to see something, that's cool. Just take me with you. That's the unbreakable rule. Don't leave me behind."

"Is that like my duty?"

"Sure is. Will you promise me that?"

His wide eyes pinned to David's as he nodded solemnly. "Promise."

The grip on David's lungs released, and warmth spread beneath his sternum. He smiled and stood, and they spent a moment more taking in the myriad colors and shapes, and the calming movement of the fish.

When they made their way to a tank of hermit crabs with colorfully painted shells, Thomas found his voice. "I want to use the money Regina gave me on a new shell for Herman. But I don't know which one he'd like best. Look at that one with the blue swirlies on it."

"Ooh, that one looks fun all right. Did you see this one that looks like a soccer ball?"

A breathy chuckle. "Wow. That's cool." The grin he shot up at David made something in his chest tighten and flop about. "The last pet store didn't have this many and that's why Doris said that next time"—his smile went out— "well, never mind."

A muggy breeze rustled through David's soul, and he tossed up a prayer. What to do with a reserved, vulnerable kid? Eyebrows lowered,

David scratched the hollow of his cheek. "I heard about the McMillans. That's got to be tough. I'm . . . real sorry."

"I don't wanna talk about them."

"Okay. Sure. We don't have to."

"I gotta find Herman the perfect home. He has to change shells a lot." Thomas sorted through the colorful shells, his serious face contradicting the carefree picture of childhood that every kid deserved.

"Pastor David? Did you move a lot when you were a kid?"

"Um . . ." An image of his bedroom penetrated his memory, the details of each crack that snaked across the ceiling above his bed, the Incredible Hulk poster hanging on the wall, the rumpled green bedspread adorning his mattress before the army taught him how to properly make a bed, it all appeared in vivid detail.

He shook his head and swallowed against the tightness of his throat. "I lived in the same house until I graduated high school and joined the military."

"You're lucky then. I'm tired of moving. I've moved twelve times that I can remember."

And as soon as Miss Johnson found a place, he'd have to do it again.

"Ya know bud, sometimes going somewhere new, even though it's scary and hard, is a good thing."

"Yeah, yeah. I know. I just wish I could stay in one place long enough to make friends."

David pressed his lips together. "Are you not getting along with the kids at Grace House?"

"That's not what I mean. I mean like real friends that you hang out with, and you visit their house, and they visit yours and maybe your moms are friends and ride in the carpool together. And you trade lunches and Pokémon cards and talk about your favorite cartoons." He sighed and set down a chipped hermit shell. "You wouldn't understand; you never moved so you probably had a bunch of friends, but I'm always the new kid. It's better not to bother with friends if I'm only going to have to leave them anyway."

And there it was. The reason he'd stopped playing with the other kids. He didn't want it to hurt too much when he had to say goodbye.

This kid was so different than David as a boy. Total opposite end of the spectrum. David had always acted out, found trouble everywhere. But Thomas just retreated into himself, *hiding* from as much trouble as possible.

While Thomas looked through packages of moss and food pellets, David squinted out the store's glass walls toward the horizon. Treetops swayed against a backdrop of fluffy white clouds and a bird took flight. Would it help the kid to know they shared one thing in common?

"I didn't have a lot of friends growing up, Thomas. But not because I moved a lot like you. I just wasn't very nice. I was kind of a troublemaker. But inside I was still very lonely." Thomas gave him a sad look. Whether he was feeling sad for David or for himself wasn't clear.

David confirmed with a nod and canted his head at the boy. "See, people are built for relationships. We're not meant to go through life alone. So, you've got to focus on today, on who is in your life right now, and let yourself enjoy the blessing of their company. However long it lasts. Know what I mean?"

Thomas looked at him for a moment and twisted his mouth to one side. "Yeah, I guess so."

Gingerly holding his choices for Herman, Thomas pulled David toward the checkout lanes. He waited in line silently, then stepped up to the register and plopped down a handful of cash for the pet supplies. David kicked in more for a few extras that had caught Thomas's eye.

He'd gone quiet again. The kid had said more to him this afternoon than he had since the day he'd arrived, but apparently, he only ventured so far before withdrawing. And right now, it was like he'd fled the building. Just like Alli.

Realization exploded in David's mind like a grenade blast. The social worker was just like her charge. Keeping people, the *world*, at a distance. Retreating from whatever caused her discomfort. Like how she hurried out when he said he was a pastor, and how she'd avoided him since. Might that be why she seemed extra-protective of Thomas?

Because she related to him on that level? But why? What made her a runner?

As they walked out the door with their purchases, he let his eyes skim over Thomas's soft brown hair, ruffling in the midday breeze. Rejected. Unwanted. Neglected. Let down. This kid wore it on his sleeve, unlike the guarded teens David was used to. Unlike most adults, too.

Did Alli feel that way, rejected from the start? By God? And that a pastor would reject her friendship?

Well, maybe God's purpose was to show her that wasn't true.

Must be, because David had no other reason for her to be in his thoughts as often as she was. It was not her golden hair, her slender legs, the hazel eyes reflecting depths she seemed intent on hiding. No. It was the pain he knew God could ease, and nothing more. And maybe now that he had a clue, he'd be able to pray for her better, understand a bit about of how she—and Thomas—ticked.

Then surely the grip she had on his thoughts would ease. He hoped so, anyway. His ministry focus was teen boys. Young men. Not beautiful women. And not little kids. David didn't know what to do with either.

The delicious scent of chocolate cake greeted David and Thomas as they opened the door of Grace House. "Smells great, Regina!" David called out.

Thomas tipped his head up at David. "Are you gonna eat with us?"

"How can I not?" He grinned at the boy then nodded toward the family room. "But right now, why don't you go show Herman what you got?"

"Okay." He hesitated, then swift as lighting grabbed David around the waist and squeezed, pulling a grunt from his lungs. David patted the boy's back in return. Then just as quickly as he'd embraced him, Thomas ran off.

"Well, that's a positive sign." Regina strode over, Kyle beside her. "So, how'd it go?"

"Made some progress—baby steps, I think. He's a very reserved child. Holds a whole lot inside."

Kyle's eyes crinkled. "Seems he's decided you're worth letting in."

"Maybe. I'm going to go get some work done, but I'll stick around for dinner if that's all right."

"You heard it was lasagna night, didn't you?" Kyle grinned. "Regina should be sliding it into the oven here shortly. You're always welcome here, you know that."

"Thanks. Looking forward to some garlic bread."

"I'm looking forward to the chocolate cake," Kyle wiggled his eyebrows.

"Judging by your huffing and puffing under the sink earlier, you might consider skipping it." David pasted on a cheesy grin then gave a nod. "See ya, bro."

David spent the last part of the afternoon in the solitude of his makeshift office at the back of Grace House. Praying, thinking.

Pastor Ron had emailed him the date for the Men's Breakfast where David was expected to tell his story. The fact it was still three months out didn't keep the tense thoughts at bay. Revisiting the past was bad enough. He avoided it whenever possible. But inviting others into it posed big questions about what he should share. How much detail. What could the average person handle hearing. And was there a true benefit to any of it? Was it possible it could even save lives?

He thought of Quincy, the pain he must've suffered leading up to his tragic choice, and David's immediate sense that maybe talking to him, connecting with him in that darkness, could've made a difference. There were several men at the church who had served in the military. Plenty more who had backgrounds that could be compared to war zones. David wanted them to know they weren't alone.

But how much exposure could *he* handle? Where was that line and how did he go about finding it when his instinct was to lock it all up in a cage and throw away the key?

When the sun had shifted lower in the sky, lancing through his windows, David shut down the laptop—and his ruminating thoughts—to head out to the dining room. That first whiff of garlic and oregano sent his salivary glands into production. How blessed he felt to be welcomed to this family table. Not just because Regina made the best lasagna, but also because it beat eating alone.

The packed dining room was surprisingly well-organized. Portions were distributed cafeteria-style, with everyone coming together at the table plates-in-hand. Kyle led them in prayer, and at the sound of the kids' *amen*s, David's cheeks lifted in a smile. Their voices raised in conversation, laughter, and minor bickering gave him such a sense of fulfillment, like there was nowhere he'd rather be. Even Rueben seemed to have softened some of his rough edges. He thanked Jake for passing the garlic bread! Jake muttered a "no problem," in reply and David wanted to watch the replay. Instead, he offered a private nod to each of them to say *well done*.

The only thing that would have improved the meal, was if Thomas had engaged—with the other kids, with David, with anyone. Instead, he chewed in silence, observing the conversations around him with a detached interest and forcing a smile when he couldn't avoid eye contact. One of the first to finish eating, he was excused to carry his plate to the sink and return to his room.

David finished his meal soon after and headed down the hall. He rapped his knuckles on Thomas's door then turned the knob only to find the room empty.

Forehead wrinkling, David's gaze swept from one wall to the other, finally landing on a sneaker-clad foot poking out from under the bed. He walked over to it and knelt to give the foot a shake.

"Hey, whatcha doin' down there?"

A sniff and muffled whimper were his reply. David's heart lurched a little and a warning sounding in his head that he was getting too close, too emotionally entangled. But hadn't he just resolved to pay attention when someone was hurting? He gentled his voice. "Come on out, Thomas. Let's talk."

Thomas scooted out on his back, regarded David for a moment, then rubbed damp eyes with the heels of his hands. So much hurt in this boy. It rolled off him in huge, crashing waves. David sat on the bed and patted the space beside him. A somber-faced Thomas climbed up to join him.

David angled his head to see the youngster's face. Thomas could be a stoic child. Silent. Reserved. But right now, the kid he'd taken to the pet shop, the one who had started opening up, was back in plain view. Heaviness pulling down the corners of his mouth, David cupped his hand on the side of the boy's head. "What's bothering you?"

Thomas gave a tiny dip of his chin, his throat bobbing. His words were barely audible as they dropped from his lips. "Nobody…nobody wants me."

A band tightened around David's ribcage, and he felt an uncomfortable stinging in his eyes.

"Aw, Thomas, that's not true." A primal protectiveness reared up within him—different from the way he related to the teens. "I know it can feel that way sometimes. But I promise you it's not true. All of us here at Grace House may only just be getting to know you, but we like you a lot and we're glad you're here."

The boy didn't move, didn't lift his eyes, just stared at his lap and picked at his thumb nail.

"And you know who else wants you and loves you more than anything?"

Without lifting his gaze, Thomas shook his head and remained silent.

"Jesus."

Thomas's eyes flicked to David and then away again.

"It's true, Thomas. The truest thing you can ever know. God loves you and wants you to know Him. He will always be with you—no matter what else happens. Did you know that? No matter where you live, or what people come in and out of your life."

The boy shrugged one small shoulder and fixed his gaze to the center of David's chest.

Unexpected emotion clogged David's throat making his voice go rough. "God promises that He will never, ever, *ever* leave us. His love for you is bigger than the ocean. Than *all* the oceans. He says He is thinking about you all the time. More thoughts than there are grains of sand on the planet, isn't that amazing?"

Thomas twisted his mouth to the side and expelled air through his nostrils. "Do you really think God loves me?"

A smile eased onto David's face. "I *know* He does. He made you and He has a plan for your life. A really good one."

Thomas's gaze finally drifted up to David's, hope and longing reflecting back at him. David laid a hand on Thomas's shoulder. "Hey . . .how about coming to our morning devotions tomorrow? We'll talk more about God and what He has to say to us. Would you like that?"

Thomas nodded. "Yeah. Okay." His little mouth curved up and he wrapped his arms around David's chest. "Thank you, Pastor David."

Pressure built behind David's eyes and his arms slowly came to encircle the child. He rested his chin on the top of the child's silky head. "Any time, bud."

His heart felt like it could explode out of his chest. He didn't understand it, and it made him a little afraid, but this kid . . . this shy, nearly invisible boy . . . David knew in that moment, he would do anything for him.

He swallowed against the rock in his throat and whispered again, "Any time."

Chapter Four

The morning was cold and dewy, and the sun had yet to pierce the clouds as Alli parked in front of Grace House. Insides quivering, she pressed a hand to her sternum and closed her eyes. She'd been on countless parental visits, many of them emotionally fraught and unpleasant. It was part of the job, and she'd always charged into the battle without hesitation. But right now, she felt utterly devoid of the strength for it.

Thomas's mother was a harsh, vindictive, combative woman who hated the system that had taken her child and forced her into rehab. And hated Alli in particular. Even when sober, the woman was no ray of sunshine. For Thomas's sake, Alli hoped she'd turn her life around, but instinct told her it was unlikely. There were two kinds of parents in Alli's line of work: Those who wanted to change, and those who didn't. Patricia Cooper, Alli feared, fell into the latter camp. And facing that truth today, in the wake of all that had happened to Thomas in the past week, was the absolute last thing Alli was prepared to do. But she had no choice. Thomas needed a warrior, and she was it. Her heart did a stress-flutter as she counted to five, took a stabilizing breath, and opened her eyes.

Alli approached the front door and lifted the knocker on the "Peace To All Who Enter Here" plaque. This was not a house of subtlety, she'd give them that.

"Hey, Alli." The sudden voice behind her made Alli suck air and spin on her heels. David was heading toward her with a box of donuts and a smile, his shoes crunching in the gravel.

"David, hi." Why this guy? Why today? She looked down at her feet, shifted her weight.

"Did I startle you?" He chuckled.

Her mouth tilted on its own and she shrugged. "Maybe a little."

Lines creased his forehead. "I hope everything is okay; you seem a bit distracted."

"Yeah. I guess I am." She combed her fingers through the hair at her crown. "I'm taking Thomas to visit his mom today. It's not my favorite."

"Yeah, he told me. Well, here, can you hold this?" He handed her the box of donuts, his tattoo peeking into view, but not quite long enough for her to make out the design. He pulled a set of keys from his pocket, turned the lock, then swung open the door and motioned for her to enter ahead of him.

"Thanks." She took a step forward and her breath caught. The masculine scent of spicy sage with notes of pepper made Alli want to lean in and inhale. As she passed, her eyes skipped to his. He looked down at her, *into* her, something inscrutable crinkling the space between his eyebrows. Then he smiled.

Her face flushed. Alli swallowed hard and slipped past, putting distance between them. She raised the pink pastry box. "So . . . kitchen?"

"How'd you guess?"

Smart Aleck.

With David following behind, Alli went to the kitchen to set the box down then leaned a hip against the counter. The pastor propped himself across from her, an easy manner about him, and all she could think of was how cold their last interaction had been. Not that it was her fault, he'd been the one teaching troubled teens how to make their bodies better weapons. But there seemed to be more to him than that.

"So"—she scratched at the surface of the counter with her index finger—"Regina says you've been spending extra time with Thomas, helping him . . . adjust." Whatever else this man may be, he was a friend to Thomas, and that meant something. She pressed her lips together and nodded. "Thank you for that."

David angled his head at her, taking a good long look that made her insides squirm. "You're welcome." He pushed off from the counter and moved closer, then opened the pastry box. "I enjoy hanging out with him. He's quite a character. We went to the pet shop the other day and he probably could've spent the whole afternoon staring into all the tanks and cages." Amusement danced in his eyes. "And the kid notices everything. He's always analyzing, thinking deep thoughts."

Alli's eyes crinkled with her smile. "Yeah, that sounds like Thomas. I love that about him."

"So do I." David reached around her to pull a paper towel off the roll. "Excuse me."

"No problem." Arms folded across her chest, she leaned out of the way, but not far enough to miss out on another whiff of his spicy cologne. And the head-to-toe tingling sensation that came with it. She clenched every muscle to hold back the shiver threatening to fan out from her lower belly.

He placed a glazed chocolate donut onto the paper towel. "This is for Thomas. I promised him donuts if he could beat me at backgammon." He looked at her from the sides of his eyes.

One side of her mouth inched up. "So, you let him win?"

"No way. He's just crazy good at it."

She chuckled despite herself, trying to remember that she didn't like this man. She didn't like his beliefs, she didn't like his affinity for fighting sports, and she didn't like his soft approach with violent kids.

But she did like the way he looked out for Thomas. Took a personal interest in his wellbeing. And for some reason, she was itching to see the rest of that tattoo. Her gaze traveled the length of his arm, bicep to fingertips and a tiny tremble slipped past her guard.

"Want one?" He gestured toward the box. "Take your pick."

"Um. Okay, sure." Looking over the confections, her gaze snagged on the maple bar. *Oh, yeah. Come to mama.*

She reached for it, but David smacked her hand. "Hey!"

"Yeah, sorry. You don't want that one."

Round-eyed, she stared at him. "Uh, yes. I do."

"Mmm . . . no. That one is currently unavailable, sorry."

"Currently unavailable?" She held in a chuckle. "Let me guess— that's the one you wanted?"

"Hmm. How about this nice custard-filled? Or perhaps the rainbow-sprinkled?"

She crossed her arms and sent one eyebrow winging upward. Had he, or had he not, told her to *take her pick?*

He made a sweeping motion over the box with his hand. "You may eat of any of the pastries in the box, *except* the pastry in the center of the box. You shall not eat it or even touch it—"

"Lest I die?" She smirked and tipped her head. Yes, even *she* could recall the Garden of Eden story.

His forehead wrinkled in what could only be described as a pout. "Come on lady, look again. There's an apple crumb, cinnamon, an eclair. Mmm, delicious. Yeah?"

She lifted her chin. "I'm not in the mood for any of those."

"Ah, come on, Alli. That's *my* maple bar. You're killing me."

Somehow, hearing him call her by her first name, like they were old friends, made her heart leap a little. Before plummeting to the bottom of her stomach. She tucked her hair behind her ears as he stroked his chin.

"Okay," he said. "This isn't easy. But . . .I suppose I'd be willing to split it."

She gave him an appraising look through narrowed eyes, then nodded. "Deal."

" . . .75/25," he coughed as he reached into the box.

"I don't think so!" She smacked his arm before she could catch herself, then, mortified, looked up at his face. Was she flirting? Oh, sweet mercy, she was. Kind of. She didn't mean to… but the cologne and the muscles and the backgammon… and she wasn't giving up that donut now.

David rubbed at his arm, his lips pressed together in a bemused, half-cocked grin. "Now, now, no need to get testy."

"Me? You practically took my arm off when I reached for that donut. Now give. Me"— her hand plunged toward the prize but he body-blocked her— "my"— she tried to reach around him without success, and laughter bounced his shoulders.

Alli planted her hands on her hips. "I'm questioning your integrity, *Pastor.*"

His eyes sparkled. "You're funny when you're angry."

"I'm not angry. I'm disappointed." She let out an exaggerated sigh and shook her head. "I thought a preacher would be a man of his word, but I guess I was wrong."

He hissed air between his teeth. "Ooo, that's hitting below the belt."

She shrugged. "Just calling it like I see it. Isn't part of your job description to put others first?"

"Part of my job is to lift others up. And I think I'm succeeding."

Her forehead wrinkled and her eyes narrowed. "What're you talking about?"

"Well, since you've been talking to me you don't seem as stressed or distracted about visiting Thomas's mom. Am I right?"

So that's what this was? She bit the inside of her cheek. "Maybe. But you still owe me half that maple bar."

"No problem." David leaned toward her with a conspiratorial smirk. "I don't even like them."

Her mouth fell open.

"Good morning!" Regina breezed into the kitchen. She glanced back and forth between the two of them. "Am I interrupting?"

Alli arranged her features and tucked her hands into her back pockets. "No, of course not."

"Have time for a cup of coffee then?" Regina's bright tone showed the invitation was in earnest.

"Believe me, I wish I did. Sounds much better than what I'm in for this morning."

Regina gave Alli's arm a light squeeze. "I'm praying for you, Alli. That things go well today."

Praying for her? Alli blinked, unsure how to feel about that.

Grateful. She settled on grateful. For the woman's concern. "Thank you, Regina."

As she checked the time, her brain kicked into gear. If they didn't leave now, they were almost guaranteed to be late. She started reaching toward the pink box, pausing to eye David as if he might take a swing at her. When he tilted his head and gestured to proceed, she grabbed the pastry and a paper towel, then looked at each of them in turn. "Gotta get going. I'll have Thomas back in two hours or so."

Regina dipped her head toward the main interior of the house. "He's in the living room with Kyle. He's expecting you. Afterward, you're welcome to stay for dinner."

"Oh. Sorry, I can't. I have… plans." Thank goodness she had that date and didn't have to make up a lie. "Thank you though."

"Nice chatting with you, Alli." David handed her Thomas's donut. "Give this to him for me, would ya?"

"Sure." Alli nodded and turned away.

Regina pointed at Alli's hands. "I can't believe it. He let you have the maple bar? That's a miracle right there." She chuckled softly as she turned to the coffee maker.

Alli flashed rounded eyes on David, who shrugged and gave her a half-cocked smile that sent her heart fluttering. She lifted her chin and slowly sank her teeth into the sweet, doughy confection. Licking bits of maple icing off her lips, she wiggled her eyebrows then turned and walked out.

In the living room entryway, Alli stopped and took in the scene. One kid lounged in a recliner with an iPad, and another hunched over a textbook on the couch. Kyle perched on the other end of the couch working on something at the coffee table, while Thomas knelt on the floor nearby watching. She stood silent, relieved to see the personal interaction that Regina and Kyle had with the kids. With Thomas.

Kyle looked from the table to Thomas. "So then if we fold this corner right here . . . and again on the other side . . . we'll have a more stable plane." He held up the paper airplane. "See?" He sent it soaring across the room in Alli's direction.

"Cool!" Thomas's gaze followed the flight path to where it whizzed over Alli's head. When he saw her, he smiled. "Hi, Miss Johnson."

"Hey, kid. You ready to go?" She held his donut out to him.

"Uh huh." He put some crayons back into their plastic tub then waved to the other kids hanging out in the room. "Bye, guys."

"Bye, Thomas," they answered in near unison.

"Bye, Mr. Kyle."

"See you soon, bucko."

Alli smiled to see how well he was getting along here. Thomas traded her a folded drawing for his donut and took a bite. "I won this beating Pastor David in a game he taught me."

"Yeah, I heard. Good job."

She hooked her arm across his shoulders as they made their way out to her car. "So, you doing okay?"

"Yeah, I think so. I really liked the McMillans, but maybe my mom is better now. Pastor David says God works everything out for the best if you love Him. So maybe God will fix my mom, and we could be a family again."

Alli bit the inside of her cheek and blinked several times. "I hope so." The boy—and the pastor—had no idea what he was talking about. And she had a feeling his faith was about to be crushed.

Thomas seemed to have accepted the loss of the McMillans, thankfully, and he chatted Alli's ear off during the drive over to Autumnwood Recovery Center. He told her all about the activities at Grace House, the kids he liked to play with, and David. David this and David that. Took him to the pet store. Taught him a new board game. Helped him with his schoolwork. Thomas had *really* taken to the pastor. Alli wasn't surprised. Thomas could be quick to latch onto father figures, and David certainly had a vibrant aura about him. A spark of light in his chocolaty eyes…

She blinked stupidly, then ran her fingers through her hair, tidying both her waves and her thoughts.

As they pulled up to the building and parked, Thomas grew quiet, his fount of words drying up. Alli understood—coming here was like walking into a minefield. Would there be an explosion this time? No choice but to go find out.

"Okay, kid, we're here." Alli pulled her key from the ignition and got out of the car. Thomas did the same, hopping from his booster seat down to the asphalt. He dragged his feet as he walked beside her, creating scuffing noise on the gritty blacktop. The walls of New Start Treatment Facility loomed above them as they approached.

Inside, everything was white and bright, and Thomas's mother sat at a table fidgeting with her hands. When she caught sight of Thomas, her face brightened. "My baby!" She opened her arms for him. "Come give me a hug, my big boy."

Thomas glanced up at Alli like he wasn't sure what to do. Alli smiled and nodded in her direction. "Go on."

He shuffled across the room, his mother's ice-cold gaze cutting to Alli as she waited for him. "You don't need her say-so to give your mama a hug." When he reached her, she pulled him close for a moment, then released him and placed her palms on either side of his face. "Oh, let me look at you! You're getting so handsome."

Thomas smiled shyly, eyes sparkling.

Alli presented her with a pleasant smile. "Good morning Patricia. How are you?"

Mrs. Cooper shot dismissive eyes at Alli. "Fine and dandy, Miss Johnson."

She didn't sound fine and dandy. She sounded bitter and angry. As usual.

"I'm glad to hear it." Alli took a seat across from Patricia at the table.

Patricia then turned to Thomas with a wide smile that showed her stained teeth. "How have you been?

"Fine." His voice was hesitant, shy.

"Let me look at you." She held him at arms' length and beamed at him. "I think you've grown. So, tell me what's new."

"Did you know I got a pet?" He shrugged and looked up at her through his lashes. "A hermit crab."

"A *hermit* crab? Why on earth would you want one of those?" She laughed and Thomas seemed to shrink a little.

"I dunno. He's cool."

Alli's toes curled in her boots. She put a protective hand on Thomas's shoulder. "He's *really* cool. He's got a painted shell and everything, and Thomas takes excellent care of him. Don't you, kid?" She smiled reassuringly and he blinked back at her.

"Yeah. I'm all he's got. I feed him and keep his cage clean and take him out and let him play."

His mother hummed. "Well, when I get out of here and you come home, we'll get you a real pet. A dog or something, huh?"

Thomas's throat bobbed, but he nodded. Alli's blood began to boil.

Uncomfortable silence stretched among them. Patricia crossed her legs. "So, come on. Tell me what you've been up to. What are you into these days?"

"Um, I'm learning to play soccer and basketball. That's fun."

"They taking good care of you, then?"

"Uh huh. And Miss Alli let me have McDonald's for breakfast."

"Oh? Is *that* what Miss Alli did?" She shot needles at Alli. "That doesn't sound healthy. I thought you were supposed to be providing my kid with high-quality nutrition. Wasn't that what you all said he needed?"

Alli ground her molars. As if the woman had ever served him a healthy meal rather than let him forage through the cupboards while she was passed out cold on the couch.

Thomas's eyes widened as he realized his mistake. "Well, it was only because she didn't have any other food at home. Except the Pop Tart. So, we got McDonald's."

"At home? You mean, Miss *Johnson's* house? You were there with her?"

Alli's heart leapt to her throat. She coughed. "Yes, he had nowhere else to go for a night after he left the McMillans."

Patricia narrowed her eyes in Alli's direction and sneered. "You trying to play house? Like you're his mom? You hoping to keep me shut up in here so you can have him for yourself, Miss Johnson?"

Alli shook her head. "No, nothing like that—"

"If that's what's going on in that perky little head of yours, you better watch out. Cuz I'll hire a lawyer the second you try to have me severed just so you can have my boy. Don't think I won't."

"Patricia. Calm down. I care a great deal for your son but I'm not trying to steal him, I'm seeing to his needs. That's my job. You want me to do it well, don't you?"

Lips pulled to one side, Patricia looked Alli up and down. "What happened to the McMillans?"

Alli was certain an update on Thomas's living situation had been sent to Mrs. Cooper. She obviously hadn't read it. Her gaze cut to Thomas's downcast eyes. She raised her brows at his mother. "Mrs. Cooper, I'll be happy to talk to you about all that, but how about after your visit with Thomas, hmm?"

Patricia ran her tongue over her top teeth and vaguely sneered. "I'm watching you, Miss Johnson." Patricia Cooper's gaze returned to her son. "I miss you so much, Thomas. Every day. You miss me, too?"

Thomas nodded slowly. "Yeah."

"I'm getting better, baby. Working real hard here this time. Very soon, I'll be outta here and we'll be back together. And *nobody*" — her eyes cut at Alli — "will ever separate us again."

Thomas smiled, mute. But Alli caught it, recognized that fear. She'd seen it play out a thousand times. Children wanted nothing more than to believe the promises their parents made. But he was afraid to believe her. Afraid she either wouldn't complete the program . . . or that she *would,* and he'd be back living with her, always wondering how long it would last, and feeling guilty because of it.

Mrs. Cooper stroked his face and gazed at him again before chilling Alli with an icy glare. How could they work together for Thomas's benefit if the woman couldn't thaw out toward her? She wasn't the enemy.

Alli cleared her throat. "Thomas, why don't you give her the gift you brought?"

"Oh yeah!" He opened his backpack and pulled out the construction paper card he'd made. Patricia admired it but shot more ice at Alli. So Alli stepped away to give them a little space. And to grab a breath.

She looked out through the window and took in the yard, the people, all with stories to tell about what addiction had stolen from them and how they ended up coming to a place like this. For Patricia Cooper, one stint hadn't been enough to turn her around. She glanced back over at them. Would it work this time? How many shots at this should the woman get? How many years would Thomas languish within the social system, his future a big, black question mark? Thomas deserved so much more.

The next forty minutes went by in fits and starts of conversation. Silence would hang in the air, then suddenly the pair would start in on a topic they both found something to say about, and they'd keep that going until it petered out.

Finally, Alli checked her watch and stood. She meandered back over to the pair and interjected herself with a light touch to the boy's shoulder. "I'm afraid we have to get going."

Mrs. Cooper pressed her lips together. "I can see it pains you."

Thomas stood and wrapped his arms around his mom's neck, and Alli's gut fisted.

Patricia opened her eyes when he pulled away, then stood and faced Alli. "I want some answers before you go, Miss Johnson."

Alli pulled in a breath. "Of course." She nodded toward the other side of the room. "Thomas, wait for me by the door. I'll be right there."

"'Kay. Bye, Mom."

"Bye, baby."

Patricia crossed her arms over her chest and speared her gaze on Alli. "So, if he's not with the McMillans, where is he staying? With you?"

"No. That was just for the night. He's at a group home now. A good, Christian place. Until another foster family is found, he'll stay there." She rubbed her lips together. "He likes it. He's doing well."

She seemed to ponder this a moment, her lips twisting to one side. "Well, what'd he do to get kicked out of the McMillan house?"

"He didn't do anything, Mrs. Cooper. And he wasn't kicked out. Another of the kids in their care acted out and the McMillans decided to step back from fostering. Look, Thomas will be okay. I promise."

"Acted out? What does that mean?"

Alli's shoulders rounded. There was no avoiding the full truth of what happened in that house. "He attacked Doris with a kitchen knife. He's now at the juvenile detention center. Doris will be fine, but she's shaken up."

Mrs. Cooper blinked stormy, mistrusting eyes at Alli. "You say you're seeing to his needs. How could you let this happen? That could've been my boy instead of the mother."

Alli moistened her lips. She'd thought the same thing multiple times since that night. But she ignored the barb, hiking her purse higher on her shoulder. "Look, you should be focused on cleaning yourself up, if you care about him as much as you say you do. Focus on that one single thing. That is your sole job right now. And try to trust me with your son until then. I only want the best for him. That is my job."

Patricia stared at her. "How would you know what's best for him? Because some suits give you a piece of paper saying so? That doesn't make you an expert. Not in my book. Not with my son."

Alli's jaw flexed but she let the comment roll off her. "I wish you well in your recovery, Patricia. Truly."

"I will get him back, Miss Johnson."

Alli held her gaze and drew a breath. "We'll see you soon. Take care of yourself, Mrs. Cooper."

Hopefully, she'd never have to face that woman in court.

As she and Thomas walked back out to her car, he took her hand and looked up at her. "I don't think she's better, Miss Alli."

More of those deep thoughts of his.

Alli tipped her head and looked into his sweet face, searching for the right thing to say. But before she could answer, he wrapped his arms tightly around her waist and pressed his cheek to her belly. "I'll never have a real mom."

Hesitatingly, her arms came around his shoulders and she caressed his hair, her heart twisting right along with his. She didn't have an answer for him.

David sat in the New Life administration office with his ankle propped on his knee twirling a pen through his fingers. Around him sat the ministry heads and a few of the church elders, along with pastor Ron. Coffee, water bottles, and pastries were laid out on the table for their monthly meeting. They'd each report on the various church activities and ministries and to pray together for direction, and this month David had updates to give on Grace House in addition to the usual youth group activities calendar.

Brushing crumbs from his lower lip, he clicked his pen and looked down at the clipboard in front of him. After the usual youth group points of discussion, the list shifted focus to Grace House. He'd itemized it and broken it into categories such as the ministry's immediate practical needs, challenges with the kids, and personal prayer requests for Kyle and Regina. He reviewed the list as he half listened to the current person speaking. After all, it was the women's ministry update. Since he had no woman in his life, it didn't much affect him.

The first woman in his life had run away. Left him behind when he needed her most. The familiar bitterness began a slow simmer in his gut. He reached for a water bottle from the center of the table, uncapped it and swallowed down the cool liquid. Ruminating was no good, especially during meetings.

"Thank you for the update, Sandy." Pastor Ron nodded at the women's ministry leader. "If that's all, I think we're ready to move on to the next item. David?"

"Sure." David scanned the bullets on his clipboard.

First up, next summer's youth retreat. They needed to start planning now and David really wanted to get the cost down. Not all the kids in his youth group could afford to go or had parents with the money to spare. Instead of going bigger and better every year, David wanted something simple and affordable. No archery or indoor rock climbing, no jam-packed, pre-planned agendas at pricey facilities— as much as David appreciated organization. Those were great fun, but it was on his heart to just get the kids, especially the boys, out of town for the week and focus on relationships. On God. To experience quiet, to disconnect from their frenetic pace. Get out into nature. Maybe a rental cabin. He knew there'd be hesitance on the part of the church staff, doubt about something like that being enough to draw the kids in, but he proposed it anyway.

After making his case, David looked around the table at each member of the church staff and splayed his hands. "I hope you guys will pray about that, consider it."

Matthew, one of the assistant pastors, chimed in. "Absolutely."

"Great. Now, I want to run through some immediate needs over at Grace House." He referred to his clipboard. "First, they could use some new winter coats, gloves, beanies, scarfs. Weather's getting nippier and some of the kids don't have what they need. Second, they'd appreciate help restocking the pantry. That one's a constant need. I have a wish list here from Regina." He pulled it from the clipboard and passed it to his right. "I thought we might post it in the foyer and let people sign up for specific items."

"Good idea. Love it," said Danae, the children's ministry coordinator.

"What Grace House needs most though, is prayer." David dragged his gaze down the sheet, making sure not to overlook any need. Kyle and Regina's challenges, the emotional strength they needed to keep doing what they did. He mentioned Jake's struggles, as well as Reuben's, and each of the kids coming to his karate class. And Thomas. Especially today with his visit to his mom.

Assistant Pastor Matthew leaned back in his chair as he listened, a knowing look in his eyes. "You really enjoy working with those kids, don't you?"

"I do." Thomas came to mind and a wistful smile touched his lips. "The newest kid, Thomas, has really latched onto me. Always excited to see me, sit by me. Gotta admit it's kind of cool. God has a purpose for him at Grace House, and I'm glad to be a part of it." The boy's grin and increasing chatter filled his imagination. "The little dude has really come out of his shell with me, and it's…very rewarding."

Twirling the pen in his hand, he let his thoughts hover around Thomas. Today he was visiting his mother in a rehab facility. Alli's instincts on Patricia Cooper came to mind, and a twinge of anger prodded at him. It grew and morphed into a hot poker digging into his chest. That broken bond between mother and son might be the most difficult to endure, to make sense of.

The simmering in his gut returned and threatened to boil, but David didn't have time for the emotional provocation. He caught himself squeezing the pen he was holding, his thumb going white as he pressed against it, a crack in the plastic sheath already forming. The gauzy flashbacks of his own abandonment had already compromised his focus.

Wrangling his emotions, David shoved them into tidy boxes and pressed forward with the remainder of his list in a clipped military tone.

"David, the church has some pantry donations ready to send to Grace House now." Sandy gestured in the general direction of the kitchen.

"Awesome, thanks."

Pastor Ron canted his head toward David. "Before we wrap up, I want to reconfirm your participation in the men's breakfast. You'll give the message? Share your testimony?"

By participation, he of course meant talking about his past. Digging it up and putting it on display. The tidy boxes vibrated and threatened to bust open again, but David wouldn't allow it. With a crisp nod, he replied, "Yes, sir." He'd meant it when he told God he would follow His leading wherever it went.

As the meeting closed in prayer, David sat before the Lord in full awareness that he was letting the past affect him and his treatment of others.

God, I trust You. Help me to lay this down and have more self-control. The devil plays me too easily sometimes. I don't know how to stop it, but I know You do. You have more peace and healing to give me. Even though I can be so difficult, and I blow it more often than I succeed.

He opened his eyes and stood. They shook hands and said their goodbyes, then David left the administration office and made his way to the kitchen. If he ran those donations over to Grace House now, he'd be able to see how Thomas was holding up after his visit with Patricia.

And hopefully catch Alli before she left. She might need another mood-boost too. And that thought made his mouth twitch up.

"TGIF, huh?" Linda puffed out her rosy cheeks.

"Yeah. TGIF." Alli checked the time on her phone then looked again at the stack of case files on her desk. Just a few more reports, a couple more calls. Then she'd head home.

"Sticking around then, are you?"

"Just for a little while." Call it nerves, call it duty.

Linda followed Alli's gaze to her files. "I know. The work never ends."

"Ain't that the truth?"

"Hey, how's that boy? The one at the Group Home? Is that working out?"

She filled her lungs as she thought back to her visit there. Alli had stayed longer than expected when she dropped Thomas off at Grace House. The confrontation with Patricia had sapped her strength, and she'd let Regina talk her into staying for a cup of coffee and a breather before she headed out.

It did help. Regina offered encouragement and understanding about the stress and tension involved in advocating for kids when their own parents fought against it. She'd added whipped cream to Alli's cuppa, just to give her a reason to smile.

Meanwhile, David had been there dropping off supplies—some generous donations from his church—and his interaction with Thomas had somehow lightened the burden weighing on her heart. He'd even asked how *Alli* was feeling after the dreaded encounter and made her laugh by expressing his willingness to wrangle up more donuts to fight over if need be.

David's Maple bar, Regina's prayers, Kyle's paper airplane… How was Thomas? She tipped her head toward Linda. "He seems fine for now. Getting acclimated."

"Good!"

"Yeah. I'm still hunting for a family situation for him, though. Something closer to normal, ya know?" And the longer that took, the more settled into a routine he got there, the harder it would be to move him. The sooner he was out of there, the better.

Linda nodded in understanding.

"I'd hoped to have something by the end of the week but, well, you know how it is. Never enough foster parents to go around."

"We have our work cut out for us, don't we?" She exhaled. "Well, I'm gonna go home and take a nice, hot bath, then binge-watch The Crown."

Alli smirked. "Have a good night, Linda. See ya Monday."

"You, too."

Linda's departure left Alli as the last one in the office. The silence reverberated against her eardrums, kicking up her pulse. She tried to distract herself from the sense of isolation and focus on the file in front of her, on the photo of a little blonde girl with a splotchy red-and-blue bruise along her cheekbone. It was like looking into a mirror. She blinked but couldn't look away. It was the eyes. They spoke to her. *Will anybody protect me? Does anybody see? Or care?*

Alli's breaths grew shallow, and she ran her fingertips across her lower lip, flinching at the tiny scar nobody noticed. Her eyes squeezed shut and her muscles tensed. *"You get to choose this time, you stupid brat. Closet or bathtub. And shut up because nobody cares about your crying."* Alli breathed in through her nose, out through her mouth. She tapped the space behind her ear, then opened her eyes back to the casefile.

This child's bruises would fade. She would remember how to smile. But she would be scarred. Would she always feel alone in a crowd? Unable to trust? Would she startle too easily at random things?

Would the life get beaten out of her until there was nothing left of her but an empty shell?

Alli signed her name on the psychologist's report then closed the folder and gently laid it aside. She didn't want to feel empty anymore and she had a date to get ready for. No excuses.

When she got home, she unlocked her front door and stepped in, kicking her shoes off as she headed down the hall. She changed out of her jeans and into an A-line skirt, reapplied her deodorant and lipstick, and combed her long waves into submission. She shellacked the whole 'do with hairspray and assessed her reflection. Did she look the part? Close enough.

Okay, Alli. Try not to blow this.

Tipping her head to the side, she adjusted the decolletage of her lacy top. That should help. She practiced smiling in the mirror then turned off the light.

Show time.

At the restaurant, Garrett was already seated with a glass of wine in front of him, the bottle on the table. He stood when she approached and, smiling, pulled her chair out for her. "Alli, you look . . . wonderful."

Judging by his roaming eyes, Alli wondered if she'd overshot the mark with her attire. She sat and scooted her chair farther in. "Thank you. You look nice too."

"Wine?" He reached for the bottle.

"No. Thank you, but I don't drink."

"Ever?"

"Not usually. I never know when I'll get that late-night call to pick up a kid or something, so I just don't. Sorry."

He passed her a sincere smile. "No need for sorries. I'm just real glad you're here."

"Good. Me too. To tell the truth, it's been a rough week and I could really use a night out to take my mind off things. That kid I left to pick up last time—" She shook her head, "—he lost his foster family, and I haven't found him a new one yet."

"That's terrible."

"Yeah. It is. I just hope I can find a family for him soon. I don't like him having to stay in a group facility, you know? He's only seven. And his mom . . . she's a mess."

Garrett scanned his menu. "I'm sure you're doing your best for him." He set the menu down and reached for her hand. "But for tonight, why don't you set your worries aside and try to enjoy yourself."

"Oh. Yeah, sure. You're right." She smiled and shook her head. "Sorry." Her gaze moved to their two hands. How could she open her menu without pulling away? She licked her lips. "What are *you* getting?"

"The crab Alfredo here is fantastic."

"Okay. That sounds good, I'll get that too."

The waiter arrived and Garrett released her fingers. Alli unfolded her napkin, spread it across her lap, and stored her hands there.

Her gaze traveled the restaurant. The low lighting, the flowers on the tables, the votive candles in sparkling cups. A far cry from the karaoke bar. He was upping the ante.

"And for you, Miss?"

"Same. Thank you."

"Very good." The waiter dipped his head and turned to go, leaving Alli and Garrett alone again.

Alli pulled her shoulders back and sipped at her ice water. She could do this, right? Bond with someone. Or at least give a convincing approximation.

"So, I thought after dinner we might take a walk along the lake." His eyes sparkled at her, piercing. Blue as a robin's egg.

"Sounds nice. But it's pretty cold out." She hadn't brought her down jacket.

"Don't fret, I'll keep you warm." He winked.

She shifted in her seat. "Okay, slow down Casanova." She smiled and held up a stopping hand.

He laughed. "There's that spunk I'm so taken with. Don't worry, I'll be a good boy."

At her raised eyebrow he put on a faux wounded look. "What? I will."

Alli gave him a lopsided grin and shook her head. "I'm watching you."

"I hope you like what you see."

Her gaze roamed his handsome features. "Mmm, too soon to tell."

He smirked at that. "I'll have to ask you again later then."

Alli tipped her head in response.

Conversation flowed smoothly throughout the evening, a good mix of banter and information swapping. Garrett's birthday was May 30th. A Gemini. So astrologically, they were compatible. His father was a history professor and his mother a trial lawyer. He had two younger sisters, a niece named Molly, and a Golden Retriever he called Biscuit.

Things seemed to be going well. Alli was glad she'd said yes to the date. Even the walk along the lake was nice. Comfortable. True to his word, Garrett was a good boy. And he made her laugh, which was important.

They made it back to the bistro parking lot and stopped beside Alli's car. She unwound his scarf from around her neck and held it out to him. "Thanks for letting me borrow this."

"Sure. Couldn't have such a pretty neck getting cold." Garrett reached out his hand and Alli froze, willing herself to accept his touch. He ran his finger down her cheek and stepped closer. Her breath caught. It was coming. Did she want this? She didn't know. Maybe?

In the span of two heartbeats, Alli ran down the list of all the reasons Garrett was good for her. The reasons she should take a chance on a relationship.

Goosebumps rose as his breath fanned her face. When his lips touched hers—soft, warm—she turned off her brain. Closed her eyes. Let herself enjoy the sensation of his kiss. She tried to imagine this as a part of her everyday life. Being held. It wouldn't be so bad. Quite nice, actually.

But it was time to wrap it up. She placed her palm on his chest and gently pressed him away, smiling to reassure him. "I had a good time tonight. Thank you."

He released her and stepped back. "Any time."

Alli tucked her hair behind her ear and turned to unlock her door. Garrett stood watching until she was buckled up and had the engine on. Then he finally made his way to his own vehicle. Alli puffed out her cheeks and rested her forehead on her steering wheel.

Well, it was a start. Still, shouldn't she feel something? It was a nice kiss. She couldn't think of a single thing about it that was substandard. But it lacked a certain . . .spark. Or something.

What was wrong with her? Why was she doing this? She was just setting herself up to be alone for the rest of her life. What more did she want? What was it that kept her locked up inside herself this way?

A honk startled her, and she lifted her head to see Garrett's car pulled up beside her, window rolled down. She rolled hers down too to hear him. "Didn't realize my kiss was so powerful it would knock the wind right out of ya. You okay?"

She cocked her head and smirked. "I'm fine. Get out of here, Casanova."

"Yeah. Hey, maybe I can give you a call tomorrow night?"

She shrugged one side of her mouth. "I told you, Saturday's no good for me. Sorry."

"Right. So you did. Well, I'll . . .call you soon then. Drive safe."

"You, too." She held her hand up in goodbye, rolled her window up, then pulled out of the parking lot behind him, and drove home.

Fifteen minutes later, Alli walked into her house and kicked the door shut behind her. Dropping her veneer, she tossed her jacket on the couch, then plopped into a dining chair and rested her head on her arms with a groan. Wasn't she supposed to be "floating" after a first kiss? What was missing? Maybe she was incapable of having "that feeling" for anyone. Maybe this was as good as it got for her.

Or maybe she needed more than a checklist and a skilled set of lips.

She reached across the table and plucked the folded piece of paper that had sat there for two days. She unfolded it and looked at the picture Thomas had given her the day she'd delivered the news about the McMillans. A blue sky, a house, and two people—one shorter with brown hair, and the other tall with long, yellow-blonde waves. They were both smiling . . .and holding hands. Above their heads he'd written "you" and "me." Alli's throat constricted as she traced her index finger over the crayon smiles. If she knew how to cry, this would surely do it.

Her supervisor's words echoed in her mind . . . *you two are like peas in a pod.*

Sometimes there's a kid you just want to take home yourself.

A pang shot through her belly. It was stupid. Even if some primordial part of her was drawn to a child, she never could, even without the red tape. She couldn't hack it. She wasn't parent material. She didn't know how to *nurture.* She was no *mom.* Her role was advocate, friend—warrior when needed. Definitely not mother.

Her stomach dipped at the reminder. Family had never been in the cards for her.

Why? Alli could play just about any part, fit in with any crowd. So why couldn't she connect? What more did she need to do?

Look at me! Too messed up on the inside to be of any good to a child or anyone else.

Which was why she sat in this dark kitchen after a successful date just feeling . . .hollow.

She blinked a few times, then pulled her gaze from the drawing and sent it across the room. She stared at the nearly finished final chair. It stood off in the corner of the dining area, with a drop cloth under it. One more coat of varnish and it'd be ready.

Just in time, too.

She pushed back from the table and stood, regarding it. With a sniff, she walked over and pried the lid off the nearby can of varnish. Without even removing her sexy sling-backs, she knelt and dipped in the brush. She ran the glaze back and forth across the seat of the chair, then each spindle on the back. And slowly, her mind cleared of all thoughts of her date, her empty soul, everything but this chair that had once been ready for the dump and now gleamed in the light of her chandelier like a work of art.

Fixed up, restored. Given brand new life.

Must be nice.

Blinding sunlight pierced Alli's closed lids, shouting *get up! the day is here.* She flopped onto her other side, back to the window, and pulled the blankets over her head. Surely, she was allowed to sleep in today, right? Her only plans were with herself. Not that she was celebrating the solitude. Maybe she should've accepted Garret's dinner invitation after all. Something to write on the calendar. But she wasn't ready for that. Yet.

Her breathing went rhythmic, and sleep was just beginning to pull her back in when her phone buzzed. With a start, she blinked open her eyes then stretched across the bed to grab the phone off her nightstand. Linda's name lit up the screen. Curiosity and confusion wrinkled Alli's forehead. Linda rarely called. Never without a good reason. Surely it wasn't because . . .

She rattled the sleep from her brain and pressed the receiver to her ear. "Hey, Linda."

"Morning, Alli. Guess what?"

"What?" Anticipation flooded her at the sound in Linda's voice.

"I think I found the perfect family for the Cooper kid. Maybe."

Family for Thomas? Alli pushed herself up to fully sitting. "Yeah?"

"They've just gotten their clearances done, they live in West Grove, have successful careers."

"West Grove?" Alli's heart quickened. "That's a really nice area." She chewed her lip as she tucked her messy hair behind her ears.

"Yeah. I'm sending you their file. I thought you might want to reach out to them."

"Thank you. I do." She scrambled out of bed and went to her laptop. "How many other placements are chomping at the bit to get in there?"

"None yet. But it won't take long."

Alli tapped in her password and was soon skimming the family profile as Linda continued.

"Dan and Marylou Haskell are a stable, married couple with one child of their own, an eleven-year-old boy. The husband makes six figures as a surgeon and the wife runs a profitable web design business from home."

Promising. Very promising.

Alli ran her index finger along her lower lip. "Their address is in a nice part of town, *and* in a good school district."

"Yep."

Alli jumped up and rushed to pull on her favorite pair of jeans while balancing the phone with her shoulder. "Okay, I'm gonna call them now. Thank you, Linda. Fingers crossed!"

"Fingers crossed."

The call ended and Thomas's sad declaration crossed her memory. *I'll never have a real mom.*

Alli wanted nothing more than to find him one. If she could accomplish that, today would be the *best* day ever!

She dialed the Haskells, and they agreed to an eleven o'clock meeting.

Alli pulled out a box of frozen blueberry waffles and put two of them into the toaster. When they popped up, hot and toasty, she dropped them onto a plate and doused them with syrup. Then she drew a happy face on them with whipped cream and added a cherry for the nose. Thomas's freckled face grinned in her imagination, and she could almost hear him asking for the stem. And wondering if hermit crabs could eat waffles.

After breakfast, Alli pulled a royal blue top over her head, scrubbed her face, then headed out the door.

Truth was the Haskells didn't require another home visit. They were cleared to take in a child already. But Alli wouldn't place a client anywhere without checking out the family herself, seeing if they were a good match.

Traffic was on Alli's side as she traveled into the affluent neighborhood. Manicured lawns and homes with turrets dotted the picturesque roads. She pulled into the Haskells' driveway and shook her head at its beauty. Custom stamped walkway led to a large, double-doored entry. Alli knocked and was welcomed into a sunny living room.

"So nice to meet you. Please, make yourself at home." The woman looked to be in her early thirties. Her hair was shiny, her eyebrows impeccable, and her smile bright. Her husband was equally fine-looking as he stood smiling beside her.

"Thank you."

Alli was offered coffee and pumpkin cookies, which tasted divine but left crumbs on her paperwork which she had to brush off. The couple seemed very grounded. Loving. Their home was tidy without being stuffy. Alli learned they valued hard work, an entrepreneurial spirit, and the power of kind words.

"Miss Johnson, we hope you can see how much love we have to share. We're eager to open our home to those children who need it most."

"I can tell you do, Mrs. Haskell." Alli smiled. "I only wish you felt you could take more than one."

"Perhaps down the line. But being new to this, we really feel it best to only commit to one child to start with."

"I completely understand. That's wise." She glanced at the family photos on their wall. "Can you bring your son out now? I'd like to meet him too."

"Yes, of course." Mr. Haskell stood and left the room, returning a moment later with a boy with blond spiked hair and a gamer t-shirt. "Miss Johnson, this is our son, Tyler."

Alli shook his hand. "Nice to meet you, Tyler. How old are you?"

"Eleven. But I thought you already knew that."

Alli chuckled. "Yes, you're right. I do have that written in the file somewhere. What sorts of things do you like to do in your free time, Tyler?"

The boy glanced at his mom and shrugged. "I dunno. Normal stuff, I guess. Xbox, my BMX bike."

"BMX? Sounds pretty cool." She tilted her head. "So, tell me Tyler, what do you think about having a foster child move in with you?"

"I think it's great. I mean, we have so much, and some kids have, like, nothing. And it's real hard for them, you know? So, we should help them. And I've never had a brother or sister so it might be cool to have someone to hang out with."

Alli smiled. "Thank you, Tyler." She looked at his Mr. and Mrs. Haskell. "You've got a real good kid, here."

"Yes. We do." Mrs. Haskell ran her hand over Tyler's head in a maternal gesture that put an ache in Alli's heart.

"Alright then. I think we're finished." She stood and slung her purse onto her shoulder.

Mrs. Haskell drew in a breath as she rubbed at her thighs and stood. "Okay. I'm excited-nervous." A little laugh puffed through her lips.

The Haskells walked her to the front door and Mrs. Haskell held onto it after Alli stepped out to the porch. Mr. Haskell put an arm around his wife. "So, when do you think you'll have a child to send us? You mentioned a boy . . .?"

"Yes, I have one in mind who I can see doing very well in a home like yours." Her insides stirred with excitement. "It could be as early as Monday, but I'll give you a call first, with specifics."

"Wow." Mrs. Haskell grinned up at her husband then returned her gaze to Alli. "So quickly. Thank you—very much." Anticipation gleamed in her eyes.

Saying her goodbyes, Alli dipped her head, then stepped down from their porch and walked toward her car. A buzz of adrenalin filled her belly. They were perfect for Thomas. Absolutely perfect.

Now Alli wanted to celebrate.

West Grove boasted some amazing antique stores and thrift shops, and it would be a crime not to do some browsing while she was in the area. What better way to spend the afternoon?

After shopping, she threaded her way through an old, familiar neighborhood Then, on a lark, stopped at the nail salon and indulged in a pedicure. What could be better?

Back home, she unpacked the Chinese takeout she'd picked up, dished out her plate at the table and smiled to herself.

But the silence of her empty house muted her joy.

Chow Mein was still delicious even when alone, but how nice would it be to have someone to celebrate with?

Her mouth was full of orange chicken when her phone rang, and Janelle's name lit the screen. Alli hurried to answer, swallowing the half-chewed chicken. "Hey, you."

"I can't believe you haven't called me! Was it good? It was good, right? Did you kiss him?"

Oh, right. The date. "It was fine. And not that it's any of your business, but yes. We kissed good night." She twirled Chinese noodles onto her fork.

"What about good morning? Did you kiss him good morning, too?"

"No, Janelle. Come on, seriously?"

"Kidding! Sort of. But hey, you gotta keep me in the loop here, okay? I set you up. I have rights."

"Mm hmm, sure ya do. Next time, I'll wear my Go Pro, so you don't miss anything."

Janelle laughed on the other end of the line. "That'd be interesting but might ruin the mood."

"Probably. So, hey . . ." Alli glanced around her apartment, a tightness growing in her throat. "You wanna pop by for a brownie? Double Fudge."

"Oooh. I'm salivating just hearing the word. But I'm sort of on my way out. It is Saturday night and all. Eric and I have reservations. But call me next week and maybe we can set up a double date!"

The noodles slipped off her fork. "Oh. Yeah, of course." She set the utensil down, her shoulders wilting. "Tell Eric I said hey."

"Will do."

The call ended and Alli pushed her plate away. Loneliness nibbled at the edges of her spirit. Across from her stood the newly refinished dining chair, a bright red bow tied to the top. As she looked at it, she huffed a deep breath, then stood and put her plate in the sink.

She should still be feeling over-the-moon happy that Thomas was going to get a new family. That's all that mattered. And it *was* reason to celebrate. Even if she was alone.

Pulling open a drawer, she rummaged around for the lighter and lit the pink-and-white striped candle on the double fudge brownie sitting on her counter.

Hunching down to rest her chin on her hands, she studied the tiny dancing flame, then closed her eyes and blew it out.

"Happy birthday to me," she whispered.

Chapter Five

Alli arrived at Grace House with her portfolio in hand, eager to see Thomas. The transition would be bumpy—it always was—but good things were about to happen for him, she just knew it.

She reached toward the knocker and paused, hand midair, as the *Peace to All that Enter Here* sign snagged her gaze. Her fingers curved and she rapped on the door directly instead.

The door opened and Regina greeted her by pulling her into a hug.

Alli stiffened, blinked, returned the squeeze. "Good morning."

"Good morning, Alli! Come on in." Regina's wide smile was contagious, and an unnamed longing poured through Alli. "How was your weekend?"

Alli tightened her hold on the portfolio, as if to hug it the way Regina had hugged her. "It was great, how was yours?"

"Wonderful. Wonderful. If you'll go ahead into the office, we'll be there in a jiff."

"Take your time." Alli turned down the hall to the office and opened the door, expecting to find it empty. Instead, she found David, sitting alone in the room.

He hopped up when she entered. "Alli. Good morning." The sound of his voice sent a fizzy feeling through her veins. He gave her a warm smile, his presence seeming to fill the entire room.

"Morning to you, too." She lowered herself into the second chair and he took his seat again beside her.

The air crackled with the hum of silence. Alli cleared her throat. "So… how are you?"

"I'm okay."

Regina entered and handed Alli a cup of coffee, Kyle right behind her. They took seats on the other side of the desk.

The scent of pumpkin swirled beneath Alli's nose. She'd remembered. "Thank you, Regina."

"You're welcome." Regina grinned. "So. This is it, huh? You found a family for Thomas to stay with."

Alli hummed through a sip of her brew and nodded. "I did. And I'm super excited for him. How has he been?"

Regina's eyes lit up. "He's doing really well. He's a very polite, creative little boy." Her gaze traveled to her husband. "We'll miss him."

Alli knew how they felt, but it was part of the drill. The job they'd all signed up for. "Anything I should know? Any hiding or anything like that? I know sometimes he retreats after visits to his mother."

"No, no hiding. David, any observations?" Regina's gaze went back to Alli, but she inclined her head toward him. "Thomas has really connected with David, he clings to him like ivy."

David's eyes crinkled. "Yeah, he's my little buddy, my second shadow these days." Something sparkled in the man's eyes and sent a rock to the pit of her stomach. "He even likes to keep me company when I'm working on my sermons sometimes. Just reads Bible stories right alongside me. Never had anything like that before." His Adam's apple bobbed then he seemed to return from whatever scene had been playing in his mind.

His face turned serious. "He's making friendships here. Smiling more every time I see him." He glanced down. "He loves chapel. He told me Saturday that he asked Jesus into his heart."

Alli's spine tingled but she forced a smile. "If that makes him happy, then . . .good for him." But she knew that happy feeling wouldn't last. He'd stayed here too long and now he'd have one more disappointment to add to the list. One more source of empty dreams. At least Alli could help fill some.

David cleared his throat. "Alli…Do you mind if I ask a question?"

She took a sip of her coffee to help her refocus on the here and now. "No, go ahead."

"The Haskells . . . do they go to church?"

Alli pressed her lips together, her neck muscles tightening. "I don't believe so, no."

"Do they live close enough for Thomas to continue coming to our weekly chapel meetings?"

Her skin felt too tight, too small for her frame, as pressure built up within her. She ran her tongue along her teeth. "I'm afraid not."

David wasn't finished. "It's just that Thomas has really been getting a lot out of the Bible messages. I think it's given him hope."

Invisible fingers wrapped around Alli's windpipe. She did her five-count as she pondered her reply. "Hope is important. And he is free to bring a Bible story book with him, if you'd like to send him with one. But he'll be fine with the Haskells. They're a great family and they'll treat him well."

David nodded slowly. "Miss Johnson, I'll be blunt. I wouldn't move him. He's flourishing right here."

It was *Miss Johnson* now, was it? No more donuts and spicy cologne, he was all Holy-Joe now. Well okay then.

Alli pinned him with her gaze, her blood sizzling. "Mr. Porter. I get that your faith is important to you. And that your concern for Thomas is sincere. But a boy his age shouldn't be stuck in a group home when he has the chance to join a nice, two-parent family. You have to trust that I know what I'm doing here."

Silence stretched between them and Alli thought she'd gained the upper hand. But David shook his head. "I don't have a good feeling about him going."

Regina uncrossed her legs and leaned forward. "David. Don't."

"Don't what?" David glanced from the house parents to Alli. "Look, his mother is on course to regain custody, right? She's close to completing her residential treatment. Thomas is happy here. Why bounce him around more than necessary if he's going to be going home soon anyway? It seems like a bad move. That's all I'm saying."

Why was this idiot even in this meeting?

Alli swallowed the words burning in the back of her throat and pulled in a cleansing breath. "There are no guarantees when it comes to his mother." Patricia was *far* from a fit parent, according to everything Alli had observed. *And* shared with the pastor. Thomas deserved a good family. And she had sworn to find him one. "Thomas *is* going to the Haskells'. And I promise you I wouldn't do anything that wasn't in his best interest."

Kyle cleared his throat. "Alli, I apologize if we've crossed any lines. Please excuse David's . . .fervency. I'm sure he means no disrespect to the Haskells. Or you."

David leaned forward in his chair and loosed a frustrated sigh. "Of course I don't. I just *know* this is the wrong call. I feel it in my gut. And I hate to see these seeds of hope ground to dust."

Alli's jaw clenched, and she had to work to maintain a civil tone. "I am not grinding his hope to dust. I'm fulfilling his hopes. Fulfilling my promise to him. I would never do anything to hurt Thomas. Whether you realize it or not, I'm good at my job, *Pastor*. I suggest you stick to yours." She broke eye contact with David and looked at Regina. "Does Thomas know I'm coming?"

Regina's voice was soft. "Yes, we spoke with him last night. I'll get him now."

"No," David interjected gruffly. "*I* will."

Alli's lips pressed hard together as David strode out the door. She closed her eyes and quickly counted to five, then opened them again and offered her most sincere smile. "Great."

Kyle had an uncertain, but apologetic look about him. Regina lifted her mug and Alli followed suit. Good distraction. *Let's segue out of that unfortunate exchange, shall we?*

When David returned with Thomas, the boy was clutching his hermit crab habitat with one hand and David's hand in the other. His face was utterly blank. The smile he gave her, empty. He dragged his eyes up to David.

"Go on." David nudged him toward Alli, then tousled his hair.

There was no hint of animosity left in him, and Alli's body felt confused. Uncertain whether to fight or melt. So, she focused on Thomas instead. "Hey, kid. How's my main man?"

This garnered a shy grin from Thomas. Alli stood. "Okay, let's get going. You wanna say bye?"

"Bye, Regina. Bye, Kyle." As he looked at David, his face fell. "Bye, Pastor David." He took a deep, shuddering breath.

David ran his thumb down Thomas's cheek. "Take care, kiddo." He held Thomas's bag of things out to Alli.

Not a plastic trash bag this time, he'd come out with a canvas duffel bag.

She blinked at it, offered a closed smile to David in acknowledgment, and took it. A hum shot through her when her fingertips brushed against his. Stepping back quickly, she led Thomas out of the office, down the hall, and away from Grace House.

David watched through the kitchen window as Alli and Thomas loaded into her car and drove away. His gut churned with worry for Thomas. Frustration toward Alli heated his neck. And reigning over all of that was deep, deep disappointment in himself.

He shouldn't have been so gruff. The woman was just doing her job, and it was obvious how much she cared about Thomas. What did David know about little kids anyway? Was he suddenly an expert? His ministry was teens. Had he forgotten that so quickly? He'd opened himself up to try and do some good, but he was getting in too deep. Thomas probably *would* be better off with a more traditional family unit.

And now, whatever aversion this woman had to Christians, to faith, to *God*, he'd just reinforced it tenfold by his . . . lack of self-control. Who was he kidding? He'd flat-out strong armed her. Or tried to. So much for *just giving it to God*. Would he *never* change?

"I'm sorry, Lord." Shame weighted his gaze downward and he ran his hands over his face. "Help me. Please. I don't want to be this way."

As much as God had turned his life around, changed and healed him, there were times David was acutely aware of the darkness still lurking within him. That 'old man' that refused to die and kept rising from the grave gasping for breath.

Alli didn't believe in God. What evidence had David shown to convince her otherwise? She had no reason to come back anymore so he wouldn't be able to apologize. He'd just ended things on that sour note.

Kyle appeared behind him and laid a hand on his shoulder. "All we can do once they leave us is to pray for them, David. There comes a point where we have to release them to God's sovereignty and trust Him."

"I know. You're right." A gust of wind left his lungs. "I was out of line with Alli. Pushed too hard." He shook his head. "Sorry if I embarrassed you and Regina."

Kyle patted him on the back. "Don't worry about it. And Alli will be fine. She's a good advocate for her kids. Passionate. Strong."

"Hmm. She *is* passionate about her clients." But David didn't think she was as strong as she made herself out to be. He'd looked into those hazel eyes of hers and seen the lonely little girl beneath that confident exterior. "But I think she's just about as lost as these kids are."

And instead of helping, he'd sent her running. Again.

As they cruised down the street, music pumped through the speakers and Alli tapped her steering wheel to the beat. The conflict at Grace House had been left behind and outside, the sun was burning off the morning dew and shimmering off the golden leaves of the trees lining the street. Alli smiled into her rearview mirror at Thomas who was holding Herman's habitat up to the window as if sharing in the view.

He looked up and caught her eye. "Miss Alli? Do you think they'll like me?"

"Of course, I do."

He smiled and turned back to looking out the window.

Her heart was full of hope when she parked in front of the Haskell's home, but she could see the fear in his eyes. "Come on. Let's go meet these rascals." She winked, then unloaded him from the car and led him up the steps to their porch. "You wanna do the honors?" She nodded toward the doorbell.

Thomas shook his head *no* and drew closer to her side, the fingers of one hand gripping the dog tags hanging around his neck.

Alli rang the bell and almost immediately the door flew open. Mr. and Mrs. Haskell stood beaming at them.

"Come in, come in." Mrs. Haskell stood back to give them entry, then closed the door. Hands clasped below her chin, she leaned toward Thomas and smiled. "Hi, Thomas. I'm Marylou. It's *so* nice to meet you."

Thomas blinked at her and hid behind Alli's arm. Mr. And Mrs. Haskell exchanged worried glances.

Alli rested her hand on his back and cleared her throat. "Why don't we all go in the living room and get to know each other?"

"Good idea. Honey, the cookies." Marylou waved Mr. Haskell into the kitchen then extended her arm toward the living room. "Right in here. Make yourselves comfortable."

Alli and Thomas followed her into an open area, bright and airy, with furniture and decor straight out of Beautiful Homes magazine. They took a seat on the couch and Thomas sat with his leg flush against Alli's, Herman on his lap.

Mrs. Haskell came to him. "Thomas, can I take that for you?"

Thomas clutched the habitat and looked up at Alli.

"It's okay." Alli rubbed his back and Thomas held out the box to Mrs. Haskell.

Marylou peered inside with wide eyes. "He's so colorful! I'll put this right here where he can see everything." She set the box down on the extended brick hearth and Thomas's gaze went back and forth between her and his pet. Calculating, pondering whether to trust.

Mr. Haskell appeared and set a plate of cookies on the coffee table before settling in next to Marylou on the opposite sofa. "Tyler should be home soon. He's got guitar lessons on Mondays after school. Do you play any instruments, Thomas?"

Thomas shook his head.

"If you'd like to give it a try, just let us know." He put an arm around his wife and the two of them looked at Alli.

"Maybe we can see Thomas's room?" Alli suggested.

"Oh, yes! Of course." Marylou breathed a nervous laugh and stood. "Right this way."

After touring the middle of the house, the Haskells showed Thomas to his room. He had a dresser, nightstand, desk and chair, and a big window looking out to the backyard. Thomas silently took it all in.

Alli stayed to help him unpack his things. While Mrs. Haskell hung his jacket in the closet, Alli folded his three pairs of jeans and laid them in the dresser drawer, followed by his long-sleeved shirts and then his two sets of pajamas. In the bottom of the duffel bag, she found a Children's Bible, its bright cover achingly familiar.

She'd had a similar book once. Alli had loved the brightly colored pictures of the smiling man in white robes and a beard. She glanced over her shoulder then opened the cover. A note was written inside. *To my friend Thomas. Remember that Jesus loves you, and so do I. Love, Pastor David.*

A cauldron of emotions bubbled in her gut. Nostalgia, longing, and bitterness whirled together. She closed the Bible and set it on Thomas's nightstand.

Had David really overstepped his bounds and tried to bully her, or had *she* overreacted to his resistance? He wasn't a bad guy. He obviously cared for Thomas.

She bit down on her lip. Nothing wrong with the kid believing in Jesus. Hadn't she said so herself? It was no different than Santa Clause. Like all children's fantasies, Jesus could bring warmth and light into a child's world. Maybe it would do him some good to read these stories.

Marylou was sitting beside Thomas on his bed, and he was quietly showing her his new bag of marbles—a gift from Kyle. She oohed and ahhed and Thomas watched her face, pleased with her reaction.

Alli smiled. They were going to get along just fine.

A pang of envy struck her as she watched them together, already looking something like a mother and son. She shifted her weight and slipped her hands into her back pockets. "Well…it's time for me to go."

Thomas turned widened eyes to her, paused, then nodded. He wiggled down off the bed and came to her, and Alli knelt in front of him. He looked deep into her eyes for a moment, glanced back at Marylou, then hugged Alli tight around the neck. "I wish you could stay," he whispered, his breath warm against her ear.

Alli closed her eyes and wrapped her arms around his little body. *Me, too.* She arranged a smile, then pulled away and gave it to him. "I'll see you soon, kid."

Alli woke the next morning with a smile on her face. But as she finished blow drying her hair, the joy faded. She chalked it up to professional instinct. There were other kids who needed the same kind of help. Time to focus on the next one. Tim would want an update at their meeting this morning, so it made sense that her thoughts were shifting away from the triumph of a successful match for Thomas Cooper.

The fact she had no appetite for breakfast had zero correlation to closing the chapter on Grace House. To not sharing pumpkin spice coffee with Regina, watching Kyle make paper airplanes, or ever getting a full view of David's tattoo. No, it was totally normal to crash after a big win, for the exhaustion to hit all at once.

That's what she reminded herself as she sat in her boss's office, updating him on her caseload. He'd stationed himself at his desk in his leather chair, his monitor open to the Cooper case. She could make out the skewed reflection of Thomas's photo in Tim's reading glasses.

"So, you got Thomas squared away with the Haskells?" Tim crossed an ankle over his knee and lifted his coffee cup to his lips.

"Yep. Sure did." Her lips pressed together as she gripped the slippery sense of victory she'd carried around the day before.

"I finished reviewing your report last night. You did good work with that case this month, Alli. You should feel good about that."

Yes, she should. She did. "Thank you."

"So, let's look at the rest of your caseload. Any specific and immediate concerns?"

Seriously? With a tip of her head, Alli gave Tim a dull stare.

"Right, I know. It's all specific and immediate in foster care. But you know what I mean. Anything really jumping out at you that I should be aware of?"

"Nothing more pressing than anything else, no. But you should really start calling these meetings at the end of the day rather than the beginning. My answer might be totally different then."

"True." He set his mug down on his desk, uncrossed his legs, and leaned forward. "Alli . . ." He rubbed a palm over his balding head. "How are *you* doing?"

Her forehead wrinkled. "Me? I'm fine. I'm great. Why?"

His eyes pinned to hers, his brows arched high above them. "Because I know how close you are to the Cooper case, and I imagine these last few weeks have taken a hefty toll on you."

Her chest thudded. "I can handle it just fine, don't worry about me." *Thud, thud.* "Have you ever seen me tap out on my job?"

"No, I have not. You've always done superior work. Doesn't mean you're immune to the struggles that come with this job." A poignant smile touched his lips. "I just wouldn't want to lose one of my best case workers."

"You won't. Like I said, I'm fine. Business as usual."

He reached for his mug and leaned back in his chair. "Okay. I'm glad you're okay."

"Thanks." Alli leaned forward and splayed her hands on her thighs, preparing to rise. "So, are we ready to wrap up this pow-wow? I've got kids to help."

"Yes, go ahead and get to work."

"You got it, boss." Alli stood and left Tim's office folder in hand, mentally preparing for the day ahead. Linda was waiting for her in the hall wearing a silly grin. "Morning, Linda."

"You didn't tell me you had a new man in your life. Good for you."

"What? First of all, I don't. I mean I do, but I don't know what we are yet. Second . . . how do you know about him?"

Linda bit her lip and tipped her chin down conspiratorially. "He dropped by to see you. He's in your office now and, oh my, he's . . ." She fanned herself. "Whew! I wish I were so lucky."

Alli's eyebrows twitched toward each other. "Thanks?"

"Go get 'em, tigress."

Alli rolled her eye as Linda spun around and walked away. *This* was why she didn't like talking about her personal life. Not that she had much of one anyway. But what was Garrett doing here? It made her uncomfortable. This was her place of work; now she had to switch gears. She pulled her shoulders back and put on her 'I'm datable' smile then opened the door to her office.

Her smile faded in favor of a furrowed brow. "David?" He was dressed in warm layers and looked like he belonged at a snowy cabin chopping firewood.

"Hey, Alli."

She couldn't stop staring at him. "What are you doing here?"

"I brought a gift for Thomas. And I, uh, wanted to apologize."

"Apologize?" The dark brown of his soft Henley played off his eyes, which were full of regret. "What for?"

"For getting upset the other day, for pushing too hard. I was out of line; I lost my cool." He looked her in the eye, making her stomach tighten. "I should trust your judgment. I'm sorry."

"Oh." Alli didn't know what to say. Yes, he'd ticked her off; but she'd never think to expect an apology like this one. It was too sincere. Threw her off kilter. She shifted her weight and folded her arms, hugging the folder to her chest. "It's fine, David. Thank you though. That means a lot."

He didn't move closer, but somehow it felt like he did. They stared at each other in awkward silence until he snapped out of it with a swift inhale and turned to grab a package off the chair beside him.

"Yeah so . . .here's this. Next time you see him." He pulled out a soccer ball covered in signatures and short messages, like a yearbook, and handed it to her. Alli's throat tightened as she skimmed a few of the messages.

"Everyone signed it. His friends all say 'hello.'" A wistful expression curved his lips and stretched his stubbled cheeks. "We already miss him."

Thud, thud. "I'm sure he'll love this." She pulled her gaze up to meet his and managed a smile through her throbbing emotions. Why did he have to be so thoughtful? She was trying to hate him.

"I also have something for *you.*"

"Me?" She launched an eyebrow in disbelief.

"Yeah, I didn't want to leave things on a sour note." He looked almost shy as he produced a small, white paper bag and set it on her desk. "Well . . . guess I'll see ya around."

She gave him a pinched look, her curiosity sufficiently piqued. "Yeah. See ya around."

His eyes brushed across her face before he smiled and let himself out.

Alli opened the bag and peered inside. *A maple bar.* She breathed out a laugh and covered her smile with her hand. The jerk. He was impossible to stay mad at.

Her eyes snapped to the door, and she rushed into the hallway. "David?"

She stopped at the end of the hall, and he turned back to her. "Yeah?"

Alli studied his face. The scruffy jaw, the fine lines at the corners of his eyes, the smile teasing his lips. She swallowed. "Thank you." *For everything.* "I didn't have breakfast."

He acknowledged her with a dip of his chin, then turned and walked out the main doors.

Chapter Six

"Okay class, fall in."

Everyone hurried into formation on the mat and assumed an attention stance—backs straight, feet parallel and touching, hands at their sides.

"Great job tonight, I'm really proud of all of you. Keep your heads up this week, stand tall. Know your worth and where it comes from. Respect yourselves. All right, now be safe and I'll see you all next time."

"Yes, Sensei!" the room chorused back. They bowed to David before scrambling to peel off their pads and helmets and pack up their gear.

A smile softened David's face as he looked on. Classes at the YMCA were going well; Adam's students had been quick to accept David as their new instructor, and a couple kids from the youth group had since signed up. The class was near capacity. He felt great.

Except for the times that he didn't. Which was usually when his thoughts strayed to Alli. To her guarded eyes, her crossed arms used as a shield. And to the smile he'd managed to pull out of her before leaving her office.

That was a week ago, and still her face regularly popped to mind. How was she doing since they last spoke?

Entrust her to Me, son.

Good reminder. David often needed it with situations and people he couldn't control or fix on his own. For some reason he tended to feel like it was all up to him, rather than humbly accepting whatever role the Lord—the One really in control—might choose for him. David straightened up the empty dojo while he straightened out his thoughts.

He'd done what he could while she was in his life. And he continued to pray for her—and Thomas—every day. Beyond that he shouldn't think about Alli anymore.

He flicked off the lights and locked the door, adjusting the duffle bag on his shoulder. His growling stomach quickened his pace as he cut through the building. Down the hallway, hang a left, past the glittering, blue pool, into the lobby where a brightly lit vending machine begged him for change. But David had plans to meet Liam for a late-night bite, so he bypassed the machine and pushed out the door.

The cold night air felt refreshing after an evening in the stifling YMCA classroom-slash-dojo. He hit the unlock button on his key fob and watched his car's headlights flash from across the lot.

A scuffling sound tugged his attention to the left, where a group of teens were standing around. No, not standing around. They were forming a tight circle, and the scuffling he'd heard was shoes dragging on asphalt.

Pivoting their way in a cautious approach, David squinted through the dim night to see a guy pinned to the side of a car, his shirtfront wadded into the fists of a taller kid.

Liam?

With the recognition, his muscles surged. Every sinew tight and alert. What kind of trouble was the boy in?

Close enough now to be noticed, David made no bones about the fact he'd taken in the whole scene. He could still sense the old instinct to leap into action, but he'd mastered the impulse. "What are you guys up to?" Jaw firm, he let the duffle bag slide from his shoulder and land with a thud. "Everything all right?" His voice was strong, challenging, controlled.

"Yeah, we're cool. Just messing around." The kid who had pinned Liam released his hold on his shirt and draped his arm around his neck instead. "Right buddy?" He grinned at Liam and laughed, his sidekicks chuckling along with him.

David's eyes narrowed across each of them before settling on the leader. "Why don't you go ahead and let go of him then." It wasn't a question. He took a casual step closer, and the kid stiffened and dropped his arm.

Liam shoved the guy away from him, and David threw up a halting hand. Raw, teenage adrenaline and testosterone filled the air, but all the boys held themselves in check, like pit bulls on a tether. The leader stood there, chin high, shoulders back, as if weighing options.

The parking lot lamp flickered as David raised a questioning eyebrow and took another step forward. "*Are* we cool, or do you still feel like messing around?"

His eyes narrowed. "We're cool, bro. We're cool." Without looking away from David, he jerked his head to the left and addressed his buddies. "Come on guys, let's go."

As they scuttled off, David took a power stance next to Liam and, arms crossed over his chest, watched them until they'd piled into a car and left.

Liam's breaths were still coming a little fast. "Man, I wanted so bad to throw a side snap kick to his—"

"And that would've put you on his same level. Be better than that."

Liam growled. "But it would've felt so good." Then a long breath left him, and his shoulders sank, his chin along with it. "I'm…glad you were here."

"Me too." David gave a thoughtful nod. "God knew exactly where I needed to be tonight." And He always knew what He was doing. He squeezed Liam's shoulder then walked over to his duffel bag and hiked it onto his shoulder. "I don't know about you, but I'm hungry. Why don't we finish this conversation over a burrito?"

As Liam blew a chuckle and followed, David reminded himself he had a rich, full life. A calling to be *here*. He needed to shift his focus from Thomas and Alli and entrust each of their futures to the Lord. God knew what they needed and would be a far better friend than David could ever be anyway.

Cold fog dampening her airways, Alli sipped her Starbucks coffee and wandered to the other side of the home's dormant lawn.

"Hey, check it out," her friend called. "What do you think?"

She turned her head to see Janelle sporting a very large, very pink, Derby hat. Alli raised her brows and, holding back a laugh, shook her head *nuh-uh*.

"Hmm." Janelle plucked it from her head and checked the price sticker. "Three bucks. I'm gonna get it."

Alli bit her smile with a shake of her head. "Well, if that's your thing."

"At garage sales, it is. You find anything good?"

"I'm not sure yet." She raked an eagle-eye over the yard's contents.

"Well, I'm freezing my fanny off out here, so can we pick up the pace a little?"

"I'll try. But remember, you're the one who insisted on coming with me today."

"A mistake I won't make again. When you said 'early,' I thought you meant like eight. Not o-dark-thirty."

Alli puffed air from between closed lips. "The best pieces will be picked over by breakfast. I take my garage-saling very seriously. It's how I roll."

"You're just weird."

Probably. Alli brushed her fingers across the wood shelving of a bookcase, tipped her head, then moved on to a beat-up cabinet. She needed a new project, a distraction. The sooner the better.

It was that stupid group home. She wanted to forget about Grace House. Put it behind her. But it consumed her thoughts day and night. Instead of feeling relieved to be extricated from the religious tentacles snaking through everything that went on there, Alli had a hole in her heart. A hole where the people of Grace House had been.

" . . .so, I told him to shove off."

"What?" Alli sucked foam from the rim of her cup and turned to Janelle. "Sorry, I missed that."

Round, scolding eyes flashed at her. "Alli! You've been off in la la land since you picked me up."

So very true. Alli had been distracted all morning. She'd brewed hot water without coffee, and nearly left the house with mascara on only one eye.

"Yeah, I know. Sorry, Janelle."

Her brows dropped, transforming the scolding gleam to one of concern. "You okay?"

"Of course." Alli pretended to examine a bust of Beethoven's head sitting on an old end table, then lifted her paper cup again to her chilled lips.

She missed having coffee with Regina, watching Kyle fold paper airplanes with Thomas, and even—yes, she had to admit it—even getting riled up at David. Most surprising of all, she missed being hugged—though she wouldn't want to admit it.

She'd never been a hugger before. As a rule, they made her quite uncomfortable. But Regina made her feel almost… like *family*. And that was something hard to come by. Alli hadn't realized at the time just how much she liked the feeling.

When she was there last, Regina had squeezed her hand and told Alli she'd be praying for her. And Alli believed her. These weren't the religious wackos she'd known as an adolescent; these people were the real deal. It triggered an uncomfortable churning in Alli's chest that no antacid could fix and made her think too often about Pastor David and that stupid maple bar. Stupid, insignificant, delicious maple bar.

If she visited again and Regina hugged her, Alli would return it.

But she had no reason to go back there again. Thomas was in a family now and doing well. She was happy about that.

And not so happy.

"Could this preoccupation have something to do with a certain hot lawyer?"

Alli drained the last of her coffee and said nothing. She'd gone out with Garrett again over the weekend—lunch at a local cafe—and he'd sent flowers the next day. It was sweet, made her smile.

"You guys are such a cute couple. Come on, tell me what you like best about him."

Alli took a breath. "Uh . . .his eyes. Or maybe his smile."

Janelle's grin widened. "Oh, look at you, all gah gah for Garrett. I love it!"

Alli gave her *the look*. "I don't do gah gah."

"Sure, ya don't. So, when are we doing another double?"

She sighed and picked up a Pokémon lunchbox, then set it down. "I don't know, Janelle."

Janelle scrunched her forehead. "Ew, I don't like that tone. What's the dealio?"

"Nothing. It's just . . ." she rubbed her lips together. "Yeah, I like him. But I want to take it slow. My life, my job, is pretty crazy. I just need to take it one step at a time."

"Okay, but can't the next step be a weekend getaway up at my grandparent's cabin?"

Alli rolled her eyes.

"Kidding."

She bunched her lips into a half-grin. "Sure, you are." Alli checked the time. "I've got to be at court at eight. We should wrap it up here."

"You buying that?" Janelle pointed to the cabinet Alli had been examining.

"No, not this. But I'll take the semi-circular table." Alli picked up the two-foot table and carried it to the person manning the money box.

"Oh! Alli, look at this. This is so cool." Alli looked to see Janelle climb inside a claw-foot tub. "Wouldn't you *love* to have something like this in your bathroom?"

Gooseflesh poured down Alli's arms, her lungs burning with panic a second before she grounded herself. Years of practice made the process quick enough to hide her shudder. "Come on, crazy woman, I've got to get to work."

After dropping off Janelle and unloading the table from her car, Alli changed into a skirt suit and headed to the courthouse, arriving with ten minutes to spare.

Children's Court was the usual hustle and bustle as she made her way to the waiting room. Her pre-teen client arrived shortly after she did and plopped into one of the brightly colored plastic chairs. At twelve, Kevin had the swagger and defensive attitude of a sixteen-year-old. His foster mother, Ann, greeted Alli then sat and expelled a long breath.

Alli gave him a quick once-over. "How ya doing, Kevin?"

He twisted his mouth side to side and shrugged. "Don't know yet."

Alli nodded. "Yeah." Obviously, that depended on what the judge decided today.

She smiled and took the seat beside him. Bins of toys lined one wall and a toddler stood digging pudgy hands through the limited selection.

Kevin's foster mother crossed her legs. "We aren't late, are we?"

"Nope, you're right on time. Thank you for coming."

"Of course." Ann smiled tenderly at Kevin. "Just hoping for the best for my man here."

Warmth unfurled in Alli's chest. "Me, too." She looked out the door into the hall, watching for the last member of their party. Kevin was hoping to go live with his grandfather and the judge would decide that today. She hoped it worked out. How lucky he was to have family who wanted him.

Kevin's grandfather bustled in the door five minutes later, looking a bit overwhelmed but determined. Alli offered him the chair beside Kevin and after a few moments' chatter, they all fell into a fidgety silence. Nothing ever happened on time in the social system. Nothing. Often, the hoped-for happy ending never came at all.

Alli's stomach churned. "I'm going to go find out how much longer until we're up. Be right back."

She made her way over to the desk and asked for an update. The clerk turned form her screen and rifled through a thick stack of papers. "Looks like this hearing has been postponed. Sorry."

Alli groaned and headed back to break the disappointing news. Sitting across from the trio, Alli leaned forward and exhaled. "I'm sorry, Kevin. The hearing has been postponed."

Kevin shrugged his thin shoulders and dropped his head. Alli guessed he was used to this by now. At least to a certain extent. In some ways, you never got used to the feeling of crushed dreams. She looked at the grandfather. "We'll contact you with the new hearing date. I'm so sorry for your trouble."

"Kevin's no trouble." The man wiped his eyes then hugged his grandson, cupping the boy's head with his weathered hand. "Don't worry, Kev. Everything will be fine." His voice was husky with emotion and Alli felt the blood whooshing in her ears. If only all her clients had that kind of love. If only *Thomas* had a grandparent like that.

She checked the time then excused herself to head across the street for a quick bite before her next appointment. She really hoped for something positive to happen today. Polishing off a breakfast burrito, she reviewed the case facts, before returning to the courthouse. Turning a corner, she nearly collided with someone heading the other way.

"Whoa. Sorry," came the familiar, masculine voice.

"Garrett?"

"Fancy meeting you here." He winked.

"I suppose it's bound to happen from time to time."

A beat passed as Garrett stared into her eyes. "It's good to see you, Alli. When are you going to let me take you out again?"

She raised her shoulders. "When are you going to ask?"

He laughed. "I thought I was. Hey, listen, there's a karaoke contest down at our spot on Halloween. I think we'd nail it. What do you think?"

"Sounds fun. But give me a call later, okay?" She looked up at a clock on the wall. "I can't keep my clients waiting." Sophie and Vivienne had already waited a long time for this day. They were hoping to go home to their mother, who'd just successfully completed a drug program.

"I know how that is. Good luck."

She smiled. "Thanks."

Alli snaked her way through the paths of lawyers and social workers, all walking with purposeful strides, and found the two blonde pixies in another waiting room, identical to the first.

This time, the court was ready to hear the case as planned and they all filed in and stood before the judge. Statements were given, the judge addressed the mother, and then Alli gave her recommendation. "Your honor, in light of the extraordinary progress, and dedication to her children, displayed by Ms. Brennan, I fully support the reunification of this family. I recommend the girls be returned to their mother, with continued support in the way of counseling and parenting classes." She held her breath and stood erect as she awaited his response.

With a nod of his gray head, the judge replied, "The court concurs."

Alli's lungs released their air and she beamed at the Brennan trio.

Tears were shed and little hands clapped as the judge spoke. The hearing concluded with some of Alli's favorite words as the court officially reunited two of her sweetest clients with their clean and sober mother. After an emotional embrace with the foster family, the Brennans walked out the door in a mass of intertwining limbs and Alli's heart soared.

Ms. Brennan stopped her in the hall. "Thank you, Miss Johnson. For everything." Her eyes shimmered and filled Alli with a sense of accomplishment.

No other words necessary, Alli smiled and nodded, then watched them head toward the big glass doors and out into their new world. It was cases like this one that made the job worth it. Made her life feel worth something.

As if on cue, her phone rang, flashing Tim's number. "Hey, boss."

"You sound happy. Good report?"

"Yes." She grinned. "The Brennan case just wrapped up and the girls were able to leave with their mother. Love days like this."

"That's wonderful news, Alli. I'm afraid *my* news will pop your balloon though."

"Uh oh. What do you got?"

"CPS called. They have two kids, a brother and sister, in need of emergency services. I'm assigning them to you."

"Okay, give me the rundown." She pushed through the courthouse doors, stepping into the dwindling daylight.

"Liz and Toby, ages eleven and eight. Mom took off a week ago and hasn't returned. Not the first time she's done this, but the girl finally called because they'd run out of food two days ago."

"Oh, geeze." She dug her keys out and approached her car.

"Mm hmm. I forwarded you the full CPS report. They're expecting you. Oh, and Alli? Hit a drive-through on the way. They're hungry."

"Roger that." But first, those kids would need a place to go. Smiling, Alli scrolled through her contacts. She had a call to make.

Alli approached the two children sitting on an office sofa and knelt to meet their sad eyes straight on. "Hi, guys. I'm Alli Johnson." She handed them a couple fast food bags.

"Thanks. I'm Liz and this is my brother Toby." The girl unwrapped her burger, releasing a meaty aroma, and took a huge bite. She closed her eyes in relief.

Toby jammed fries into his mouth. Several ends stuck out and wiggled as he chewed.

Alli offered a warm smile. "Nice to meet you both. You ready to get out of here?"

Liz nodded, mouth full.

The kids had been at the CPS office for hours. Waiting was always the worst. Not knowing what was going to happen, where you were going to be taken. As they stood to leave, Alli scanned their appearance. Their clothing needed a wash, shoes peeling apart at the soles, but they seemed to have kept up their personal hygiene. Hair looked clean and brushed, though framing dull, distant eyes.

Their plastic bags didn't look very full. Likely they had been rushed out their door. Neither of them was even wearing a jacket. Compassion filled Alli's heart.

"You need anything from home first?" Alli held the door open for them to step outside.

Toby looked up at her, then at Liz, eagerness in his eyes.

Alli tipped her head. "If you have a key, we can stop and pick up a couple more things real quick. Extra clothes, jacket, a favorite book maybe."

Their heads bobbed and they looked at Alli as if taking her in, trying to figure out who this woman was, and whether or not to trust her.

"Come on, let's get in the car where it's warm." Alli pulled out her keys. The sun would set soon, and the temps were already taking a dip into the high forties.

The children exchanged a glance, then followed Alli to her car and piled into the back. Their burgers were polished off by the time Alli pulled up to the rundown building that was their home. Alli escorted them inside, assaulted by the stench of garbage. Decay. Mildew. She'd need to set up a doctor's appointment for them in the morning.

Liz placed a hand on Toby's back and guided him into his room, then hurried into hers. Alli watched from the hall as they went to work stuffing things into their bags. Toby pulled out a box of Pokémon cards from a drawer and Alli recalled the ones she'd seen just that morning at the garage sale. Any chance they were still there?

She peered into Liz's room and watched her gather not toys or games, but extra socks, a turtleneck, winter boots, a journal, and a photograph. Practical. Responsible. Alli pressed her lips together. At eleven years old, Liz had already left childhood behind.

"Come on, Toby. Hurry up," the girl said. "Don't forget your striped sweater."

"I hate that thing."

"It's the only one that still fits you and doesn't have holes, so bring it. Your hat, too."

"Got that already."

"Okay, let's go then."

Liz scampered past Alli to a rinky-dink closet and pulled out coats for herself and Toby.

Toby's eyes turned worried. "Liz, what about Thor?"

Another toy?

Liz ignored her brother's question and zipped up his coat.

"Liz?"

"I told you." She put her hands on Toby's shoulders. "Thor's just gonna have to take care of himself, Toby. I filled his bowl earlier. He should be okay for a few days."

Not a toy. *Oh, boy.*

"But then what? What if we're not back by then? What if we *never* get to come back?"

Liz looked away. "Mom will turn up. Everything will be fine."

"But Liz . . ."

An empty hole opened inside of Alli. She cleared her throat. "Who is Thor?"

"Our cat." Toby turned pleading eyes on Alli. "We can't leave him here all alone."

So that was the other smell. "Maybe your neighbor can take him in."

Liz shook her head. "They have allergies. And the people on the other side of us have dogs." She gave a stern look to her brother. "He'll be *fine.*" Her tone was firm, but her eyes gave her away. She was worried, too. "Sorry about my brother, Miss Johnson."

Toby dropped his head but not before Alli spotted the tears gathering in his eyes.

"No, no. That's okay." Alli chewed the side of her thumb. "Maybe . . ." Unable to believe what she was doing, she exhaled and looked at the children. "Maybe I could bring him home with me. Temporarily."

"Really?" Both kids' eyes brightened.

Alli shrugged. "Sure. I'll pick up a carrier tomorrow—"

"We already have one." Toby ran down the hall and Liz went for the kitchen. She emerged with food bags, bowls, and treats.

It took several minutes to wrangle the orange tabby into the carrier, but they eventually succeeded. And then they were on their way again.

Thor sat in the carrier up front with Alli, while the siblings huddled together in the back seat.

Alli watched them in the mirror, saw the despair in their faces as their home fell further away. She powered up the radio. "You like Taylor Swift?"

Liz's eyes skidded to the mirror, and she nodded. "Yeah, sure."

"Me, too." Alli turned on her phone's Bluetooth and started her Taylor Swift and Friends playlist, filling her car with the tune of "Shake It Off." The world may have moved on from that song, but it was still one of Alli's favorites. Could be the theme song of her life. Something she fought to do every day. Shake. It. Off.

She saw the effect on Liz, and even Toby, as the upbeat melody "shook off" a measure of the heaviness hanging over them.

Twenty minutes later, Alli flipped on her blinker and exited the freeway, turning onto a quiet, winding road.

"So where are we going?" Toby spoke around a mouthful of fries he must've found abandoned at the bottom of the bag.

"Somewhere with plenty of food, and games, too." Alli hadn't bothered with the Crisis Shelter. As soon as Tim called, her mind had gone straight to one place. "It's Grace House Children's Home and it's the best there is."

Huh. She believed that. Maybe it was because of the way they'd treated Thomas. And her. They'd say it was God. And who knew— maybe, despite her cynicism, it *was* something about the Jesus business. Whatever it was, they were doing something right over there and Alli didn't doubt it was where Liz and Toby should go.

She pulled up in front of the Home and opened the car door for the kids. They quietly walked behind her and waited while she rang the bell. The door swung open a moment later.

"Hi, Kyle." Alli raised her hand. "It's us."

"Come in, Regina put out some hot cocoa." He led them to the dining room and served the kids their chocolate. "Would you like some, Alli?"

"Oh. No, thank you. I only have a minute." Thor was still in her car and who knew what adventures her evening at home with him would bring?

"Alli?" David's voice behind her made her stomach dip.

She turned to find him grinning, his eyes sparkling at the sight of her. Or so it seemed. Shoulders back, posture perfect, yet somehow totally relaxed. He looked happy, warm, at peace with himself. Envy spiraled through her.

She curved her lips into a smile. "Hi, David."

His eyes didn't leave hers as he took a step closer. "I didn't think you'd be back."

"Yeah, well." Tipping her head toward the kids, Alli stuffed her hands in her back pockets and shrugged. "Look, I want to apologize. I was pretty harsh with you last time I was here."

"You weren't harsh." Somehow, they had drifted closer together, close enough she could detect his scent.

"Well, I think I kind of was—"

"Trust me, you weren't."

The finality in his tone closed her mouth, furrowed her brow. "Okay. Thank you." Tension eased from her shoulders. A tension she hadn't been aware of till just then. Had she been so concerned about what David thought of her?

Apparently, yes.

"So . . . water under the bridge?"

She smiled. "Yeah."

His gaze whispered over her face, touching her lips, her eyes. "It's good to see you."

At the low hum of his voice, warmth flooded her core, and her belly somersaulted. "You, too." As the heat rose to her face, she gave herself a mental shake. "I also wanted to thank you."

"For the Maple Bar? It was nothin."

She smirked. "For the gift you gave to Thomas."

"Ah. Yes. I hope he has fun with it."

"Not just the ball, David." Alli ran her tongue along her lips. "I saw the Bible. I think it really meant something to him." And did a number on her as well.

He peered into her eyes as if he read her thoughts—and was delighted at the unspoken revelation. "You're welcome."

Shrinking away from the sudden sense of vulnerability, Alli broke eye contact and gestured toward the kitchen. "Anyway. That's Liz and her brother Toby. I thought this would be a good place for them."

Both kids sat sipping their cocoa and looking around at their temporary home. Kyle chatted with them, trying to put them at ease.

"Can't wait to get to know them. So, uh. I guess this means you'll be coming around now and then."

"Yeah. When my schedule allows."

"Good." He flashed that Robert Redford smile at her.

Good? She peered up at him.

"Come here, I have something to show you."

Alli glanced over her shoulder toward the door. Toward escape. From whatever she was feeling. "I really should get going."

"It will only take a minute. Come on." He tipped his head toward the hallway and Alli surrendered and followed.

He paused in front of the last door on the right—his office—and gripped the knob. "Maybe this will help you keep up on that schedule." He pushed open the door.

What was she was looking at? The room looked like it had been split into two spaces. On one side, a coat rack stood with a karate gi hanging on it. A T-ball bat leaned against the wall. On the other side, the room was nearly empty. A cleared off, freshly polished desk sat in the center.

"What is this?" She looked up at him standing closely behind her.

"What does it look like?" He grinned and stepped around her, entering the room. "I don't really use this space they give me. Not much. I store some stuff here and take some counseling appointments. But I don't need all this room. I thought, maybe you'd like to set up shop here. Have a place to work. A second office so you can check on the kids as often as you like."

Alli blinked. Looked for words. "What do Regina and Kyle think about that?"

"They were excited. Said it's a great idea. If you're interested."

They all wanted her there? Truly?

Wheels began turning in Alli's head. An office here would make it easier for her to keep tabs on Liz and Toby. And any other clients who might land in the home or who were in families on this side of town. It would give her a place to work at night when she didn't want to sit in an empty office building, or an empty house. She sent her gaze around the room again, finally settling it on David's face. "Why?"

His brows flinched. "What do you mean? Why not?"

"Why open this space to... someone like me? I'm a heathen, remember? Opposed to your religion, to what you stand for. Doesn't that sort of make me the enemy? An adversary?"

He looked surprised. "Not at all. You're not adversarial. You just seem . . .wounded. *I* was the adversarial one the other day."

Wounded? Alli inhaled and blinked a few times. Her jaw clenched but she hid her reaction with a shrug. "Well, I'll think about it."

Disappointment filled his countenance. "Okay. Just let me know."

"I will. Really do gotta get going now, but I'll see ya around."

"Drive safe."

"Yeah." She smiled and nodded, grateful to slip out from under his eye.

As her headlights cut through the dark night, Alli ran her fingers through her hair. David thought she was wounded?

After a quick stop at the store, she pulled up to her house and took in the pretty white fencing around the front lawn. In the spring, there'd be flowers along the wall under the living room window. It was a beautiful house.

A throaty meow demanded her attention. She grabbed the cat carrier and headed inside. Before releasing Thor from the cage, Alli put out dishes of food and water and set up a litter box in the bathroom.

When she opened the latch on the carrier door, the cat eyed her warily before slinking out. Then he ran and squeezed himself under her couch. *Great.* What if he got stuck?

Well, he came from a tough background. He'd have to figure it out himself.

Alli peeled off her jacket and kicked off her shoes on her way to her room. She stopped in front of the linen closet, opened its doors, and stared at the stacks of clean, fresh towels. *Her* towels. In *her* house. She might not have everything she wanted out of life, but she had more than she once thought possible. She liked to remind herself of that now and again.

Reaching up to the top shelf, Alli pulled down a cardboard box and toted it to the middle of her living room. First, she pulled out a long garland of Fall leaves and a burnt orange table runner. Next, she dug out a set of pumpkin salt-and-pepper shakers she'd found at a yard sale and took them to the kitchen to fill them.

Somewhere along the way, Thor had ventured out from his hiding place and found the cat food near her feet. She set the salt and pepper on the table runner and nodded at the effect. The garland went on her bare mantle which instantly shifted the feel of the room and coaxed her lips into a half-smile.

But as silence stretched out before her, the corners of Alli's mouth pulled down. She stared into the ether then sank onto her couch and dropped her head into her hands.

Maybe David was right. Because even with the clean linens, the nice house, and the cat crunching kibble in her kitchen, Alli still felt . . .empty.

David checked his jacket pockets again, but they were empty. *Distracted* was not a strong enough word for the way his attention rebelled against him lately. Students would start walking into his class at the Y just minutes from now. If he'd left his phone in the lobby, or if it had somehow slipped from his pocket, there was a good chance it'd be gone by the time class ended.

He chastised himself as he hurried to retrace his steps. What was his deal? He never lost things. But ever since Liz and Toby came to Grace House, David seemed to have lost a few brain cells.

Or was it seeing their *social worker?*

Ridiculous thought.

Pushing through the door, he rounded the corner into the lobby and found a familiar, petite blonde standing at the counter. "Alli?"

She twisted to see him. "Oh, hey. There you are."

"Here I am." He felt the goofy grin stretch his cheeks.

Leaning her weight to the side, she reached into her bag. "I have something you might want."

His blood spiked and he prayed to Almighty God it didn't show. He managed a straight pitch as he replied, "Oh? What's that?"

The top of her head was all he could see as she focused on the contents of her purse. Sunlight bounced off her hair making it shine like gold.

"You don't know? Regina thought you'd be freaking out." She lifted her face and pulled something out of her bag.

"My phone!" Relief washed through him as he took it off her. "Thank you so much. Yeah, guilty about the freak out."

"Happy to come to the rescue."

Not wanting the exchange to end, he settled a deliberate gaze on her and spoke in unhurried tones. "My class is about to start. Why don't you stay and watch?" His mouth quirked up on one side, all on its own. Was he hoping to win her over to the *sport*, or to himself? Either way . . .

She folded her arms over her chest. "That's okay. There's a Starbucks across the street and a PSL with my name on it."

Dave lifted his chin and gave her a smirk. "Come on, I insist. Stay for the first fifteen, then go get your Pumpkin Spice Latte."

She swallowed, lines of her face hard, arms still wrapped around herself. Then she dropped them to her sides and met his challenge with an upward tilt of her own chin. "Okay fine. Ten minutes."

He'd won that battle. "Right this way." He headed toward the interior of the building walking shoulder to shoulder with Alli.

"So, this is like your favorite thing, huh? Fighting? You gonna break some bones today?"

"Not 'fighting.' Martial Arts."

She bounced a shoulder. "Same thing."

"No, it's not."

The set of her jaw revealed her opinion. "You're practicing the best ways to injure someone else. Trying to hurt them. That's fighting."

"Wrong. I'm practicing the best ways to control a dangerous situation *before* someone gets seriously hurt. To stop an attacker."

"By becoming one."

His blood heated, this time for a different reason. "No."

Her nostrils flared with an inhale, and she shook her head as if brushing him aside. Her antagonism grated like gravel boring into his knees, but he stretched his neck and forced his muscles to relax.

"Through here." He opened the door and held it for her. The scent of chlorine wafted out, echoing voices and the sound of splashing water hit his ears.

She blinked at him like he was crazy. "This is the pool."

"Uh huh."

"We have to walk through here to get to your class?"

"Yup." He gestured for her to hurry and step through. With a resigned and shaky sigh, she did.

"Just keep an open mind, all right? Watch the class and see what I'm all about. You make me out to be a blood-thirsty criminal. Some might call it a bit rude."

Her jaw snapped shut and she flicked her gaze toward him. "I apologize for coming across that way. I dislike all forms of violence. But I'll try to extend you the benefit of the doubt. Okay?"

He dipped his head and kept walking. "That's all I ask."

"Pastor David! Pastor David! Look, look!" A little-boy voice echoed off the walls.

David stopped and scanned the pool on his left until he found the source. "Hey, Trevor! What's up, buddy?" The ten-year-old went to his church and was a regular at the YMCA.

"I can go all the way across the pool now with one breath. Watch." He sucked in a dramatic breath then plunged under the water.

Alli's voice came from behind him, shrill and thin. "Shouldn't we keep heading to your class?"

"Just a second." He waved her off, but his gaze snagged on her colorless complexion. Worry sliced through him. "Hey, are you okay?"

"Yeah. Fine." She lifted a hand to her forehead, where pinpricks of perspiration gathered at her hairline. The tremble in her fingers didn't escape his notice, either.

She wobbled, and concern propelled him to her side with a swift arm around her waist. "You don't look fine." Though she smelled fantastic. "Come on."

"I don't need your help," she croaked, but she let him guide her down the corridor, and into his classroom/dojo where he lowered her into a chair. Her breaths came in little shuddering gasps and her eyes had a glazed look. "Thank you. I'll be fine in a second." She dropped her head and released a slow exhale through tight lips.

"Are you sure?" David's brow crumpled. He knelt in front of her. Parted the hair that hung in front of her face. "You look like you might pass out. Do you need a doctor?"

"No. No, I'm good. A little woozy is all. I just uh . . . I shouldn't have skipped breakfast this morning. That chlorine and my headache . . . I'm fine, though. Thanks." She offered him a tiny smile that erased any previous hostility.

He liked that smile being directed at him.

"Right." He cleared his throat and stood. "Don't get up. I'll be right back."

He went to his locker and returned with a banana and a protein bar. "Here. Eat something."

Alli looked at him with round doe eyes before taking what he offered and blinking her gaze to her lap. "Okay."

David noted the crease of her brow as she unwrapped the protein bar. "What is it?"

She shook her golden head. "Nothing. I just . . ." She met his eyes and held. "Thank you." For timeless moments, she didn't look away. Finally, she lowered her lashes and David found his tongue.

"No problem." He cleared his throat and took the front of the room, which had filled with kids while he'd been focused on Alli. "Students, we'll go ahead and get started."

"Yes, Sensei."

They bowed and he returned it, then stepped into a horse stance. From the side of his eye, he caught a subdued Alli looking on.

Chapter Seven

Alone in her new office space at Grace House, Alli leaned back in her chair and tapped the end of her pen against the desk. Grounding herself to her present surroundings as her mind was tugged away. The past week, she'd spent most of her office hours here. Liz and Toby's mother had been located and put into a drug rehab program. She'd gone willingly, and if all went well, she'd be allowed a visit in a few weeks. In the meantime, Alli would be around to keep an eye on how they were handling things.

She told herself her clients were her only reason for being here, but she didn't buy her own lie.

Low volume chatter came from the other side of the house, but it was all white noise to Alli. Her thoughts had drifted back to the Y, her ears full of the sounds of lapping water.

That panic attack almost did her in. She could've passed out and tumbled right into the pool. A shudder rode down her spine even now.

But there was more to the memory, something she kept coming back to—the concern in David's eyes when his strong, steady arm circled about the waist and held her fast. He'd brought her fruit. Knelt in front of her and brushed her hair from her face. And as she watched him lead his class, she saw some things she hadn't expected. Like how he wove respect and self-control and humility into the lesson. She hadn't been able to take her eyes off him as he performed the moves, his physique and manner contradicting everything she thought she knew about pastors and religious leaders.

She gave herself a shake and turned back to the files in front of her. Sounds of activity continued beyond the door, and a few minutes later she closed the folders, tapped them straight on the desk, and stowed them in her laptop bag. Whatever was going on out there carried a buzz of excitement that made her want to investigate.

Covering the length of the hall, Alli strolled into the game room and took in its decidedly untidy state. Tons of craft supplies covered the table, and everyone was busy doing something. Looked like a fun time. She hooked her thumbs in the back pockets of her jeans. "Hey guys, what are you doing?"

"We're making a bean bag toss." Toby rubbed sandpaper over a plywood pumpkin.

Alli stepped onto the tarp spread out on the floor where he worked. "A bean bag toss, huh?" A thin layer of sawdust sprinkled around him and speckled his jeans.

"Yeah, for the party. Liz is helping make the bean bags. This is the part you toss them into." He pointed at the jack-o-lantern mouth cut out of the wood. "It's kind of splintery so I've got to smooth it."

Grinning, Alli knelt beside him and picked up another piece of sandpaper from a small stack nearby. Too bad they didn't have a sanding block instead; it would be easier on his fingers. "Here, look." She sanded with the grain for a moment then ran her fingers over the spot. "See?"

Toby reached over and touched the smooth section. "How'd you do that so fast?"

"I know a bit about wood." She bobbed a shoulder and started working again. "The key is to go in the same direction as the wood grain. See how there's lines in the wood?"

"Cool. Do you want to help finish it? After this we're going to paint it."

A warm feeling grew behind her ribcage. "I'd love to. For a little while."

Dressed in a fuzzy orange sweater, her hair in a neat braid, Liz wandered over and waved to them. "Hi."

Alli gave her a grin. "Hey there."

The girl settled on the floor nearby and began filling a fabric square with rice. She had come alive since moving to Grace House. As if a weight had been lifted off her shoulders. Some kids were like that. Especially when they'd been overwhelmed with responsibility for younger siblings. As long as Liz and Toby stayed together, Alli was confident the pair would weather the current storm.

"Alrighty folks," David strolled into the room and plunked down a cardboard box. "I need some hands. Anyone have some extras?" His gaze landed on Alli. "Adult sized arms are a plus."

Toby shortened his arms and flapped his hands in front of him. "Not it!"

"No worries, buddy. You and Liz are doing a great job with that bean bag toss. I'll find another helper." He winked at them.

Mood inexplicably light and airy, Alli straightened and went to peer into the box of decorations—lots of paper pumpkins, turkeys, and pilgrims. She raised an eyebrow at David. "The turkeys and pilgrims are a bit early. Don't you want to get through Halloween first?"

"Eh. Close enough." He rooted around and pulled a pine-cone turkey from the box. "Halloween is a week from now. And we don't like to do anything evil, scary, or gory, so that pretty much means pumpkins and leaves."

"Pumpkins and leaves are fine. Leave out the turkeys and pilgrims till next week." She snatched the turkey from his hand.

Incredulity widened his brown eyes and a smile crept up one side of his face. "That means I'll have to do this again."

"Quit whining, I'll help."

David chuckled. "Okay, fine. But that doesn't give us much in the way of party decor."

Alli selected a few paper decorations and opened a box of push pins. "So, what is this party?" She climbed up onto one of the couches and pinned a paper pumpkin to the wall above it.

"Believe it or not, we have a costume party. The staff members go out and buy a bunch of costumes—*appropriate* costumes—and then the kids go 'shopping' and choose one to wear. We load them up with candy, play games, drink cider. It's a fun night, you should come." He handed her a large paper leaf.

"Um, I don't know. We'll see." Regina had mentioned some of their annual festivities when Alli first brought Thomas in, but she'd not thought much about it since she didn't figure on being around long.

Yet here she was. Setting up shop, even. Sharing an office with Pastor David.

Pastor.

Alli would *never* have thought she'd be keeping such close quarters with one of those. But her life had always been unpredictable. This place had somehow reeled her in. She glanced at David. Had he been reeled in, too? Grace House seemed like his second home. "So, are you here all the time or what?"

"You want me to leave?"

She blinked. "No. Sorry, I didn't mean it like that. I just wasn't sure if this was full time for you or not; you said you were a pastor."

"Yeah, I am. I lead the youth services at my church Wednesday nights and Sunday mornings, teach a couple times a week at the Y, take counseling appointments whenever I'm needed, but I spend the rest of my free time here. What can I say? These kids have burrowed under my skin."

The corner of her mouth tipped. Yep, they'd both been hooked. Twisting her hair, she flipped it over her shoulder out of her way and reached for another pin, stealing a sidelong glance at David's decidedly non-pastorish physique. "When do you sleep?"

He stopped and faced her, eyes wide. "Sleep? What is this *sleep* you speak of?"

"That's what I thought." She smirked and pressed the pin into the wall. "There, I'm finished over here."

He nodded appreciatively. "Hey look at that. Good job, thanks."

"No problem." Alli smiled as a kernel of joy sprouted in her.

He checked the time. "I'm supposed to be finishing up tomorrow night's Bible Study right now." He grinned at her. "But I'm starving. I'm gonna make a sandwich or something, you want one?"

She stuck her hands in her back pockets and checked out the walls they'd decorated. "Um. Yeah, sure. Then I've got some work to do, too." She filled her lungs. "I'm going to call the Haskells and see how Thomas is doing. This afternoon I've gotta head to court." Then there'd be more paperwork before she could call it a day.

She followed him into the kitchen and leaned against the bar while he pulled out bread and cheese. "Well, you gotta eat. Don't want you getting woozy." His unreadable gaze cut to hers. "I was thinking grilled cheese today, but I can also fix you up a ham sandwich if you prefer. Or something else? Sorry no donuts today."

A smile quirked her lips. "Grilled cheese sounds great." This was now the second time in a week that the man was making sure she stayed well-fed. "What should I do?"

"Nothing. Just stand there and keep me company." His grin made her pulse stutter.

"All right."

He turned on a burner and set a pan over it. "So, Alli, what do you do for fun? Any secret talents?"

Why was he asking? They had never talked about their personal lives. "I don't know." Her lips pressed together as she shook her head. "Nothing really."

"I have a hard time believing that. Come on, tell me something about you."

Licking her lips, she flipped up her palms and shrugged. "I'm . . .decent at karaoke. There."

"I wouldn't mind seeing that." He chuckled.

"And I'm a passionate garage-saler."

"Okay, explain that one to me. I've never understood the appeal. It's other people's old junk." His smile disarmed her. "No offense."

Alli scraped her teeth along her lower lip. "I like finding things others think are useless, almost ready for the bin, and restoring them to make them beautiful again. Finding treasure that was invisible to those who held it. I like rescuing things others overlook. That is why I like garage sales." She wrapped her arms over her chest and shrugged. Why was she sharing this?

David stared at her with his hazelnut eyes. "Wow." The pan sizzled and drew his attention and he quickly flipped over the sandwiches. "Now *that* I understand. In fact, that sounds a lot like what God does."

"Riight." Leave it to a pastor to turn a garage sale into a sermon. She pivoted to the fridge and swung open the door. Pulled out a couple Gatorades, "So . . . what about you? If you had free time, how would you spend it?"

He nodded once as if acknowledging her redirection of conversation, then slid the sandwiches onto paper plates. "You mean besides Kenpo?"

Her mouth turned down at the mention of karate. Yeah, *that* one she knew. And still wasn't real comfy with, though watching him the other day at the Y almost had her rethinking her position. Almost. She puffed out her cheeks and decided to skip over that topic. "Yeah, besides that."

"I'm pretty darn good at Mario Kart." He tossed the spatula into the sink.

"I'm not really big on video games. I didn't have any as a kid and it just hasn't been something I've picked up." She traded a soft half-grin for the plate he held out to her.

"Might have to fix that one of these days."

"I think that boat has sailed. I'm too old now."

"You're never too old to rediscover childhood."

An ache formed in her throat. He was being playful, but his words touched a sore spot. Alli had missed out on so much as a child. And it was indeed too late to fix that. But perhaps some youthful experiences *were* still out there for her.

"Maybe." Alli picked up her sandwich and tore it in half, the gooey cheese oozing out the middle.

They ate their sandwiches, sharing a comfortable camaraderie that surprised her. It wouldn't last of course. But she'd take the moments of reprieve as they came.

Afterward, Alli slipped into her new office and dialed the Haskells.

"Mrs. Haskell? It's Alli Johnson. How's Thomas doing?"

"Oh, hi, Alli. Thomas is doing just fine! You know I was really worried about that first night, but it went so well. The boys have spent a lot of time together. I know there's a bit of an age gap, but I think they'll be great for each other. They're getting along well."

The smile in her heart reached her lips. "I'm so glad to hear that, Mrs. Haskell."

They talked for a few more minutes, and Alli ended the call feeling optimistic. Thomas was settling in, adjusting to the new environment. The Haskells had so much to offer him. But Alli looked forward to seeing him for herself. Just a few more days and she would, though not under her favorite circumstances. Patricia was about to complete her drug program. Next time they visited, it would be at her own apartment.

Her stomach knotted.

Her phone buzzed and Garret's name popped up on the screen. She pressed the phone to her ear. "Hello?"

"Hey, sexy mama."

Alli laughed. "You sure know how to sweet talk a woman."

"Yeah I do," Garrett said. "I only have a minute. Court's in a short recess. But I wanted to check with you about the karaoke contest."

Oh, yeah. Her gaze shot around the office, landing on the small tower of orange field cones, and above them, the wall of photos and kids' drawings on David's side of the room. She sucked air between her teeth. "I don't think I can make it, Garret. Sorry. I've got this work thing . . ."

"Oh. That's a bummer." The disappointment in his voice twisted her stomach. "But I get it. Our jobs are demanding, aren't they?"

"Ain't that the truth. Look, I'm really sorry."

"That's okay, it's not your fault. You'll make it up to me somehow, I'm sure." Flirtatious laughter carried over the line and Alli tried to match it.

She gathered her hair and pulled it over her shoulder. "Well, I should—"

"Yeah, I gotta run. See you soon."

"Bye." Alli caught her lip between her teeth as she ended the call. Had she just blown off a date for a kids' costume party? At *Grace House?*

Grace House was abuzz with excitement about the costume party. The younger ones were already getting dressed, the teens were helping with last-minute preparations. The scent of cookies baking wafted from the kitchen. David ducked into his office to stow his Robin Hood costume. He hung the hanger neatly on the coat rack then lifted a piece of the fabric for examination. What was he thinking?

"Nice tights." Alli stood in the doorway smirking. "Can't wait to see them on." Her golden hair flowed in waves past her shoulders down her arms. Her tall, fur-lined boots and ivory peacoat made her look like a wintry angel.

He hid the rounding of his eyes by squinting at her. "Har har."

Alli had been less prickly and standoffish the last couple of weeks. She'd been around a lot, too. He liked that. The glimpses he'd caught of the woman behind the granite wall intrigued him.

He thought often of what she'd said about turning trash into treasure. Whatever past she blamed God for, she didn't seem as far out of reach as he first believed. He'd noticed less flinching on her part when someone quoted Scripture or said a prayer. Once during a devotion he was leading, David thought he saw her eavesdropping. He liked to think they'd even made a connection.

He eyed her as he straightened up his desk. "And what are you dressing as?"

Expecting friendship was probably asking too much of her. But maybe he could coax her out from behind the walls she kept up with him. With everyone. Prove to her it was safe.

"Here's a hint." She reached into the bag on her shoulder, pulled out a headband with a snake on it and placed it on her forehead.

David felt one side of his mouth inch up. "Cleo!"

Alli pulled the prop off her head and stuck it in her bag. "Ya know," she said around a smile, "I'm actually really looking forward to tonight. I haven't done something like this since . . . well, ever." She tossed the bag onto her office chair and ran her fingers through her hair. His own fingers itched to know the feeling.

He cleared his throat. "Really? What do you usually do?"

Her smile faltered. "Oh, you know. Hand out candy. Maybe put on a pair of cat ears or something like that."

"Alone?"

She pulled in a breath and tucked her hands into her back pockets. "Yeah. Just me and a stack of horror flicks."

David scratched at his jaw. "What about as a kid? What did you do growing up this time of year?"

A beat passed before she spoke, eyebrows rising. "So. What else do we need to do to get ready?" A ray of light from the early-setting sun cut through the room and illuminated the discomfort on her face.

Mentally kicking himself, David closed his eyes and exhaled before opening them. "I think I'm in charge of the pizza run. The rest of the snacks and drinks should be taken care of. Then we just . . .get dressed and have fun."

Her elbows flapped. "Cool beans."

"Wanna come with me to get the pizzas? I could use another set of hands to help carry them."

Her smile felt like it was just for him, and his neck heated. "Sure."

"Great." He held the door open for her to step through, her soft, clean scent tickling his nose. "So, what do you want on your pizza?"

"Anything but mushrooms. They make me gag." She shuddered.

Half hour later, they returned carrying armloads of pizza. Long tables had been set up along one of the living room walls for bowls of snacks and treats. The whole house radiated festivity.

David slipped into the bathroom to get his costume on. Alli took a while longer to get ready. She emerged looking quite striking in her black eyeliner and gold arm bangles. Slits in the bottom of her dress showed off shapely calves that made his throat go dry.

Get a grip. Now. "Wow, look at you."

Alli arranged her bent arms one up and one down. "Walk like an Egyptian," she sang. She bobbed her head forward and back as she walked down the hall, then laughed. She had a wonderful, sparkling laugh. David hadn't heard it before. Not really. She looked as excited as the kids and her veiled giddiness did something to his insides.

Heart pounding, David bowed at the waist. "My queen, can I fetch you a glass of punch?"

"Hmm." A cute smirk played around her lips. "A scoundrel like you might be more apt to steal from me."

"Alas, my reputation precedes me. But you see," he gestured to the room, "my merry men are nowhere to be found this night. I will attempt no robberies on your royalness, I assure you. It would be against my code of honor."

She raised a brow. "Ah, a man of honor, are you?"

He tipped a nod and offered his arm. "I am, milady." *By God's grace.*

She stroked her chin with slender fingers. "All right, I'll take a chance." She looped her arm through his, and David's bicep tightened in response to her touch. Like an idiot meathead. Worse, the shy grin she lifted to him sucked the air from his lungs before he could calibrate his senses. He set his focus on the snack table on the other side of the family room and led them toward it. She must have sensed his awkward reaction because three feet from the potato chip bowl she dropped his arm like it was made of stinging nettle and sent her gaze wandering everywhere but at him.

"Looks like we did a good job in here." The room had been cleared of the center furniture and kids were mingling, smaller ones darting about, some older ones sitting on the couches that had been pushed along the walls. The bean bag toss was set up in a far corner and Kyle, aka Scarecrow, was awarding candy to the kids as they took their turn while Dorothy, aka Regina, went around snapping photographs.

"Smile, you two!" Regina, dressed in her blue checkered dress, held a camera to her eye and motioned toward David and Alli.

"Oh. Um, okay." Going a bit stiff, Alli blinked and inched closer to David's side. As he leaned in, her hair caught on his quiver of arrows and when he tried to untangle it, he accidentally knocked her serpent headdress askew. They both started snickering, Alli fending off a serious attack of the giggles that made him see her in a whole other light. As they stood there grinning at Regina, the scent of spiced vanilla met his nostrils and his pulse hammered like a middle school boy's during a game of spin the bottle.

The camera click-click-clicked and Alli stepped back, taking the spiced vanilla with her.

"Oh, that's great. Thanks, you guys." Regina moved on to the next photo subject, and David turned toward the punch bowl.

His mouth was dry as dust. He snatched a plastic cup and ladled in some red punch with rainbow sherbet, handing it to Alli. Her fingers brushed his in the pass, tripping his heart. She met his gaze and for a split second something real, genuine, and . . .intimate . . . passed between them.

And then it was gone.

"Thanks." She took a shaky sip of her punch, looking out across the room. David did the same.

Alli set her cup down. "Oh look, Liz and Toby are waving. I'm going to go say 'hi.'"

"Yeah, sure. Of course. Have fun."

"See you later, Mr. Hood."

"Okay, Miss . . . 'Patra." He groaned at his lameness.

Alli spoke through a restrained laugh. "That was bad."

"I know. But you didn't have to point it out."

With a look back over her shoulder, she snickered as she walked away.

David sucked in a deep breath, trying to clear his head of the blood pounding in it. What was happening? He wasn't interested in any relationship, and he especially couldn't be attracted to a woman who rejected the most important thing in his life: The God he'd pledged everything to, owed everything to, loved more than life itself. It could never work. He wanted her to find peace, embrace the gospel, but his feelings had to remain platonic. And they *would* remain platonic.

No matter how much those storming hazel eyes drew him in and made him want to soothe her. Hold her.

Kiss her senseless.

Argh. He scrubbed a hand over his face. Yeah, this wasn't good. He was a man with appetites like any other, and she was . . .an incredibly attractive woman. But that didn't make it okay to imagine what it would be like to . . .

No. He'd point her toward grace. Nothing more. He gulped down the cold punch and refilled the cup.

"Hey, Pastor David," a boy's eager voice came from the middle of the room. "I've been practicing my moves. Come watch!"

David nodded, grateful for the distraction. "Sure."

The boy spun toward the living room where a small cluster of kids demonstrated katas for Liz, Toby . . . and Alli.

It was ten-year-old Daniel's turn for Alli's attention. "Watch me, watch me, watch me."

"Okay, I'm watching." Alli visibly swallowed, then folded her hands in her lap and focused on the stocky redhead.

"This is Short Form One." Daniel bowed then thrust his arms into a series of blocks and stances. He fumbled and a groan burst from his throat. "Wait, I messed up. Hang on."

David came alongside him. "Step into a right neutral bow. And then . . . that's right, you got it." He nodded and backed away as the boy finished the set.

When Daniel finished, Alli surprised him with her mild applause. "Great job. Looks like some intricate choreography."

Daniel grinned. "Thanks." His eyebrows hiked up in question. "You wanna try?"

Her eyes widened. "Oh no, that's okay." She waved her hands in front of her. "You guys are the padawans, not me."

A chuckle tried to push its way up David's throat. *Good luck, kids.*

"Don't be a party pooper." This from Toby, who pushed against her arm to make her go.

"I'm not, I just . . . I don't know the first thing about Ninja Turtling."

David bit the inside of his cheek, enjoying the entertainment as the kids crowded around, putting Alli on the spot. Not so easy to dismiss a child's proud accomplishment is it, Miss Johnson?

Daniel gestured her up off the couch. "Come on, Miss Alli. I'll show you. First, stand like this and bow."

Casting David a pleading yet defeated look, Alli hesitatingly complied. David retreated a few steps to watch the interaction play out. Cleopatra sank into a horse-stance, bangled fists holstered at her hips, dress fabric stretched taut between her knees.

She looked so uncomfortable and awkward. It was the funniest thing he'd seen in a long time. Crossing his arms over his chest, he bit back a laugh as a trio of his students tried to teach her the Star Block. *Tried* being the key word. Between short interjections of "okay, got it" or "like this?" giggles slipped from between Alli's perfect lips.

He couldn't believe his ears. David drew closer and waved his hands. "No, no, no guys. You're messing her up. Look, it's like this."

Alli wore a tremulous smile as he inched forward, entering her space.

"Keep your wrist straight like this." He took her hand, ignoring the feel of her silky skin as he ran two fingers in a line from her knuckles to her wrist.

He walked her through the Star Block Set one move at a time, determined to score a win for Kenpo and nothing else.

"Okay . . ." Her voice came out low, breathy, and instantly fried his nerves. "I think I've got it. Sensei."

His throat was too dry, his tongue too swollen, to verbalize a response. Senses wide awake, David nodded and inched away.

Alli finished with a bow then smiled, gazing up at him through dark lashes and paralyzing him where he stood.

Gonna need a bit of help here, Lord. Could you do me a solid and block these urges when she's around? I'd really appreciate it.

Was Alli actually doing karate? And *not* hating it? This Star Block Set was like a form of dance, one move flowing seamlessly into the next with a certain sense of beauty.

And then there was David.

In his sage-green cloak and leather boots, Robin Hood had never looked so rugged and appealing. How could she make sense of the man standing before her: Tattooed, chiseled, wearing tights and a disarming smile? She couldn't.

But soften her position on martial arts? Maybe she could do that. It *was* kind of fun. Graceful in its own way. And watching a skilled black belt like David was downright thrilling, she couldn't deny it.

For the next few hours Alli laughed and smiled more than she could recall doing in years. Her belly ached from it, and it felt wonderful. She joined in a sack race across the lawn, she walked the 'Costume Runway,' and posed for dozens of group photos.

As Alli took a moment to stare up at the stars, David sidled up to her.

She passed him a smile. "I haven't had this much fun in a long time, Robin Hood. Thank you for inviting me."

"You're welcome. I'm glad you came."

Her smile brightened, then mellowed, because there was just one thing missing. She cast her gaze out over the woods toward horizon.

Silence stretched between them until David finally spoke, softly, as if he were reading her thoughts. "I know. I wish he was here, too."

Their eyes met and held. David always saw through her armor, behind the face she gave to the world. She hated that. How did he know when her smile was less than sincere?

David squeezed her shoulder like he sometimes did with the kids and Alli stiffened at his touch. Not because it was unpleasant, but because it *wasn't*, and she couldn't indulge that. Something must *really* be wrong with her if she was responding this way to the touch of a pastor.

She swallowed and wrapped her arms around herself, managing to nod her head instead of letting it tip to rest on David's solid shoulder.

"Last event of the night! Gather up!" Kyle shouted. Kids and staff moved toward the center of the yard and several individual buckets of water.

Alli hung back as the kids were positioned in front of the buckets, hands tied behind them. Knowing what was coming, she managed to root herself in place as the first person bobbed for an apple, but as a blond head plunged into the water, she felt the panic swirling within her. When everyone was distracted, she slipped inside and poured herself a cup of hot caramel cider, hoping to quell the shaking in her core.

"Tuckered out?"

She turned at the sound of David's voice. "Hey. Yeah, I'm wiped." Blowing across her mug disguised the truth, she hoped. But he didn't look fooled. She scrambled for something to say. "Apple bobbing grosses me out a bit, to be honest." She faked a laugh. "But the kids like it."

"It is a bit nasty if you stop and think about it. At least they aren't sharing the same bucket. We're a little more civilized these days." He picked up some abandoned Styrofoam cups and carried them into the kitchen.

"Let me help." She grabbed a plastic bag and went around gathering trash.

The party wound down, and Kyle and Regina managed to have the kids start getting ready for bed.

Alli vacuumed up crumbs and stored leftovers, then found herself back out in the yard with David, clearing apple remnants and trash. It took a good half hour, but after the last core was bagged, she collapsed onto the bench and sighed.

David lowered himself beside her, close enough for her to smell his cologne. And it spun her head, despite her resistance.

She stretched her neck from side to side. "I'd say the party was a success. Liz was excited to win the costume contest."

"She made a great pirate." David leaned his arms on the backrest. "Oh, man, I'm beat." He laughed. "Those kids, I don't know how they do it. I feel old."

She glanced at him and smiled. "You aren't old. We're just not kids anymore."

"You sure about that?" He shifted and made a face. "My tights are riding."

She laughed and covered her mouth with the back of her hand. "Oh, but they look so fetching on you."

His smiling eyes roamed her face and made her go silent as her insides lit up. She looked away and pointed her face at the sky with a contented exhale.

David leaned forward, resting his elbows on his knees. "Can I ask you a question?"

"Sure."

"What happened to keep you from believing in God?"

She pulled a breath in through her nose. "You're too direct sometimes, you know that? Why do you assume something must have *happened*? People have different opinions on things. We don't all have to drink the Kool Aid."

His eyes rounded, and red crept up his neck. "I'm . . ." He shook his head, his throat bobbed. "I'm sorry I offended you. I *am* too direct sometimes."

Her shoulders drooped as guilt punctured her lungs. "No. I'm the one who should apologize. That was uncalled for. You didn't *offend* me. It's just . . ." She set her gaze out into the thicket of trees bordering the yard. " . . .people like you are able to . . . hold hands and sing Kumbaya and chant Jesus and have that make their lives better. And that's awesome. But for some of us, that just doesn't work. And for the record, I tried. I really did. For years. It just wasn't for me."

Why was she even sharing this? She didn't owe him an explanation for her beliefs. But something made her want him to understand.

David nodded slowly. Alli felt his gaze but didn't turn to face him. A long moment passed and Alli regretted making him feel uncomfortable, lost for a response. But his voice interrupted that thought, low and deep. "God still loves you. He still wants you. And He'll never stop chasing you."

Her chest tightened and she finally dragged her gaze back to his. The depth of certainty, passion, in his eyes choked her breath.

Good. She didn't say it out loud.

Her phone rang, shattering the moment.

Alli took one look at the screen and pushed herself to her feet. "It's the Haskells. Excuse me." She took a few steps away as she answered. "Hello?"

"Alli, I'm so sorry." Mrs. Haskell spoke through broken sobs, sending every hair on Alli's arms standing.

"What's wrong?"

"The boys. They got into a fight. I don't know what happened. Tyler's always been such a good boy. He'd never hurt . . ." She started sobbing again.

Alli's heart hammered her ribs. "Mrs. Haskell, please. Calm down. I need to know what happened."

David appeared beside her, eyes wide with concern. She shook her head to say she didn't know anything yet.

"We're at the ER, we came right away. Please, Mrs. Johnson, you have to believe that we are good people."

"The ER?" She glanced at David, his mouth hanging open. "I'm on my way." She waited for Mrs. Haskell to provide details, then ended the call and shoved the phone into her coat pocket.

"I'm coming with you." David was holding the sliding door open for her, a scowl darkening his features.

"David, you're wearing tights."

"And you're dressed as an Egyptian queen." David brushed past her and headed straight toward the front door. She followed him down the porch steps and climbed into her car. Once he slid in, she peeled out onto the road, worry and guilt pressing in around her.

A broken arm, Mrs. Haskell had said. How bad was it?

David glared out the front window, gripping the door handle. His jaw muscle jerked. Alli knew what he was thinking. He'd been right. He'd known the Haskells weren't a good idea.

Alli's stomach twisted as the words eked out. "You don't have to say it."

"Say what?"

"I told you so."

"I wasn't going to."

"But you're thinking it."

His nostrils flared but he didn't deny it.

They arrived at the ER and hurried inside. Alli approached the counter. "Excuse me, I'm looking for Thomas Cooper. My name is Alli Johnson. I'm his social worker and was called about his injury."

In a blur, Alli was shown to his bedside. Though he was awake and alert, the sight of his fat lip and bandaged arm sickened her stomach. "Thomas," she said, gingerly sitting on the edge of his bed.

Thomas looked up and took her in head to toe. "What are you wearing?"

Alli's hand went to the headband on her forehead, tugging it off. She suddenly felt ashamed that while he was suffering abuse, she'd been having fun at a costume party. "It's a . . . costume." She tossed the headband and her earrings onto the nearby table then took his hand in hers. "You okay, kid?"

He blinked and looked away. "Are you here to take me away? They won't keep me anymore, right?"

Alli's stomach roiled, pushed acid to the back of her throat. "Yes, you'll be coming with me."

"I'm here, too." David. She'd almost forgotten he was there.

"Pastor David?" Thomas's tone brightened and his hand moved to the dog tags at his chest. "Am I going back home with you?"

"To Grace House, yeah. As soon as the doctor says you can. How you holding up, buddy?"

Thomas stared at him, eyes welling with tears.

"Hey, hey. It's okay. You're not alone. How about we talk to Jesus about it?"

Thomas wiped his eyes with the back of his hand and nodded.

Alli patted the boy's knee. "I'm going to talk to the doctor now, okay? But I'll be right back." She turned to David. "You'll stay with him?"

"I'm not going anywhere."

At this, Thomas's swollen lip curved upward. But Alli's heart plunged as she read the message between the lines. The thing he hadn't spoken but didn't need to say—he didn't trust her. She shoved the thought aside and went to find the doctor.

"He has a bruised collarbone and a buckle fracture of the forearm. He says the brother punched him before pushing him off the loft bed."

Alli's heart sank further, and she wanted to melt into the floor. But she determined to keep calm and composed. "Thank you, doctor. When can he leave?"

"Won't be too long. But we need to file some paperwork. Then we can release him to your care."

The doctor left and Alli took Mrs. Haskell aside. "Mrs. Haskell, looks like Thomas will be leaving with me."

Mrs. Haskell wiped her reddened nose and nodded. "I'm so sorry. I feel like my family has been torn apart. Tyler always was such a good kid. Look at me, I'm shaking." She held out a jittery hand.

"You're in shock. It's not your fault." It was Alli's.

"He's a good boy."

Alli had no reason to doubt that. "It isn't always easy on biological children when foster siblings come into the picture." She struggled to maintain her professionalism. "We try to evaluate them ahead of time, but we can't always predict what kids will act out. I'm not in any way excusing his actions, but . . .don't paint Tyler as a monster in your minds. He's your son and he needs your support to get through this as well."

Mrs. Haskell nodded and blew her nose.

"I'll need Thomas's things. Can you have them packed for me?"

"Yes. I'll call my husband to do it."

"Thank you."

As she stepped away, Alli's phone vibrated in her back pocket. She glanced at the screen. Garrett. She exhaled and pressed the phone to her ear. "Hey, Garrett."

"Hey, you still at your work gig? I thought maybe once it wrapped up you might be up for some late-night fun."

"I can't. I'm at the hospital with an injured kid. It's shaping up to be a long night."

"I don't mind waiting up."

"Garrett . . ."

"I understand, Alli. You have an important job and I'm okay with that. I respect you for it. Can't blame me for missing you, though."

Her mouth curved up. "You miss me?"

"Oh yeah. Big time. And next time we see each other, I plan to show you just how much."

She quirked a brow. "Is that right?"

"Yes, ma'am, it sure is. See . . ." his voice fell to a husky whisper, "I can't stop thinking about you. And me. The feel of your lips on mine. I still taste that kiss. I'm hooked on you, Miss Alli Johnson. And I need to see you again. *Soon*."

A heady, nervous smile tipped her mouth. "You will. I promise. I just . . . can't right now. I'm sorry."

"I know. But call me when you can. I'll be here."

"Thank you, Garret. I will."

She ended the call and returned to the hospital room where David sat at Thomas's bedside. "Hey, kid. Doc says it won't be too much longer and we can hit the road. Can you tell me what started the argument?"

"Tyler was in my room looking at Herman. He took him out of his cage and wouldn't give him back to me when I asked. He said he would smash him. Crush his shell. He laughed and called me a cry baby and ran to his room and up to his loft bed. So, I tried to get up there. To save Herman. But Tyler was hitting my arms and said *get off my ladder!* and to *go away*. I didn't belong there."

His mouth twisted as he hesitated.

"What else?"

"He said . . ." His voice was strained and quiet. "I wasn't part of their family, and I should leave and go back where I came from. Then he pushed me, and I fell."

Alli reached out and smoothed his forehead with a brush of her fingers, wishing she could fix *everything*. "What happened to Herman?"

"I don't know. After I fell, Mrs. Haskell ran in and picked me up and everything was kind of crazy. I didn't see what happened to him." His voiced pinched at the end and he sniffled.

"I'll find out, okay?"

He nodded.

Out in the hall, Alli found a chair and collapsed into it. David took the seat beside her. With a shake of her head, she dropped her gaze and took a breath. This was all her fault. She'd chosen the Haskells. She'd interviewed Tyler. She'd pretty much ignored divine warnings from the man beside her.

David covered her hand with his own. "It's not your fault, Alli." But his tone didn't match his words. More like he was obligated to let her off the hook.

She looked at his hand, then at him. "Yeah." He didn't mean that, but she wasn't going to call him on it. "But I've got to do better by him." She puffed out her cheeks and pulled her hand from his. "I need to go by the Haskell's and get his things. Find his crab. Alive, hopefully."

With a grunt, she stood then looked down at him. "Well, the good news is, he's got somewhere familiar to go this time."

"And people who will be happy to see him."

"Yeah." Warm affection softened her mood. "And he'll be around for all the holiday fun."

Chapter Eight

David could still detect the sweet scents of s'mores and candied applies as he crossed the nearly empty living room. He approached Thomas as the boy scanned the printed photos from the Halloween party tacked to a corkboard on the wall. "Hey, champ."

"Hey." His eyes remained glued to the collage. A wall of smiles and budding friendships he hadn't been a part of.

David squeezed his shoulder. "You feeling left out?"

Thomas shrugged. "Not really."

"Good. Cuz, you know they've got a jam-packed calendar of fun events from here on out, now that we're in full blown holiday mode."

"I know."

Roasted marshmallows, movie nights, and hot cider flowed daily now that November had blown in temps in the forties. He followed Thomas's line of sight to the photograph of David and Alli together at the costume party. A ball of barbed wire cinched in his chest. He willed it to release so he could draw a breath. "Guess we look pretty silly, huh? Grownups dressing up like kids."

Thomas' gaze went soft. "I think you look . . . just right."

David's back tensed, his mind resisting the implication. He'd couldn't go there, not with anybody. Not even with Thomas. He had to keep his heart reined in, his emotions in check. But he examined the picture again and had to agree with Thomas's assessment. They both looked happy. Comfortable in each other's presence for once. Like they'd settled into a well-fitted groove. Her laughter came to mind and the ball in his chest tightened further.

He nudged Thomas's shoulder. "Hey. I was thinking about some hot cider before heading into the devotional this morning. Want some?"

"Sure do."

"Come on then." He led him to the kitchen, arriving just as a couple of boys turned off the sink and bustled out.

"Morning, boys."

"Morning, Pastor David," they called as they shuffled off.

Eyes shifting to the countertop, a bemused grin had David shaking his head as he moved Regina's forgotten cup of tea aside—the woman seemed to forget, or abandon, her tea quite often. Using the hot water setting on the coffee machine, he prepared two mugs of cider.

"What are we doing today, Pastor David?" Thomas sat down, propping his casted arm on the table. It was already covered in signatures from the other kids and staff. Didn't slow him down one bit.

David set Thomas's drink in front of him. "After morning devotional, I thought we'd kick around a football out back for a bit, then I think you all have some school lessons to work on."

Thomas made a face. "We can skip that part."

David laughed. "Yeah, right."

"It was worth a try." Thomas beamed, seemingly buoyed by David's laughter. Then suddenly, smile faltering, his gaze lowered, and he ran his fingernail across the cast. When he spoke, his voice was small as a kitten's mewl. "Can I ask you something?"

Apprehension stole over David, sobering his tone. "Of course, bud. You can talk to me about anything."

"How come God doesn't want me to have a family?"

The barbed wire dug in until his heart bled.

He expelled a slow breath and chose his words carefully. "There are a lot of things we just might never understand. And I'm sorry. I know how hard that is. But God is always with you. Try to remember, you have a family, Thomas. I know it's not what you'd like. But we're your family for right now. And your mother is working to get better so you can go home to her."

Thomas's eyes flitted up then back down again. "Do I *have* to go see her?"

"Yeah, bud. You do. Don't you want to?"

He shrugged and picked at his fingernails. "I guess." Thomas reached for his cider and slurped at it, and David lifted his own mug to his lips, wishing he had the answers to all the kid's problems.

Not to mention questions of his own.

Just give it to God.

A silent moment passed, and he rested his palm on the top of Thomas's head. "Let's head in for the devotion. We can talk more about it later today, all right?"

With a resigned nod, Thomas slipped down from his chair. "Do you think Alli will be there?"

Not likely. "You never know."

Alli had yet to attend one of the morning devotionals. If she was there at the House when they took place, she kept herself tucked away in the office. She sure spent a lot of time in a house of faith for a woman who had none. And she didn't let anyone forget it either, finding little ways to remind them all of her disbelief whenever possible.

"I've been praying for her."

"You have? I bet she'd really like to know that." David knelt in front of him. "And you know what?" He lowered his voice to a near whisper. "I've been praying for her, too."

Thomas grinned, drawing one from David as well. They put their mugs in the sink, then Thomas took David's hand. The gesture was one of trust, vulnerability, need. And it stirred David in a way he wasn't used to.

Alli entered the kitchen just as they moved to leave. "Hey, kid."

Thomas hurried to her side. "Alli! Are you coming to Devotions? Can I sit with you?"

"Oh, well I have to get some work done this morning. Maybe next time." She looked at David. "Can I talk to you real quick before you get started?"

David quirked a brow at her. "Yeah. Let's go over here."

"Hang tight, kid. I'll bring him right back." They found a semi-private spot and Alli produced an awkward smile. "So. What do you have going on today?"

He scratched his jaw as the answer sprang to mind all too quickly. "I'm supposed to start preparing to share my story at church."

"You don't sound excited."

"I've just never much liked talking about my past. But I know people are curious about my military experience. They're fascinated by it, like a Hollywood movie."

"But it isn't fiction."

He nodded and looked her in the eye. "Exactly." Silence hung suspended between them, then he tipped a smile. "At least I have some notice this time. What about you?" Surely, she had a more concrete reason for pulling him aside?

Alli chewed her lip, then took a deep breath. "I just received word that Mrs. Cooper completed her drug program."

"Is that not a good thing?"

"It should be. But honestly, I don't know. Not in this case. I don't have a good feeling about it." The creases in her forehead spoke of her concern. "I foresee a bumpy road ahead, lots of upheaval. This is not her first rodeo. She still has to stay clean on her own for thirty days before she can get Thomas back, but we do have a supervised visit scheduled for next week. At her apartment.

"We were just talking about that. He asked if he had to go."

"He did? Gah, poor kid." She glanced over at Thomas and shook her head. "It's a very confusing time. So, if Thomas seems out of sorts, I wanted you to know why."

"Got it." He puffed out his cheeks. "It's stressful sometimes, isn't it? This job?"

Alli twisted her lips to the side and nodded.

"But God has His hand on the situation. I hold onto that."

"Right. Okay, well, I just want to make sure he has the support he needs in place. I guess you better do your God thing now." She gestured toward the den then headed for the coffee pot.

God thing. She flung the words out and they flitted across the vast gulf between them. And more importantly, between her and the Lord. But on the plus side, it gave David the anchor he needed to keep his head on straight. And his heart safe.

Alli poured a cup of coffee and splashed some hazelnut into her pumpkin creamer. Janelle thought her coffee consumption was reaching intervention levels, but Alli saw it as a comforting friend. She inhaled deeply and brought the ceramic mug to her lips, thoughts hovering around Thomas. He was walking a difficult road, and she hoped she could guide him through it. It helped being able to spend extra time at Grace House. She still ran around town a lot, but all that darn paperwork could now be done here, keeping her close to the reason she got into this line of work: the kids.

She was encouraged at how well Liz and Toby were doing. And Thomas was recovering from his injuries. Nurturing friendships. All of that was the good.

The trade-off was having to hear about faith all the time.

'God has his hand on the situation' was one she heard often. 'With him all things are possible' was another.

The staff here quoted Scripture and prayed together as comfortably as discussing the weather.

Speaking of which—Alli leaned across the kitchen sink to peer out the window—the forecast was clear and bright for the Bonfire later. Despite the abundance of religiosity, she enjoyed the 'family nights.' She didn't want to admit how much. The experience was like… living your whole life on tofu and finally discovering bacon.

"Morning." Regina sidled up to her and took a mug from the tree.

"Good morning." Alli popped off a grin, happy to have these moments with Regina again.

"What's your day look like?"

"I have to take a client to a counseling appointment and try to catch up on paperwork before my boss blows a gasket."

"The files and forms are endless. But you're doing a solid job with these kids."

"I hope you're right. Liz and Toby seem to be mostly happy. I think they knew for a while that this was inevitable, with their mom, and they're realizing that they landed somewhere good. I can tell there's a sense of relief there."

Regina nodded. "Kyle and I are praying for them, and their mother." She'd turned up a few days after the kids were brought in, and she was now set up in a plan to regain custody. She puckered her red lips and blew across her coffee. "I hope you'll be with us this evening."

"Oh, I don't plan on missing out on S'mores."

"Good. I know someone in particular who will be glad to have you there."

Alli smiled. "Yeah, Thomas *is* a very loyal kid."

"Yes, he is." Regina sipped from her cup and started heading out of the kitchen. She paused at the doorway and looked back over her shoulder. "But I didn't mean Thomas."

Alli's brows twitched, and heat flashed to her cheeks as Regina disappeared from view.

Her ears perked to David's voice carrying from the den where he was sharing a "devotion" with a small group of boys.

"…Listen to what Peter says: 'God has given us new birth into a living hope."

There was that word again. *Hope.*

She drank from her mug, savoring the warmth sliding down her throat. It was getting more and more difficult to tune out David's messages. His words snagged her insides somehow. New birth? Living hope? Fresh start? Of *course* that sounded appealing. Who wouldn't think so? But that didn't exist for Alli.

Still, she found herself drifting closer to the den, unable to keep from eavesdropping. David sounded so passionate, so sincere. So fully convincing.

" . . .In this you greatly rejoice, though now for a little while you may have had to suffer grief in all kinds of trials.' You see, even when we go through rotten circumstances, we can choose joy. We can choose hope. How? By holding on to a deeper truth, a truer reality than our present crummy circumstances. And that reality is that we are loved—wildly, passionately, stubbornly loved."

Alli's heart pounded like a tribal drum against her ribs. The air in the room thinned. To be wildly, passionately, stubbornly loved…? Half a second indulging the thought nearly knocked her to her knees.

She shook her head both in disappointment and to wake herself up. *Darn it, Alli. They're getting to you.*

But David's words still clung to her. Did *he* have hope and joy in the midst of grief? It seemed like they all did—Regina, Kyle, David, even some of the kids. Well, Alli tried to "choose joy" every day. She smiled and laughed and had fun when she was supposed to.

So why didn't it work for her?

She hurried back to her office and shut the door, determined to fill her mind with just one thing—work.

She mostly succeeded, sinking into the lives of each of the families in her caseload as she prepared her periodic reports. Later, she brought her laptop with her to the psychologist's office and continued working in the waiting area there. The day wrapped up back at Grace House and by the time the sun dipped below the horizon Alli had accomplished enough to shut down for the night. She crossed her fingers there wouldn't be any emergency calls, then happily joined everyone out in the backyard.

They gathered around a shallow fire pit, roasting marshmallows. Alli wasn't sure she'd ever roasted them outdoors before. It was much better than holding them over a stove on a fork. A bluesy playlist pumped through outdoor speakers. She sat bundled up with a blanket around her shoulders, a thermos of hot chocolate by her feet, and a skewer lanced with three marshmallows in her hands.

Thomas stationed himself close beside her, and on his other side, David. Liz, Tyler, and half a dozen other kids completed the circle. Despite the varying degrees of brokenness they all carried, Alli felt connected. At home. Relaxed.

Especially when she looked at David. Watched him interact with Thomas. He was so patient with the kids—sometimes too much so, perhaps. But watching his face light up as he mentored a young boy, talked to a child about God's love… it awakened a longing she'd tried to keep buried.

With his thumb and forefinger, David tested his marshmallow and hissed. He blew across it then pulled off the gooey blob and stuffed the whole thing into his mouth. Then, with cheeks bulging and white specks stuck to his lips, he winked at her. Alli snorted a laugh and dove into her own.

"Thomas, come chase me!" A young boy called.

Thomas abandoned his sticky skewer and hopped up to join the game of tag, leaving Alli and David alone on their wood bench. Alli watched Thomas running and laughing and her throat ached.

"He's such a great kid," David said.

"He is." Alli turned to him, his face awash in moonlight. "You know, my boss said something crazy awhile back. He said . . ." She stopped and clamped her lips together.

"What? What did he say?"

"He said Thomas and I were two peas in a pod. That he needed someone like me. Sometimes it crosses my mind that . . ."

He inched closer, encouraged her with a nod.

"That maybe I should raise him myself. But of course, that's crazy on so many levels." So, so many levels.

"Not necessarily." David's deep voice reverberated in her bones, hummed through her core.

She pressed her lips together and swallowed the tightness in her throat. "I just want him to be happy. To have a normal life."

"I know what you mean." David stood and held his gloved hand out to her. "Come here."

Her brows pinched. "What?"

"Come on. Let's dance."

Really? She watched him for a moment, a slow smile spreading across her face. "Okay." Unsure why she was doing it, Alli took his hand and let him lead her to an open space not far from the fire. There, he released her hand and started in on a funky dance that made her laugh out loud.

She watched for a moment, snorting laughter, then joined in with haphazard moves of her own. This was about fun, freedom, no pressure. The kind of dancing she'd normally do alone in her living room. And she loved it. No pretense, no worry about image. David twisted his hips and poked out dance fingers, then grabbed her hand and twirled her in a circle. She felt like a little girl.

Alli was breathless by the time the song came to an end and another, slower one, began. She pressed her hand to her chest to catch her breath and expected them to return to their seats. But David surprised her by taking her hand and gently pulling her closer. Her laughter faded as she found herself suddenly in his arms, swaying back and forth, his hand at her waist. She blinked and smiled as she placed her hand on his shoulder.

Silliness gone, David kept a decent pocket of air between their bodies as though they were waltzing. For a moment she became Cinderella dancing at the ball.

But she was no Disney Princess, no matter how much she longed for her own happy ending. Her stomach hollowed. This wasn't her, it wasn't real, she was performing again. And the stifling awareness nearly choked her.

When the song ended, she gave a playful curtsy, then hurried back to the bench.

David followed on her heels. "What's wrong?"

"Nothing at all."

He settled beside her, concern written on his features. "You sure? There was a moment there where you seemed to suddenly shut down. Sort of put yourself on autopilot."

Alli forced a laugh, hating that he read her so easily. "Don't be silly. I'm having fun."

Just then, Thomas hopped onto the bench between them and wiggled in. Alli made room for him, relieved at the distraction. "Hey, kid. You enjoying yourself?"

"Yeah! But Kyle said only ten more minutes, then time to go to bed." He pouted.

David rustled his hair. "We'll do it again, don't worry."

"Kay." Thomas smiled first at David, then at Alli. It wasn't lost on her, the picture the three of them made together.

"Besides," she rubbed her hands together and blew into them, "in ten more minutes I'll be a Popsicle."

"Here. Let me." David removed his gloves and reached across Thomas to take both of Alli's hands. His were warm and strong, completely engulfing hers. Leaning forward, he brought their hands up to his mouth and blew delicious, warm air into them. Her stomach dipped. Her numb fingers tingled as his warmth thawed them, and her heart skipped a beat when he looked up at her, no trace of playfulness in his eyes.

She pulled her trembling hands back into her lap. "Th-thank you."

"Teeth chattering too?"

Eyelids flickering, she produced a closed-lip smile and nodded. "Yeah. *Told* you I was freezing over." But that was a lie. It wasn't the cold making her stammer; it was the heat.

"So let me ask you something." Alli put Janelle on speaker and ran a mascara wand over her lashes.

"Shoot."

"Do you ever feel attracted to someone you would never, ever, *ever* have a relationship with?"

"Yes. Often. Why?"

"No reason." She tossed her mascara into her makeup bag.

"Who are we talking about here?"

"Nobody. No one." Just a hot-flash inducing pastor was all.

"Uh huh."

"Hey Janelle, I gotta go. Talk to you later?"

"Oh, you better."

"I'm hanging up now. Byeeee." Alli looked away from her reflection, turned off her bathroom light and headed to her front door.

When she got to Grace House, she helped herself to a cup of coffee. Extra pumpkin. And whipped cream. She needed it.

"Whipped cream this early? You must be stressed." Regina entered wearing sweats and slippers and popped an English muffin in the toaster.

Alli slurped at her coffee then she lowered herself into a kitchen chair. "I'm taking Thomas to visit his mom today. At her apartment."

"Ah. That explains it." She pulled the muffin out and slathered butter on it. "We'll be praying it goes well."

Alli took another slow drink. "Thanks."

David joined them and poured himself some coffee. "Thomas is just waking up. You have a few minutes yet, don't you?"

Alli nodded. "Yes. I just wanted to give myself plenty of time. Go over my to-do list for the day."

And, if she got up the nerve, maybe sit in on David's morning devotions.

Male voices sounded at the front door, then Kyle appeared in the kitchen entry. "Alli, looks like you have a visitor."

Alli's eyebrows pinched together. "*Me?*"

Garrett stepped into the kitchen and scanned the room, his expression lighting up when he spotted Alli. "Hey there, beautiful." He bent to drop a kiss on her temple.

Blood rushing in her ears, Alli refused to let her gaze cut to David, though she couldn't imagine why. She cleared her throat. "Garrett, hi." She stood on noodle legs. "What are you doing here?"

"I was passing by and thought I'd surprise you. I brought you a treat." He held out a brown paper bag to her.

"Thanks." She reached in and pulled out a blueberry muffin. Her heart sank. In her periphery, Regina, Kyle, and David looked on, making her feel awkward. Disoriented. "This is everybody. Everybody, this is Garrett."

"Hi, Garrett," said Regina with a grin and hooked a thumb to her right. "This is Kyle. And that's David."

David approached and offered his hand, along with a stiff smile, to Garrett. "Nice to meet you, Garrett."

"Nice to meet you too."

"Next time get a maple bar. They're her favorite."

Garrett glanced to the muffin in her hand, a wrinkle forming between his eyebrows. "Really?"

"Yep."

Alli swiveled toward Garrett, muffin held aloft. "These are great, too. Thank you, Garrett. This is sweet of you. Can I call you tonight?"

He was still staring at the muffin but at her question flashed a smile. "Yeah, of course. Just wanted to say hi to my gorgeous girl. I have to meet with a client in an hour anyway." He leaned in for a kiss, but Alli turned to take it on her cheek. He looked at her with questioning eyes, the wrinkle deepening.

She held up her mug. "Coffee breath. Sorry."

A loud scraping noise made her shoulders jump. David pushing his chair in. He nodded toward Alli. "I've got to get ready for devotions. Have a good day, Alli. You too, Garrett."

Alli's throat went gritty as he left the room. Regina's brows rose and she herded Kyle along too.

Garrett jutted his chin at David, then turned a small smile on Alli. "Okay then. I'll talk to you later."

As soon as she heard the front door close, Alli's breath whooshed out of her. She had no reason to feel so off-kilter. But she did. She headed on shaky legs to the den where David was preparing for the devotions, a few kids already settling onto the couches.

David barely glanced up at her. "So. It's Garrett, right? Your boyfriend?" His voice had a hard edge to it.

She leaned a shoulder against the doorway and crossed her arms. "I don't know what he is."

"Typical." He chuckled but she didn't like the way it sounded. David's chest seemed to be rising and falling more rapidly than it should.

"What's wrong, David?"

He shook his head as he looked at her. "Nothing. I just find it odd you've never mentioned him."

Was she supposed to? Her face screwed up, her hackles instantly raised at his accusing energy. "Why? Why is my personal life anybody's concern?"

He scraped his teeth over his bottom lip. "It's not. I just thought . . ." He shook his head and looked down at his Bible. "Forget it."

"You thought what?" She stared at him. Was he jealous? "That you and I . . .?"

"*No.* Of course not. Not that but . . ." He pushed his hand through his hair. "The boundaries feel different between us. I don't know. It just doesn't seem right. You should've told me."

She cocked her head at him. "What it seems like to me, is that you're wound way too tight. You've wired yourself to assign deep meaning to every stinkin' little thing. But not everything has to be precious and deep and meaningful, David. Sheesh, lighten up. Garrett and I have been out a handful of times, that's it."

"So that wasn't meaningful either? Might want to tell him that. I get the feeling *you* mean something to *him.*" David released a long breath, uncaring or oblivious to the attention he was starting to draw. "You think I'm wound too tight, that I make a big deal out of every little thing. But here's what I think. I think *you* like to keep things shallow. Because you're afraid. You won't let anyone really get know you, you put on a show because you don't want to take a deep look at yourself."

Alli faked a laugh. "Okay, whatever. I'm shallow and afraid because I didn't mention to my *coworker* that I date. Newsflash: I have a life." *Oh, what a lie.*

"No, that's not what I meant." He stared hard at her, and the fire in his eyes cooled, the tension in his shoulders bleeding away.

"Look, I have to get ready to take Thomas over to see his mother." Surprisingly, that sounded preferable at the moment. "I hope you have a good day."

"Yeah. You too."

Alli shook her head, fighting the lump in her throat, as she headed out of the room. She certainly *wouldn't* be sitting in for the devotional this morning.

Alli locked her car doors and cast a furtive glance down the street as she led Thomas along the cracked sidewalk. Graffiti covered the boarded-up windows of a building across the street. Flowers and candles created a makeshift memorial at the corner light post.

Thomas held tight to her hand.

"Come on." She found a smile for him as she led the way up his mother's front steps. Which were starting to crumble. The peeling paint of the front door also spoke of its age and lack of upkeep.

The door opened and Mrs. Cooper all but ignored Alli as she pushed open the screen and ushered Thomas inside.

"Welcome home, baby!"

"Hi." He'd brought Herman for an introduction and stood now with both hands wrapped around the habitat, his gaze painting the room.

Patricia shut the door behind Alli and proceeded farther into the interior of the house. She fidgeted about the living room, straightening pillows. "Have a seat. Get comfortable. This is your home, too, ya know."

Thomas set Herman on the coffee table and perched on the edge of the sofa while Alli took a seat in the faded recliner nearby and set her purse by her feet.

Mrs. Cooper's eyes lit. "Oh, and I made your favorite cookies." She scurried into the kitchen, returning with a plate of Oatmeal Scotties.

Alli offered an uncomfortable smile. "Thank you, Mrs. Cooper."

"They're not for you." She glared at Alli. "They're for Thomas." She grinned longingly at her son and nodded to the plate. "Go on, you can take as many as you like."

Thomas cast a questioning glance at Alli then reached for a cookie. "Thank you."

Patricia's brows dipped. "Hey, what happened to your arm?"

Thomas's eyes widened with worry, and he chewed his lip. "I . . . I fell down."

Well, that was true. Alli cleared her throat to break the tension. "How are you doing, Mrs. Cooper?"

Mrs. Cooper shot sarcastic eyes at Alli. "Fine and dandy, Miss Johnson. Haven't you heard? I'm rehabilitated."

She didn't sound fine and dandy. She sounded bitter and angry, as usual. "I'm glad to hear it."

"Now you tell me the truth." She pointed a finger toward Alli's face. "What happened to my boy? Someone knock him around?"

"Not exactly. He did fall, from a bunk bed, during a tussle with another boy."

Her eyes widened. "A tussle? You mean this boy *pushed* my kid off the top of a bunk bed? Was he trying to kill him? He could've broke his neck."

Alli's gut twisted. "Mrs. Cooper, you don't have to worry. Thomas is no longer with that family. He's safe and back at the group home. We're taking excellent care of him."

Eyes narrowed, Mrs. Cooper shook her head at Alli. "That's what you told me last time."

"They really are, Mom."

The woman huffed. "Well, not for long. You'll be home real soon, I promise. No more group homes, no more CPS, no more social workers up in our business all day long."

"But I . . . I like Miss Alli."

"Well, you won't need her."

Alli surreptitiously blew air between pursed lips then touched her fingers to Thomas's shoulder and set a steady gaze on his mother. "It'll be some time yet before he comes home permanently. And we'll provide ongoing support services, for both of you, afterward. We'll still have a presence in your life, Thomas. No need to worry."

"He's got nothing to be worried about. Not anymore. I'm clean and I'm staying that way."

Alli let a beat of silence pass before speaking. "I do hope so."

Dismissing Alli, Patricia plastered on a smile for Thomas and moved to sit beside him. She circled an arm around him and pointed to Herman. "So, tell me about this crab of yours."

Thomas grinned and nodded. "His name is Herman."

"That's a nice name. What does he like to eat?"

Thomas was happy to launch into one of his favorite subjects, telling his mom all about the care and feeding of hermit crabs. He visibly relaxed, and mother and son fell into a comfortable back-and-forth that Alli had never witnessed before.

"Is it okay if I use your restroom?"

"Second door on the left." She spoke without looking at her.

Alli stood and moved toward the hall, taking the opportunity to examine the surroundings. The carpet had some stains but had been recently vacuumed. The walls were clean of smudges. A photo of Patricia holding Thomas the day he was born was in a frame on the small entertainment center.

The hallway displayed a few more photos, and some crayon sketches he'd made for her over the years.

She did love her son, Alli could see that. But whether she loved him more than she loved her own pleasure, her next high, that wasn't as clear. Would she really be able to care for him?

In the bathroom, Alli turned off the tap and dried her hands, then quietly opened the drawer, and scanned the contents. Just brushes, bobby pins, makeup.

Thomas's voice carried from down the hall, talking about soccer, and wanting to show his mom how far he could kick the ball.

Alli opened the medicine cabinet. A toothbrush, toothpaste, moisturizer, a few prescriptions. A half-empty bottle of cough syrup. She checked the date and tried to determine how recently it had been purchased. She hadn't noticed Mrs. Cooper coughing. Effervescent vitamin tablets caught her attention. A common hangover cure, they pinged her radar even further. But Patricia wasn't dumb enough to store anything obvious out in the open.

Turning the tap back on to obscure any noise, Alli gripped the sides of the toilet tank lid and gingerly lifted it. She bit her lip at the slight scraping sound it made, then peered inside. A bottle!

Seriously? Already?

Alli's fingers shook and lost grip of the lid. As it clattered back into place, she winced, then froze. Silence hovered in the air. Heart pounding, she turned off the tap and strained to listen.

A car door slammed. Alli's head whipped toward the window and the sound.

"Herman! I need Herman!"

Her eyes widened as an engine roared to life.

At the sound of tires squealing, Alli's lungs seized. The blood drained from her face. Black spots crowded her vision.

"Thomas!" She burst out of the bathroom and into an empty living room.

No. No, no, no!

She grabbed Herman's habitat and frantically scanned the floor by the reclining chair. Where was her purse? *Her keys?* A sick feeling washed over her in one strong wave and the room tilted.

Patricia and Thomas were gone.

David sat in his office kicking himself for how he reacted to Alli's boyfriend. After she left and he'd cooled down, he realized she'd come into the den that morning for the first time. If he'd behaved better, would she have sat in on the morning's devotional? A sinking feeling told him she would have. But no. She fled to her office. Because of him. And he couldn't blame her.

He kicked his chair away from the desk and stared out the window into the backyard. What was his problem anyway? He couldn't even begin to understand his response to Garrett. Yes, Alli was pretty. But he wasn't interested in her. He couldn't be. He massaged the back of his neck.

Alli was bright, sensitive yet tough, with a huge heart. She was also more attractive than he wanted to think about. And he did feel a tenderness toward her, saw a wounded lamb when he looked at her. But that was his pastor's heart wanting to reach the lost and see them made whole.

Right?

His jaw flexed. Maybe the motives for his attentions *had* been inappropriate. If so, he needed to repent of that. He was in her life to be a friend, a light pointing to God, and to serve the children together as a team. Not to fall in love with her. And he *wasn't* in love with her. Especially when the one thing he knew for sure about the Alli who lived behind the walls she kept up was that she did not believe in God.

It is not the healthy who need a physician.

He pushed himself up from his chair. What he needed was a cup of coffee and some time in the Word.

He opened his office door to the sound of Kyle speaking on the phone. "Have you called the police?"

The tension in his voice triggered an alarm in David. He approached in silence, eyes round in question.

Kyle covered the phone and addressed him. "It's Alli. Patricia Cooper took off with Thomas."

What?

His pulse rocketed as Kyle returned to the call. "Yeah, I'm still here. Okay, keep us posted . . . I know. I know. The police will do their work, try not to panic. Okay." He hung up and looked at David. "Gather the staff."

When every volunteer had assembled, Kyle delivered the news and led the group in prayer. There was nothing else they could do.

Their intercession was interrupted by a cacophony of alarms as the Amber Alert chimed on everyone's cell phones at once. David's gut clenched in response, urging him to act. To do *something!*

Thomas must be so afraid. Just *how* unstable was his mother? And Alli . . . his muscles swelled. Alli was a champion when it came to the kids, but he'd seen the guilt weighing on her at the hospital. She'd blame herself for Thomas's abduction.

"Regina, Kyle, I need Cooper's address." He had to know that she was all right. "Someone should be there with Alli."

Regina nodded and wiped moisture from her eyes.

When he arrived, Alli was standing on the porch speaking with a pair of officers. No tears, no hysteria. But her calm and cool exterior didn't fool him. The woman was a chameleon, trotting out different personalities for every social occasion. Herman's habitat was clutched in her hands, her whitened fingers the only evidence of her fear.

The officers concluded their questioning and David made his way toward her. Their gazes met, terror behind her warrior's eyes, and David wrapped an arm around her shoulders. She did little more than allow it, but he felt the tremble running through her.

He smoothed her hair beneath his chin. "God, we need You. We need Thomas safe. We need strength to get through this." David prayed aloud over Alli, not caring whether she believed it would help or not. He'd have faith for both of them.

Reluctantly, he released her. "What happened?" Kyle had filled him in, but he wanted to hear it from her mouth.

She licked her lips and went into autopilot, relaying facts in detached precision. "We were sitting in the living room. Things were going fine. I asked to use the restroom. I was examining for any evidence she was using when I heard the car-"

"Are *you* okay?"

"What? Yeah. I wasn't in the room when it happened." At those words, she sucked in a breath.

"But are you *okay*?" He framed her face and looked into her eyes until she blinked and nodded.

He shook his head. "No, you're not. Come here." He led her inside to the couch, pried the hermit crab from her grip, then went to get her a glass of water. Kneeling in front of her, he brushed the hair away from her face then pressed the glass into her hands. "Here."

"Thank you." She didn't make eye contact as she brought it to her lips.

He slid into place beside her and wrapped an arm around her shoulders. "It'll be okay, Alli. We have to believe that." The thought of Thomas disappearing into the mist coiled his stomach. His muscles twitched. *Oh, God, help me entrust him to You.*

The sense of helplessness overwhelmed him. He needed answers. "Stay here. I'll be right back."

She nodded, and he left her there to go back outside and find an officer. Ask questions. Do something.

Across the street, a thin man in ragged clothes watched the house, chewing his fingers, looking much too interested. David's brows pinched. A nosy neighbor, or someone who'd seen something? He checked for traffic then headed toward the man, who got jittery the closer David got.

"Hey, man," David called out. "You live around here?"

Sunken cheeks and red facial sores accompanied the man's rotted teeth, raising a host of red flags. "Did Patty make it?"

David tensed, stomach coiled tight. "Excuse me?"

"Did she get her boy?"

"What do you know about it?" The veins of his neck swelled; his shoes scuffed over chipped concrete as he stepped closer.

The man shrugged and fidgeted. "Nothin', man. I don't know nothin'."

"How do you know Patty?"

"Known her for years." Another shrug. "We party sometimes."

David ground his molars, trying to remain calm. "Do you know where she's taking him?"

A creepy smile stretched his scabby lips wide. "I told you. I don't know nothin' about no kid."

"You just asked me if she got her boy." Blood pounded in his temples, anger heating his neck. He was losing grip on his patience. At this point he was flirting with insanity. He straightened to his full height, eyes narrowed at the scrawny mess of a man. A weasel more like. "Tell me what you know. Right now! Where did she go?"

"I don't got to tell you nothin'." The man laughed in David's face, washing putrid breath over him. "She done it. Ha ha!" he cackled. "You ain't gonna ever find em."

He *knew* something. This man *knew*!

His brain snapped, and an inferno ignited within David's body.

The man reacted, eyes going wide as he shuffled backward on frantic feet. "Hey. Don't you touch me, man! Don't you touch me!" He threw a wild punch and instinct took over.

With a quick inward block, David deflected the guy's bony arm, threw a straight punch to the ribs, kneed him in the gut, then grabbed him by the hair and took him to the asphalt, face first. Pulse roaring, David pressed a knee to the man's shoulder blades and pinned his arm behind him. "Where are they!" Was he ready to listen yet?

"Come on. Let me up, man." He sounded like a whimpering child.

David wrenched his arm tighter. "I will when you tell me what you know!"

The man winced and cried out, and David wanted nothing more in that moment than to snap the skinny limb like a toothpick.

The scuffling of shoes on pavement.

"Mr. Porter!" Strong arms grabbed at David from behind and pulled. "That's enough."

His feet skidded beneath him, and David jerked against the grip on his shoulders.

"Settle down," came a deep, stern voice. "We'll take it from here."

Chest heaving, David blinked and took in the faces of the officers surrounding him.

The one holding him from behind spoke in his ear. "Okay man, I'm gonna let you go. You good?"

David turned toward the house and saw Alli staring. Her shocked expression said it all. He'd gone too far. Completely lost control. Regret cooled the anger in his veins. He nodded. "Yeah . . . yeah, I'm okay."

They released their hold and David pointed to the man on the ground. "But this one knows something."

"He's lying! I don't know nothing about Patty. Or her kid. You better let me go or I'm going to use my laser on all of you. I swear, I'll do it!"

"No, you won't, Percy."

David tugged his shirt and rolled his shoulders. "You saw him come after me first, right?"

"Yeah yeah, we saw it. But it's best you go and leave the investigation to us."

He nodded. "Sure." As the cops hauled the man up and put him in a squad car, David jogged back to the Cooper house and hurried inside. "Alli?"

No answer.

He found her in the kitchen, refilling her water. Her back was to him, but he saw the glass shaking as she held it under the tap.

David pointed toward the street. "Alli, that man knows something. Something that could help us find Thomas."

She turned off the water but made no move to turn around. The thick silence was punctuated by the sound of his own breathing, and the pulse beating in his temples.

"Alli, look at me." He softened his voice. "Please."

"I . . . I can't." She drained her glass then leaned her hands on the counter in front of her. Other than dropping her head, she didn't budge.

David took a step closer. "I know I went a little too far. Okay? But I'm worried about Thomas, and that crackhead has the key to getting him back." His heart rate began to climb back up. "And he wouldn't *tell* me anything. Alli, I couldn't get him to tell me anything." He felt so frustrated, so desperate. Couldn't she understand that? "He swung at me, and my training took over. Should I have just *let* him hit me? Should I have given up on Thomas? On getting information to help find him?"

Her shoulders sagged. "No."

Finally, he was getting somewhere.

"I'm scared, David." She turned and pierced him with her fathomless hazel eyes. Eyes that had never reflected more emotion than they did right now. "I'm scared. *I* did this. Don't tell me it's not my fault because that's a lie." Her lower lip trembled, and she jabbed a finger to her chest. "I was his mediator, his defense. I was here to supervise the visit. But I dropped my guard, and now . . ." She shook her golden waves and wrapped her arms around herself.

"Alli . . ." he murmured.

She flung her hand toward him, then the window. "And now you're out there going kung fu on the neighbors, and everything is just

. . . wrong. Because of *me*." She blinked. "David, if they don't find him-"

"They will."

"I have to *fix* this; I have to make it *right*. But I can't. I can't do *anything* but sit here, and replay it all, and wonder, and imagine, and watch pastors beat up junkies and I don't know what I'm supposed to do right now. I just feel out of control and just . . ."

"Powerless?"

She dropped back against the counter and nodded.

"I know. Me too." David moved close and gently took hold of her shoulders. "That's when we have to remember Who has the power." He said it as much to himself as to her, a reassuring calm beginning to emerge beneath the panic, like a steadying anchor.

Alli shook her head and looked away. The gesture fell short of an eye-roll, but David felt it anyway. And grieved for her. He shared her fear, but he couldn't make her share his faith.

The screen door clapped, and an officer's radio crackled. "Repeat. Subjects have been found."

Alli's wide eyes snapped to his, which must certainly have matched hers in size. They collectively held their breath.

"Ma'am?" The voice of the same officer who had pulled David off of Percy called from the living room.

"Yeah." She pushed off from the counter, into his space. "We're right here."

He didn't miss the look of trepidation in her eyes just before she stepped around him. David followed her out to the living room where the officer waited. His heart was beating hard in his chest. "Did I hear that right?"

He gave them both a subdued smile. "Yes, sir, you did. We've got him."

Alli lit her fireplace and settled onto the couch with a blanket. Thor rubbed his head against her arm. She scratched behind his ears as she stared into the flames.

She'd really made a mess of things today. Because of her, David had morphed into a vigilante and Thomas had been traumatized. They'd been lucky to get him back. But what if they hadn't? She couldn't stomach the line of thought.

Once he'd been checked out by a doctor and released safely back to Grace House, Alli had left. She wasn't up for a family meal, for being social. Her head was spinning, and she just needed to be alone to process everything. Let the paperwork wait; she had too much on her mind.

Thomas's abduction. The fight with David. Both had stirred up feelings she needed to examine.

She ran her palm down Thor's silky back, taking comfort in the vibration of his purring. He looked up at her as she rubbed his head.

"The kid deserves better from me." She let the flames mesmerize her again. "Far better."

But what he truly needed was something she couldn't give, even if she wanted to. And she realized now that she *did*.

Her tongue darted across dry lips. A few foster parenting classes wouldn't hurt anybody, right?

She shook her head and pulled in a cleansing breath. No. She should tuck this feeling away and focus on her job, on not failing him again.

And then David . . .

You like to keep things shallow. Because you're afraid.

Her shoulders ached with tension, and she squeezed the back of her neck as David's words replayed in her mind. He was right. She *was* afraid. Afraid of looking too deep and realizing . . .there was nothing there. That Alli Johnson didn't exist. It was all an act. Smoke and mirrors.

The thought terrified her. A voice in her head screamed, "I am here!" But was she? David had said she was shallow and maybe she was. But it was the only way she knew to get along. If she didn't keep relationships surface-level, she wouldn't have any at all. Let someone in and they'd take one look around, realize she had nothing to give, and leave. So yes, she was afraid of letting people in and getting hurt. Losing them. She didn't even know how to be that vulnerable.

A pit formed in her stomach, then twisted, reminding her she hadn't eaten all day. She heaved the cat off her lap and padded to her kitchen for a frozen burrito. The microwave dinged and she pulled out the burrito, covered it with salsa, then poured herself a glass of cola.

Her doorbell rang and her brow furrowed. If Janelle was supposed to come over, Alli had totally blanked on it. And wasn't up for the visit. She went to the door and pulled it open.

Alli blinked at Garrett, standing there on her porch. He wore a half-cocked grin. "Hey there, gorgeous."

"Hi." Her brows pulled together. "I thought you were gonna call." She winced internally at her lack of filter and rushed on, "I mean, not that I'm not glad to see you. I'm just surprised."

"Pleasantly, I hope." He lifted a bouquet of flowers she had somehow missed in the shock of seeing him.

A twinge of guilt ran through her. "Thank you. Um . . ." she glanced back over her shoulder at her living room and opened the door wider. " . . .come in."

When he stepped inside and looked around, Alli pressed her lips together. She hadn't prepared the house for company and felt . . . exposed. He turned back toward her and gazed into her eyes. "I've missed you."

"Yeah, sorry. There's been a lot going on with work. Today was . . ." she took a breath, "rough." She headed for the kitchen, and he trailed behind.

"I get that. Alli, I know. But if we're going to make this work, we have to find a way to figure it out. I mean, how can we be together if we can never be together?"

She reached up to open a cupboard. "I know. You're right." She pulled down a vase and deposited the roses into it, then filled it at the kitchen tap. She set them on the kitchen table and rubbed her hands on her thighs. "These are beautiful."

Garrett came and stood in front of her and placed his hands on her shoulders. "Not as beautiful as you." He brushed the hair from her forehead and gazed into her eyes. "You're important to me, Alli. I hope you see that."

She swallowed. Yes, she was beginning to see that. But the idea caused panic to swirl in her gut. She nodded and gave him a small smile.

Slipping a hand behind her neck, he pulled her mouth to his and claimed her lips without ceremony. He tasted of mint mouthwash as he deepened his kiss. His urgency built, and Alli tried to match his passion, to focus on the moment. It seemed like a significant one. But her eyes opened, and her gaze traveled over his shoulder to the burrito on the counter, and she realized she was more interested in eating it than in kissing Garrett.

The kiss ended and she rested her hand on his chest and smiled, then stepped back toward the kitchen. "I should offer you a snack, or something to drink. Should I make coffee or get you a soda or something? I think I have some cookies in the cupboard."

"Alli." He came up behind her and rested his hands on her hips. Spoke into her ear. "I just want you." Alli stiffened as he nipped at her earlobe and ran his hand across her belly, flattening the curve of her back against his firm chest. "Don't you want me, too?" He brushed her hair over her shoulder exposing her neck and dragged his fingertips along it, sending a shiver through her.

She swallowed but couldn't get an answer to her tongue. So, she tipped her head for him as he trailed kisses up along the column of her neck. Her body was trembling, though she felt disconnected from it. From everything.

Gripping the edge of the counter to try and ground herself to the moment, Alli turned her face toward his. When his mouth took up the invitation, she returned the kiss. The moment called for passion. It could be beautiful if she embraced it.

Garret's arms wrapped around her, rotating her body to face his and pulling her close. She told her arms to wrap around his neck without faltering in her kiss, but found her elbows pulling together like magnets to create a barrier between their bodies. He didn't seem to notice, so she commanded herself to keep going, to relax in his hold. To try.

But when his fingers found the hem of her shirt and grazed the skin of her lower back, she stiffened. Lips stuttered closed against his mouth of their own accord. She lectured them to go soft, reminded her body it was supposed to melt into his, but it refused. Instead, she found herself halting him with a hand to his chest and a leaning away.

Garrett pulled back and looked into her eyes. "What's wrong?"

"I just . . .I think we should slow down."

"Slow down? It's been over a month; I'd say that's pretty slow. Worth it, don't get me wrong, but slow." He pressed his lips to her jaw, coaxing her to continue. "Don't worry Alli, I'm gentle."

No doubt he was, but sadness welled up in Alli's chest. She closed her eyes, took a step to the side, and forced out the words she knew he didn't want to hear. Words she didn't want to say but had to. "I'm not ready."

To his credit, he backed up and pulled in a deep breath. "Okay. It doesn't have to be tonight." He looked into her eyes with a soft smile and stroked her cheek with the pad of his thumb. "I really want to make this work."

Grief and sorrow flooded her. She tilted her head, eyebrows drawn. "I'm sorry, Garrett." A rock formed in her throat. "But I don't think it's going to."

"What do you mean?"

She forced her shoulders back. "Us. I don't think we're going to work out. As a couple."

He rattled his head. "Wait. You're ending it? Now? Just like that?" The hurt in his eyes gutted her.

"I . . . I'm sorry."

His mouth hung open. "Wow." He raked a hand through his hair and pointed his face to the floor. "I totally misread you. I feel like an idiot."

"No, Garrett, don't. You're a *great* guy."

He held up a hand and gave her a wry smile, eyes narrowing with justifiable anger. "It's okay, you don't need to do that." He swept his gaze over her one last time then shook his head and marched out of the room. "Take care of yourself, Alli." The door slammed and reverberated through the room.

Alli hung her head and scraped her teeth along her lip. Why did it always end this way? Pressing a hand to her middle, she looked up at the roses on the table. She'd had a good man right in front of her, offering her love and intimacy, and she pushed him away. She squeezed her eyes shut. But she had to. He wanted too much of her.

Her jaw clenched. Why couldn't she just have given it? *Why?*

Hurt, angry, confused, she stormed to the vase and screamed as she threw it across the room. Glass shattered across the floor. Water dripped from the wall.

Alli dropped into a chair and lowered her head. She didn't want to be this way. She wanted normal. Love, family. A man to hold her in his arms at night and wake up beside in the morning. She wanted to let someone in.

But she simply. Didn't. Know. How.

Chapter Nine

From his vantage point in the courtroom, David watched Alli face the judge. Spine locked, chin up, she wouldn't allow Patricia Cooper to see her tremble, but David noted the slight quivering of her body. In truth, his own muscles twitched with anticipation of the verdict.

Alli's voice was steel as she finished delivering her statement. "Therefore, in light of the full history, culminating in these recent events, my recommendation is that Patricia Cooper's parental rights be severed."

The judge wore a stern, somber expression. "Thank you, Miss Johnson."

Alli dipped her head in acknowledgment then took her seat to await the court's decision, along with David and the rest of the room. He wished he were sitting beside her.

His gaze shifted, jaw clenching tight. Not ten feet away, Mrs. Cooper sat in handcuffs beside her court-appointed counsel, glaring at Alli. Patricia had leveled accusations of impropriety and conflict of interest against her, claiming interference and charging her with influencing her child against her. But in addition to the abduction, she'd also been found with drug paraphernalia in her car, and blood tests indicated she'd used within twenty-four hours of the visit.

David wasn't a lawyer but surely, no judge in the world would send Thomas back to that situation. Even so, David's stomach would remain unsettled until he heard it from the bench.

The judge cleared his throat, and the room held its breath. "Mrs. Cooper. I abhor tearing families apart. It nauseates me when I have to sever parental rights, and I will take every recourse available to the court before making such a determination."

David noted the firm set of Alli's jaw. Watched her clench shaking hands in her lap. David's had formed fists as he sat in a similar pose.

"However, you have spit in the face of every chance you've been given. You have resisted change and put your son in harm's way too many times for this court to allow. It is therefore my decision that your parental rights be permanently and irrevocably severed, and a restraining order be issued against you immediately. You are to have no further contact with Thomas Cooper. As for the charges of kidnapping and child endangerment, you will be remanded to the State's custody to await trial in criminal court."

The air dumped from David's lungs in a whoosh. But as the gavel came down, Patricia Cooper leapt to her feet, hurling obscenities at the judge and her lawyer. When she shifted to Alli, his muscles swelled with protective fury. Alli's rounded eyes stared back, unblinking, as the vulgarities flew. Fire licked at his veins and David's heart thumped against his ribs, urging him to let his tongue fly on its own and tell the woman off. Or leap over the table and throw himself between them as a shield.

His mouth dried as the bailiff escorted the woman out of the courtroom, heaping abuse and attempting to spit on Alli as she passed by. David's eyes flung wide, molars gnashing, and he was grateful Thomas wasn't there to witness the entire display. And even more, that this woman wouldn't have the chance to hurt him again.

Step one complete. What would come next for the boy?

David thumbed in a text to Pastor Ron about the outcome. The elder board, all the New Life staff really, would be anxiously awaiting the update.

He watched Alli leave the courtroom next, noting the striking contrast between her and Patricia. One of them wore a mother's heart on her sleeve, and it wasn't the one that came to it by way of DNA.

Family was a choice. David knew that firsthand. In the army, the men in his squad were his brothers. Always would be. In civilian life, his church had become his family. The *only* family he had on Earth. His chest burned at that thought, that *truth*. But God had made Himself a father. Adopted, rescued, and healed him of so many deep, psychological wounds. Traumatic military experiences. And more.

Jumbled thoughts and feelings bounced around inside him all the way back to Grace House. So, once he got there he shrugged out of his coat and closed himself in the office for the next hour, just sitting with God in prayer. Specifically lifting up Kyle, who was tasked with letting Thomas know what had happened in court. When he spotted Thomas in through the window in the backyard, alone, staring at nothing, David realized the news must've been delivered.

David rose to his feet with a shake of his head and left the office. As he passed the kitchen, he noticed Alli at the table. She stared into space, a bowl of soup in front of her, a dull, blank look on her face. Much like Thomas's expression.

His chest ached for her. "Hi, Alli."

She jerked and looked up. "David. I didn't see you there."

He pointed a thumb over his shoulder. "I'm on my way out to see Thomas."

"Ah." Her lips pressed together, and she stirred her minestrone.

"Kyle gave him the news about his mother. He's taking it pretty hard."

Of course, he was.

Alli just bit her lower lip, scraped her spoon along the bottom of the bowl.

He canted his head in concern. "Hey. You okay?"

She cast him a sidelong glance then stared into her soup, throat bobbing. "I wish I could fix it for him. I know where the road leads. His future is disintegrating in front of me. He has so much potential, but if he doesn't find somewhere soft to land, put down roots soon, it will be too late. And that kills me."

David pulled a chair out for himself. "It's never too late, Alli. For any of us. There is always hope, and a future. God came to give us abundant life."

She groaned, eyelids fluttering closed. "Please don't. Not right now. God isn't going to walk through that door and present a set of parents for Thomas. That kid's been let down so much already and if it were up to me . . ." Her breath hitched.

He already knew what she wasn't yet ready to say. "If it were up to you," he murmured, "you'd take him home and never let him go."

She met his gaze, hers swirling with surprise. "Maybe," she admitted. "But that's not how this works."

He let silence have its say, then shook his head. "I'm sorry, Alli."

"For what?"

"All of it. Attacking you the other day. Tossing platitudes at you just now. I'm sorry for the pain you're in."

The bands of her neck tensed. "This isn't about me. But . . . thank you." She took a sip from her spoon, but made a face, then stood and went to the sink. After dumping the rest of the bowl, she planted her hands on the counter and hung her head.

Kyle poked his head in. "David, Thomas is out back. I told him you were on your way."

David cleared his throat. "Okay. Thanks."

Kyle left, but David didn't make a move. "Trying to spend some one-on-one mentoring time with Thomas."

Back turned to him, her answer was muted. "That's good. He needs lots of support right now." Alli turned and gestured toward the back door. "You shouldn't keep him waiting."

He recognized the strained emotion in her voice, her desire to be alone. So, he nodded and licked his lips. "Yeah. But one more thing. I *am* sorry about the platitudes; I know how they can sound sometimes. But the thing about it is, they're also true. Maybe I don't have the right words, maybe it comes across flippant, but I believe with every ounce of my soul that it's never too late for anyone to find hope. And for what it's worth, I think you'd make a great mother." He tapped the door frame. "I'll see you later."

Her voice was hushed, tight. "See ya."

David's spirit churned. It was clear how deeply Thomas's case affected Alli, *and* how powerless she felt to change his situation. He got it. Thomas was special to him, too. And right now, the child was hurting.

He crossed the yard to where Thomas stood under a tree, stomping at the ground, a scowl marring his young face. Drawing closer, David saw that it was ants he was stomping on. With ferocity. And a whole lot of anger. David recognized that inner rage, and concern lowered his brows. He squeezed Thomas's shoulder and the boy stiffened.

"Hey, Thomas." David knelt beside him. "I thought we'd have some special time together today. What do you say? You wanna toss a ball around?"

Mouth a straight line, he shrugged. "I guess."

"Great." He stood and directed Thomas to the expanse of dormant lawn. *God, show me how to help him.*

As the baseball passed back and forth between them, David tried to get Thomas to crack a smile. To laugh. He tried to find that exuberant boy whose face lit up when he talked. But that boy had retreated, like that first day they'd met.

On his next throw, Thomas chucked the ball hard, sending it into the shrubbery separating the yard from the woods beyond.

"I'll get it, buddy." David shook his head as he walked over to recover it. After fishing the ball from the bushes, he looked out at the light patches of snow stretching into the distance. And he prayed. For wisdom. For insight. *Answers.*

He turned to jog back to the center of the yard. "You've got a strong arm there, bud!" David grinned but Thomas just kicked at the ground. Nothing was working.

With a lung depleting exhale, David lifted his arm. "Come here."

Thomas dragged his feet as he approached, his face tight.

David lowered to a knee before him. "Hey, what's going on? You okay? Wanna talk?" Silence passed between them, and David looked into his guarded eyes. "You know, you can tell me anything and I will still be right here."

Thomas's narrowed gaze flicked to his and then away again. His cheeks flushed red.

"I mean it. Even if you think I won't like what you have to say, you can still say it. I will still care about you. No matter what. Is there anything you want to say?"

Thomas stared at him, eyes glowing with raw, irrational emotion. His breaths came faster, and David braced for the explosion. "I hate you!"

There it was. The irrational offense. David nodded, waiting.

"I hate everyone! Even God!" he spat.

Ribs aching, David rested his hand on Thomas's shoulder, but he shrugged it off.

"Don't touch me! I said I hate you! I hate everyone and everyone hates me. You're all stupid and I hate you all so much." Thomas swung a hard fist toward David's chest.

David didn't flinch. Didn't move. He absorbed the blow and waited for the next.

Thomas looked up at him, his eyes full of hurt and anger and confusion, no doubt wondering why David did nothing. He hit him again, hard. And again. "I hate you! I hate you!"

David refused to budge.

Over and over, Thomas struck until gradually, the blows lost their power. Finally, his bottom lip jutted out, his face crumpled, and David reached out to him again and squeezed his shoulders.

"It's okay," he whispered. "I'm not going anywhere."

Thomas threw himself against David's chest and sobbed. Deep, body-wracking, little boy sobs. He wrapped his arms around David's neck and held on as if for dear life.

Eyes stinging, David patted his back, stroked his hair, and let him cry. "I've got you, buddy. I've got you." In that moment, the words felt like a forever promise.

Alli couldn't breathe around her shattering heart.

She gripped the back of a kitchen chair as she watched them through the window. The way David held Thomas in his arms, a steady rock.

Deep longing rose within her. A multi-layered yearning she fought to keep buried. She'd needed that as a child. Desperately. Someone who wouldn't be pushed away. And Thomas was pushing *so* hard. She'd never seen him this way, so full of fire and pain. She wanted to run out there, scoop him up and promise him the world.

She clutched her stomach and turned away, unable to take any more. His pain was too familiar. Raw. And watching David comfort Thomas made her ache for things she shouldn't. Like a real, complete family.

That picture stayed with her, wouldn't budge. The best she could do was try and rearrange it, sans David. She spent the rest of the day in her office, thinking. At home that evening, she found herself clicking the link to the upcoming Foster Parent Information Meetings. Checking the Partners In Parenting class schedule. Reviewing the required steps.

Was she really reading up on this? Her pulse tapped in her throat. She'd never believed she could be a mother.

But David *did*.

David… believed in her.

Her mouth tipped. That had to be worth something, right? Maybe she wouldn't be the 'great' mother he thought she'd be, but she'd certainly be a better one than Mrs. Cooper. Or the Jacobs, the Pennells, the Schneiders . . .

She closed the laptop and chewed her thumbnail, stomach dipping. Her hands twitched for something to do just in time for her latest furniture project to beg for attention.

After donning her rubber gloves, Alli opened the mineral spirits, picked up a rag, and got to work scrubbing. Miraculous the way it cleaned years' worth of buildup.

If only there was a way to simply strip off the gunk that clung to her life. But if not her own life, what about someone else's?

She poured more liquid onto her rag and pressed it into the grooves of the woodwork, using her nail to dig in. Layers of old lacquer gave way until the grooves became intricate garden vines. She leaned back and smiled at the beauty she'd uncovered. How many others had overlooked this piece? How many owners had it in their possession and never knew what was in front of them?

Just like the kids she worked with. Like Thomas. He was slipping away, buried under layers of hurt and anger. Thomas needed someone to dissolve the painful crud that was distorting who he really was. He needed *her*. Regina, Kyle, David, they were good to him, they cared. But nobody loved that kid as much as Alli did, and she never thought she'd be able to love like that. She sat back on her heels and chewed her lip at the direction her thoughts beckoned.

Then she followed them.

It might take months, and in the end, she might be denied. After all, she was single, she worked unpredictable hours, and she was his social worker. But if she somehow hurdled all the roadblocks and got the green light . . ., would she really do it? Would she actually become Thomas's foster mother?

Hope budded in her heart and made her blink.

Because, yes. She really would.

In a nanosecond.

Chapter Ten

David's apartment was packed with teenage boys. Loud, messy, fun-loving teenage boys. They filled the living room with the scent of popcorn and body odor.

"If no one's going to claim this last piece of pizza, I'm taking it." Liam swooped toward the box and grabbed the hours-old slice, then proceeded to fling off the olives into the box with a flick of is finger. "Oops!" He smothered a laugh as one of them sailed off course and landed on the bill of Declan's hat, who remained oblivious as he thumped a fist to his chest and burped.

Those who saw it began barking with laughter, while Declan looked at them with narrowed eyes like they were crazy. "That one wasn't even that loud."

David had planned this as a sort of "Friends-giving" for the Heir-Born Youth Group guys, with beef jerky instead of turkey, pizza pie instead of pumpkin pie, and hours of ridiculous jokes, games, and bodily noises.

Right now, they were vying for the loudest, longest belch—much preferred to the contest they'd been having earlier, with sounds emanating from another source. At that point he'd decided the windows would remain *open* the rest of the evening. He'd had to stop one kid from adding a lighter to the competition and setting his apartment on fire.

Nothing like some good, clean fun among upstanding youths, right?

But David loved that they were having a good time. That they were so comfortable with him. That he'd had a distraction, something uplifting to occupy his focus for a few hours.

As the party wound down and kids began to file out, images of Thomas's reddened face pried into his thoughts.

If family was a choice, why did it have to be so hard? So painful to let go and leave behind the family you never should've had? How long would it take Thomas to heal?

He rubbed his chest, where bruises were sure to form—he'd never again underestimate the force and intensity of a hurting child's flailing fists. Those little knuckles could cause some real damage.

Gut twisting at the memory, the urge to help, to intervene, overwhelmed him.

"Pastor Sensei, I stacked up the board games on the coffee table. Not sure where they go." Liam's voice cut through his thoughts and pulled him back to the present.

"Perfect, thanks for doing that." He socked him lightly on the shoulder. "Pastor Sensei, huh? That's new."

He shrugged. "Seems fitting."

Amusement jetted through David's nostrils. "Glad you could make it tonight, bud. Things must be going pretty well at home?"

"Yeah, not too shabby. I get my car keys back next week. Finally." His eyes lit up with anticipation of that freedom.

"Just in time to take yourself shopping and get your folks a nice Christmas gift, huh?" He grinned and slapped Liam's chest with the back of his hand.

"Pfft. Who goes *out* to shop anymore? I do it all online."

"All of it? Where's the fun in that?" David enjoyed Christmas shopping. He loved the atmosphere, the greetings. Scoring a door-buster deal or two.

Liam shrugged then looked at his buzzing phone. "My mom's outside. I gotta go."

David said goodbye then turned to assess the state of his living room. Declan, the last man standing, carried a black trash bag around tossing in empty soda cans, paper plates, and pizza crusts.

For a second, all David could do was stand there, stunned. Then he grabbed another trash bag and joined him. "Thanks for helping, Declan. I wasn't looking forward to tackling this sty on my own."

He chuckled. "No prob, man."

Turned out he could be quite thoughtful that way. Declan was a pretty good kid. David had witnessed some real changes in him in the last few weeks. And knew *he* couldn't take any of the credit. The reminder whispered across his spirit.

I am in control. And I make all things work together for good.

Yeah. And David just needed to allow God to use him however *He* wanted. Without wrestling for control.

He needed it embroidered on a pillow or something. Maybe another tattoo. Across his forehead. He'd struggled for years with this need to control. Or more precisely, he struggled to willingly *give it up*. He knew God wanted him to, the prodding growing stronger and stronger. In the privacy of his own heart, he could even admit to knowing God wanted him to be more open about it with others. To let people into that part of his life. That it was time.

He just didn't want to.

You are not your own. You have been bought with a price.

A steep price, too. The life of Jesus. But it was hard. Really hard. He would ask himself why if he didn't already know the answer.

A cold gust blew through the window, and he shivered. "Don't need this open anymore." He walked over and pulled it closed, then looked over his shoulder at Declan. "Or do I?" He raised a questioning eyebrow.

Declan snorted and shook his head. "I did have a lot of sausage but nah man, I think you're safe."

He grinned back at him. "Phew. Glad I made it out alive." He closed the remaining windows, then wiped down the kitchen counters.

While Declan pushed the couch back in place in the living room, David carried the trash downstairs to the dumpster. He grabbed the mail on his way back and stopped at the entryway table to sort it.

Bills, coupons, junk mail, personal correspondence, everything had a stack. The quantity of junk mail had been on the rise with all the holiday sales ads. Felt like a greeting card was in there too.

David pulled the red envelope from the midst of the stack and froze. The sharp, jagged handwriting scrawled across the front turned his stomach. Shot acid up his throat. Weakened his knees. His jaw clenched so hard he thought his teeth might crack. He didn't need this right now. Why? What point was there?

As he stood there like a paralyzed possum, Declan appeared at his shoulder, and he startled. Declan pointed at the return address. "Porter? I thought you didn't have any family left. Is that a cousin, an uncle…?"

"Something like that." Hands shaking, David stuffed the card in a drawer and clapped it shut. Mentally padlocking it and wondering if there was anything he really needed in that drawer. Maybe he could avoid opening it ever again.

Behold, I stand at the door and knock.

"Canned goods over on that table; Pumpkin cheesecake right here." Alli directed traffic at the downtown office staff party. They called it a party, but really all it was was a fifteen-minute dessert-grab injected into the day. And someone was always missing— out on a visit or service appointment.

Cardboard boxes full of canned cranberries, green beans, corn, and stuffing mix mounted up on a table against the wall. A little help for some of the families in crisis that they worked with. Alli grabbed a Styrofoam plate, supporting a lovely piece of pumpkin cheesecake, and chunked off a forkful.

"There's a rumor going around about you." Tim reached for a plate beside her.

"Oh?" The silky-sweet pumpkin perfection danced on her tongue.

"Someone mentioned you attended the Orientation meeting last week."

Oh. Filling her lungs, she looked him in the eye and responded with a single nod. She'd known it wouldn't take long for this to get back to her boss.

"It doesn't take a rocket scientist to figure out what you're trying to do." Tim looked at her from under raised brows. "Alli, are you sure you know what you're up against?"

She bit the inside of her cheek and nodded again. "Yeah. But you said yourself, we're like peas in a pod. We belong together."

"I'm all for you taking the classes." Tim had polished off his whipped dessert in two bites and now tossed the plate into a bin. "But, what you want, it's highly . . . unorthodox." Had he wanted to say *improbable?*

"I know. I realize that." Alli popped another bite of heaven into her mouth. Small comfort from the odds he was mentioning.

Tim slid his hands into his pockets, his eyes fixed on some distant point behind her. Brows drawn, he returned his gaze to hers. "I've got to be blunt here, Alli. It's a long shot."

"But it's a shot I've got to take." She blinked rapidly as her insecurities mounted. "Just . . .I don't want anyone else knowing yet. Please keep it on the down low." If she crashed and burned, she didn't want any attention drawn to it, and she certainly didn't want Thomas to find out and get his hopes up.

Tim's eyes crinkled around the edges as he gave her arm a squeeze. "Okay then. Good luck. And mum's the word."

"Thank you." The pressure in her chest released and she scooped up another bite.

"If you don't want to be alone on Thanksgiving, you're always welcome to join us. Marie would love to have you."

She lifted her chin. "Actually, I have plans this year." And that thought alone gave her spirit a boost.

Alli came early to Grace House on Thanksgiving Day. When she pulled up, David's car was already parked. A soft white blanket of snow lay over the trees, the roof, the grounds. Like something out of a movie.

She smiled as she tugged her coat belt tight and walked up the footpath to the front door. David had mentioned that his church was closed, and he didn't have any sermons to give that week, or classes to teach at the Y. So, he was here all day.

There was nowhere else Alli'd rather be either.

Fresh coffee greeted her with its scent as she walked in the door. The turkey would likely fill the house with its aroma within an hour. Alli couldn't wait. She hadn't had a real, home-cooked Thanksgiving dinner since she was nine years old. And no precooked turkey meal deal could replace the drool-worthy scents coming from a family kitchen on Turkey Day.

Getting cozy on the family room sofa, she held a steaming mug of coffee in her cold hands and watched through the window at the scene playing out. Free of his cast, Thomas made full use of both his arms as he played. David and half a dozen boys and girls worked on making snowmen out back.

She smiled at the sight of Thomas's pink cheeks and David's red nose. All the kids had been given snow gloves and scarves, donated by David's church. She also noted new boots and a coat on Thomas that she knew he didn't have when he arrived. The generosity warmed her insides more than the hot coffee ever could.

David straightened to stretch out his back and caught her watching from the window. He grinned that boyish grin and waved to her to come out and join them.

Play in the snow? A smile crept up her face. Sure, why not? Leaving her mug on the table, Alli pulled her hat over her head and gloves over her hands and hurried outside, wrapping a scarf around her neck as she nearly skipped out to join them.

"Alli!" Thomas ran and squeezed her around the waist. "Look at my snowman I'm making." He pointed to two blobs of snow stacked together, a third ball nearby waiting to be added.

"It's coming along great, kid." She rustled his hair and he hurried off to finish it.

Her inner child begged to play and Alli bent to scrape together a ball of snow, then started rolling it larger and larger. And larger. "Give me a hand," she called to David, who was pushing a stick arm into his snowman.

Eyes bright, he jogged over and helped her push the ever-growing snowball in a wide arc through the yard. They laughed puffs of steam as they passed by several snow-people in various states of creation, receiving oohs and ahhs from the kids. By the time they returned to her original point of origin, her snowman body was in need of some serious diet and exercise—and her throat ached from sucking cold air.

David chuckled. "Need me for round two?"

"Let's do it." They made shorter work of the second and third snowballs, then took a moment panting before she waved him off. "I can take it from here." She shot him a grin then glanced around for props. She dug her gloved fingers into the snow for some rocks and used them to create a face and buttons down the chest.

"Hey, not bad." David's voice called from behind her.

"Thanks." She cocked her head at the snowman, then removed her scarf and wrapped it around its neck. "How's that?" She turned to look at David and a snowball smacked her in the shoulder. She gasped and flashed him wide eyes. "No, you did not!"

Scooping up a handful of her own, Alli dashed toward David before he could duck behind the storage shed. She lobbed the snowball in a straight shot, splattering his chest with ice.

"Go, Alli!" Liz squealed.

Thomas chased David behind the shed with his arm cocked. "I'll get him!"

"Come on, we have to move fast." She and Liz got a team together and began stockpiling snowballs.

"They're coming!" Toby yelled.

David and Thomas ran out from their shelter, arms loaded up with half a dozen snowballs each.

"Thomas! You little traitor!" Alli laughed, as she got whacked on the behind by the first missile. Her sides ached as she rounded a tree and returned fire, pelting Thomas in the leg before taking aim at David. Her shot whizzed through the air in perfect trajectory, hitting him square in the face.

A collective gasp sounded from the kids.

Alli froze, mouth and eyes wide open. Uh oh.

David cocked his head and sent her a fierce look that said *I'm coming for you.* Eyes rounded, Alli did what she always did in the face of danger. She ran.

Alli screamed as David lunged toward her. He emptied his arms of his remaining snowballs in rapid fire. Her eyes watered as she ran— a combination of cold air and laughter. She desperately tried to scoop up more ammo while on the run.

"Oh, no you don't!" He was right there, smacking the unformed snow out of her hand, then grabbing her from behind before she could bend down for more.

The kids were all exchanging snow-fire now, and there were casualties among the snow-people.

Alli wasn't going to be one of them. "Let me go!"

"Are you gonna behave?"

"Release me and you'll find out." She chuckled and panted, cheeks burning with cold.

"I want an answer and that isn't one."

"You can't always get your way, David." She wriggled as he pinned her arms to her sides, his hands clasped like a lock around her.

"And you can't always run."

"We'll see about that." Remembering one of the Kenpo moves the kids showed her on Halloween, Alli stepped backward, throwing David off balance. But he was a master. Rather than resist, he propelled himself into the fall and took her down with him. She landed on her back on top of him, blue sky smiling down at her. Kids clapped, pointed, and howled in laughter.

David's breath warmed her cheek and earlobe as he panted beneath her. His scruff pressed up against the back of her neck. Her belly dipped and Alli cleared her throat. "Well, this got awkward."

David relinquished control and scrambled up, dusting snow off his very well-fitting jeans. "Sorry. Didn't think that move through."

So now she knew his weakness: Fear of impropriety. "That's okay. One thing, though." She pressed her lips together to hide the smirk trying to form.

"What's that?"

"I win!" She vaulted the snowball she'd managed to sneak together as she was standing up. It hit him square in the chest and she raised her arms in victory. Behind her, the audience of kids cheered.

"Ach!" David laughed and held his hands up in surrender. "Okay, okay." Crinkles formed around his eyes and Alli's stomach dipped a second time.

This moment, right here, came the closest to perfection she'd ever been.

Dropping her gaze, she sucked in lungfuls of crisp air and pressed a hand to her side as she lolled over to the bench and plopped down into it. Her belly still felt the tingle of laughter. And it felt sublime. Had she ever belly-laughed like this in her life?

Her nose burned with cold, and she could no longer feel her fingers even in her gloves. David joined her, his face split with a smile of his own.

"This is fun, David." *Fun* didn't begin to cover it. This was . . .living. Her throat suddenly constricted. "Thank you." She flashed him a grin to hide the depth of her emotions. Snowball fights weren't supposed to be deep.

He looked at her, eyes twinkling, and nodded. "I love this time of year, don't you?"

She shrugged. "Not usually, no. I love the idea of this time of year, but the reality has never lived up to its potential. Until today." She hadn't meant to share that tidbit. She pushed herself up and rubbed her arms. "I'm freezing my fanny off. Can't feel my toes at all anymore, they're probably going to be frostbit when I peel off my socks." She lifted one side of her mouth then inclined her head toward the house. "I think I'll go warm up. See if Regina needs any help in the kitchen."

"Yeah. Me, too."

They walked together to the sliding door and Alli cast a look over her shoulder at the kids. At Thomas. She smiled. Being here, in this place, she almost believed she *could* have a different life. That maybe she wasn't as broken as she felt.

A Scripture-engraved garden stone poked up through the snow and she paused. Surrounded by these people who placed their faith so squarely in God, Alli almost found herself longing to believe, too.

David opened the door and held it for her. "Hey, uh, Alli?" He cleared his throat. "I don't suppose you'd be interested in a pre-dawn Black Friday shopping venture, would you?"

Alli blinked in surprise. "Uh . . ." A smile softened her face and she nodded. "Sure. Might be fun."

"Okay. Good." He grinned then headed toward the fireplace, tugging off his gloves as he went.

Why would David invite her shopping with him? Her forehead wrinkled, but her frozen fingers and toes shortly had her hissing in pain, and she headed for the fire herself.

Soon, the longed-for smell of a roasting turkey, rolls, and sweet potatoes made her stomach growl. In the kitchen, she caught Regina sneaking a sliver of turkey from the platter where Kyle was stacking the slices he carved. He tickled her side and she darted away, licking her fingers, while Alli took it all in, smiling.

When everything was ready, Alli stepped into the dining room and leaned against the wall. It was a beautiful sight. Fall leaves and scented candles, pinecones in a basket in the corner. The table was decorated with red place mats and the plates rested on gold chargers.

Handmade turkeys and cutout leaves covered one wall, each labeled with things the children were thankful for. Things like shoes, friends, food to eat. And for Grace House.

Kyle and Regina called everyone to the room where they stood in a circle and began linking their hands. Alli barely flinched when Regina and David each took one of hers. She wasn't the touchy-feely type, but this somehow felt okay. Kyle led them in a beautiful prayer.

"God, thank you so much for all the blessings you have poured out on us. A warm, sturdy house, people who care about us, food for our bellies, and most importantly for your son, who You sacrificed in order that we may be adopted as Your children. We are not left as orphans in Your kingdom. We are your sons and daughters. Give us grateful hearts and fill this evening with joy and laughter. In Jesus' name . . ."

"Amen!" everyone shouted. And Alli smiled. It felt good to be a part of this hackneyed family.

"Amen," she whispered, and took her seat.

The meal was loud, and chaotic, and delicious, and everything she always imagined a family Thanksgiving should be. And she soaked it all in.

"Pass the rolls, please." David grinned at her, and she passed the basket of rolls his way. He must have noticed the light in her eyes because he cocked his head and gave her a genuine smile.

She drew her gaze from his face to the others around the table and landed on Thomas's. He was talking with a mouth full of sweet potatoes and his eyes were dancing.

This is how it should always be.

He looked like a normal seven-year-old boy, more so than she'd ever seen him, and her heart glowed warm at the sight. He wasn't completely broken. He still had a shot—if the right someone stepped in and gave him a chance.

Would *she* get to be that someone?

That thought kept springing up to dance around the edge of her consciousness throughout the meal. A private, wonderful hope. Maybe together, the two of them, they'd spend every Thanksgiving together. They'd be each other's family.

As the meal wound down, David pushed away from the table and stood. "Hey guys, I need to head out. I promised my buddy I'd stop by their place after this."

The room swelled with replies from the kids.

"See ya, Pastor David."

"Glad you could make it."

"Happy Thanksgiving."

"Aw, do you have to?" This from Thomas, whose disappointment was clearly visible. And endearing.

"'Fraid so, bud. Besides, his wife, Ginger, makes her pumpkin pie from scratch and I cannot pass that up."

"Something wrong with *my* pumpkin pie?" Regina looked at him from the tops of her eyes and feigned indignation.

"You mean the one you bought frozen from the grocery store? Not a thing."

"Shh!"

"Don't worry, your secret's safe with me." David winked and flashed her a grin, then slipped on his coat.

"Give Adam and Ginger our love," Regina said on a chuckle.

"Will do." He flipped up his collar. "Hey Alli. We're still on for black Friday, right?"

She was still confused by the invitation, but her mouth ticked up as she nodded her answer. Did he want help with gift ideas?

"Perfect. See you in a few hours then."

"Okay." She didn't know what to think, but she was too nervous and skeptical to hope the invitation was…social.

Once the aforementioned pumpkin pie had been devoured and the kids began drooping as their blood sugar crashed, Alli helped wash the dishes while Kyle and Regina facilitated nighttime routines and tuck-ins of the littlest ones. By the time they all finished, she was happily exhausted and found her thoughts taking an unfamiliar turn.

God . . .if you're there . . .thank you for a wonderful Thanksgiving.

David stood in the aisle of the big box store, watching Alli examine the entire selection of Christmas decorations lining the shelves. He'd been eager to head to the electronics section, but her face glowed so bright at the sight of the home décor he couldn't bring himself to rush her. The thrill of finding a great piece for her mantle, or for the wall of their office at Grace House, he wanted to experience it all with her.

A length of pre-lit garland hanging over the crook of one arm, she lifted a white wicker snowman and gave it an approving smirk.

She looked at David. "Thoughts?" She jerked her head toward Frosty.

He shrugged. "It's a snowman."

She gave him a dull look, then tipped her head toward Frosty in a conspiratorial manner. "What do you think?" She paused and nodded sagely. "Hmm. I agree. He's spent his patience. Let's give him a break."

She approached the shopping cart and laid both the snowman and the garland into it, alongside the candles and tabletop Christmas trees she'd collected earlier. "He may not be as big and fat as ours, but I say he's perfect. And he's coming home with me."

"Mazel tov. Glad that's settled. So…you good?" He glanced longingly toward the wall of glowing TV screens across the store.

"Yep. This should be a good start for my bare, undecorated house. Lead the way."

Hopefully, they weren't sold out of that new video game console by the time he got over there. At the advertised sale price, he was considering getting one for Grace House *and* one for himself. For youth hangout nights, of course.

The thought of the most recent hangout night reminded him of Declan spotting that letter and how David hadn't opened that drawer back up since. That knowledge was the only stain on an otherwise enjoyable holiday, so he cut that reel. Replayed the highlights instead. Holding Thomas's hand for the Thanksgiving prayer, listening to the children's laughter, wrestling with Alli in the snow. His face heated and he was glad Alli had her back turned.

That memory probably shouldn't have made the highlight reel. But even while hanging with Adam and Ginger, stuffing his face with the best homemade pumpkin pie in the world, David had been eager to wrap it up and get to the shopping. With Alli. And later, as they carried their bags to their cars, he wasn't ready for the night to be over.

Hands shoved deep in his pockets, he watched as Alli loaded the last of her haul and closed the trunk. "You…wanna get some coffee?"

Her eyes flared in surprise, and she smiled. "Sure. I'd love some."

"Good." They exchanged an unhurried smile then pivoted back toward the shopping center and its coffee shop.

Inside, the place was warm and cozy, and holiday music pumped from the speakers overhead. Judging by the fair number of customers, staying open all night had been a good call on the shop's part.

A rather stiff-looking Alli sat across from him at the table, hands wrapped around a steaming caramel-pecan latte.

David ran his thumb along his paper cup, soaking in its warmth and smiled at her. "Thanks for coming tonight."

"Of course. Thanks for asking." She smiled, but her brows dipped down.

He tipped his head. "What, are you sorry you came?"

"No, not sorry. Just…"

"You're wondering why I invited you."

"Yeah. A little."

He wasn't a hundred percent sure either, but he gave her the answer he'd given himself. "Well, I figure, we spend a lot of working time together at Grace House, but we never really…just talk." He smirked. "Unless I'm doing something stupid to make you mad."

One side of her mouth lifted. "You're an expert at that."

"Everyone's good at something."

The other side of her mouth lifted into a full smile before she pressed her pink lips to the edge of her cup. She set the cup back down, a bit of whipped cream clinging to her cupid's bow.

David swallowed hard then shifted his gaze to her forehead. "Speaking of stupid, I owe you an apology for that idiotic outburst of mine. The day Garrett came by." Such an idiot response.

Her head started shaking in dismissal, but he kept speaking. "After blowing up at you like that, I did some prayerful soul-searching. And discovered something about the David Porter who spoke that way to you." He took a sip of his drink, mostly to buy himself time.

"David, it's okay. Really. We don't need to go over this again, it's under the bridge. Besides, you were right."

Huh?

He tipped his head, brows lowered.

"You were right. I *don't* have deep relationships with people."

His teeth clacked as he clamped his mouth shut.

"I- I never have."

He grasped for what to say in the face of this sudden honesty. "Well, you have Garrett."

A dry laugh shot from her nostrils. "No, I don't. We ended things last week." She shook her head. "No, that's a half-truth. *I* ended it. Things were getting too intense and... I ran. Like I always do." Lowering her face, she dropped her gaze to her lap. "Because I stink at relationships."

A cappuccino machine hissed in the background. "I don't know what to say. I'm sorry." For her pain, not so much for Garrett being out of the picture.

"There's nothing to say. It's just how I am." Her gaze found his and held, air expanding her ribcage. "How a lot of . . . *us* . . .are."

He quirked a brow. "Us?"

"Uh huh." She broke eye contact and scratched at the table with her thumb nail. "I grew up like the kids we work with. Spent virtually my entire childhood in the system until the day I turned eighteen."

He looked at her then. Really looked at her. The stiff body language, the protective shell. It made sense now. So much sense. He leaned back in his chair. "I didn't realize."

Her shoulder lifted, then fell. "I don't talk about it much." She donated a reassuring smile over her cup of java.

Was she letting her guard down with him? The sounds of the coffee shop seemed to fade as their eyes carried on a conversation of their own for interminable seconds. Hers seemed to be saying, *here I am*. And he hoped she got his message of, *I see you*. "How about we walk a bit, hmm?"

"Sounds nice."

They followed a sidewalk path at an unhurried pace, past a half dozen shops serving customers in the middle of the night with their Black Friday Doorbuster Sales.

"What was it like for you?" he ventured.

Alli tugged up the collar of her coat, her contemplative gaze scanning the horizon. "I don't know how to answer that." She downed the rest of her drink then tossed the cup in a trash bin. "There's no permanence in foster care. You're always waiting to be sent away . . .or worse."

The last two words held an ominous tone and David's stomach churned, a question souring his tongue. One he didn't know how to ask.

As if sensing it, she scraped her teeth along her lower lip and shot him a sideways glance. "I'd hear stories. An older kid using a younger one for tackling practice. Meals withheld until an impossible list of chores was done. Foster parents holding a child's head under water in the tub in some sick form of punishment they called *baptism*."

What? Lord, no, please.

Her throat bobbed and though there were no tears, David read her pain. His cheek muscle twitched as his suspicions took shape. Her reaction at the pool at the Y. To the apple bobbing. These weren't stories she'd heard from others. No. They'd happened to *her*.

A hot, sick feeling writhed inside him. Part of him wanted to tell her he knew the truth, but he refused to call her on it. Her past was hers to divulge or to not, just as his was. So, he simply nodded for her to go on.

She licked her lips. "But being sent back was just as bad. It's common for kids in the system to pick up certain skill sets along the way. I guess I'm no exception. In every home I just wanted the family to like me. Keep me. So, I learned to fake a smile, laugh at jokes, be quiet or outgoing, whatever they wanted me to be." She blinked several times then lifted her gaze to his. "The thing is, I ended up lost in all those identities. You said I don't know how to be real, and you're right." Her voice dropped to a strained, desperate whisper. "Because I've never figured out what that *is*. I don't know who I am. I'm just this hollow shell."

David inhaled through his nostrils, seeing Alli as if for the first time. Understanding why she seemed to slip into and out of personas so frequently. The silence grew weighty as the desire to comfort her welled up in him.

Alli fidgeted beside him and looked away. "I don't talk about my past in the system. I don't know why I just did, but . . ." She shrugged, like she was trying to shrug off the heaviness of the topic.

"I'm glad you did." His brow wrinkled, some of his scattered thoughts turning inward. "Ya know, the only thing I used to feel was rage. From the time I was little. But Jesus changed that. Gave me a fresh start."

Alli nodded, but was she listening? David wanted to grab her by the shoulders and make her hear the truth.

"Don't give up hope, Alli. You *can* find meaning, and connection. I know you can because I know the God who wants to connect with you. He's the one who can give meaning to your life and relationships. He's the one who can fill those hollow places inside you."

She blinked at him, swallowed, blinked away. "I don't know, David."

"*I* do. That'll have to be enough for right now."

They were almost to the parking lot, but David wasn't ready to go just yet. The moment was too precious to waste. Who knew if he'd have another chance to talk to Alli in this way again? "Here, let's take the path through the Christmas lights before we go."

They turned down an interior pathway between shopping buildings, trees lit by strands of twinkling white lights. Alone, he paused in the center to look up at the silent, starry sky through a break in the tree covering. "Alli, you said you don't know who you are. Do you want to know what I see when I look at you?"

She kicked at a twig on the ground then smirked. "A pitiful, emotionally stunted girl?"

"No." He smiled. "I see you through God's eyes. Hurting, sure. But I see a woman who is strong, smart, determined, fiercely loyal . . ."

She gulped and then forced a small laugh, looking away. "Wow. I sound like quite the catch. Unfortunately, my whole life I've always been a 'catch and release' kind of girl, if you get what I mean." Her attempt at humor didn't mask the longing in her voice. She was so broken, and everything in him wanted to put all her beautiful, shattered pieces back together.

He wrapped his fingers around her hand, giving it a squeeze until she looked at him. "I wasn't finished. I see a woman with a big heart and a great capacity to love. Someone who pours her life out for those who have nobody. A woman who's funny, and braver than she realizes." He scanned her face, watching her breath form clouds in the cold air that mingled with his own. "I see . . . beauty." He turned to face her head-on. "You're beautiful, Alli," he whispered.

Alli stared back at him with hazel eyes that looked like Autumn and Springtime. Cinnamon and Mint. His gaze whispered over her face and his pulse revved as he admired the delicate tip of her nose, the soft crest of her lips. "So very beautiful." He lifted his fingers to brush away a strand of golden hair that was whipping about her face, and her breath hitched. The atmosphere shifted, sizzling with electricity, and somewhere in the murky recesses of his brain, David knew he should take a step back. Turn. Stop this while he could.

Instead, he tucked the hair in place behind her adorable ear and ran the pad of his thumb across the apple of her porcelain cheek, the feel of her silky skin making his head spin. She swayed forward, eyes glued to his. Almost imperceptibly, she tilted her chin up in subtle invitation. Heat shot through his limbs and before his brain could catch up with his body, David had leaned in and found her mouth. Sweet. Supple. And shockingly eager.

He stifled a groan as her fingertips slid up over his chest, his shoulders, traced the hinge of his jaw, then found their way to his hair, teasing the sensitive skin behind his ears. He was breathing so hard his chest burned. But who needed oxygen when Alli was in his arms? Nothing existed beyond her lips moving on his, grasping, caressing, and searching for more. He'd move the world to give her what she wanted. Her sweetness filled his senses, shook his core, and he angled his head and deepened the kiss.

Rocking up on her tiptoes, Alli wrapped her arms around his neck and pressed against him, sending waves of desire shuddering through his body. Needing her closer, he pulled her tighter to him, the exquisite sensation of her soft curves spiking his blood. *Not enough*. He needed all of her. Like a slave master, his body demanded gratification. Hands and lips itching to explore, seizing control, cutting off reason.

He was powerless.

A gust of icy wind finally cut through the fog in his brain. His hands stilled, buried in her golden tresses. With a gasp, he broke away and stumbled backward, eyes wide. "Alli, I'm so sorry." His lips still tingled; his body still craved. But he'd only meant to reach out with God's love, not testosterone-fueled urges. He wasn't an animal. But he'd acted like one. "I shouldn't have done that." He hadn't just crossed the line, he'd raced past it on all cylinders.

Alli's lips were swollen, their color a deep scarlet. "It's more than okay, David. I didn't know pastors could kiss like that." Her hungry eyes drank him in, and it *wasn't* okay.

"No. It's really not. That . . .that was a mistake. A huge lapse in judgment. I can't . . ." How could he be so stupid? So weak? "I'm so sorry."

The light in her eyes shuttered and she pulled away, stiff and straight. She flicked her wrist. "Okay. Breathe, David. I get it. I'm not changing my Facebook status or anything, and I don't kiss and tell. You can relax."

"I shouldn't have taken advantage—"

"You didn't. I'm a big girl. Even when taking trips down memory lane."

He shook his head. If he'd just become a stumbling block . . .

"To be honest, it's not the first time I've indulged in a sloppy kiss with a friend. It happens. At least in my world. I know yours is different. But I assure you, it doesn't have to be a big deal unless you make it one."

"I just don't want you to think I said all those things just to—"

She shrugged. "We got caught up in a moment. Enjoy it for what it was, but please don't make it out to be more than that. Okay? You really don't need to feel guilty." She canted her head and smiled like she almost felt sorry for him. "It's freezing, let's get outta here before I turn into Olaf."

A nervous chuckle stuttered out of him. "Okay." They turned and began walking back toward where he'd left his car and he bumped her shoulder with his. "You're sure you're okay?"

She waved her hand in the air. "Yeah. It was a one-time thing. And you were good. Really good," she muttered, "but you and me . . . we're not peas and carrots. We both know that. I know you're a god-fearing man, but this seriously is no big deal. Don't put so much weight on it."

David cleared his throat. "I just would hate for things to get . . .weird." They stopped in front of her car. "I meant everything I said tonight, Alli."

To that, she just smiled in reply. "I'll see you tomorrow." She slipped into her car, started the engine, and pulled away.

Oh, Lord, I'm so sorry. I blew it. Badly. Could this be fixed? She was finally opening up, listening. Had he squashed a seed of faith just as it was about to bloom?

A few neighbors' lights were still on when Alli pulled into her drive. She controlled her shaking legs as they carried her to her porch and into her house. What a fool she'd been. She turned the deadbolt and rested her forehead on the door. Her life had seemed to be turning a corner. The parenting classes, Thanksgiving. Her heart kicked against her ribs like a martial arts master. Sucking in oxygen, she slid down the wall in her entryway and dug her fingers into her hair.

One. Glorious. Moment.

For that brief space of time, she'd almost believed she could be part of David's world—the one filled with hope and Bible songs. Believed someone like him, a pastor of all things, could feel something for her in a way no one ever had. Not even Garrett in all his determined persistence. David had seen her weakness, seen her for what she was, and reached for her anyway. Called her beautiful. And he was oh, so convincing. He looked into her eyes, and she'd *felt* beautiful. Worth something.

But she was an idiot.

A moron.

A mistake.

She'd been nothing but a charity case he'd gotten carried away with. He didn't love her. How could he? The idea was laughable. He was a pastor; how could he ever be with a woman like her? How could anyone?

Alli tipped her chin up toward the ceiling. She was a total mess. Nobody should have to carry her trunk-loads of emotional baggage. She wrapped her arms around herself; her insides felt so cold. *Why* had she opened up to him? Shared so much? Stupid.

She banged her head against the wall.

Stupid, stupid, stupid.

David's world looked wonderful, enticing. But Alli was from somewhere completely different. She didn't belong. And, clearly, he knew it too.

Chapter Eleven

After the staff meeting, Alli asked to speak privately with Tim. In his office now, she handed him a folder. He stood there a moment looking through its contents, before taking his seat. Alli remained standing and tried not to fidget as the clock ticked of the seconds.

Finally, Tim looked up at her over the paperwork in his hands. Paperwork transferring Thomas to another caseworker. He held it as if it weren't real, as if it were a fatal diagnosis. A sentiment Alli halfway shared, considering she might fail. But the other half felt giddy at the chance to live a rich, full life.

He arched a concerned brow at her.

She reassured him with a soft smile. "I'm fine, Tim. Really. We belong together and this is the only way I can even have a shot at making that happen." Last night she'd realized which world she belonged in, and it wasn't David's. It was a broken one, a land of misfits, full of harsh realities. The same one Thomas came from. He shouldn't feel alone in it. Her mission now was to eliminate every obstacle she possibly could.

He nodded at her, expression cautious. "Alli, you realize you can't petition his placement until you complete your licensing, which, even expedited, can take months?"

She bit her lip. "I know. But I'm halfway through the classes already. It'll be tough not being his caseworker, but I'm at Grace House all the time. I have other clients there, so I'll still see him."

Eyes dropping back to the paperwork, he ran a hand over his head and squeezed the back of his neck. "You might not pass the home study. You're a single woman working a very demanding job that takes you away from the home at all hours of the day or night."

Her belly dipped. "That's why . . ." she cleared the ball of nerves from her throat, "I need to start thinking about transitioning out completely. I'll have better chances in a nine-to-five job, and I'm sure I can get a position as a children's therapist—maybe at Grace House, or somewhere else. Still demanding, but the hours would be regular."

Tim scratched his beard then latched his gaze to hers. "If you do that, Alli, you'd be leaving a hole in our department."

Alli shifted her weight to her heels and licked her lips. "I know and I'm sorry. But I have to do this. And it's not like I'm walking out *today*. Like you said, it will still be months. Plenty of time to find a replacement and have me train them."

"That's not what I mean." He set the folder on the desk and stood to face her. "I mean, we'd miss you."

A smile stretched her lips. She didn't try to stop it. "Thank you, Tim. I'd miss you, too. But… I have to do this."

"I can see that." Fatherly concern warred with the warmth shining in his eyes. "Have you thought about what happens if you succeed? There's schooling and discipline and lots of healing to be done."

"I know." Was he trying to discourage her? Scare her? "I also know about every resource available to me—parenting classes, therapy. Plus, I know what it's like to wade through trauma and live to tell about it." Heat flushed her cheeks as her tongue moved faster than her brain could guard it. "I understand what makes an eight-year-old wet the bed, hide in a closet, or push back against authority. I understand Thomas better than your average parent would because I've *been* him."

She swallowed past her hammering pulse and released the air trapped high in her chest. "So, I'll figure it out." Because they belonged together. She knew it in her bones. She was done denying it.

Tim smiled at her, teeth gleaming. "Good girl. I'm proud of you." He wasn't quite old enough to be her father, but Alli suddenly realized he was closest thing she had to one, and she felt like a daughter basking in his approval.

The tension in her body eased and she slanted a smile back at him. "Thank you. And now . . ." she raised her brows and jerked her head toward the door. "I have to see him."

The kid she hoped to one day call her own. She didn't need David, or any man, to accept her how she was. She and Thomas could do that for each other. It made perfect sense they should be family.

Alli breezed into Grace House feeling lighter than she had in months. She bounced down the hall and poked her head through the office doorway. "Hi, Regina! Hi, Kyle!" Entering, she hugged each of them—very unlike her—then plopped into a chair and grinned at them. *Come on, ask me.*

The couple turned their attention to Alli with looks of surprise on their faces.

"Well don't you look happy." Regina gave her a curious smile.

Alli's foot bobbed back and forth. "I am. I made a decision today."

"You did?" Kyle exchanged a look with Regina.

"Yes." She glanced over her shoulder toward the hallway, checking for little ears. The magnitude of her plan required a tight lid. "I haven't mentioned this yet, but I've been taking the foster parenting classes for a couple of weeks now. Today I decided to do everything I can to get Thomas." A grin stretched her cheeks wider than she thought they could go.

Kyle and Regina's eyes widened.

"Really? My goodness, this is wonderful news!" Regina's brightness dimmed. "Oh, but it won't be easy. You're his social worker."

"It won't be easy, no." Had anything in her life been easy? "I'll need to make some career changes, which is why I told my boss this morning to get ready for my departure; I'm looking for a different position. And..." This was the scary part. The giant leap from the airplane with nothing but a parachute. Stomach fluttering, she lowered her volume a notch. "Thomas's case is being transferred. You'll probably hear from another caseworker within the next few days."

Regina's eyes rounded. "Wow. Alli, that's quite an announcement."

Yes. It was. "There's still a big question mark, and I don't know if I'll succeed, so don't say anything to him yet. But today I decided I'm all in. I'm going for it. And I had to tell you before I burst." With that,

Alli popped up and gave them another grin. "For the next hour I'll be in the sunroom making Christmas wreaths with the kids if you need me."

"Well okay then." Kyle breathed a laugh. "See ya."

"Not if I see you first." She winked then slipped out of the office. Those wreaths weren't going to make themselves, and her blazing holiday spirit wanted to enjoy it all.

"Do you like it, Miss Alli?" Thomas grinned up at her from his seat at the craft table.

Stepping closer, Alli leaned over his shoulder and studied all the details and nuances of the Christmas design he had painted onto his wooden ornament. Every carefully placed brushstroke a reflection of him. "I love it. You're an amazing artist, kiddo. And when it's dry, I'll add a layer of varnish to protect it and make it shiny."

"Really? Cool."

She rubbed his back as his adoring smile made her secret burn her insides and beg to be shared. "Why don't you go on and play. I'm going to catch up on some work." Before her goofy face gave her away.

"Okay." He wiggled off his chair and looked proudly again at his handiwork.

Keeping the plan to herself was proving even more challenging than she'd expected. In addition to the classes, Alli had poured herself into reading all kinds of parenting books, articles, blogs. It felt more real every day.

She studied up on the care of hermit crabs, too. And toyed with the idea of a friend for Herman when the time came. Maybe they'd even get a cat or dog. She was getting used to Thor greeting her at the end of each day and had to admit she would sort of miss him when Liz and Toby were ready to take him back.

For now, though, life had a comfortable rhythm, going to Grace house daily, spending time with Thomas, dreaming of their future. She still saw so much hurt in the world, so much heartbreak. But having a future to look toward relieved a lot of that strain.

Maintaining some distance from David was getting easier, too. They'd somehow found a way to be professional, appropriately friendly without pushing each other's buttons. Important since he was still an influential part of Thomas's life.

Alli was hunched over a stack of paperwork, nibbling a gingersnap cookie when a knock sounded on her office door. Regina poked her head in, looking all serious. "Alli, can we have a chat in my office?"

At her solemn tone, Alli's eyebrows slashed down. "Sure." She followed Regina on leaden legs down the hall to her office.

Kyle was waiting there, face grim. "Hi, Alli. Have a seat."

"Oh . . .kay." She took a chair and waited. Regina and Kyle exchanged a nervous glance that sent Alli's stomach plummeting and drained the blood from her face. Her gaze pinged from one of them to the other. "What's wrong?"

"Nothing's wrong exactly. Just . . .hard." Regina moved to the seat beside Alli's and took her hand in both her own. "It's about Thomas."

Alli's throat went dry. "What do you mean? What about Thomas?"

Regina offered a sympathetic smile. "DCFS has found relatives. In Arizona."

A sharp ringing sounded in Alli's ears. She shook her head. Relatives? Had she heard that right? Alli blinked stupidly several times as a cloud of confusion swirled through the room. "What?"

"An aunt I think it is. They hadn't been considered while Mrs. Cooper was working the program to get Thomas back. But now that her rights have been terminated . . ." she let the sentence hang and settle on it's obvious conclusion. Alli's mind whirled as she grappled with what she'd just heard. What she couldn't comprehend.

Thomas was... leaving.

To Arizona.

Hundreds of miles away.

No. Alli hadn't even gotten to Home Study, and she'd already lost him?

Kyle and Regina's voices merged in placating tones, but she made out none of it.

She brought her hand up to her forehead and rubbed at the grooves there. This made no sense. "H-how can this be happening?" Her eyes snapped to Regina's. "How will I tell Thomas?"

Regina flicked a glance to her husband and squeezed Alli's hand. "His new caseworker is talking to him now."

"Wait, what?!" She sprang to her feet, horrified. "Why didn't she talk to me first? I haven't even formally met the woman."

Regina sat head bowed, wringing her hands.

Kyle stood and came to take steadying hold of Alli's shoulder. "Considering the circumstances, she thought it best you not be included in the meeting. Conflict of interest."

"Yeah, but Thomas doesn't know that!" She flung out her hands. Desperation scorched her dry eyes as the full implications mounted. "He won't know why I transferred his case; he'll only think I've rejected him."

Never.

Sweat dampened her chest as she ran out of the office, dashing through the house to find Thomas and his new social worker. They weren't in the living room, or the game room.

Finally, she spotted the caseworker pushing her arms into the sleeves of her coat. The little boy was nowhere in view. "Where's Thomas?"

"You must be Miss Johnson." The woman smiled as she finished wrapping a scarf around her neck and adjusted her purse onto her shoulder. "I'm Mrs. Warner, it's nice to meet you in person." She offered her hand.

Alli's fingers twitched with impatience as she accepted the handshake. "Nice to meet you, Mrs. Warner. Can you tell me where Thomas is?" *Now, please.*

"Once we finished, he wanted to go to his room. I told him that was fine." She seemed to sense Alli's agitation. "Miss Johnson . . .this is good news for Thomas."

But not for her. "Thank you." With a curt nod, she hurried down the boys' hall and rapped her knuckles on Thomas's door. She had to make him understand. Alli hadn't thrown him away, she'd tried to make him her own.

Thomas didn't answer. She knocked again, called his name, then turned the knob to go in. But something was blocking the door.

"Thomas?" She pushed harder and the door budged slightly, the sound of something large scraping along the carpet on the other side.

Alli pushed until the door was open enough for her to squeeze inside. A nightstand had been pushed in front of the door as a blockade. "Thomas? It's me. Alli." She got on her knees and looked under the bed. Nothing. "Come out so we can talk."

"No."

She spun toward the muffled voice. "Thomas, please come out. I want to see you."

"No, you don't."

David poked himself halfway through the partially blocked door. "What's happening?"

Alli shook her head. "Nothing. Thomas just doesn't want to talk to me right now."

David pushed the door farther open and squeezed inside. He lifted the nightstand and returned it to its place. "Thomas, where you at?"

Alli pointed toward the closet and David nodded. He went to it and spoke in a gentle but firm voice. "Thomas, come on out so we can all talk."

Alli crossed her arms, frowning at his intrusion. He wasn't going to get anywhere. Thomas needed *her*. And she needed to talk to him herself. "Thomas, I know you're hurt and confused, but I promise I can explain."

"Thomas," David began again. "Remember the story I told you about Jesus standing at the door and knocking? He said if you hear His voice and open the door, he will come in and dine with you . . .we're here at the door, buddy."

Alli shot him a look. Of course, he knew they were knocking! What did Jesus have to do with it? But it worked. Thomas slid open the closet door. But he hustled farther back behind the coats and sweaters until only his shoes were showing.

Alli stepped inside, pushing through the hangers, and sat beside him, knees to her aching chest. "Thomas, don't be mad."

"You gave me away, too."

A knife stabbed her heart. "No, Thomas. I didn't give you away. I'm right here."

"That lady said she was my social worker now instead of you."

"There's a reason for that. I . . . I can't tell you what it is but it's not because I was giving you away. I care for you very much. I'm still right here, aren't I?"

He hid his face in his arms. "I don't want to go to Arizona. I want to stay right here! With you and Pastor David." Sobs shook his body.

Alli reached out and rubbed his back. "I know," she whispered. Her heart felt like it would shatter into a million pieces if it didn't bleed out first. How could she let him go? She loved him. "But . . .God will be with you wherever you are."

Did that sound right? Adequately comforting? She slid a glance at David, whose eyes reflected his awe. Perfect. Now, he was going to think she was climbing aboard the God wagon. *So not important right now.*

"Do you believe that, Thomas?" David asked softly.

Thomas shrugged without looking up. "I just don't want to go. Please. I'll be good, I promise." He looked up with tear-soaked cheeks and a runny nose. "I'll do all my chores and work real hard at school and I'll never bother anybody for anything."

Alli dried his cheeks. So soft, innocent. He was dealing with so much for such a little guy. "You already *are* good, Thomas. But you have a family to go to."

Thomas crawled onto Alli's lap and wrapped his arms around her, squeezing tight. "You're my family."

His small voice in her ear nearly undid her. As she held him close, she closed her eyes, blew out a breath, and carefully counted to five. He needed something from her right now. Something maybe only she could give.

"I'm your friend and I care about you very much, but I am not your family, Thomas." She'd tried and failed. But right now, he needed to believe everything would be okay. "Come on now, it's time to get out of here." She pulled his arms from around her and set him on his feet, then stood and exited the closet. "Go with David and wash your face. It's almost dinner time."

David looked from her to Thomas and held out his hand. "Come on, bud. I hear we're having turkey casserole tonight."

As he led a sullen Thomas out the door, he caught Alli's eye. The look he gave her felt like compassion. Alli nodded once and waited for them to clear the room. Then she leaned over, hands on her knees, and took a series of deep breaths trying to calm the storm inside.

She didn't believe in superheroes or fairy tales. And she was not climbing aboard any wagons. Because sometimes, God was a nightmare she wanted to escape. Other times, a dream just beyond her reach. If God actually did exist, he'd been beyond cruel to her.

David didn't know what to make of the scene he'd just witnessed. Alli was hurting. Bad. Talking about God? His heart had leapt, but, well, he didn't want to read too much into that.

He led Thomas to the bathroom and wet a washcloth for his tear-smudged face. "I know you're upset right now, but no matter what happens, you have whole gobs of people who care about you and are looking out for you. And Alli is right—God is always with you." He wiped the boy's face then handed him some tissue to blow his nose. "Ready for some turkey casserole?"

Thomas scraped a sleeve across his snotty nose and nodded.

"Come on." He offered a slight smile as he shepherded him out to the kitchen where Kyle was grating cheese. "Not quite ready. How about we play a game of Connect Four while we wait?"

His answer was a noncommittal shrug.

They played a subdued game until it was time to gather at the dinner table. The adults all seemed to be on the same page with keeping up light, normal conversation. But, though Alli tried to hide it, David could tell she was struggling.

After the meal, she lingered to help with the dishes, then volunteered to read a bedtime story to Thomas. Seemed to David she didn't want to leave until Thomas was asleep, safe and sound.

He stuck around too, hoping for a moment to talk to her. Make sure she was okay. Especially after that kiss. *Foolish, man. Real dumb.*

He wouldn't tell her that he couldn't get the memory of it out of his head. Being made of flesh and blood really got in the way at times.

He almost missed his chance to catch her when he heard Alli at the front door wishing Regina a good night.

He hurried to catch her in the entry way. "Alli, hold up."

Alli flipped out the collar of her coat and freed her long hair. "Yeah?" Her voice was drab, exhausted. He hated seeing her so depleted.

"Let me walk you out. I want to talk to you for a minute."

She hesitated, shifted her weight, a look of resignation on her face. "Sure."

It tweaked his conscience, but he had to admit to himself that right now he was grateful she could never say no.

David grabbed his own coat and gloves and keys then smiled at her. "Ready."

Snow dusted the pavement as they descended the steps to the large circular driveway where their cars were parked side by side.

"So, what did you need?" Alli glanced toward her car, not hiding her eagerness to get into it and shut out the cold. Or him. Maybe both.

"I wanted to make sure you were okay?"

"Sure." Arms wrapped around herself, she kicked the toe of her boot into the white powder. "Why wouldn't I be?"

"Well, Thomas for one. Me for another." A puff of fog came from his nostrils. "Things have been different ever since . . . my blunder." And now he was thinking about it again. Probably emitting even more steam.

She blanched, but quickly recovered. "I told you that wasn't a big deal." A false-sounding chuckle. "I could never date a pastor. No offense. But you live in the world of the Cleavers, and me, well, I have more of a Mommy Dearest background."

"Alli." David's gut torqued. "I did not grow up with the Cleavers."

"It wasn't an accusation, David. I just meant that . . .I never thought of you that way either."

Somehow that admission jabbed more than it should have. He worked his jaw, shook his head to rattle the sting away. "And Thomas?"

Her face clouded. "Yeah, that one's harder."

"Alli, why did you transfer his case?" It didn't make any sense.

"I had to." She bit her lip and shifted her gaze away.

"What do you mean? Why?"

"Because I . . ." Her eyes flicked to his, then up at the stars. Like she was searching them for something. "I wanted him. I was going to try and get him."

David lifted his shoulders. *So . . .?*

"So, it's a conflict of interest for his caseworker to handle his placement. He needed to have another social worker on record. I had to start creating some layers of distance if I wanted him placed with me. Especially if I wanted to…adopt." She hugged herself more tightly and pointed her face to the ground.

Understanding dawned. Sadness crashed a moment later. "Oh, Alli. I'm so sorry."

"Yeah." She nodded out toward the horizon, then shot keen eyes at him. "He can't ever know, David. The move is hard enough as it is."

"Yeah. You're right."

Lord, what are you doing? What's your plan?

Thomas would've thrived with Alli, he was sure of it. And Alli would've opened up and found herself through the act of loving this child.

Alli's head dropped, and she rubbed at her nose. On instinct, David raised his hands to her shoulders to comfort, but she stiffened and shifted away from him, a curtain falling over any trace of vulnerability.

"I'm fine." She dug her keys out of her pocket. "Keeping a child with blood relatives is always the preferred outcome, so long as they are stable." Her voice pinched. "There's a reason we aren't supposed to get too close. I needed reminding. Anyway, thanks but it's really not your concern. Have a nice night, Pastor." With a polite smile, she turned and unlocked her car door, leaving David feeling a bit stunned. And rebuffed.

"Good night," he managed. "I'm praying for you."

She stilled, hand on her door handle. "Don't." She closed her door and started the engine.

An ache threatened to swallow him whole. Alli was retreating, running, not just from him but from God.

He watched her roll out of the drive, steam billowing from her exhaust pipe. He'd really thought, *hoped*, she was edging closer to faith. But this thing with Thomas must have affected her on a very deep level.

What could he do to help? She wouldn't let him in.

David stuck his key in the ignition and started for home. Worry etched his forehead as he drove. Did he push through her barriers or give her space?

He allowed a thought to form. Maybe if he talked to her about *his* history, before he became a pastor or even a Christian, she'd listen more. Put more stock in what he had to say and realize she could have that same peace and joy. Learn to release her past.

Like he had?

His conscience pricked. Avoiding toxic family members was not the same thing as releasing his past. The man lived only half an hour away and David hadn't seen or talked to him in eons.

At the thought of it, his muscles bunched, and his mind seized. Some things were just too difficult. David had turned to Jesus, allowed God to change him from the inside out, to radically alter the direction of his life. He loved the Lord with all his heart.

But he still couldn't face his dad. Nothing good could come of it.

Back home, he flipped on the heater before peeling off his coat and heading to the kitchen to tear open a package of Swiss Miss. The cold temps seemed amplified by the conversation with Alli. And his racing thoughts chilled him further.

Steaming mug in hand, he went to his recliner and propped up his feet. Memories knocked on the door of his mind. Painful memories, enraging memories. Flashes of images tattooed on his brain—steel-toed boots seen from under his bed. The stairs leading down to the basement as they rushed toward him over and over. The red glow of a ciGarrette just before it burned his skin.

And the sounds . . .the bellowing shouts of an angry drunk and the sick thud of fists hitting flesh. Worst of all was David's own pitiful whimper and begging.

Even now the memories caused his teeth to clench. How could God expect him to ever simply "let that go?" That couldn't be what the Lord required. Could it?

He blinked burning eyes, regaining awareness of his surroundings. Looking down, he found he was white knuckling his lukewarm cocoa. David forced himself to relax his jaw muscles and took a long drink of chocolate.

There was only one thing to do when the demons of his childhood came clawing, so he bowed his head and called on the name of Jesus. "I'm still such a broken man, Lord. Full of fear and weakness. I can't fight off the memories, and what they do to me. They're like stains in the fabric of who I am." Resentful tears sprang to his eyes. "You've washed me of my sins, can you wash me of these memories? This pain?"

He sat in silence and dragged in a breath. His gaze drifted to the worn leather book sitting two feet away at the top of a stack of commentaries. Maybe there'd be something in there that would speak to him. Something God wanted to say. Shoving aside his cold mug, David reached for the Bible.

Alli was still shaking forty-five minutes after coming home. She'd set the shower level to as hot as she could handle and stood under the stream, skin turning red, but still she shivered. When the water grew warm then cool, she shut it off and stepped out into her steamy bathroom, dried herself with a thick towel. She dragged her palm across the mirror and watched her empty eyes for signs of life.

Come on, Alli. Pull it together.

Thomas was never hers to begin with. And he had family.

Now, even in flannel pajamas and wool socks, she still felt cold. It was a coldness that seemed to emanate from deep within, not something she could fix by kicking the heater up a few degrees. How did she ever let it get this far? To let herself think, even for a moment, that she could make a family for herself. Like a normal person. But she was far from normal. She knew that, so what was she thinking letting herself hope?

Death of hope was the worst form of pain Alli could imagine. And something she'd never wanted to feel again. But hope was a stubborn thing, like a weed. It sprouted in the deadest of hearts if given just the tiniest bit of encouragement.

"Not anymore." She couldn't go back to the group home. If she did, they'd only find a way to make her hope again and she'd have to feel all this pain again.

Several hours after crawling under her covers, she hadn't found sleep. She checked the time—just after eleven. Too late to call anyone but she texted Janelle anyway.

Hey, you up?

Yeah, catching up on Netflix. What's up?

Rough day. Needed a distraction.

Come over and watch Gilmore Girls with me.

I'm already in my pajamas.

Me too. Come on over. It'll be fun.

Her thumbs hovered over the keyboard . . . *Okay.*

Alli bundled up and headed across the street to Janelle's. The soft glow of her TV shone through the blinds. She knocked then bounced and rubbed her arms as she waited for the door to open.

"Come in! Quick." Janelle waved her in and closed the door behind her.

Janelle's house was a mirror image of Alli's floorplan but stepping inside felt like stepping onto foreign soil. Her friend's place was decorated with an Italian motif. Lots of grape vines and metalworking. A picture of the Trevi Fountain hung above her fireplace, twin sconces on either side. Her kitchen held a wine rack, and in the corner was a large, hand-painted ceramic vase. This house felt like a home, not just a place to eat and sleep.

"Want some hot chocolate, coffee, something stronger?"

"Chocolate. Definitely. It's been that kind of day."

"Tell me while I make it." Janelle pulled out the milk and poured some into a saucepan, clicking on the burner.

Alli let her gaze drift to the windowsill where little potted herbs struggled to survive winter. How depressing that she envied them. Because Spring would eventually come to them. While her life remained barren. She wasn't sure how much time had passed when Janelle's voice brought her back.

"So…" Her friend eyed her as she continued to whisk the cocoa. "Is this about Garrett?"

"What? No."

"He told me you cut him loose. I just thought maybe you were having a hard time with that."

"No. Garrett and I just didn't mesh. This…this is a lot bigger than that."

"Now you have me curious." She suddenly looked up from the simmering saucepan, worry pinching her brows. "You're not sick, are you?"

"Depends on your definition of sick."

Janelle's face froze as if bracing for a terminal diagnosis.

Alli lifted a halting hand. "No, I'm not."

Releasing her breath, Janelle turned off the stove and opened a cupboard. "Good. I was scared for a second there."

Alli tried to muster a reassuring smile for her friend's sake but, for once, it wouldn't come at her command. So, she directed her dull gaze at the stream of chocolate flowing from the saucepan into an olive-green ceramic mug. "I just allowed myself to believe I could have a future that's not mine, and today was reminded that I can't." She bumped a shoulder and stared at nothing.

"Hmm. In that case." The fridge door opened. Pressurized air whooshed. Whooshed again. The fridge closed.

When the kitchen came back into focus, Alli saw large mounds of whipped cream where the chocolate steam had been.

Janelle pushed a mug into Alli's hands and pulled her to the couch in front of the fireplace. "Now tell me everything."

Alli gave a stiff smile and inhaled. "Thomas is moving to Arizona. Some aunt I didn't know he had is there, and I had thought that I could have him. I actually believed it would happen, despite the odds." She shook her head in amazement at her own foolishness.

"Thomas? Is he why you dumped Garrett?"

"No. He's a child. One of my cases. But it doesn't matter anymore, what matters is that now I know, beyond a doubt, that I'll never have a normal life."

"Alli, you're not making sense. Of course you will, you *do*. Look at you, you're smart, funny, successful. You own your own home, you have friends."

"No. Janelle. I don't, not really. Nobody knows the real me. I never let anyone in and when I try it always goes horribly, horribly wrong." She pushed away thoughts of Pastor David and his kiss. "It's me. Something is wrong with me. And I don't know how to fix it. David would say I need Jesus, but every time I turn around it's like God is playing tricks on me."

Janelle's forehead wrinkled. "Is David another one of your cases?"

Alli shook her head. "No, David is a pastor who volunteers at one of the group homes. The one Thomas has been living in. Anyway, he's the one who had me going there for a minute. Believing there was hope for me when there's not." Anger swam through her veins. If it weren't for David and the rest of the religious zealots at the group home, Alli never would have pursued fostering Thomas. She never would've opened herself up to this pain. Really this was his fault.

"Ah, okay. Pastor, gotcha. Well . . . you know . . . Jesus isn't such a bad idea."

Alli stared at Janelle. "I had no idea that you were, you know, a *believer.*"

Janelle twisted her lips together as guilt blew across her features. "I guess I'm not a very good one. Haven't gone to church in years. But deep down, Jesus is there." She shifted to face her better. "But look, Alli, it's clear that this didn't just start with this kid. It sounds like something you've been carrying for a while." Janelle rested her hand on Alli's knee. Alli stiffened then relaxed. "Like what's that about? Why do you do that? You react like that every time I touch you." Concern flashed in her eyes like she was looking at Alli clearly for the first time.

Alli shrugged and sipped her drink. "I didn't grow up in a very affectionate family, that's all."

"Neither did I, but I don't flinch every time a friend touches me." She set down her mug on the coffee table. "Alli . . .is there something in your past that you maybe haven't told me?"

Alli looked at Janelle for a long while, remembering what happened the last time she opened up to someone. Then she counted to five and offered a well-meaning smile. "No."

Janelle looked unconvinced. "You sure?"

A knot coiled in her belly. "I mean, I grew up in foster care but that's it. Not uncommon. But could be why I'm not good at connecting."

Her brows hiked. "Foster care? You? No wonder you chose social work."

Alli shrugged. "I know what it takes to survive the system. I just don't know what it takes to survive life outside it afterward." Her lashes beat rapidly. Had she just said that? Out loud? Her back rounded and she looked away. Everything felt too raw and exposed, and she didn't like it. Needed it pushed back into iron-plated boxes.

Janelle's voice was a husky whisper. "Alli. You'll be fine."

Alli shook her head. She grabbed a breath that sounded way too shaky with emotion. "I'm not fine. I will never be 'fine.' Don't you see? I'm defective. I can never have a normal life, a family, because I'm not normal. I need to accept that, stop dreaming, stop hoping for more than what I have. Because I had begun to hope for more, but now . .

." She pressed her lips together. "Now I'm just having everything ripped away again. Like I did with every foster family that didn't keep me. And I think of Thomas getting on that plane to Arizona and I can't breathe." She pressed her hands into her abdomen. "Janelle, I'm drowning." Alli knew that sensation, and there was no better word to describe this feeling.

Janelle's face was shrouded in worry. "I don't know what to say, Alli. I'm so sorry." She grabbed Alli's hand and squeezed. "You have to hang in there. Give it time. Things always look better with a little distance. I'll . . .I'll pray for you."

Alli's gaze popped to her, brows drawn. *Janelle* wanted to pray for her? Was this the Twilight Zone?

"And maybe you should talk to this pastor of yours some more."

She looked away, eyes wide. "Trust me, that's *not* what I need." She tucked her hair behind her ears. "When David told me he would pray for me, you wanna know what I said? I told him 'Don't.' I'm pretty mad at God right now. But . . .I won't tell you the same thing. I'm glad you're my friend, Janelle."

Janelle smiled. "So am I."

Alli pushed herself off the couch and licked her lips. "It's late and I should really get going. Thanks for the . . .girl time. Not something I've had a lot of in my life. I kinda like it." She gave a half-felt smile and carried her empty mug to the sink.

"Me too." Janelle stood and pulled her into a hug. Alli closed her eyes, feeling loved. Cared for. It was nice.

"Call me tomorrow?"

"Yeah. Good night."

"Night." Janelle walked her to the door and helped her back into her coat.

It was well after midnight by the time Alli climbed back into bed. She was exhausted enough this time for sleep to find her. Despite the temperature, the shaking had stopped, but though she still felt the impression of Janelle's hug, the emptiness remained.

Chapter Twelve

Taylor Swift blared through the speakers as Alli pulled up to the Child and Family Advocates office. Taylor always made her feel better, but Alli was giving the singer a run for her money today.

Sunlight glittered across snowy patches on the curb strip and planters as she yanked the parking brake and powered down the car, allowing silence to fill the space. She took in the office facade, Tim's familiar gray Chevy—reindeer antlers attached the side mirrors, and the folder sitting on her passenger seat, as she steeled herself to face this day. And all the changes it would kick off.

Bells on the door jingled merrily when she entered. Bypassing the candy dish, she offered greetings to her coworkers and made her way to Tim's office.

He looked up from his computer. Pushed his chair away from the desk. "Alli. Good morning. I knew I'd be seeing you sometime today. Have a seat." He gestured to the chair across from him, but she had no plans to settle in for a lingering chat.

"No, thanks. This won't take me long." Alli hooked her thumbs in her back pockets as she paced back and forth in front of his desk, letting the words form in her mouth. "I was originally going to come in here and ask you *why*. Why was I left out of the loop on this, left to find out only after Thomas had been told. Why you shut me out of whatever meeting must've taken place upon discovery of these mystery relatives. Why you let this happen at all, Tim."

"Alli . . ." His voice held an apologetic tone, but Alli held up her hand to cut him off.

"But I'm not going to do that. Relax. Truth is, I can guess why I wasn't brought in, even if I don't agree. Which I don't, for the record. So instead," she stopped pacing to face him straight on, "what I'm here to tell you is that I still plan to transfer out of casework. As soon as possible. I've been up this morning since an ungodly hour reviewing my clients' files, writing summaries, considering recommendations for who I think should take each case. Yeah, I know that's not really up to me, and I didn't have to do that but . . .I'm responsible for these kids and I want to make sure they're taken care of before I move on."

Forefingers steepled at his chin, Tim gave her a somber nod. "You've always been hands-on with your cases. A real advocate." Sadness filled his eyes, but Alli broke away from it.

"Yes, well, I hope you'll go with my recommendations. I found a couple open positions and will be sending my resume out today. I'd like to start getting the new caseworkers up to speed on my clients, if I can get your expedited approval."

He made no reply, nothing to postpone the rest of what she had to say. She swallowed the giant rock in her throat. "They'll have Thomas on a plane within a day or two. As soon as that happens, I'm leaving too. Even if I don't have another job to go to. I just need you to understand. I have to go."

She raised her chin and eyed him, waiting for whatever argument he might throw at her to try and talk her off the ledge. Talk her out of leaving. Whatever demand for two weeks' notice or attempt to compromise or negotiate.

Silence hovered in the air for a long moment, and then he gave a wordless nod. He must've realized that she needed the clean break. To leave this place of false hope in order to survive. Rising from his desk, he came and took her hand in a warm shake. His eyes held kindness, understanding. Affection.

Thanking him with a quick dip of her head, she turned and opened his office door. "I'll email you my case recommendations."

In her own office, Alli opened her desk drawer and began emptying it, removing contents into a cardboard box. Pens and highlighters, a few mint candies. The desk could've belonged to anyone really. Just like her house, it lacked any personal touches. Except for the baby cactus Linda had given her a year ago. She added it to the box when her gaze snagged on a bit of crayon artwork poking out from under a file folder. Her jaw flexed as she pulled it free from the pile and stared at one of Thomas's pictures.

Eyes fluttering closed, Alli hung her head and propped her hands on her desk. She had to be strong. Endings were not new to her. She was just a hermit crab who'd outgrown her shell. Time to find a new one.

The sooner she booked a flight, the better.

She unlocked her phone and dialed Grace House.

"Good morning," Kyle greeted.

"Hi, Kyle. I just wanted to see how Thomas is doing this morning."

"Hey Alli, he's hanging in there. Eating breakfast at the moment, engaging with the others now and then. He's a bit subdued but David's here with him so I think that's helping. Are you coming by today?"

The thought of seeing David sent pain through her middle. "Yes, I'll be there in a bit."

"Alrighty. Alli… Regina and I want you to know we're praying for you. I'm sure this is exceedingly difficult. We know how excited you were about fostering him."

Hearing him say it aloud made her ears go hot. "That's the way these things go sometimes." She rolled her lips together. "Kyle?"

"Yeah?"

"Has a day been set yet for Thomas to head to his aunt's?"

"Yes. His flight is booked for Saturday."

Throat aching, closing off, she rushed to the end of the call. "Thanks. See you soon."

"See you."

Four days. Then this chapter of her life would end.

A few hours later, Alli pulled her coat tighter as she stood in front of Grace House, staring at the nativity in front of the big bay windows, willing herself to go in. Knowing she'd be leaving soon made it hard to be there. Hard to see them. It might be easier to just go. But she wouldn't do that. Not this time.

Frigid air chilled her knees with each step forward as she approached the porch steps. The closer the front door got, the more eager she felt to get inside, though she dreaded telling Kyle, Regina, and David.

Especially David.

He looked at her with those eyes that saw past her painted shell and said things that spun her head and confused her heart. Hauling air into her lungs, she straightened her backbone and grabbed the knob.

A wall of delicious scents enveloped her. After shrugging out of her coat, she followed her nose to the kitchen, where a group of kids were gathered around a bent form in front of the open oven door.

"Smells delicious," she said to announce her arrival.

The children all turned toward her, faces glowing, and for the moment her nerves were forgotten.

"Hi, Miss Johnson!"

"Alli!"

"Want a Snickerdoodle?"

Their voices merged and curved her lips. Her smile grew wider when she saw it was David pulling a sheet of cookies from the oven.

"Hey, Alli, you're just in time."

"David. I didn't know you could bake."

"There's a lot you don't know about me." His smile already had her head spinning.

She pointed at his torso. "Nice apron."

David looked down at the pink-and-white gingham apron tied around his waist. "I do wear it quite well, don't I?" He grinned and picked up a spatula. "You'll have to try a sample." He slid the spatula under a fluffy golden cookie, and gently deposited it onto a napkin. He fanned it with his hand as he brought it to her. "It's still hot and might fall apart. Be careful."

He handed her the napkin and Alli blew on the cookie before lifting the cinnamon-laced dessert and sinking her teeth into it. "Oh my gosh," she said around a mouthful of hot deliciousness. "I've died and gone to heaven. This is scrumptious."

His eyes sparkled. "Glad you like it." Then to the kids, "Okay, let's get these onto the cooling racks."

She inclined her head toward the hall. "I'm gonna finish this in my office. Thank you."

"Thomas is in the game room." He passed her a significant glance then looked back down at the cookie sheet.

Alli swallowed another bite to ease the ache in her throat. "Okay. Thanks."

She headed down the hall to her shared office, sat down and closed her eyes. Being here was a hundred times harder than she thought it would be. Even while feeling a hundred times better than not being here at all. None of it made sense. Not her feelings, not her thoughts, certainly not the series of events leading up to this one.

"Knock knock." David poked his head in.

"You don't have to knock David, it's your office."

"I didn't want to disturb you," he said, stepping in and closing the door.

"You aren't."

He leaned back against his desk and crossed one foot over the other. His eyes penetrated hers, their depths drawing her in. "How are you doing today?"

"I'm fine."

He cocked his head, clearly calling her bluff.

Exhaling a rush of air, she shook her head. "How can you stand to . . .to bake cookies right now?"

He spread his hands out. "What else should I be doing?"

"I can barely function. How are you still going, knowing that...?" Her throat clicked on a swallow.

"That Thomas is leaving? Yeah, it's difficult. But that's part of what we do. We unite families. Doesn't he deserve a shot at getting to know his family? If he has blood relatives to go to, that's more than most of the kids here have."

He was right and she hated it. "We don't know anything about them. We can't vet them. I haven't seen their home or how they are with their other kids or . . .anything."

"Well, someone did." David's voice fell to a patient whisper. "I know. It's hard. No denying that. But Alli, Thomas needs our confidence and optimism going in."

Alli rolled her eyes. "Optimism. Right." She caught his scolding look and backtracked her tone. "No really. You are right. I'm obviously having a hard time separating my emotions the way I normally would. I've gotten too close; I see that now. Which is why I'm leaving."

His back straightened out of its slouch. "What do you mean, leaving?"

"I mean I'm making a career change, moving out of the city."

"What? You can't be serious." He pushed away from his desk, standing tall and straight like the soldier he was.

"Not until Thomas goes, but yes I am. I need to break away from all this and clear my head. Start fresh."

David blinked at her like he'd been slapped. Placed his hands on his hips and turned away, then back again. "But . . .I don't want you to go."

Her stomach clenched. *Why?* Why was he doing this? He saw her so clearly most of the time, couldn't he see what he was doing to her now? "I have to, David. I can't stay here."

His brows knotted and he stared at the wall as if he could find all life's answers written in the paint. "What about the other kids in your charge?"

"Transferring them to other caseworkers. Listen, this is the way it has to be." And she had to escape this room, *now*.

She made a show of straightening a pile of paperwork on her desk and pushing in her chair. "Excuse me. I want to let Thomas know I'm here."

David stood in shocked silence as Alli breezed out of their shared office. Out of his life soon, too, if what she'd just announced came to be. Would she really leave?

"David? What's going on, is everything okay?" Kyle stepped in, forehead lined in worry. He pointed a thumb toward the hallway. "Alli just rushed past me in the hall. She seemed… agitated. Did you two have an argument or something?"

Still dazed and dumbstruck, David shook his head. "No. But she . . .she says she's leaving." After everything they'd shared, the thought of her not being in his life just didn't compute.

Kyle looked at him and pressed his lips together. "Hmm. This has been especially hard on her. Opening up her heart only to be rejected yet again."

"But she can't just leave. Not when—" He clamped his mouth shut. Silenced the words in his head.

Kyle cocked his head. "Not when what, David?"

He hauled air through his nostrils. "She still has a job to do. Other kids she's in charge of. What will happen to Liz and Toby if she up and leaves?"

"Alli wouldn't go without having all her ducks are in a row. She'll make sure each case is transitioned to a new worker before she moves on."

David nodded absently. "Yes of course."

"But that's not what you were thinking of, was it?"

David's jaw muscle jerked. "Why wouldn't I think of it? I care for the kids here."

Kyle laid a hand on David's shoulder and looked him in the eye. "You also care for Alli. A great deal."

David's nostrils flared. He turned his head away. "She's a lost sheep without a Shepherd."

"David… have you told her?"

"Told her what?" His words flew out hot as he whipped his head back around.

A smile played on Kyle's lips. "How deeply you care for her."

"I don't." He scoffed then gripped his forehead and massaged his temples.

"Regina and I have both seen the way you look at Alli." Kyle squeezed his shoulder muscle and gave it a shake. "Have you considered you might love her?"

"No," he snapped, then deflated. He pinched the bridge of his nose.

Darn it! Despite the lies he told himself, maybe he *was* in love with her. But she was still an unbeliever. Without a faith of her own, they could never share a life, a heart. A growl formed in his throat and escaped between his teeth. "It's not right." His gaze bored into Kyle's. "She hasn't given her life to Christ. I *cannot* give her my heart."

"Nevertheless, you do have feelings for her."

He puffed out his cheeks. "If you're right . . .then maybe her leaving is best for everyone." David didn't want to believe it.

"Maybe. But whether she stays or moves on, you should be honest with her."

"Should I? Kyle, I'm a pastor. And she wants nothing to do with church or with Jesus."

Kyle shrugged. "So maybe nothing will happen between you. Or maybe she's closer to embracing grace than you realize. You know what that's like more than most."

He did. David had railed against God until the day he called on Him for mercy. "Even if that were true, and she were to give her heart to the Lord, she doesn't feel that way about me."

Kyle smiled like he had a secret. "I'm not so sure about that. But you'll never know if you don't talk to her."

David looked up at him. "I'll pray about it."

"Good enough for me." He patted his arm.

Yeah, he'd pray about it all right. Pray that God would clean him of any trace of weakness for the woman. Pray for strength to keep in control. Keep on the narrow path. "I need to take off. Head over to the church. Get a few things done."

Kyle nodded his understanding. "Alright man, I'm praying for you."

David went straight to the church and tried to distract himself with Bible study, with straightening the youth Launch Pad, with working on a sermon. But Alli invaded his thoughts through it all. So, he'd hopped in his car and started driving. Just driving and thinking.

Alli was leaving. Quitting her job. Moving away. From her house, from her friends, from him. Just erasing it all.

How could someone uproot their lives, just like that? Run away from everything, everyone, trying to build a new, pain-free existence by ignoring the past? Pretending it never happened, it didn't exist?

Bewildering… irritating… and somehow, in the farthest corners of his mind, familiar.

Because the past *did* exist. And facing it—with support and with God's help—was the only way to heal.

He pulled up to the curb and put his car in park. Who was he to talk? When he still slammed the door on the ugliest memories and refused to deal with his own trauma. He was running too. When it came to his father, it's all he'd ever done.

So here he was, staring over the steering wheel at the dirty blue stucco house across the street, trying to get up the nerve to walk up to the door of his childhood home.

Snow crunched beneath his feet. Scraped the sidewalk with a push of the gate. And every muscle in his body tightened, braced for confrontation. Hands in his pockets, he stood there and stared up at the porch covering above him.

His stomach was in his throat, threatening to evacuate should his knuckles make contact with the door. *I can't do this. I'm not ready.*

I will be with you, always.

On that whisper of assurance, a small measure of strength came over him. Before it could evaporate, he knocked on the door. Sounds of shuffling feet came from inside. David stretched out his backbone, jaw tight, and waited for the door to swing open.

When it did, the familiar stench of stale nicotine hit his nostrils, but the man who stood before him shattered every conjured expectation. His father was feeble, hunched, with oxygen tubes running from his nose to a tank beside him.

He stared at David with yellow, glassy eyes, wide with shock. "You're here. I can't believe it."

"Yeah, me either."

They just stared at one another. David took in the stained robe, the deeply lined face, the wasted muscle.

"Want to come in?"

For some reason, David answered *yes*.

His father moved aside, and David stepped over the threshold onto the exact same carpet he'd walked on as an eight-year-old. The years had further worn down the fibers, deposited more filth. Though he was certain he was looking at many of the same stains he recalled from his childhood. Made by himself. Associated with punishment.

They veered left into the living room where his father cleared a space on the couch, brushing debris out of the way. "You can sit here."

David lowered himself to the edge of the cushion, sitting stiff and alert.

CiGarrettes littered the coffee table, a TV droned, the whole place was a wreck. David took it all in, the sight before him smudging with his childhood memories.

Silence stretched as he waited for his father to say something. His nostrils flared. His father stared at him, blinking stupidly. "So, how've you been?"

"Good."

"Yeah, you look it. Not like me, huh?" He patted the tank of oxygen then went on about his health issues, complaining about doctors and insurance and how he wasn't getting what he needed.

Anger began a low boil in David's blood as his father continued with awkward small talk. It burned in his gut until it parted his lips and erupted. "I don't want to dance around the elephant in this room, *Dad*."

His father's flapping lips came together and stayed shut.

"You know why I've stayed away all these years. Or do you need a reminder?" David pushed up his sleeve and thrust out his arm. Do you remember giving me this scar? This was the first ciGarrette. I was *five*." He bent his head and pointed to the back of his skull. "How about this one. Where you cracked my head open. Or *this*?" David held up a crooked pinky finger, broken during one of his father's rages and never set properly. "We both know it didn't get caught in any door."

His mother had had a similar "incident" and assured him it would heal, like hers had. But she never healed, she *left*. And she didn't take him with her.

David glared at him, daring his father to tell him he was talking crazy. Imagining things. Remembering things worse than how they were.

But as David's eyes shot daggers, his father's filled with moisture. His lips trembled, and when he finally found his tongue, he said, "I'm sorry. I... I feel terrible for what I did to you."

Primed for confrontation, for a fight, David's body didn't know how to respond. A confusing, frothy mix of grief and frustration washed over him in a wave, but his muscles released in emotional exhaustion.

David took in the form of his pathetic father, and for the first time felt . . . pity.

Pity, but not forgiveness.

He rose to his feet. "I hope someday I can reply with 'I forgive you.' But that won't be today. For now, I can only manage, 'I'm glad.' And 'It's about time.'"

Dear Mrs. Johnson,

Your experience and references are impressive, and we would be delighted to have you interview for our Children's Counselor position. Would you be available to fly out to see us at the end of the week?

Okay, this was good news. If she was lucky, there'd be no gaps in income during her transition. Or at least, only a small one. She immediately sent her reply.

Mr. Hanover,

Thank you for your interest. Yes, I am available and would love to come out and interview with you. When would you like me there?

Alli had emailed back and forth with a private agency in New Jersey during her lunch hour. Now, having set a time for her interview, she was online booking a flight for Saturday. Same day Thomas was leaving. Which was good. It would help distract her.

After booking her flight, she packed up her computer, said goodnight to Regina and Kyle, and headed home. As she pulled up in front of her white picket fence, she sighed.

She wouldn't see the flowers this Spring. This wasn't going to be her life anymore.

Well, at least she wouldn't have to worry about how to spruce up the inside anymore.

She turned on the heater and connected her phone to her living room speakers via Bluetooth, and started some music playing.

Time for a fresh start. Again.

Holiday tunes followed her down the hallway where she flipped on the bathroom light. Foot tapping to the beat, she examined her reflection, pulling some hair down in front of her face and assessing the effect.

Alright, let's do it.

She combed her hair straight and grabbed the scissors. Music pounded through the living room and down the hall to where she was as she snipped into her hair. Snip, snip, snip, she cut across her forehead at the line of her eyebrows, checking and rechecking that she was making it straight. She smiled and turned her head to the side. Not bad. After texturing the ends, she fluffed them with her fingers and made a pouty face in the mirror. The fringe suited her, she decided.

"Lookin' good, Alli." Hmm. She frowned. Maybe she'd switch back to *Alison*. Either way, she was already feeling better. Next, she opened the box on the counter. She'd stared at a wall of hair colors for twenty minutes before finally settling on this rich chocolate brown. She pulled on the gloves and got to work.

Half an hour later she was heating up some packaged apple cider and bopping to Christmas carols on Pandora, her dye-saturated hair piled on top of her head. Mug in hand, she leaned a hip against the kitchen counter and looked toward the empty corner in her living room. Just to the right of her fireplace. She'd looked forward to putting up a tree this year. It would have finally made it feel less empty in there. She shook off the thought and sang along to a few bars of *Mistletoe*, until David popped into her thoughts. Without meaning to, she replayed his lips moving on hers, the puff of fog created by their shared breath. Evaporated by the word *mistake*.

She shuffled to another song and settled on her couch and tucked her feet up under her, careful not to let the back of her head touch the cushions. Thor rubbed against her leg. He'd need somewhere else to go too.

Alli blew across the top of her cider and took a sip, lyrics about the savior's birth filtering to her ears. She swallowed the rich warmth as the words wafted over and through her soul. At one point, she'd believed them with everything in her. The manger, the donkey, the star in the sky. But she was a hurt little girl then who didn't know any better. Now, she was a hurting woman who had learned a few things.

But what would it be like to let herself believe again? Just for a moment?

David had said that hope was 'the realization of truth, that fills the empty places in our souls.'

Well, it must be nice to be as 'filled up' as he was. But he hadn't walked in *her* shoes. He didn't know what that was like. Her demons were a little harder to shake. Alli didn't have empty 'places,' she had an empty soul.

The kitchen timer dinged and Alli headed to rinse out her hair.

She tipped her head into the stream and the dark, slippery stain washed away in her own form of baptism. Of becoming a new person.

Chapter Thirteen

"Looks like you're just about packed." Alli's gaze traveled around Thomas's room, landing on a box full of Hot Wheels peeking from under his bed. "Hey, don't forget this." She pulled it out, smiled at him, and tucked it into his new suitcase—a gift from Regina and Kyle.

"Thanks," he answered glumly.

Alli reined in her own emotions and cocked her head at Thomas. She lightly bopped his shoulder. "Come on, kid. It'll be fine. Do you know it's sixty-eight degrees in Arizona today? I checked. You could probably wear shorts."

"I like the snow." He zipped up his backpack and sighed.

It was happening, this was it. And Alli was determined to be make it as easy as possible for him. She'd keep it together, she'd demonstrate strength.

Alli twisted her lips and stuck her hands in her back pockets. "Is that everything?"

"Yeah. Just Herman." Thomas looked up at her with concerned eyes. "You don't think they'll take him away from me, do you?"

"No. I told Mrs. Warner to make sure she talked to them about it. They said it wasn't a problem. They love pets and even have a dog." She widened her eyes in forced enthusiasm.

"I guess that's cool."

"Yes, it is." Was she trying to reassure Thomas…or herself?

She checked the time on her phone then slipped it back into her pocket. Her own flight left an hour earlier than his and time was slipping away.

She sat on his bed, reached into her bag, and pulled out a small box wrapped in superhero paper. Her nose stung as she held it out to him. "Got you something."

His eyes sparkled as he took the box from her. Alli propped an arm on the mattress and leaned into it, soaking up his eager anticipation. Tearing open the gift, Thomas took in the several painted hermit crab shells inside. He touched each of them before looking up at her with a smile that cut her to the quick. "Thank you. These are cool."

"Thought you'd like those."

"I have something for you, too." He went to the head of the bed and reached under his pillow. When he pulled his hand out, he held a picture and a sealed envelope with "Miss Alli" printed across it.

He climbed up beside her and handed her the picture first. "Here."

Alli's throat ached as she examined the drawing, drinking in every detail his heart had driven him to add. She recognized the scene immediately. Snowmen. Three of them stood in a row on one side of the page and on the other side, three people holding hands and smiling. "It's really beautiful."

"That's you." He pointed. "And that's David. And that's me in the middle."

"This was the day we played in the snow, isn't it?" She smiled down at him.

He scooted closer to her, and she wrapped a loose arm around him. "Yeah. It was a good day."

"It was. You know what I'm going to do? I'm going to get a frame and hang this on my wall."

He beamed up at her like she'd just given him the world. Alli pointed to the blue envelope he still held. "Is that for me too? I see my name on it."

He looked at it. "Yeah. But . . .I don't want you to open it yet. Do it at home or something, k?"

Her brows pinched in curiosity, but she nodded. "Of course. Whatever you want." She checked her watch again. "I think it's time for me to go."

Thomas looked at her, then flung his arms around her waist and hugged her tight. Alli closed her eyes and bent to press her cheek to the top of his head for the last time.

"Take care, Thomas."

"You won't forget me, will you?"

Her nose stung. "Never."

Their arms were still around each other when Regina appeared in the doorway. "Everyone's waiting for you in the game room, Thomas."

Alli squeezed him tight once more before releasing him.

Thomas slid down off the bed and gave her a shy look. "I . . . I love you." His words were whispered, hesitant. And once spoken, he turned and quickly grabbed his things and hustled toward Regina.

Alli wanted so badly to answer. To say she loved him too. To tell him she wished she could be his mom. The words were clawing at the back of her throat, looking for a way out. But that would only make things harder for him. So instead, she drew on all her strength to smile at him sweetly as he walked away.

Alone in his room, Alli fought to steady her breaths, trying not to implode. The pressure in her chest and behind her lids was nearly unbearable. She squeezed her eyes shut, striving for composure. Just long enough to make it to the front door and out of this house.

Footsteps neared from down the hall and Alli hurried to smooth her face. Her lungs stuttered on an inhale just as David appeared in the doorway.

"Hey," he said.

"Hey." She blinked, trying to brighten her eyes.

His gaze pinged to the top of her head. "Whoa, your hair."

"Oh. Yeah, I've got bangs now." She glanced up and finger-combed her fringe.

"And the color, too."

She bobbed a shoulder, feeling inexplicably shy.

"I like it."

Alli lifted her eyes to meet his gaze. She wished she hadn't. His eyes were saying something confusing, frightening. Something that made her want to run… and also stay. All at the same time.

She somehow managed to break away and pushed herself up off the bed. "Thanks." Her strangled voice didn't lend much strength to her legs. Or her heart. The pressure in her chest surged. She had to get away. Now. Grabbing her bag, she moved toward the door—closer to him.

"*Alli . . .*" His voice sounded intimate, knowing.

Her breath caught and she froze. She pressed a hand to her chest trying to hold everything in place. But she couldn't. Her heart cracked. Her nose stung.

She lowered her head as moisture pooled in her eyes.

David closed the remaining distance between them and locked sturdy arms around her. "I know."

She sniffed, felt her face contorting. She couldn't look up at him. Didn't have the strength to endure seeing his face, seeing him see her. She just leaned forward until her head bumped his chest, and let his strong frame hold her up. Let him be her strength as she succumbed to the tears that refused to be stopped. Tears that had been trapped inside her for decades.

Alli wrapped her arms around his back and clung to him as sobs overtook her and emotion warped her face. Her lungs burned for air as she fought to at least keep quiet enough that nobody—including Thomas—would hear her. "He's leaving," she sputtered.

David tightened his grip. She expected him to say 'shh', but he didn't. Just held on and stroked her back. Pressed his cheek to the top of her head. "I'm not going anywhere." His fierce whisper brought on another round of sobs she couldn't explain. His lips brushed her temple.

It seemed a long time that they stood like that, until Alli's breathing finally evened out. She didn't want to let go. The center of his chest seemed made for her cheek. If she could stay that way forever, she would.

But this was a goodbye and she had to go.

Pulling away, she swiped at her cheeks and under her eyes. "I don't cry."

"Clearly." He was still so close, and he rubbed his hands up and down her arms.

"I mean I haven't for a really long time. Since I was like eight or nine. Guess I just made up for that." She tried to laugh but choked on it. She was so tired of faking it. Tired of running to stay ahead of the storms. Tired of being so alone behind the walls she built up.

David ran the pads of his fingers along her forehead and down her cheeks, framing her face. For a second, she thought he might kiss her, but that was a foolish notion.

"God saves them all, Alli. Your tears." He swiped his thumbs under her eyes, drying some moisture left there. "And He promises never to walk away. To never leave you as an orphan."

Alli blinked and worked her throat. She remembered that verse from years earlier. It had been shared with her by a Sunday School teacher and she'd memorized it, repeating it to herself often. Before she realized they were just pretty words.

David looked at her hard, like he wanted to say more, but she pulled his hands down and rushed to fill the silence. "Thank you, David." She squeezed his fingers then released them. "But I have to get going. I have my own plane to catch." She hitched her bag up on her shoulder. "I have an interview in New Jersey."

His Adam's apple bobbed, and he stuck his hands in his pockets as he backed up. "Of course. I'm going to ride up with Thomas and Mrs. Warner after the little going-away shindig out there."

Alli stopped at the door and looked back over her shoulder. "Take care of yourself, David."

He nodded, jaw muscles flexed. "You, too."

David's insides wrenched painfully as he watched Alli turn the corner and walk away. From Grace House, from him, from everything. But he had to entrust her future to God and untangle his heart.

An ache moved down his throat as he listened to her say goodbye to Kyle, heard the front door open and close again. Only then did he head for the game room.

Stockings, garland, and snowflakes had been put up for Christmas, so the room already had a festive vibe. And cookies sat on the counter, along with juice boxes and potato chips. The kids had all grown to like Thomas in the past couple months and he would be missed.

David wouldn't have his little shadow anymore.

Connecting with Thomas these past months had been a God-ordained privilege.

David watched from a distance as Thomas hung back toward the farthest corner of the game room, looking small and uncertain. But a couple kids approached and coaxed a reluctant smile out of him, joking around and pushing a cookie into his hands. The little guy was wearing his reserved, serious face but he did bite off half the cookie in one go. Clearly, his love of Oreos held steadfast. David's heart warmed to see him munch down the other half and take a second from the table.

After about fifteen minutes of mingling, David relegated himself to the edge of the room. He exchanged a few nods and smiles across the gathering but had no stomach for party snacks and conversation proved difficult. Too many tangled thoughts. He remained a passive observer, stationed on the sidelines until a wave of melancholy washed over him and sent him down the hall to his office where he could hide out and nurse his battling emotions. And hopefully find his game face.

He closed the office door behind him and went not to his own desk, but to Alli's. Eased into her chair, the soft leather conforming to accommodate its unfamiliar occupant.

When the ticking minutes had rounded half the clock, his gaze skimmed across her desk, pausing on the little snow globe she'd purchased on their Black Friday shopping venture. His heart stuttered at the memory. Next to the globe, a small photo collage of her case kids—and the pic of them at the costume party. Tongue turning to clay, he propped his elbow on the desk and leaned his forehead to his palm.

Seeing Thomas off to his family was bittersweet but watching Alli walk away was something else. Was it less than an hour ago she'd cried in his arms? His hand drifted to his chest where she'd laid her head and wept. The tears had since dried, but he almost wished they hadn't. Evidence of her increasing distance, and how he wouldn't be there to see what the Lord would do in her life. He just prayed she'd find peace. And connection.

God, please be with her wherever she goes.

A text message buzzed his phone. He looked down to see Mrs. Warner's name. *I'll be there in five.*

He thumbed in his reply. *All right, five minutes.*

Listening to the children's voices, the chatter coming from down the hall, he spent those minutes in prayer, wishing he could give Thomas more time than that with his friends. A weight pressed on his shoulders as David pushed himself out of Alli's chair and to his feet, then headed for the office door.

These changes had come about so quickly. Trying to wrap his head around it all made him dizzy, like his brain had a glitch. He paused with his hand on the knob, drew a readying breath through his nostrils and blew it out of rounded lips.

Regina was just opening the door to Mrs. Warner as David reached the foyer. After greeting Regina, she looked to him with expectant eyes. "Ready to head out?"

"Yeah. I'll grab Thomas." Breathing out resignation, he carried himself to the game room, scanning for the freckled face and brown hair. Groups of children and adults clustered and ate and talked, but Thomas wasn't with them. The corner he'd planted himself in earlier was empty as well.

David returned to Mrs. Warner in the foyer and dipped his head toward Thomas's suitcase standing by the door. "Can you take his suitcase to the car while I track him down?"

"Sure."

David wandered through the game room, the living room, the kitchen. Each area populating a memory of Thomas, Alli, or both.

"Thomas, we gotta go, bud!" He meandered to the back door and looked through the glass. Remnants of slushy tracks led from the back steps out across the yard, but people came in and out that door all the time.

David hailed Toby. "Do you know where Thomas is?"

The boy shook his head, cookie crumbs clinging to the corners of his mouth. "No. Sorry."

"Okay. Thanks bud." He opened the back door and scanned the area. "Thomas? Are you out here? It's time to get going."

No reply.

A shivering fear rocked his gut. David hurried back into the house and to the game room.

"Hey, listen up!" He held up his arms until he had everyone' attention. "Who knows where Thomas is?"

Heads whipped back and forth, but no one spoke up. *Oh no.* "How long ago did someone see him?"

"I saw him at the snack table earlier. But that was a while ago."

"I said hi to him when he came out of his room."

"We all did."

David licked his lips. "Anything more recent?"

When nobody answered, David clapped his hands together once. "Okay everyone, I need you to do something. First, I need you to pray. Second, I need everyone looking. Any hiding place you can think of in this house, I want you to check it. But stay indoors."

"I've got the engine running, Mr. Porter." Mrs. Warner came in from the foyer and stopped when she saw everyone standing quiet as statues. "What's going on?"

David forced down the sour taste in his throat. "It's Thomas. He's missing."

"What?" Panicked eyes stared back at him.

Regina hurried over. "I don't see his backpack."

"And his hermit crab is nowhere to be found either," Kyle added, a firm grip on his wife's shoulder.

David turned to the social worker. "He's a hider. Just start looking." He pushed past her and headed for his office. Once there, he grabbed his coat from the back of his chair and shoved his arms into it then charged back out down the hall.

Mrs. Warner's brow wrinkled. "Where are you going?"

"Just going to look around outside a little bit." He'd give himself two minutes to circle the house. Then they'd need to start making phone calls.

Alli sat at the terminal with her carry-on at her feet and stared out the glass onto the tarmac. Her eyes felt tired and puffy from her cry, and she couldn't stop thinking about David and Thomas. The way each of their arms felt around her. Nose tingling, she opened her bag for a tissue and saw the blue envelope staring at her. She'd almost forgotten about it.

She pulled it out and ran her fingertips over her name, written in little-boy handwriting. Sacred. Opening the flap, her trembling fingers eased the letter out. She closed her eyes as she unfolded it. Hardly able to bear finding out what he'd had to say to her. But on a bracing inhale, she began to read.

Deer Miss Alli,

Tomorrow I am leeving on a plane to Arzona to live with my ant. I probly wont ever see you again and that makes me sad. Your my best frend since I was little. Like, 5, wich is a long time ago. When parents don't want me anymore you come get me. You always make me happy and you like hermit crabs and you never get mad at me or ignored me and you say reel smart things like pop tarts for breckfast. So I figured it out Miss Alli. Your like my mom. The best one I ever had. Like moms are sposed to be. You lisen to me and care about me and you never hit me or make fun of me. So that's why I think your the best mom. And even if my ant is nice I still will wish I was with you and I can never forget you. I don't want to go to Arzona. I want to stay with you. Forever. I would be the happyest kid in the hole world if that happend. But I know I have to go. I hope they ar nice. But if not then maybe I can come back and see you again. Eether way, I will pray for you evry nite.

Love,

Thomas

Moisture sprang to her eyes, hot and sudden. What was with all the tears today?

She carefully refolded the letter and pressed it to her chest before securing it back in its envelope. Thomas had thought of her as his mother already. Just like she'd thought of him as her boy.

But, like always, she was being separated from those who would be family to her.

"Now seating rows fifteen through twenty-five." A woman's voice came over the microphone.

Body heavy, Alli gripped her bag and carry-on and got in line to board. She was supposed to be more excited about this. New opportunities, the chance for a fresh start. It would kick in when she landed.

An airline worker scanned her pass and she headed down the breezeway to the plane, greeted the flight attendants, and squeezed down the aisle toward her seat.

She smiled at the man in her row before opening the overhead bin and stuffing her carry-on inside. "Excuse me." Sliding past his knees, she lowered herself into the window seat.

The man nodded an acknowledgment then turned back to his iPad. Alli released a deep breath and settled back against her seat. She pulled her earphones out of her bag and stuck them in her ears then started some Taylor Swift to try and shake off the dark cloud over her head.

Absently watching the ground crew through the window, she began going over her interview answers.

I'm not going anywhere. David's voice echoed in her memory, and she clenched her fingers. What had he meant by that? Was he quoting Scripture to her?

I will never leave you nor forsake you.

I will not leave you an orphan.

But He *had.* A very long time ago.

She refused to start crying here on the plane. But her chest ached, and her throat closed. God had left her all alone. Every person she'd ever cared about had been taken from her. From the time she was born she'd been abandoned, rejected.

Can a mother forget the baby at her breast and have no compassion on the child she has borne?

Though she may forget, I will not forget you!

The words snagged in her mind, but she couldn't remember where she'd heard them. She leaned her head against the glass and turned up her music. All she wanted to do was put this whole year behind her.

A tap on her shoulder wrenched her attention to her seatmate and Alli pulled out one of her earbuds.

He pointed to her bag. "Your phone's ringing. Gonna get in trouble with the flight attendants if they hear it." He gave her a half-grin.

"Thanks." She turned off her music and pulled out her phone. The ringing had stopped but she had two missed texts. She frowned and tapped her messages folder. But before they could load, the phone began ringing again, and David's name appeared on the screen.

"Ma'am. I'm going to have to ask you to power off your phone. We're about to take off."

She looked from the phone to the flight attendant. "Yeah, of course. Sorry about that."

As soon as the attendant stepped away, Alli swiped the screen and answered, hoping it wasn't too late. Stubborn hope sprang up inside her. "David? My flight's about to—"

"Alli! Oh, thank you, God." Fear replaced the hope she'd had a moment ago. "Alli, it's Thomas. He's missing."

"Missing! What do you mean, missing?" A wave of gooseflesh poured over her.

"I think he ran away to avoid going to the airport."

"He hides—"

"We've looked everywhere. I found fresh footprints out in the backyard. I can't be certain they're his, but the rest of the kids have been inside all day."

"Ma'am, you can't be on the phone now."

Alli sliced a panicked glare at the woman and continued speaking into the phone. "Have you called the police? How long has he been gone? What else do you know?"

"I don't know anything else. The police are here now, questioning everyone in the house. They're trying to get a K9 unit sent over. We'll be putting together a volunteer search party."

Search party? Her head felt dizzy.

"Ma'am. I must insist."

The plane jerked backward and began pulling away from the gate. With a gasp, Alli shoved to her feet. "Stop!" She climbed over the man in the aisle seat. "Stop the plane! Please!"

"Alli, are you there?"

Lungs pumping fast, she pressed the phone to her ear. "I'm coming, David." She hung up and dropped the phone into her bag. "Tell him to stop the plane!" She practically shrieked at the wide-eyed attendant.

"I don't think we can stop now, ma'am. The door has already been secured. It's too late."

Her jaw hardened. "No, it's not. This is an emergency. My . . .my son's gone missing." She yanked her bag from the overhead bin and heard the flight attendant tell someone to get word to the pilot.

A wave of nausea gripped her, trying to sap strength from her limbs. But a surge of adrenaline wiped it out. *God, if you really haven't forgotten me, now's a good time to show up.*

Chapter Fourteen

David huddled the kids together in the living room, holding onto the necks of those on either side of him. "We just gotta keep praying, guys. Keep praying." His voice cracked. "Bow your heads with me, guys." They did and the words began pouring out of him.

"Lord, lead us to him. Keep him safe. Give us all wisdom and courage. Thank you for the officers and volunteers that have come to help us find Thomas. Give us strength. In Jesus' name." Adrenaline had his heart kicking hard and wild against his breastbone. He had to keep a clear head. Think. Take charge. He couldn't lose—

A hand landed on David's shoulder, and he turned to see Jake's determined gaze.

"Don't worry, Pastor D. God's in control here. You taught us that."

Voice strangled, David reached up to his shoulder to pat the back of Jake's hand. He needed to hear that.

"Yeah, God's gotta listen to your prayers. You're legit, man." This from Reuben. "You stick around even when we give you crap." Was this the same Reuben who'd needled Jake mercilessly just months ago? "I seen you with that little dude and . . . straight up, you'd make an awesome dad."

Jake nodded. "For sure."

Dad? A lump formed deep in his throat. "Thanks, guys. That means a lot."

Reuben clapped him on the back. "God's with him. He'll bring him home."

Through his clamped windpipe, David forced a confidence he didn't feel. "I pray you're right."

He wished Alli were there. The terror in her voice still twisted his gut, made him want to keep her close. Protect her.

I'm coming, David.

But how quickly could she catch a return flight back? Could the search still be going that long? A wave of nausea rocked him at the thought of Thomas still being out there by the time she arrived.

Regina led the kids to sit and passed out hot chocolate to try and keep their spirits up, while Kyle followed David out back to where a small band of local residents had gathered to wait for instructions. The police would give formal directions, but all eyes seemed fixed on him. The pastor.

How do I lead a thing like this?

Jake's words repeated in his mind. 'Don't worry, Pastor D. God's in control here."

Straightening his backbone, David stepped forward and lifted his chin. "Thanks for coming. You don't know how much I—*we*—appreciate your support and willingness to help in this search. We're all united in our concern, uncertain of the task ahead, but our hope is in God. His strength and mercy are unfailing. We can count on that.

"The cops are bringing in K9 units to canvass the area, but in these conditions there's no telling if the dogs will pick up a trail. But it's getting cold out here folks, and there's a little boy out in it that we need to bring home." He handed out photos of Thomas that he'd printed off. "Take this photo. This is the jacket he'd be wearing. He may not be trying to be found. So, look everywhere, even if you've gotten no response to calling out his name. Just to reiterate what the police said— do not venture out alone. Please stay in groups of two or three. We don't want to lose anyone." *Else.* The unspoken thought seared the faces of Thomas and Alli on his brain. How he longed to have them both here right now, safe and sound, throwing snowballs and laughing. And if not that idyllic image, then to at least have Alli there at his side right now.

God, I'm leaning on You here. But Lord I wish she were here.

David's eyes burned with emotion. He took a moment to rub them and when he opened them again, he thought he was seeing things. Alli was running toward him, fire in her eyes.

"David!" She flew to him.

"Alli, you're here." Heart knocking in his chest, he held her face and pressed a kiss to her forehead. "We're just about to head out. Stick with me."

She nodded once and pulled her hat down farther over her ears.

"Okay everyone. Let's get this done!"

Everyone fanned out, calling Thomas's name.

David raked their surroundings and turned to Alli. "Let's go this way."

She followed his lead as he scanned the ground for prints or signs of any kind. But the hard-packed snow, and frozen mud beneath, only confused the eye.

"How did you get here? I thought you were already on the plane."

"I was."

He read the determination on her face. The fierceness. "You… made them stop the plane?" That would mean making a scene, applying pressure, going against the current.

Her brows knotted as she combed the horizon. "No way could I leave knowing Thomas was out there somewhere, alone."

David nodded, a smile inching his mouth upward. They ducked into some trees, snow and twigs crunching beneath their feet.

"Thomas! It's Alli. I came back for you." Her voice broke and she stopped and leaned over, resting her hands on her knees.

"You okay?"

She shook her head. "Definitely not."

David rubbed her back. "We'll find him, Alli. You have to have faith."

"You don't understand. Kids like Thomas, and me, we aren't like the rest of you." Her voice went steely. "Uncertainty about what's going to happen to us, it isn't just a vague disquiet. It's a crumbling of who we are. I know what Thomas is feeling right now because . . .I feel it too. It's hard to explain if you haven't lived through it."

David's gut churned with guilt. He should've told her about his own past long ago. Instead of trying to bury it, pretend it didn't touch him.

Alli straightened and started marching again, swatting a branch out of her way. "And I did this to him." She moved like a warrior going into battle.

"What? No. Alli, no. This isn't because of you, it's because he's afraid of going to a new home. It's because his mother was a drug-addict, it's because he's been through more than a kid should ever have to. But it's not because of you. You've been the one constant in his life."

She stopped short and looked at him with big eyes, full of guilt. "Don't you get it? That's exactly why it's my fault. *I* left." She turned and kept walking. "Thomas? Can you hear me?"

All David had wanted was for Alli to be there, so he could know she was okay. Now here she was, distant and hurting and he couldn't do a thing to help.

A crunching, rustling noise sounded nearby and they both froze, straining to listen. David turned toward the sound. "Thomas, is that you?"

Alli gripped his arm as she stepped slowly toward the direction the sound had come, then jumped, gasping, when a squirrel darted across the clearing and up a nearby tree. The short-lived hope weighted their shoulders.

"Come on. Let's look that way." He pointed with his chin.

They'd been at it for a couple hours when David's cell phone rang. Fingers numb from cold, he fumbled to answer it. "You have him?"

"No. I'm afraid not, David." Kyle's voice sounded strained and sad. "But people are getting cold, some have had to go home. I'm suggesting we warm everyone up inside for thirty minutes, then head back out."

"Good idea for the volunteers. But I'm not sure Alli will stop. I'll stay with her and keep going."

"I understand. But David, be smart. You can't help Thomas if you're both frozen solid and suffering from hypothermia."

David tugged on his coat. "I'm geared up pretty good. So's Alli. But I'll bring her in if it comes down to it. Even if I have to toss her over my shoulder."

"Okay. Be safe. We'll be back out there soon."

He ended the call and looked at Alli. "That was Kyle. The search party's going to warm up for half hour and then get back out here."

"I gathered that." She stamped her feet and shivered. "If we're this cold, how cold must Thomas be?"

A stone dropped through his core. David put his hand on her shoulder and gave it a squeeze.

"I'm fine." She trudged off, stepping out from the grove.

Snow had begun to fall while they were under the cover of trees. Whether that might improve their chances of finding tracks, only God knew.

Alli trudged up a small hill and stopped at the top. "David, look."

David looked out toward the horizon where a cabin home stood in the distance. "You think he'd head there?" Hope surged through his veins.

"It's cold. He doesn't want to be found but he needs to warm up. He might've seen that and headed toward it."

"Let's go." He proceeded first and offered Alli his hand for support. She took it and together they sidestepped down the incline.

"When I picked him up from the McMillans after the kitchen knife incident, I found Thomas hiding in their shed in the backyard. Huddled in the dark, hugging the hermit crab cage. You want to know the saddest part of that?"

David looked at her, watching her breath puff out from her pale lips.

"The saddest part was the thing upsetting him most in that moment wasn't the fact he'd just witnessed a knife attack. It was that he knew they wouldn't want to keep him anymore."

David blinked away the sting in his eyes.

"And as you know, he turned out to be right."

David's gaze dropped to his boots as they sank into deepening snow. "If there's a storage shed or woodshed at that cabin, that'd be the first place we should look." He took her hand again, even though they had reached flat terrain. "You have to have faith, Alli. We both do."

Lord God, we need you. In so many ways.

Alli tightened the scarf around her neck as she kept pace with David. Her thighs had begun to burn from trudging through snow, and her nose was running. David said they had to have faith, and boy, did she want to. She'd been praying nonstop since she got the call on the plane, trying to trust. Revisiting the faith she'd had as a child, trying to grasp it again. It wasn't coming easy.

A breath of icy air burned her throat. "I've been praying, David. The faith part is in short supply, but I have been praying. I can tell you that much."

"Good." His eyes told her it meant a lot to hear her say that.

She ventured further. "When I was eight, I spent a year with a minister and his wife. They bought me gifts at Christmas and my birthday, took me to church, gave me chores, read to me at night, treated me like their own. They were the best foster parents I ever had." An ache moved down her throat at the memory.

"What happened?"

"She got cancer. He had to take care of her, she declined fast. The state wouldn't let me stay even though they wanted me. So, I was removed."

"I'm sorry."

"It's just one more placement, one more link in the chain, piece of my puzzle, however you want to put it." A breeze slapped her face, and she adjusted the shield of her coat collar. "But I do sometimes wonder what it would've been like if they'd adopted me. I'd probably be more like you." Her gaze flicked to him. "Believe like you. The truth is, I want to. I'd give anything to be able to trust in something like the Bible and Jesus." She sucked air into her aching lungs. "Feel that love I see on all your faces at Grace House. Have that hope you talk about all the time. But my past . . .it's shaped who I am. I can't change that."

David was silent beside her, his eyebrows pulled down in a near-scowl. "Alli, there's so much I want to say to you. About the past. I understand—"

"No." Alli refocused on the destination ahead. "You *can't* understand and that's okay. I just wanted you to know that I'm praying for Thomas and trying to have that hope."

They were approaching the cabin now and Alli circled around to the front. "I don't think anyone's here." She knocked on the door and waited but nobody answered.

David exhaled great puffs of white. "I want to see if there's anything in the back. Shelter of any kind." He headed around and Alli followed, her weary legs stumbling in the snow.

The snow was falling heavier now, and the wind was picking up. She shook out her hands trying to keep the blood pumping. She couldn't feel her fingertips at all. Alli stuffed her hands deep into her pockets and encountered something made of paper.

The blue envelope.

"There's a covered slant house for wood but nowhere for a boy to fit." David crossed his arms and stuck his hands under them. "I don't like this weather."

"Think the owners would mind if we were able to get inside this place?"

"You want to stop?"

"No. But I can't feel my fingers or toes and I need to think."

"I don't think they'd mind, under the circumstances."

They tested the door, but it was locked. No key under the mat. While David tried the front window, Alli opened the envelope and pulled out Thomas's drawing. She stared at it and sniffled. *Thomas, where are you?*

His crayon face smiled back at her, and their clasped hands made her wish for the real thing. Suddenly, her eye snagged on a detail that made her gasp. "David, come here!"

"What? What is it?" David appeared at her side in an instant.

"This picture. I thought it was the backyard of Grace House, but it isn't. Look." She pointed to the feet he'd drawn on the three of them.

"Skates?" David's brow puckered.

"Yes. We're skating. On a frozen pond. And this big tree on the right . . ." She spun around, scanning the area. "Look!" She pointed to an enormous tree a short distance away. Her heart was pounding. "Is there a pond or lake over there?"

David shielded his eyes and squinted. "I don't know. I can't see anything through this snowfall. But Regina has mentioned a pond somewhere nearby."

"She mentioned it to me, too." An urgent prodding rose inside. She folded the picture and stuffed it back in her pocket. "We have to get over there."

"Are you sure you don't want to warm up for a few minutes?" Concern intensified his appraising gaze. "You're freezing, Alli." He circled his arms around her, and his warm breath washed over her face.

"So is Thomas." She pushed away and started marching.

While they walked, David pulled out his phone and struggled to dial. Alli heard him telling Kyle where they were. Surely, someone would get an ATV out this way, and they'd be fine.

"Look!" She pointed to three vertical blobs of snow that were obvious attempts at mini snowmen. In front of one of them was a box about the right size to be a critter habitat.

They hurried to the scene and Alli bent to confirm that, yes, it was Herman. "He's *got* to be here!"

David's eyes rounded. He cupped his hands around his mouth. "Thomas?"

Alli spun a circle, struggling to make out the shapes of trees from what might be the shape of a little boy through the swirling white expanse in front of her. *Please, Jesus. Lead me.*

Turn around.

She turned. The wind died. A figure appeared in the snow. She started running. "Thomas!"

The figure moved. Thomas's fearful eyes locked onto Alli's. He struggled to his feet. "Alli?" His voice carried to her on the breeze.

"It's me, Thomas. I came back for you."

He moved stiffly toward her and Alli felt a flood of relief. They ran toward each other, snow slowing their feet, until an ominous creaking sound stopped her in her tracks.

She sucked in a breath and looked around them. "Thomas, don't move!" He stopped and stared at her. "Be as still as you can, okay?" Kneeling slowly, Alli brushed a hand through the snow at her feet, heart sinking fast.

They were standing on the frozen lake.

And it was cracking.

She took one timid step and then another. She saw David running toward them and her eyes widened. She held her hand up. "Stop!"

"Alli?" His plodding legs halted, and he looked around. Understanding dawned on his face. "What do we do?"

"I'm going to try to get to Thomas very slowly, then guide him out. You keep an eye out for the ATV."

"Alli, we don't have an ATV coming."

Not good.

She blinked stupidly, then shoved that news away from her thoughts. Right now, they had more immediate concerns. She distributed her weight and slid her foot forward.

"I-I'm scared." Thomas stepped toward her and another long *craaack* rent the air. Thomas whimpered.

Panic tore through her lungs, flipped her stomach, chained her limbs. Pushing air out her nostrils, Alli closed her eyes and counted to five. Then she lifted her gaze to Thomas and smiled. "It'll be fine, kid. Just gotta hold still, like freeze tag."

He nodded.

She inched closer, gaining confidence. "You see how I'm moving? I want you to do the same thing. Slide one foot forward real slow."

"Okay," he whimpered. He slid one foot forward then brought up the other.

Alli smiled encouragement. "See? We're almost there."

They inched toward each other. Just a few more steps and she'd be able to reach him. As Thomas moved his foot forward again, a loud crackling noise sounded from below him.

"Miss Alli?" The crackling continued and Thomas's round, frightened eyes pierced her heart.

"Thomas, don't move!" She struggled to hold back the cry in her throat as she hurried to slide toward him.

"I'm not!" He shouted over the continued cracking.

And then . . .

The ice gave way and down he plunged into the water with a shriek that ended too abruptly.

"Thomas!" Alli screamed. She tore off her jacket and tossed it away.

"Alli, what are you doing?" David's voice barely registered in her ears.

Alli dove into the icy water and flailed her hands in search of Thomas. Her fingers found his coat and yanked him to her. She looked up but all she saw was a ceiling of ice. Her muscles wouldn't obey as she commanded her legs to kick. Thomas panicked and struggled within the tight embrace of her left arm. With her right, she pounded on the ice above them, reaching and stretching to find the opening.

Jesus, save us!

When you pass through the waters, I will be with you.

Summoning the last of her dwindling strength, Alli kicked toward where she thought the opening should be. Her starving lungs burned, and her heart thrashed as the ghost of a punishing hand held her under, its harsh voice muffled by the water filling her ears. *Useless child! I'll purge the sin out of you yet.*

Please, please! Help me!

Daughter...I Am.

At the command of the quiet voice, the monster's arm let go and disappeared. Whispered words pushed her forward then transformed to the faraway, muffled sound of a human voice. She reached up, her fingers breaking the surface.

The way out!

Alli hoisted Thomas's head up out of the water and felt him lift away. To safety. *Oh, thank you, God!*

But her limbs seized, locked up, refused any command to move toward the surface for a taste of oxygen. And her frenzied lungs jerked, rebelled, and opened.

Reality distorted when Alli jumped into the water after Thomas, and the blood drained from David's head in a rush. A surge of mind-numbing panic froze him more than the cold weather ever could. Then propelled him into action. He dropped to his stomach and began an army crawl along the path she'd taken, arriving at the jagged opening mere seconds before Thomas's head emerged from the water. David yanked him out onto the ice where he coughed and spluttered. Water sluiced over him, and the shock was near paralyzing. He gasped and whipped back for Alli, but she was still submerged.

And sinking.

"No!" He plunged an arm into the water, desperate fingers grazing the hand floating above her head. Adrenaline tore through his veins as he strained against the limits of his reach. The finger hold was not enough. Begging for strength, David fought to haul her up with so little leverage.

God was merciful. She floated up, and he scrambled for firm clamp around her wrist. When her head breached the surface, he grabbed hold under her arms, pulled her toward him, and scooted back toward where Thomas now crouched. Cradling her head in his lap, David wiped the dark hair from her porcelain face. "Alli?"

Dear God, no. Please.

"This way," he called to Thomas, as he dragged Alli to the bank. Quaking with cold, he tugged a finger of his glove with his teeth and pulled it off, then tipped up her chin. Holding her nose, he covered her mouth with his and blew into her lungs.

Oh, Lord, don't take her. Don't take her!

Thomas stared unblinking, shivering.

David blew into her lungs again, tears filling his eyes. Her chest spasmed. He drew back in time for her to retch water through blue lips.

She sucked in a beautiful, rattling breath. Rolling onto her side with a labored gasp, she coughed up more water, inhaled, and sputtered again.

"Alli. Oh, thank God." Without thinking, David pressed his lips to hers. "We have to get you both warmed up, fast."

Shaking violently, Alli nodded. She managed to get to her feet and David hoisted Thomas up into his arms. Together, the three struggled through the biting wind. As they passed the snowmen, the boy's gaze pinged to the habitat. He mewled, and David slowed his tracks. "I'll get him, buddy." He scooped up the box and plunged ahead, not stopping until they reached the cabin. He set Thomas on his feet. This time, David didn't bother checking for open windows. He elbowed one, breaking the glass. "Just give me a second." He climbed through the window then came out the front door to usher in Thomas and Alli. Both were shaking so badly David feared they were going into shock.

"Sit over here, you guys. I'm going to find some towels and blankets."

He managed to find not only towels and blankets, but a change of clothing for Alli and a large men's sweater that Thomas would swim in but was better than the wet things he had on now.

He took Thomas into the bathroom and peeled off his clothes, then dried him off and pulled the sweater down over his head. His fingers were like ice.

"I'll make a fire in a minute, okay bud?"

Thomas nodded. "Th-thank you." His voice was small and sad.

"Hey," David looked into the boy's eyes and gave him a smile. "We're okay."

"But we w-wouldn't be here if-f I hadn't r-run away."

"That's not important now."

"And I k-killed Herman. He w-wasn't moving." A fat tear rolled down his cheek and collected on his protruding lower lip.

"Aw, bud." He pressed a kiss to the boy's frigid temple. "We don't know that for sure. But you're way more important to me. Let's wrap you up in a blanket, okay?"

Thomas shook uncontrollably as David carried him to the living room couch and tucked a blanket around him. He pressed a hand to the boy's forehead and breathed out a prayer.

Turning back, David found Alli shivering in the hallway, a blanket draped around her, still holding the clothes he'd found for her.

"You'll feel better once you're dry."

"I. Can't. Move."

Oh, boy. David gulped but put an arm around her shoulders, walked her into the bathroom and sat her on the toilet seat. He bent to remove her waterlogged boots and freezing socks. Her feet were white as death, but her toenails were painted red with white polka dots, and he couldn't help but smile. He squeezed each foot to warm them, then straightened on his knees in front of her. "We have to get you out of those pants."

"I . . . didn't think pastors . . . said those kinds of things." Her mouth tipped with a tiny smirk.

At least she still had a sense of humor.

She managed the button and David placed a big fluffy towel over her lap as he tugged at the ankle of her pant leg as she shimmied out of the clingy denim. He tossed the jeans across the tub then faced her again.

Her teeth chattered as she watched him. He pulled the sopping hat from her head, grabbed the hand towel from the counter, and squeezed the water from her hair. Her eyes never left his face, mere inches away.

Pulse tapping at the base of his throat, David kept his eyes focused on Alli's as he tugged at each sweater sleeve until her arms were tucked inside.

Sweet heavens, hadn't this day been enough of a trial?

His fingers found the bottom edge of her sweater, brushed against her waist, and he hesitated. Cursing his biochemistry, he took a second to wrangle his erratic heartbeat with a full, deep breath.

"David . . . I'm cold."

"Not me," he muttered, but not quietly enough. He pressed his lips together and shook his head at his foot-in-mouth. "I'm sorry, Alli."

Her colorless lips curved up slightly.

David cleared his throat and decided the only way to get through this was to move quickly. He reached up and pulled the heavy sweater over her head, trying very *very* hard not to notice the skin in his peripheral vision.

His body burned, but he draped another towel across her and got the new sweatshirt over her head without any more skin exposure. That finished, he exhaled a sigh of relief.

Alli looked down at the shirt and frowned. "It's. Backward."

"Tough luck." He helped her step into the leg holes of the snow pants, and she pulled them up behind the privacy of the towel. David felt like he'd just run a marathon. He'd never in his life expended so much energy to resist his own wandering thoughts. Pure agony.

"Thank you." Alli peered up at him with crystal blue eyes and lips whose color was just starting to return. Her teeth still chattered.

"You're welcome." He framed her face and looked into her eyes, wanting so badly to kiss some heat into her. Instead, he hugged her, then supported her by the elbow as he escorted her back out to the living room couch with Thomas. She smiled up at him as he tucked a blanket around them.

His head swam with feeling. Whirling, intense feeling. "I'm going to get a fire going now. There's some wood out back."

Alli nodded and pulled Thomas closer.

The trip out into the snow for firewood helped cool him off, along with some pleas toward Heaven. He returned with an armload of logs and had a fire going in short order.

Flames roared up in a welcome blaze, heating his bones. "All right. Now we're cookin'." He looked back at Alli and found Thomas's head on her lap, eyes closed. He was fast asleep.

The floorboards creaked as David stood and went to them. He laid a hand on Thomas's cheek. "Think he's warm enough?"

Alli smoothed back his hair with her fingers and nodded. "I think he will be." She shuddered and hiked the blanket up higher around her neck.

David settled beside her and put an arm around her shoulders. "And what about you? Are you warm enough?"

"I . . . could be warmer." She turned her face to him and the air between them sizzled as she looked into his eyes. Firelight danced in the shades of blue, reflecting back…longing. Desire. Invitation. She leaned in, killing any doubt about what her eyes were saying to him.

Breath trapped in his chest, David stroked her cheek with his knuckles. An ache moved down his throat. "I was so scared today, Alli," he whispered. "When you and Thomas both went under…I almost lost it. But you," he brushed a strand of hair from her forehead and tucked it behind her ear, "you were so brave. You didn't even hesitate. You jumped in…"

"My kid was in trouble." As that statement hung in the air, her eyes misted. "Something happened down in that water, David."

"Oh?"

"I think God spoke to me."

David's pulse pounded against his eardrums. "What did He say?"

"He said, 'When you pass through the waters, I will be with you.' I don't remember where I heard that verse, but it's from the Bible, right?"

David nodded, his throat tight with emotion.

"I just wanted Thomas to be safe, to live. I would've done anything for him in that moment. I'd die for him. And it's like God said, 'this is what My love looks like. I dove in for you.'" Her throat bobbed. "I swear time down there moved slower because He said a lot of things to me, and I know I wasn't down there that long."

"What else did He say?" David whispered.

Alli sniffed. "He said, 'Even when you run away, I will search for you. And when you're in over your head, I'll pull you out.'" She used a corner of the blanket to swipe at a tear. "Ugh, I'm such a blubbering idiot today."

"You're not an idiot. And your emotions are nothing to be ashamed of." He turned her face toward him and pressed his lips to each of her eyelids. "Your tears are beautiful, Alli. They reveal your heart. The real you."

She gave him a watery smile. "I didn't know the real me cried so much."

David let his gaze soak in her face. He wanted so badly to pull her closer, taste her lips.

But the pastor in him knew she was just taking her first wobbly steps toward faith, and a kiss like that right now would only cloud her way. He pulled his gaze away and fixed it on the flames.

"I guess you see a lot of this, doing what you do."

He nodded. "I've watched God work miracles in many lives. Starting with my own." His mouth went dry, and he knew. It was time to tell her. To share…everything.

Alli's heart pounded so hard it echoed in her head. Probably good for the hypothermia. But she was confused. The way David looked at her, the energy buzzing between them. Was she the only one who felt it? Why hadn't he kissed her when she practically begged him to? Still was.

She blinked out of her trance and repeated the mantra to herself. *He's just not that into you.* He was her friend, maybe even her pastor. Nothing more. She knew this.

They were too different anyway. She freed a hand from under the blanket to run her fingers through Thomas's hair. This, right here, was enough. Thomas was safe, snuggled on her lap. And David was taking good care of them both.

She had a lot of stuff to process about God, too. She believed. Oh, yes, she did. But it felt different than when she was a little girl. Pretty sure it would take a long time to unravel all the tangled beliefs in her heart. She still had very little idea who she was. But she already felt some of those hollow places inside her beginning to fill up. And that gave her something more valuable than anything else in the world, including David. It gave her *hope.* The kind that meant "realizing a truth that filled her up" as David had said.

Her gaze went to him, staring into the fire. His jaw firmly set, the muscle there bulging with tension. He cleared his throat and turned to her, something like fear in his eyes. Her stomach knotted.

"There are things you don't know about me, Alli. Things from my past. Things I didn't want to talk about. You've often said that I couldn't relate to the kids we work with. You see a Bible in my hand and the title "Pastor" in front of my name and you think that means I grew up in some idyllic home, but that isn't true."

Alli's brows twitched, and she adjusted to see him better. David removed his arm from around her shoulders and leaned his forearms on his knees. Creating distance. His ribs expanded with increasing breath as he stared ahead.

Worry began to niggle at her. "Did you grow up in the system, too?"

He shook his head. "No. I almost wish I had. I grew up with an abusive father and a permissive mother who watched it happen and did nothing."

The statement sank into her slowly, then sent tentacles of concern twisting and stretching through her body. She peeled her tongue from the roof of her dry mouth. "Abusive . . . how?"

He pointed his face down and toward her without looking her in the eyes. "I'm not going to list all the twisted details, but it went beyond the whole 'daddy whooped my butt a little too hard' when I got in trouble." That jaw muscle bulged again as his gaze fixed to some unseen image. "There were broken bones. There was a basement." With a flick of his eyes toward her, he pushed up his sleeve and turned his arm over. "There were lit ciGarrettes."

Buried in the design of the tattoo she'd always wondered about, Alli recognized several ringed scars. Punched out flesh. As she reached out to run her fingertips along the scars, hot tears filled Alli's eyes and smudged her vision. Her lower lip trembled. "I'm so sorry," she whispered. All this time thinking he couldn't relate. That he'd had an easy upbringing. She'd said such idiotic things to him!

"Something else about me . . .I was a bully. A real mean one. Picked on small kids, got into fist fights." Shame clouded his features. "I needed to not feel powerless and that was how I did it. I controlled people. I *hurt* people." His Adam's apple went up, then traveled back down with an audible click.

He slid a glance to her, but Alli struggled to find words.

She took in his honest, caring face and shook her head. "That's really hard to imagine, David." Pushy, sure. Short tempered when a child was threatened. But a bully?

The image of David patiently accepting Thomas's blows, taking the pounding of his angry fists until the boy broke down and clung to David's neck, sprang to mind. "You're nothing like that now."

"Sometimes I am. I'm still working through all of that, and I don't know how long it will take or if I'll ever be able to fully forgive. But I've come a long way. I gave my heart to God at the beginning of high school. He saved not only my soul, but my life. I went into youth ministry wanting to help others who were like me." He took a breath and leveled a gaze at her. "So. I understand better than you think. About rejection by those who are supposed to love and care for you." He sniffed and rubbed at the inside corners of his eyes with his thumb and forefinger.

Her heart wrenched at this raw display of emotion, drawing her closer. He'd invited her into his pain and the moment felt . . .intimate. When she ventured a gentle touch on his shoulder, David reached up and clasped her hand. For an instant she saw the little boy inside the man.

The unguarded pain in his eyes made her want to love him. But she could never be what he needed. If she were, he would have kissed her when she all but asked. Maybe he saw her more as a sister. She could be that.

He settled back against the couch and put his arm around her shoulders again. After swiping the heel of his other hand across his eyes, he reached toward Thomas's head and smoothed his hair. "I hope he has an easier time than either of us."

She looked down at Thomas's sleeping face and the sadness stirred again. Alli was still going to have to say goodbye. He was still facing a great unknown and she still had zero say about it, no influence in what happened to him because she was no longer his caseworker. But she tucked all of that away for tomorrow.

Today was about something else. Something *more*, if that was possible.

Leaning her head against David's chest, Alli watched the flames flicker and dance, casting shadows on the wall. His fingers played up and down her arm, comforting her.

But confusing her even more.

Sitting beside Alli in front of a crackling fire, Thomas sleeping beside them, David felt a sense of rightness he'd never experienced before. But brushes with death and lingering hypothermia were bound to bring about all kinds of unusual feelings.

Herman's habitat sat on the coffee table in front of them and David stared at the crab's unmoving form and prayed for a Lazarus miracle. But if the crab was the only casualty, he'd thank God.

Sooner or later, they'd have to get back to Grace House, they'd have to reschedule Thomas's flight, and he would go to Arizona. Barring a miracle, that was the only outcome ahead for him.

Alli shifted beside him, her eyes drooping.

What about her? Would she reschedule the interview for that job in New Jersey? Did she still want to move on, away from the group house? And him?

David took a deep breath, released it, and prayed. He had to have faith. God had plans for his life. All their lives. And they were good plans, whatever they were. He had to trust that. Had to give it all to God.

He checked his phone, wondering what was taking Kyle so long. It had to have been two hours since he'd put in the call.

With Alli drifting off beneath his arm, he was loath to move. But he had to make this call. He scooted over and off the couch, laying her head on the arm rest. Then he found a bedroom and dialed Kyle.

"David? Thank God. Where are you?"

"We're in the cabin at the edge of Clearwater."

"Okay. The roads are closed but I was able to secure a couple ATVs. We'll head out now. Did you find him?"

"Yeah. He's safe." David's conscience nipped. Why hadn't he thought to call it in sooner?

"Is he all right?"

"He will be. He fell through some ice. Alli went in after him. They're both okay now, I have them in front of a fire, warm and dry. They're both fast asleep."

"Praise Jesus. They found him!" David heard a round of applause carry over the line. Why hadn't he thought to call sooner? But all he'd been focused on was warming them up.

Or maybe he wanted a little more time with them all to himself.

Kyle came back on the line. "Okay, David. Hang tight and we'll be there soon. This snow is about to hit blizzard strength but we're eager to have everyone safe under one roof."

"We're fine here for now, so wait for a break in the weather if you have to."

He ended the call and walked out to the living room, put another log on the fire, and sat in front of the hearth until his face grew too warm. Then he got up and adjusted the blankets around Thomas and Alli, kissed each of their foreheads, and lowered himself into a recliner.

His eyes drifted closed and next thing he knew, someone was knocking on the door and voices were calling his name. With a series of hard blinks, he shook the sleepy fog from his head. "Coming."

He opened the door to see Kyle and a group of rescuers standing with thermoses in hand. Kyle pulled him into a hug and patted his back. "You did good, David."

David gave a quick nod then inclined his head toward the couch where Thomas and Alli still lay sleeping. "They're here, safe and sound. I'll wake Alli." He went and knelt in front of her and gently shook her arm. "Alli, wake up. It's time to go home."

Alli rubbed her eyes and pushed herself up to sitting. "David." She smiled at him, and he wished they had just a little longer to be alone, to connect.

"Hey you. Kyle and the gang are here to take us back. And looks like they brought something hot to drink."

Kyle stepped forward. "How you feeling, Alli?" He opened the thermos and poured her some hot chocolate.

"I'm okay, thank you." She rubbed Thomas's back. "Hey, kid. We got hot chocolate. Better wake up before I drink it all."

Thomas yawned and rubbed sleep from the corner of his eye. "Better not."

Within fifteen minutes, after leaving a note for the owners of the cabin explaining what happened and promising repair to the window, they bundled up and headed outside. Thomas and Alli were loaded up on two ATVs with a couple of volunteers to drive them back. Kyle would walk back with David.

Kyle looked hard at David. "Hard to watch them go, huh?"

"I'll see them soon."

"Mm hmm. But it won't be the same."

"I don't know what you mean."

"Quite the cozy little setup back there. I saw how you looked at her. At both of them." There was a twinkle in his eye that made David uncomfortable. Because he was right. But David couldn't admit that.

"I'm just thankful God provided for us. There was a moment I thought things might turn out very different." A rock lodged in his throat as the vision of Alli's breathless body, white as death, flashed in his memory.

Kyle's eyebrows pulled together. "You didn't tell me much about what happened. They fell into the water. But that's not all, is it?"

David coughed to clear his emotion-packed airways. "I almost lost her, Kyle." He buried his hands in his pockets and watched the horizon as they walked.

"Please tell me you're going to elaborate."

"She went in for Thomas under the ice. Had trouble getting back to the opening but she finally did and lifted him up to me. I pulled him out and when I turned back for her . . .she was gone." He blinked rapidly but moisture leaked from the corners of his eyes. "Almost couldn't reach her. It was the scariest moment of my life. When I did get her out, she wasn't breathing."

Kyle didn't speak, but the serious look of shock on his face was enough to send David right back in time. Every detail returned. Not just visually, but every eternal second of fear and desperation that had coursed through his body. "I had to give a few rescue breaths before she came to. But it could've gone the other way, if not for the grace of God."

Eyes round, Kyle shook his head. "Praise God."

"I don't know if I could've handled it, Kyle. I really don't."

Kyle nodded his understanding and patted David on the back.

"I love her." David looked over at him and held his gaze. "I'm in love with her."

Kyle smiled softly. "It's about time you admit it."

David looked up at the white sky and pulled in a chest-expanding breath. "Not sure what to do about it."

A laugh shot from Kyle's nose. "Want me to pass her a note in Study Hall?" He punched David's shoulder. "Tell her, you doof."

"Did you call me a doof? Look, you know it's not so simple. I'm a pastor. I'm supposed to point her to God, not to myself. I don't want to stand in the way of her journey toward faith. I think He's moving in her heart. She shared some pretty profound things after her little swim."

"That's awesome to hear! So . . . what makes you think that loving her would hinder her from finding God?"

How to put it into words? "I...I don't want her to mix up God's love with mine. I'm a very imperfect man. If I let her down, she might blame God and shut Him out completely."

"Or . . .?" Kyle's eyebrows hiked up.

"What?"

"Or she'll see that she doesn't have to be perfect to belong to Christ, to be loved. She'll see that God loves us warts and all. Do you really think you're doing her any favors by hiding your flaws?"

David exhaled. "I didn't mean it that way."

"I know you didn't. You have a good heart, David. Just don't hide behind your job. Tell her how you feel. Seek the Lord. See what happens."

"Even if I wanted to tell her . . .she's moving."

"Maybe she just needs a reason to stay."

"You don't know how much I'd like that to be true."

Chapter Fifteen

Wind-slapped and frozen, Alli's nose and cheeks burned with cold when the ATV arrived back at Grace House. She dismounted and offered a quick thanks to the volunteer who drove her in, then directed her stiff legs to carry her inside where she could warm up.

Regina came running down the hall toward her. "Oh, Alli, I'm so happy to see you!" She hugged her and rocked her back and forth.

So. Much. Hugging. Though right now, Alli welcomed it.

"Ah! And you, too!" Regina knelt to embrace Thomas, who had come in behind.

Thomas tucked a worried chin to his chest. "You aren't mad at me?"

"No, dear. I'm not mad." Regina framed his face and held it in her hands. "I'm just glad you're safe. Come on, let's get you two something warm to eat before we take you to the hospital. You must be hungry."

Alli's groaning stomach answered for her on the last point, but she didn't feel like getting poked and prodded. "I don't need a hospital, Regina. I'm fine."

"Don't you start. You need to get checked out and they're already expecting us."

Alli sighed in surrender.

Regina served them tomato soup and grilled cheese sandwiches, and the other children flooded out from various parts of the house to see Thomas. To pat his back or give him a hug. Alli took it in, smiling, but ever aware that today was only a delay in the inevitable. Goodbye still awaited. Looming larger than ever.

An hour later, Alli sat in a hospital room pulling a sweater over her head while Regina sat beside her on the bed.

"You were both lucky," Regina said. "Doctor says your blood oxygen is normal and your airways are clear."

"Good thing David was there." She flipped her hair out of her sweater, trying not to recall the feel of the water pulling her under. Blocking her air. Burning her lungs. Bringing back all her darkest nightmares. "That's definitely not the way I want to go." She managed a casual tone for Regina, ignoring the traumatic memories and reaching for a change of subject. "What's going to happen with Thomas's trip? Has the flight been re-booked yet?"

Alli would have to do the same. If the company still wanted to interview her after her abrupt cancellation.

"I haven't gotten an update on that. But Mrs. Warner said she'd call this evening to start sorting it all out."

"Keep me posted, if you don't mind."

Regina looked knowingly at her. "Of course."

"Thank you." She smeared lip balm over her chapped lips. "Now I'd like to go home. All I can think about is a hot shower and a thick blanket."

"Don't you want to wait to see David? He and Kyle should be here any second."

"No. Please. It's best if I just left now. You wait with Thomas; I'll call a ride."

Regina looked into her eyes and nodded. "Okay. Get some rest."

Throughout the ride home, Alli's thoughts were a kaleidoscope of images that wouldn't stop spinning.

A ceiling of ice. David's face when she first opened her eyes. The scars in his tattoo. Thomas's face as he went under. Her own hand reaching for the surface of the water.

Slippery porcelain. The faces of the monsters who held her under in the tub.

The man on the plane tapping her shoulder.

What if she hadn't answered?

Once home, Alli took a hot shower, long enough to thoroughly thaw. Nearly cook even. Then she put on her warmest pj's and thickest socks, cuddled up with Thor, and called Janelle. She told her everything.

"Oh my gosh Alli, are you sure you're okay?"

"I don't know." She dropped her head into her hand.

"Maybe you should've let them keep you at the hospital overnight."

"No, I mean about David."

"Oh."

"After he rescued me and helped me change out of my wet clothes, maybe I was just in a weird head space, but I kinda sorta came onto him." She sighed heavily into the phone. "And he totally shut me down."

"Seriously? You came on to a pastor?"

"I know, I know, I'm an idiot. But it felt right at the time."

"What did you think would happen?"

"Nothing bad! A kiss would've been nice. Ugh, I need to die. What if he wants to talk about it? Oh, please just kill me now."

"Don't worry about it. If it ever came up, you could just blame the near-death experience and get a free pass. The bigger question is, do you have real feelings for him?"

Alli rubbed her lips together. "I . . . I don't know. He makes me feel things nobody ever has."

"And the Jesus thing?"

"Actually, I've been talking to Jesus, too. Don't make fun, but I felt God with me in that water today and nobody can tell me it wasn't real. "

"I wouldn't make fun, Alli." Her voice was low and earnest. "I believe you. And I think it's wonderful."

Alli rubbed her nose. "Thank you." She yawned. "I'm wiped. I think I'm going to go to bed now. Thanks for letting me talk."

"Any time. Talk to you again soon."

She climbed into bed but before turning out the light, Alli decided to do something she hadn't done in many, many, years. She opened the Bible.

She'd kept it from Barb and Pastor Roy all these years as a token of her time with them. Her pulse pounded in her ears as she skimmed the pages in the middle. The Psalms. Proverbs. Verses of poetic truth. Verses of holding on and walking in faith. And she felt something.

God, thank you for being with us today. For being with me. I do believe You're real, and even that you love me. But I don't have a clue about what to do about it. Do you have a plan for me? If so, what is it?

Her cell phone rattled on the nightstand. Alli snatched it up and answered. "Hello?"

"Miss Johnson? It's Mrs. Warner."

Alli sat up straighter. "It's late. Is everything okay?"

"Oh, yes. Things are fine. In fact, I just spoke to Regina, and she said to tell you they think Herman is alive. Looks like the cold sent him into hibernation but you all got him warmed back up in time."

"Oh, what a relief! Thomas was devastated." Another blessing!

"Yes, Regina said he was really excited and wanted to stay up to watch for any other signs of movement but conked out within five minutes of getting into bed."

"I can imagine he did."

Mrs. Warner cleared her throat softly. "Um, listen. I know you'd been hoping to get Thomas yourself. I know that's why you moved his case to me. And I hope you know how badly I felt on your behalf when the relatives were found in Arizona."

Arizona. Her heart dipped at the reminder. "Uh huh." Yes, yes, Alli understood. Just didn't help.

"Well, I knew you'd want to hear this right away. I've been talking to the family all day. First, to let them know we'd be missing the scheduled flight and why. Then with updates as the search continued. And then this evening I called to work out the details about rescheduling his arrival. But it turns out, after all this stuff today, they . . .don't want him. Refuse to take him actually. They said . . ." she cleared her throat . . . "they aren't up for any drama, and he sounded like too much trouble."

Fire singed her veins and made her teeth clench. "How could they say that? He's a scared boy!"

"I know. It's terrible and I can't understand people like that. But the point I'm making is this. You're free to pursue him again."

Alli's heart gave a little leap. "What?" She covered her mouth with her hand. The possibility was too wonderful. Too unexpected.

"Yes. When you get your classes done you can apply to be his foster parent. I doubt you'll be blocked in any way."

Alli's eyes filled instantly, moisture leaking from the corners and down her cheeks. She sure was making up for lost time. "Thank you."

"You're very welcome."

The call ended and Alli dropped the phone onto her lap, covering her mouth with both hands, eyes squeezed shut.

God, is this the plan You have?

Christmas carols played through the speakers as Alli and Janelle wandered through the bookstore.

"So, how long until this is all over?" Janelle asked.

"The foster licensing? Three, maybe four months if I'm lucky. Six months or longer if I'm not." Alli picked up a book and skimmed the back cover. "I'll also be transitioning into private practice during the first quarter of the new year." She pushed the book back into place and chose another. The plan sounded good, but these months would be torture. She couldn't even tell Thomas what she was doing.

Janelle eyed her over the shelf display. "Private practice, parenting classes, *Bible* shopping. Somehow this is not where I imagined you'd be this Christmas. But I'm inspired, Alli. Truly."

Alli gave her friend a soft grin. "Thanks. Can I tell you something?"

"What?"

"I'm hoping that Thomas will get to be home with me before the first week of May." Her throat bobbed. "For Mother's Day." Her eyes misted and she looked down again at the shelf of Bibles in front of her. "Too much?"

"Not at all."

"I'd love to bring him home now, for Christmas, but Mother's Day is a good goal I think."

"Totally." Janelle grinned.

Alli drew a lungful of anticipation, smiling to herself as she meandered over to the gift section. Her gaze traveled meticulously over the knick knacks. But what kind of gift should she give to the man who saved her life?

A shelf stocked with Christmas ornaments drew her attention. She scoured the display until one popped out at her. A snort of laughter escaped as she picked it up. *Too perfect.*

Janelle peered over her shoulder. "What's so funny?"

"I found the perfect gift for David."

Janelle pointed. "That thing? Seriously?"

Alli nodded and bit back her snicker. "Absolutely."

"So, have you talked to him yet? About . . ." Janelle dropped her voice low, "you know?"

Alli tensed, face flushing. "No. I can't. I'm just going to focus on Thomas. He's my future."

David hadn't called her out on flirting with him at the cabin, so it was safe to say he wasn't planning to. They could be friends; she could do that.

For sure.

Eyes narrowed, Janelle twisted her lips to the side. "Yeah, I don't know. But hey, it's your decision."

Her decision. That's right. And she'd decided the foster parenting was as big a heart risk as she could take.

After they paid for their purchases, they grabbed a cappuccino and a couple scones from the in-store coffee shop before heading out to the parking lot.

Alli turned to Janelle in her fur-lined hooded coat and matching scarf. "So, we still on for Sunday morning?"

Janelle's frame expanded with a deep breath as she nodded. "Yep. I'll be ready with bells on. Haven't been to church in six years but I think it's time."

"Pfft. I haven't been in twenty and I *know* it's time. I'll see you Sunday. Eight o'clock sharp."

"Okay. Drive safe, hun."

They parted ways to their respective cars and Alli dug out her keys. After cooking dinner, she'd spend the evening in her PJs in front of the fire wrapping gifts and listening to Christmas music. Cooking was another skill she figured she should develop. Fast food and breakfast cereal weren't going to cut it once she was a mom. But spaghetti should be easy enough. And she had months to learn.

Months and months and months.

She released a sigh, then shook the thought and reminded herself to focus on the good. On choosing joy.

Morning fog enveloped Alli as she stepped out of her car. She bumped the door shut with her hip then balanced the boxes in her arms as she picked her way through the snow up to Grace House. She'd come early, eager to tuck her gifts under the tree.

After hanging up her coat, she crossed the still, empty room and knelt to arrange the presents.

"Morning." David's voice startled Alli.

She twisted to look over her shoulder at him. His brick red thermal Henley hugging his chest acted like a magnet tugging on her imagination. "Morning." She could practically feel the fabric beneath her fingertips.

"Anything for me under there?" That sparkling smile and those grinning eyes made her insides light up like a Christmas display.

Yes, her *friend* was certainly attractive. *Friend, friend, friend.*

Lips bunched to one side, she arched a single brow. "Maybe. Gotta wait for Christmas Eve."

His smile turned to a frown. "Actually, I don't know yet if I'll be able to make it over here that night. We have a candlelight service at the church, and I think they need me to help set up." His eyes held something like an apology as they moved across her face. "I might be able to stop by here first on my way over though."

Her chest ached but she just smiled. "I hope you make it."

"*Do* you?" One brow spiked higher than the other, making her burn. But Alli knew better than to take his playfulness as anything else.

"Well, yeah. I mean, the kids would be bummed if you weren't here."

"Oh, right. The kids."

"Yes." She stood and smoothed her clothes. "Speaking of the kids, I better get started prepping today's activity—gingerbread houses." She beamed at him, then turned toward the kitchen. "See ya."

"Have a good day, Alli."

Alli rounded the corner into the kitchen and pressed a palm to her belly. How long would it be until that man didn't affect her this way?

"Alli? That you?" Regina's voice came from down the hall.

"Yes, it's me, Regina."

"Can I talk to you for a sec?"

"Of course." She made her way to the office. "What is it?"

"Have a seat." Regina looked nervous, and Alli didn't like nervous.

Stomach turning over, she lowered herself into a chair and waited as Regina's gaze bounced around the room. "I know you feel strongly that a normal home life, a private family, is best for children when available. As would we all."

"Yes."

"You made a strong case about it being best for Thomas when he was to go to the Haskells."

"In that instance I was wrong, but generally speaking, yes that's my feeling on things. Ideally, children should live in a family unit rather than a dormitory-like setting. That's what's best."

"Including Thomas, I assume."

"Of course."

"The licensing procedure will take you months, is that right?"

Her heart bucked against her ribs. "Yes . . ." Where was this headed?

Regina canted her head to look at Alli. "So how would you feel about him going to live with another foster family while you take the classes?"

Alli blinked surprised, dry eyes. "Why would you . . ." She tried to swallow the stone in her throat. "I mean, I don't think that'd be a good idea. Too many transitions. Just as he got used to it there, he'd be leaving again to come to me." The path before her started to crack. What claim would Alli have? None. If he went to another family, they might fall in love with him. A child wouldn't be removed from a family without reason, even a foster family. And certainly not so he could go live with his former social worker. "Why are you asking me this, Regina?"

"Well. Because someone *has* shown an interest in Thomas."

The air sucked out of the room in that moment as fear grabbed hold and pulled her under. Alli's heart crashed against her ribs at the sensation of drowning. Unable to reach the surface, though she kicked and reached and swam.

Regina was giving her a look of great concern. "Alli, it's only an inquiry right now. Nothing more. It just got me thinking is all. It's not up to either one of us, obviously. But don't panic."

Right. That was in Mrs. Warner's discretion. And she'd been the one to call and encourage Alli to pursue this. Alli blinked herself back to the present, commanded her lungs to do their job. She moistened her parched lips. "Yeah. Okay." She jutted a thumb toward the door then stood. "I gotta get out to the dining room."

"Yeah, the gingerbread houses. I'll come join you guys in a bit if I can." Regina smiled and reached for a stack of papers.

As she left the room, Alli reminded herself to relax. Put it out of her mind. Nothing had changed. Not really.

The kids were already gathering at the table, bouncing with excitement when Alli entered the dining room Their glowing faces put a smile on her lips as she set out the bowls of candy and frosting and passed out paper plates. Each kid got an empty milk box and a stack of graham crackers.

Alli opened her phone and scrolled through the instructions she'd gotten online. "Okay I gotta let you guys know that I've never actually done this before. But it looks pretty simple." She spread frosting on a cracker and pressed it to the side of a carton. "See? 'Kay, you guys go ahead."

Everyone dove into their designs. Some kids seemed to be more 'hands on' than others, meaning they had more frosting on their fingers than the house. Some took great care with their candy patterns while others preferred to just pile it up.

As Alli went around checking on each one, giving encouragement, thoughts of Thomas with another foster family kept washing over her in periodic waves. But each time they did, she shut it down. Didn't allow herself to think about what Regina had shared. And kept smiling.

Until she came to Thomas's. "Looks great, kid!" She leaned over his shoulder and admired the house.

"Thanks. It's the cabin where you and me and David went."

"Oh, right. Yeah, good job." Alli's nose tingled, and she rubbed at it with the back of her hand.

He stacked mini marshmallows to make a snowman and stuck it to his plate in front of the house. "That's gonna be me. This one over here is you. And David is over here by the window so he can break inside."

Alli swallowed a chuckle. "Yeah, he did do that, didn't he?"

Thomas nodded and pushed a gumdrop onto the roof of the house. A small sigh escaped him.

She ran her hand over his hair. Funny how easy that came to her now. "What is it?"

He shrugged then whispered, "I just wish I was spending Christmas with a real family."

A real family. An image came to mind of Thomas with a faceless couple—a mom and a dad. And the thought crashed over her like a wave. He was eligible now for adoption. That opened an entire database of stable young couples who weren't looking to foster. Couples looking to build a permanent, *real family.*

"But… this is okay, too." He smiled up at her. "At least you're here."

This is okay, too. Somewhere out there might be a storybook family for Thomas. A couple much more suited for parenthood than *she* was.

Would any social worker take that chance from him? Would Alli want them to? He deserved more than *okay*. She was drowning again, flailing in confusing, swirling waters.

A knot formed in her chest. "Christmas will be wonderful, Thomas. We all have each other and most important, we both have Jesus. And that's something we can celebrate under any kind of roof. No matter where we go."

She straightened. "Why don't you finish up and put your house on the counter for the frosting to dry."

"Okay." He grinned and pushed another candy into place.

A shuddery breath left her as she blinked tear-burned eyes. "Excuse me a minute, guys. I'll be right back." Moisture distorting her vision, she bit her lip and made her way back to Regina's office.

Regina looked up when she entered. "You guys done already? That was fast."

Alli shook her head. "I can't go through this again. Getting my hopes up, making plans, only to have them snatched away with one simple phone call." She took three quick breaths and sank into the office chair.

Regina came around her desk in front of Alli and leaned a hip against it. "Okay don't get ahead of yourself, Alli. Maybe I shouldn't have told you. I only wanted you to be in the loop. You've always known nothing was certain, that you're taking a risk. It's why we don't say anything to Thomas."

This was different. Not only did she have a long way to go in the process, but she would be up against a different kind of competition. Real, permanent families. If he wasn't taken away from her first, she'd be taking away any chance he'd have for something better than *okay*. It had to be a sign from God. Every time she took a step toward gaining Thomas, a roadblock went up. Like swimming for the surface only to be held under, dragged deeper.

"Thank you for keeping me in the loop, Regina." If a couple was interested in Thomas, one Mrs. Warner believed in, Alli owed it to him not to stand in the way. Maybe God was sparing her the big build up;

how much worse would the heartbreak be a couple months down the road?

She pushed herself to her feet. An email was in her in-box right now, about potentially rescheduling her missed job interview. She could still reply, book a new flight. Or she could always take her plans for private practice somewhere else. Anywhere else.

After Christmas . . .she'd go.

She hurried to her office and opened her laptop, then stared at the screen. Did she want to do this? No. But it made the most sense. For her, for Thomas. And everybody else. Everything here was full of pain and unrealized dreams. And distractions. Surely God could provide a life for her somewhere else. She was learning to trust Him, so she'd practice that now. By trusting Him with her future, apart from Thomas and Grace House and…everyone.

Alli opened her email and composed her reply.

"There you are."

She looked up at the sound of David's voice. "Oh, hey. I didn't even hear the door." She quickly hit 'send' and closed her computer. Throat a tight knot, she dried her palms on her thighs. "Are you heading out for the Y?"

"No, not till January. I have to get over to the church though. Just need to grab something from my desk real quick."

She tucked her hair behind her ears. "Oh?"

"Yeah." Slanting his head, he gave her a curious look, then took a seat. "So, what are you doing in here? I thought you'd cleared all your paperwork so you could hang with the kids all day today."

"Just had to send an email." She bit her lip and looked away from his concerned gaze. But David always knew when she was hiding something. And she owed him the truth. Drawing a deep breath, she squared her shoulders. "I'm going to be moving, David. After the first of the year. Like I'd previously planned."

David's eyes rounded. He cleared his throat. "I…I thought you'd decided to stay? I'd heard . . .well, something about private practice."

She hadn't talked to David about opening a private practice. Had he been checking up on her? "I can open a practice anywhere. And it's time I move on."

His brows formed a V and his mouth opened, then closed. His jaw muscle twitched. Was he angry?

Tearing his gaze from hers, he cleared his throat and stood abruptly.

Alli blinked up at him. "I thought you said you needed something."

He grabbed a folder off his desk. "Yeah, I got what I need. I'll see you later." He marched out, lobbing a stiff smile her way. "Good luck with your plans."

Chapter Sixteen

Thor purred softly as Alli ran her palm along his back. The rhythmic sensation helped to calm her. All the mental and emotional whiplash of the last days had her thoughts spinning and her feelings in a confusing tangle.

Her Christmas playlist had ended so she sat in silence on her couch, feet propped on the coffee table, wiggling her big toe through the hole in her fuzzy pink socks. The fire had mesmerized her for a long while, but it was now dying down. Alli lifted Thor off her lap and threw aside her blanket as she sat up. Her new Bible lay on her nightstand, and she wanted to poke around in it before going to sleep. Maybe it would help.

Yawning, Alli dragged herself to the bathroom to brush her teeth. The thought of her warm, heavy bedspread weighted her eyelids as she turned on the tap. Beyond the splash of the water running, another faint sound. A knock at her front door.

Way too late for a salesman.

Still scrubbing circles on her teeth, Alli went to the door and stuck her eye to the peephole. She nearly choked on the minty foam in her cheeks.

Heavy eyelids now flung wide, she cracked open the door. "David . . ." she spoke around a mouthful of toothpaste, heartrate ticking upward. There he stood in his well-muscled glory while she... "One sec." She held up a finger then ran to the bathroom and spit out her toothpaste, rinsed, and hurried back out to the entryway, making a conscious effort *not* to look down at her feet. *Oh, please don't notice my ratty pink socks!*

Mercifully, his gaze fixed beyond her to her living room. "Sorry I didn't call first."

"It's okay." She waved him in and tucked her hair behind her ears as questions bounced through her mind. She might've expected Janelle to knock on her door this late. Or the cops maybe. But no one from Grace House. Especially not *him*.

His brows pressed low, a vertical groove forming between them, and his mouth compressed.

Worry niggled its way to her tongue. "What's wrong?"

"Nothing's wrong. Well, not like you mean. I just had to talk to you." A muscle in his jaw jerked, tension flared his nostrils. But when his gaze returned to her, it wasn't anger simmering in his eyes. More like, resolve.

She studied the tiny creases around his eyes, the determination carved into his forehead. "You're sure nothing's wrong? Because it's after eleven o'clock. And you just saw me at Grace House."

"I know, but," he stepped close, peering at her with purpose. With an intensity that bolted her in place. "I need to tell you something."

Surrounded by his scent, she blinked up at him, heart tripping and sputtering, lungs picking up speed. The rest of her paralyzed. His gold-flecked gaze washed over her, penetrating her soul, and a sultry silence thickened the air.

"What—" She struggled to push out her voice. "What do you need to tell me?"

"This." In one bold move, he took her chin between his thumb and forefinger and bowed his head toward her.

Her breath caught. Her pulse revved at his nearness, body heat rising as his mouth drifted ever closer. He paused when his lips hovered just above hers and the dizzying effect sent a rush of blood to her head.

Tingles raced along her skin crown to tiptoes as their quickened breath mingled. And then . . . contact.

His lower lip brushed along hers, making her go up in flames.

Soft and warm, his lips molded and danced with hers. She gasped as the plying of his mouth became more urgent, yet more deliciously restrained. More purposeful.

He moved with confidence. No hesitance, no uncertainty. A thousand butterflies beat their wings against her ribs as he led the waltz with beautiful precision. Whatever this was, she wanted it to never stop.

The rhythm of his kiss moved from waltz to rumba and elicited a hunger Alli didn't know she had. He framed her face, weaving his fingers into the hair at her temples, sending heatwaves through her middle.

Good golly, could the preacher kiss! And he was. He was kissing *her*.

Alli wrapped her arms around him and held on tight, her legs weakening beneath her while emotions rolled and crashed over her heart.

Chest heaving, David broke away, leaving her lips crying for more. He smoothed the hair away from her face and looked deep into her eyes. "I love you, Alli."

"Wh-what?"

"I'll say it again. I love you." He pressed a kiss to the corner of her mouth and her eyes fluttered closed. "I don't want you to leave." He kissed the other corner of her mouth. "I want you to stay right here. With me." He found her lips again and her belly stirred with desire. Demand.

But alarm bells rang in her head.

"David . . ." She took one more taste of his mouth before reaching up to pull his hands from her face. "You called this a mistake before."

His eyes closed. "I did but…the only mistake was my behavior. I handled myself all wrong. I was a fool in denial. Afraid to admit what I was feeling." Gaze intense, his thumb stroked along her bottom lip. "But no more. Here I am, Alli."

She swallowed a ball of emotion to make way for words. "At the cabin . . . I thought for a moment that I felt something between us." She shook her head. "But then I thought I was just crazy. I felt so stupid, imagining things that weren't there, and—"

"You weren't imagining things. But I was so afraid I'd get in the way of what God was doing in your heart. Or maybe I was just afraid of taking a chance. I don't know. All I know is that this past week I've watched your faith grow, but it's been torture being around you and not telling you how I feel. And then today you tell me you're thinking of leaving." He took gentle hold of her hips, turning her bones to jelly, and pressed his forehead to hers. "Please, don't." His breath was warm and shaky and utterly intoxicating. "Don't run, Alli. Not from me. Please. Give me a chance."

The room tilted at his words. He was here. Saying he loved her. Asking her to give *him* a chance.

Air labored in and out of her lungs.

"Alli," he murmured, "tell me you feel . . . *something* . . . for me, too."

She blinked at the realization she hadn't answered him back. "David." She laid a palm against his rough jaw. "Of course, I have feelings for you. I've been tortured this week, too. Dreaming for something just like this to happen."

She brought his face to hers and feathered a kiss on his lips. Then she pressed her cheek against his and whispered in his ear, "I thought you knew that all along. You always could see through me."

"Alli . . ." He cradled her head and held her tight. "Does this mean you'll give up the idea of leaving?"

"I was only considering it because it was too hard to be here with you and Thomas knowing I could have neither of you." At Thomas's name, her eyes stung, and she blinked rapidly.

"You've got me, no matter what. And you can't know for sure what will happen with Thomas."

"Someone's trying to take him, David." She sniffed. "I found out today. Someone else wants him. And I am months out from being able to take him in." She wiped a palm across her cheek. "I can't call dibs or put him on layaway or stop some perfect family from adopting him. And I can't put myself through that again." She lifted a shoulder and stepped backward. "I just can't."

David's throat bobbed with a click as his eyes remained locked on hers. "Alli . . . What if I told you that *I* was the one who asked about Thomas?"

"What?" Her forehead crumpled. David wanted to take Thomas from her? "What do you mean?"

Eyes pleading, he closed the pocket of distance between them. "I wouldn't do anything to hurt you, Alli. I swear I was prepared to drop the whole idea if you weren't on board with it."

She hiked an eyebrow. "Pastors aren't supposed to swear."

He choked out a laugh and shook his head. "You know what I mean. I didn't want you to hear about it this way. I told Mrs. Warner my inquiry was unofficial. Off the record. It was just an idea. I was going to talk to you first." Frustration laced his voice.

Mrs. Warner?

Alli pointed her face at the ceiling and emptied her lungs. "*Regina* was the one who told me. But I don't understand. You knew I was working to get Thomas. Why do this? I didn't even know you were licensed."

"I'd taken the classes last year, feeling like I might want to take that step sometime. I expected it'd be a teen I'd want to take in but then Thomas just sort of grabbed my heart. I thought how much I wanted him to have more than a group home, like you always said. I wanted him to have someone to belong to this Christmas. And I hoped that someone could be—"

"You. Yeah, I get it." Her throat tightened. David had a bond with Thomas, too.

She folded her arms over her chest and retreated from him. How could she compete with a pastor for the role of parent? Thomas probably *would* be better off with him.

"No, Alli." He came and uncrossed her arms then slid his hands around her waist. "I wanted it to be *us*."

Her eyes pinged to his, and what she saw reflected there melted her insides. Was he saying he wanted to . . .? No, he couldn't be. "What are you saying?"

"Alli, nothing in my life has felt so right as being with you and Thomas. That day in the cabin, taking care of the two of you. Watching you both asleep on the couch, it felt *right*. Like family. I've told plenty of friends over the years that I considered them family. I've told my church that they were family to me. But this…" he sank into her arms, "was so much more than that. It was the first time I ever experienced what a real family felt like."

Her chest rose and fell rapidly as she stared at him. "I felt it, too." The words eked out of her. "It was like a dream."

But what did it mean?

"I think we could be great together, Alli."

Joy stretched her cheeks. "I think so, too."

His gaze whispered across her face, like he was drinking in the sight of her. He paused on her lips then met her eyes again. "I know becoming a family will take time. But maybe this Christmas can be a start. If we spend it together."

Delight welled up within her. "I'd love that." She slipped her arms around his neck. "And I think Thomas would love to move in with you."

His features smoothed and he reeled her in closer. "Only if that's what you want. I'm serious when I say that."

"If you don't do this now, someone else might come along before I'm finished jumping through hoops. At least with you I know he's safe. And close."

He kissed her forehead. "I wouldn't want you feeling any added pressure to make things work with me because you were afraid of losing him."

She shook her head. "I'm too crazy in love with both of you to be afraid of that."

A slow smile spread across his features. "Crazy in love. I like the sound of that." He tipped her chin and brushed a soft kiss to her lips. "So, what do we do next?"

Alli bit her lip, head clearing. "Oh my gosh, there's so much to do. We have to talk to Mrs. Warner, you need to set up a room for him at your apartment—bed, dresser, toys, clothes. And unless you think you can continue his home studies on your own, he'll need to be enrolled in school . . ."

He pressed the pad of his finger to her lips, silencing her. "First things first. I'll call Mrs. Warner in the morning, and we'll go from there."

Lips compressing in a kiss against his fingertip, she nodded. "Okay."

"Think this will be able to happen in time for Christmas?"

"If you're already licensed and you have an established relationship with the child, yes it could happen in as little as twenty-four hours. As long as he has a designated sleeping area."

"Nothing a trip to Ikea won't take care of." He beamed down at her, eyes sparkling. "I can't believe this is happening."

"Me, either." She raised her eyebrows in amazement.

David's thumb traced over her lips. "I should go now." His husky voice raised goosebumps on her skin. "But I can't. I need one more, Alli. Something to hold onto until I see you again."

He inched closer, his breath warm on her mouth, and touched smooth, firm lips to hers. Blood pounded in her head as he ran his fingers down the sides of her face, then cupped the back of her neck. Who knew a pastor's kiss could be so . . .hot? He angled her head, his kiss becoming more urgent, more hungry. If he kissed her like this much longer, she'd be begging him to throw conviction out the window and carry her to bed.

"David…" She forced her lips to form the warning in between his bone melting kisses.

He broke off and nodded, his breath coming fast. "Yeah. Yeah, I know."

She smiled, soaking in his flushed appearance. Glad to see he was as affected as she was. "You better go. I'll see you tomorrow."

Like magnets, they started drifting toward each other again, then reversed course, sharing a knowing smile. David bounced his eyebrows and stuffed his hands in his pockets, sliding back a step. "Good night, Alli. Sleep knowing you are well-loved."

Her throat tightened, her voice emerging thick and heavy. "I love you, too."

She watched the words land. Saw his eyes darken, his chest rise and fall, his gaze deepen. And his hand reach for the doorknob behind him.

He shook his head. "Don't say it again until I'm through this door."

The butterfly wings fluttered to life again, low in her belly.

Her feet adhered to the floor as she watched him go, only carrying her forward once the latch clicked into place.

As his footfalls faded, Alli brushed her fingertips along the doorframe, rested her head on the slab of wood as if it were his chest, and whispered again, "I love you."

"Did you talk to him?" Alli pressed the cell phone to her ear and chewed her lip.

"Yes. But I didn't tell him who." Mrs. Warner's voice held a conspiratorial tone. "This is only a meeting today. Once I promised him he'd be coming back to Grace House afterward, and would *not miss* Pastor David's Advent celebration," she chuckled softly, "he relaxed. We'll head out in just a few minutes."

"We'll be here." She ended the call and lifted her gaze to David, sitting across from her at the coffee shop.

"Okay, this is it. The big reveal." He puffed out his cheeks. "I'm actually a bit nervous." He squirmed in his seat, then laughed a little.

"Me, too." She took his hand—it was becoming the natural thing to do. "But mostly excited. I can't get over the way all of this is coming together. The three of us. Heck, I can't believe I'm dating a pastor. My life looks so different than it did just months ago."

"Good different, I hope." He ran his thumb along her knuckles, making her skin hum.

Her eyes rounded and she bobbed her head. "Uh yeah. *Very* good different."

A slow smile curved his lips, and he gave her a wink. He tapped his foot and checked the time on his phone. "They should be here any minute."

"Yep."

They sat in silence drinking their coffees, occasionally exchanging smiles, until the bell above the door jingled. They turned in unison to see Mrs. Warner enter and start scanning the room. Thomas stood behind her with his face downcast.

Mrs. Warner spotted them and smiled. Then she placed a hand on Thomas's shoulder and pointed toward David. "There he is, Thomas. Let's go say hello."

Appearing reluctant but resigned, Thomas lifted his face. Then blinked. First, his smooth forehead creased in confusion, then realization dawned and widened his eyes. Alli's nose tingled as she watched the transformation. His little chest rose and crashed, rose and crashed, and he stared at them as if afraid to believe it could be true.

"Come on over here, buddy." David waved him over and Thomas came sprinting toward them.

He flung himself at David and pressed his damp cheek to David's shoulder. "Is it true? You want to take me home to live with you?"

"It's true." David's voice was rough with emotion. "If you think you want to."

"I do want to! I won't run away, I promise."

A laugh fell from Alli's lips, and she clasped her hands together in front of her mouth. The two of them went blurry through her sheen of tears.

David clapped Thomas on the back. "There *is* one thing you should know."

"What?" Thomas leaned back to look at David's face.

Mouth sliding into a smile, David nodded toward Alli. "I hope you don't mind if Miss Alli is around a lot. I invited her to spend Christmas with us." He shifted his gaze to Alli and lowered his voice to a stage whisper. "I have a big crush on her."

Thomas stifled a laugh. "I know."

"You do?" David feigned shock. "So, you don't mind then?"

Thomas was beaming as he shook his head. "Nope. I don't mind." He slid off David's lap and came to Alli's. "I always prayed that you could be my mom. This is pretty close." He squeezed her neck and Alli closed her eyes and soaked in his love.

"Thanks, kid," she murmured. "You're special to me, too." She pressed a kiss into his hair and hugged him tight. It felt natural, like she'd done it all her life.

"Herman's going to be excited too. I wanted to bring him, but he had to stay home and keep warm."

"We'll have a surprise for him then."

David reached over and rubbed Thomas's back. "How about we go home, and I show you your new room?"

Thomas looked back at Mrs. Warner. "Is it okay? Do I have to go back to Grace House with you?"

Mrs. Warner smiled. "You can go with David and Alli. They'll bring you back with them for Advent."

"Yahoo!" Thomas squirmed to his feet, grabbed Alli's hand, then David's. As they walked out to David's car, they swung him up in the air.

Alli's cheeks ached from smiling so wide. But she couldn't help it. And she wouldn't change a thing. Because right here, right now, she knew *exactly* who she was. Who she'd always been from the moment God created her.

The emptiness was gone.

Her heart was full.

AUTHOR'S NOTE

Dear Reader,

Whatever your background may be, whether you grew up in a stable home or no home, raised by loving caregivers or abusive ones, I hope that in these pages you've glimpsed the God who's been with you through it all. You are not forgotten or unloved. If you feel broken, there is hope and healing for you through the Creator of all things. It's time to let Him in to every hidden corner of your hurting past so He can set you free. The burden of your wounds is not meant for you to carry alone, forever. But His shoulders are broad and His compassion unmatched. My prayer is that you throw yourself on His grace, let Him carry you, fill the hollow places in your soul, and help you soar.

~ Michelle

1. Which character were you most drawn to? Was there one that you felt you could personally relate to?
2. Which scene in the story was most meaningful to you?
3. Do you ever feel like you're playing a part, and nobody knows the real you?
4. Alli was severely abused as a child in the name of religion. What mistreatment have you experienced by those who were supposed to represent Christ?
5. Both Alli and David are affected by what they went through growing up. What childhood wounds still haunt you today?
6. Do you have areas you block off even from God because you just don't want to face them?
7. Who does God say you are? Is it different from how you see yourself? (Read 2 Corinthians 5:17.)
8. When hard things happen, what's your usual response? Fight/Flight/Avoid
9. What truth has God been nudging you to learn/face? Did the story help you to confront that truth?
10. What will stick with you after reading this book?
11. Healing is a process that takes time, and forgiveness can come in stages when it comes to trauma and abuse. Did this story give you greater insight and understanding into your own wounds or the wounds of others you know?

ACKNOWLEDGMENTS

There are so many people who had a part in bringing this book to life, and I'd like to publicly acknowledge you here. Without you, this story would not have made it.

April Gardner, my crit partner, my editor, my cheerleader, my bestie. I love you so much. Thank you for dragging me to the finish line, cracking that whip, drying my tears, and holding me up when I feel like nothing but dead weight. You are a rock star, and I don't know how I got so lucky to have you.

Beta readers, you guys are awesome, and you mean the world to me. Thank you for your early feedback helping to shape and fine-tune this book. Denice Bridgman, Becky Canfield, Cindy Davis, Erika Wheeler, Nicki Lina, and my momma, Shawn Van Hook. Thank you!

Phyllis Helton, thank you for your wonderful support and the lovely images and quotes you put together. I love them!

Brittany Cluff, thank you for sharing your experiences with foster parenting. Your insight was invaluable to me in bringing these characters and situations to life.

Mike, thank you for your steadfast support and love. You are my pillar, my comfort, my home. There are not enough words to capture what you mean to me and how lost I'd be without you.

To my children—Brandon, Kaitlyn, Amy, and Trevor—you guys are my world. I have no greater desire in this world than to see each of you experiencing the fullness of God's love and plans for your lives, to grow closer to Him every day, and to have unwavering faith and strength of spirit as the years unfold.

Readers, thank you so much for the messages and reviews that allow me to glimpse God's work in your lives through my words. There is no greater motivation and joy than to see others being moved by the stories that have moved me. Your words are just as important as mine!

Lord Jesus, thank you. Thank you for reaching into the mess of our lives and loving us back to health. For suffering along with us in our wounds, for never giving up on us, chasing us down when we push you away and diving in after us when we're drowning. Thank you for never ever leaving us or forsaking us, for adopting us, making us your own, not leaving us as orphans. Abba, you are a Father to the fatherless in the most beautiful, incomprehensible way. My words of thanks will never be enough for everything You are and everything You do.

Michelle Massaro writes contemporary fiction soaked in grace. She makes her home in Southern California with her husband of over a quarter century and their four children. She dabbles in painting, loves family traditions, and stinks at Trivial Pursuit. Her literary tastes range from C.S. Lewis' The Chronicles of Narnia to Francine Rivers' The Mark of the Lion series. When she isn't tinkering with words, she enjoys posting pics of her dogs, having deep conversations with friends, and lazing about streaming movies. A new lipstick and a good French roast always make her happy.

Grace Series

Grace in the Flames - A prodigal, a sinner, and a saint . . . Three people. One God of grace.

Unbound by Grace - When the past holds the future captive, there is only ONE chain breaker.

Grace that's Greater Still - Secrets broadcast. Reputation lost. All that's left is the God who redeems.

<u>Stand Alone</u>

Better than Fiction (with coauthor April Gardner) - Real love isn't found in novels. It's messy, mundane, and deeper than fiction can ever go.

Hollow Places - He sees through her defenses, but she can't take off the mask for fear she's nothing underneath.

STAY IN THE KNOW WITH MICHELLE'S NEWSLETTER

Opt in at:
www.MichelleMassaroBooks.com
For behind-the-scenes news on covers, new releases, contests, FREE books, and information on how you can be part of her next Launch Team!

Connect with Michelle on social media at:
BookBub, Facebook, Instagram, and Goodreads